Once Upon a Timeless
Millennia

BY: AMIKO RIVER

First Edition
Copyright (c) 2023, Wonderstorm Publishing.
Published: December 2023.
ISBN: 978-1-7382229-0-9

Prologue

~ 16 years ago ~
~ shortly before King Earthquake's death ~

A Swan Made of Mist Following Dreams And Wishes

BlizzardTamer couldn't see her island, which she figured was a good thing. Good thing he was out there, far away from her. She wondered if LightningRoar, mother and Brightleaf made it out. She sighed and shook her head. She'd seen Brightleaf's dead body. He was gone now. LightningRoar wasn't, though. He was powerful. But, maybe he was stronger, was what BlizzardTamer worried about. She glanced around to see if Boreal or Frostfall were around. They weren't. BlizzardTamer launched herself into the air and flew towards a frozen valley. The Icelo kingdom sat beyond a mountain range. She loved the twinkling notes that come from the sky, and the ice castle figure, along with when an Icelo took a step. Those soft notes would play when Icelo dragons walked, but she never knew why. The Icelo weren't a small clan, but BlizzardTamer loved the close environment they lived in. Huge frozen spires with little caves and homes for the Icelo clan. She landed on a tall platform made of snow and ice. The lights flickered like tiny stars across the snowy Frost isle. The ice valley was just a flat sheet of ice, but across in the middle sat the Icelo Kingdom.

"Hey, BlizzardTamer," Frostfall whispered, seemingly appearing out of nowhere. "Sorry to bug you… just, I saw something you might want to see." BlizzardTamer stood up and smiled to her.

"It's quite alright," she said. "I was just thinking. About… them." Frostfall gave her a sad, concerned look and put her wing around BlizzardTamer. BlizzardTamer had pure white scales with slightly less pale blue wings. Her eyes glowed with a magical pink. Frostfall was dark, deep, ocean blue with a hint of turquoise. She had a circlet of ice spikes that was attached to a deep blue cape that flowed down all the way to the start of her tail. The circlet sat around her neck.

"They won't hurt you here, and Brightleaf will be ok," Frostfall promised her, smiling. "But… I saw that someone else won't be…" They both flew away around the mountain to the ice cave near the summit. They both landed near the entrance and saw a male ice dragon standing next to it. He was glaring out at the sea, in the direction of BlizzardTamer's island. She shivered. Not because of the cold.

"She saw something," Boreal growled, flicking his tail at Frostfall. BlizzardTamer looked at her, concerned.

"I saw something maybe kill someone?" She half asked, half said. "I'm not completely sure but it was… it might've been him." BlizzardTamer looked out to the islands beyond. She feared they would come for her, but Boreal didn't look scared. His scales were pale icy blue and had wings that resembled auroras and northern lights.

"Her magic saw it clear as water," Boreal said.

BlizzardTamer needed to see for herself. She took a deep breath. BlizzardTamer was usually cold and never really got to angry. She acted as though her dream of being queen had never become impossible and faded. She always knew that being queen meant being calm and smart, so she would be calm and smart. Boreal scowled out at the sea.

"So, may I see?" BlizzardTamer asked calmly. Frostfall nodded and went inside. She soon returned with a crystal ball floating beside her. Frostfall touched the orb, glowing with a mystic, indigo aura. Her eyes glowed the same colour. She she pointed it off the cliff at the islands beyond them. BlizzardTamer knew how this worked. She touched the crystal ball, and slowly, she could see the islands forming in the distance. Frostfall ran her claws over the orb and they all saw something huge and orange on the horizon.

It was on the fire island. BlizzardTamer remembered *his* rant on how he hated fire spirits, but she never found out why. As the orange shape lingered, something started to form behind it. BlizzardTamer suddenly realized that it was King Firebrazer, a banished fire spirit king. She felt a twist in her stomach. A huge black figure rose out of the ground and shot at the king. He twisted and shot a plume of fire at the figure. The black figure stumbled back, unharmed. It leaped at Firebrazer and pinned him to the ground. The black figure raised his claws and dug them into Firebrazer's scales, drawing his blood. Firebrazer threw the figure off of him and flew to the skies, but he wasn't retreating. BlizzardTamer would have.

More fire came barreling towards the black figure. It didn't bother to dodge it, however, it did reflect it. The king didn't make an effort either, and let it touch his scales. He couldn't be hurt by fire. The figure leaped up and dragged the king to the ground, his wings pinned by the figure's claws. It pinned Firebrazer to the ground as the Ariash king squirmed under his claws. He leaped out of the black thing's clutches and scraped his talons across its throat. The black figure stumbled back and vanished. BlizzardTamer and the other Icelo stood there, for anything to happen. Then she saw the creature rise again, this time purple lightning echoing across its scales. Firebrazer shot into the sky again, but it was no match for the powerful Shadowling. His wings were engulfed with black and purple smoke, and he suddenly dropped to the ground. The creature leaped on his back and shot a painful blast of shadow energy at Firebrazer.

The three ice dragons heard a horrible shriek of pain at the contact of his scales and the dark magic.

"Did you know the black one?" Frostfall asked, nervously. "Or was it a stranger?"

"I knew him," BlizzardTamer replied solemnly. "That was him." She hesitated. That was *him*, " she repeated

"How do you know?" Boreal asked.

BlizzardTamer closed her eyes for a moment, then opened them. She turned and met their eyes. Then spoke.

"Because I know my brother."

"How do you know?" Frostfall asked. She seemed hopeful. "It could be someone we don't know... Wouldn't that make your brother innocent to everyone but... You?"

Boreal shook his head. "That dragon is a menace. Doesn't matter who he killed; a killer's a killer. Unless he murdered the bad dragon, he's the enemy."

"But he's my *brother*, " BlizzardTamer snapped to him. Boreal looked to the ground in sorrow. *I know that isn't a defence, and I know that Boreal really likes Firebrazer, but I still love my brother.*

Don't I?

"I'm sorry, Boreal," BlizzardTamer apologized. "I know. We should take him down someday. But if it isn't his fault, please, don't blame him entirely."

Frostfall, from behind them, sighed quietly and nervously shifted on her talons.

"Yeah, you've both seen a lot, but why go after Brightleaf?" Boreal wondered.

BlizzardTamer shrugged. "He's a good little kid. He isn't any kind of threat, or anything. He was a friend to all of us."

Frostfall put a cheerful smile on herself and came up next to BlizzardTamer. But none of them seemed to have anything to say.

BlizzardTamer smiled at her.

"But if it was his fault, then what?" Boreal asked. He looked up into the spiralling snowstorm above them. The pale blue sky reflected in his eyes.

"Then we have the right to fight him, but I still want to talk to him," BlizzardTamer said. She controlled the blizzard above them, twisting it and bringing it down to her talons. It swirled around her claws like a school of fish around some coral. "But if my brother is at fault purposely, we can… Separate him from the world."

Follower of Ash, Fire and Loyalty

Red didn't know the palace very well; something his mother would praise him for. He wandered through the lower hallways, hearing his sheathed sword lightly clank against his armour. *It shocks me how the Ariash clan dragons fight in this,* he thought. *They don't need fire immunity for the volcano, they need it for this crazy armour.* Red stopped as he heard guards coming his way, and he hid out of the way. Red's blood-coloured scales were hidden behind his back robe and his armour, but he still couldn't risk being seen. He listened in on the guards.

"Prince Incinerator is acting weird again," one of them said. "Did you notice how he looked at the window the entire meeting?"

"Probably just being lazy," the other spat. "Wouldn't surprise me."

"Do you think Queen Magma will handle it like she said about Meteor?"

"'Meteor,' seriously?" The guard rolled his eyes. "Do you really believe that?"

She whacked his tail with hers. "I'm just saying, a prince talking about some whelp named Meteor when Magma *just had a whelp* has something to do with it. And besides; do you think Magma would've been talking about it like that if she had done it herself? Incinerator is lucky that he did it."

"Well if you think so, 'METEOR' is due to hatch in a few days." The guards left, and Red was astonished. He'd heard the palace rumours of Meteor, but he didn't know the details. It wasn't like he could just ask Incinerator. He'd have to pay him a visit first.

Red had to decide; Was he finding the prince first, or was he going straight to his mother? I shouldn't give the prince more time to change his mind, he decided as he found the prince's room. Red didn't really know if he would change his mind though. He had an awful life in the palace, and his mother's offer was a great way to get out of it. He wasn't too surprised at how low it was in the palace. The prince got the room next to the prison. A bit brutal, but nothing compared to the prison itself. *He's treated like he's in a prison, though...* Red slipped through the opening in the door and hid in the shadows of the room. Incinerator was hunched over in the corner, a tightly and messily wrapped bandage around his left shoulder. Red wondered what his mother had done to him. Or Incinerator's mother, Magma was a nightmare.

"Hey," Red called to him from the shadows. Incinerator jumped with a gasp and spun around, wincing at the pain in his shoulder.

"W-who's there?" He breathed. He stood up shakily and he looked weak.

"Decided?"

There was a silence at Red's question. "I... I think so," Incinerator replied. "I think I'm going with you guys." Red shared a smile with the prince, but there was a good chance he didn't see it.

Red snuck around to the corners of the room, which had almost no light at all, making this easier. He appeared next to the prince and took his hood off, revealing his face.

"Ah-Woah!" Incinerator exclaimed, obviously startled. "Sorry-I, uhm-"

'It's fine," Red laughed. "Come on, we have to find my mother."

On their way to the prison, Red asked about the whelp situation.

"So, who is Meteor?" He asked.

"My little sister," Incinerator told him. "She's going to hatch soon."

"Incinerator lead Red to the prison, and he got a glimpse of the horrible place for the first time. Black charcoal bricks made of volcanic stone and thick metal bars. The ceiling was a grate into what looked like another layer of cages, and small, spikes covered the floors of many cells. Not fatal, but Red would cry if he were trapped there even a *night*. A few prisoners lay in their cells, most sleeping at that time of night.

"Where's my mother?" Red asked anxiously.

"I couldn't forget what she looks like," Incinerator mumbled with obvious fear in his voice. Red looked at all the cells closely, stepping closer than Incinerator seemed to agree with, as he stayed back. Then he found someone he couldn't quiet see.

"Hello?" Red called inside. He could see a black silhouette in the back of the cell. Incinerator came up next to him, but still slightly behind him. The dragon at the back of the cell was sitting in a curled mess of shadows, and Red couldn't see if it was his mother or not. Two sharp, golden yellow eyes opened, glowing brightly in the dim light. Black slits fell across the dragon's eyes, Red knew it was her.

"Took you long enough," a sly voice hissed with a hint of teasing.

"Mother!" Red squeaked. *YES! Oranges, she's alive!*

Incinerator pulled a metal ring with keys on it out of a secret place in the wall, and used one of them on the door to swing open the cell. Red offered his mother his talon to help her up, and she pulled him into a tight embrace. Lassa's bright red didn't quite match Red's darker colour, but they had the same red-orange wings. Lassa always had her significant lime green hair, something she made a point to rarely cover up. *Something about defying the stupid laws that Magma created, respectable.* Red thought highly of his mother.

Red's mother turned to Incinerator. "Made up your mind, I see?" She asked.

"Y-yes, I- I think I have," he replied. "Um.. you're name is Lassa, right?" She nodded. All 3 of them turned to look at the prison entrance, which was suddenly filled with guards.

"The prisoners are escaping!" One of them called. The guards charged at them, Red and Lassa pulled out their crossbows. Lassa spun and threw guards at the cells and slammed the doors on them. Red shot at any guards that got remotely close to him, but Incinerator didn't seem as experienced.

"Red!" Lassa called to him. He looked over to her. She motioned for him to look up, and he saw wooden posts above them.

"Oh- I get it," he said, half to himself. He set one of his arrows on fire and shot it at the wooden beams. They fell on top of them all, with Lassa and Red dodging them easily, but the guards weren't so lucky. Smoke filled the room and fiery wood crushed the other Ariash dragons. *They're immune to the fire, but they hate the smell of smoke.* Eventually, they finished the last of the guards. Red aimed his crossbow at a dragon pushing their way out of the blazing wood, only to see it was Incinerator. He was wounded and bleeding a lot, nothing fatal, but painful. He clutched his shoulder as he came up to them.

"So, siding with us?" Lassa asked, her bright yellow eyes reflecting the fire dramatically.

"I think so," Incinerator said. He smiled despite his obvious pain and discomfort.

"You alright?" Lassa asked, observing his injured shoulder.

"I'll probably be fine," He replied. "This is nothing." Incinerator exhaled in pain. Lassa reached her arm out a little as he sat down.

"Now what?" He asked. "Are we going to your place?"

"You can't come with us just yet," She said to him with obvious guilt in her voice. Red could tell; the look in her golden eyes as she pitied the suffering prince, it was obviously guilt. *We don't want to leave you here.* He wanted to tell Incinerator that, but he would think they're abandoning him.

"Wait- Why not?" Incinerator asked in desperation.

"Because the prince can't just disappear. Not yet." Lassa rested her talon on his uninjured shoulder. "Believe me; You won't be here for very long." Lassa smiled proudly and nodded in respect. "Just survive for a little bit longer, alright?"

Incinerator's teary eyes stared fearfully at the ground. "I'll try... I can't make promises, though." Lassa pulled Incinerator into her wings, pulling Red close as well. After a moment, she released them. Incinerator smiled and ran across the prison to the other exit. They watched the injured, upset prince vanish into the darker side of the prison to the other door.

"What are we waiting for?" Red asked. He didn't mean when they would leave, he meant when they could take Incinerator with them.

"Incinerator is young," she replied. "Much younger than he should be for this world. Right now, he is prey among predators. We can save him now, but doing so would threaten if not destroy the entire resistance. I hate making sacrifices or making risks like this, but we can't endanger the entire resistance." Her sorrowful yet prideful gaze sharpened. "Not everyone will make it out alive though."

My father, Red's mind reminded him.

She turned to the empty doorway and then looked back at them. "Ready to get out of here?"

Chapter 1: The Calm Before The Storm

Yin And Yang

Silver had a wonderful life in her cottage home in the forest. She imagined that she would live on her own happily ever after, like a magic story. Silver had pale teal scales, even whiter under-scales and mint coloured wings. She also had dark blue tendrils on her chin, along with 2 horns, much unlike the 6-horned not-water-clan Aolite dragons. It was a rare defect, as she thought of it.

Her mother, Heaven, had told her about the enchanted sky spirit haven, high in the clouds. She always imagined what it would be like.

Silver always imagined it to be giant quartz pillars and marble floors with golden carvings of dragons in flight all over the walls. Stained glass windows that let the light into the large, long hallways with a light that brought good spirits.

Heaven had promised Silver that one day they could go see their amazing sky palace. Until then, Silver would have to stay in her home in the forest with her parents and sister. Silver and Sacrifice stood on the bridge over the shimmering pond, and Silver noticed something important.

"What's this?" Silver asked curiously, suddenly. Her sister, Sacrifice, looked over at her from her book.

"What did you find, tiny whelp?" She asked, laughing a little. She loved calling Silver 'whelp.'

"This snail shell… See the tiny things with slight green stuff in them? Silver pointed out, studying the shell closely.. "Something poisonous scared the snail out of the shell!" She was smiling and looking down at it. Her sister came up and looked over her shoulder. Her dark red scales were pressing against her side lightly.

"Ok… yes?" She asked, confused. While Silver had the abilities of the sun and sky, Sacrifice had only the power of the night. She didn't have the same sight that Silver had.

"For someone who reads a lot of words, I don't think you can see the varying problem here, " Silver joked with her..

"I don't think you know what the word 'varying' means," Sacrifice teased.

"This is poisonous," Silver remembered.

"What would you propose?" Sacrifice asked. Silver twirled her claws around the shell with sky magic. Her eyes lit up, the sunlight from her magic sparkling in her bright pink eyes. The slight green tint on the shell faded away and Silver stepped back in amazement. She looked over to Sacrifice, who wore a similar smile.

"It baffles me that you do what you do," Sacrifice said, shocked. Sacrifice's smiles were more calm and tame, while Silver's were wild and enthusiastic. She looked up at the diamond blue sky through the leaves. They stood in their backyard, a large hill going down with a small pond at the top, along with a cottage. A little bridge over the pond sat beneath their claws. Trees surrounded their yard and their cottage, and as they looked up at the sky, three birds flew overhead. Silver looked up at her sister and spread her wings to flap onto her back, laughing. It was hard to imagine that they were twins. Sacrifice was much taller, and Silver looked more... like an actual snowflake. Sacrifice's dark red scales always brought a wonderful thought to Silver's mind. She believed that others saw her as a black shadow, but if they looked closer, then they would see a beautiful red rose. Silver smiled at the snail shell on the rock

"Silver!" The twins looked up at the large cottage balcony and saw their mother, Heaven, looking around for them.

"Hey mommy!" Silver called up to her, waving.

"Are we needed?" Sacrifice asked. She picked up her book that she was reading, put her bookmark in and closed it to put it in her small brown bag.

"No, but I was wondering where you were," their mother called back, and went back inside. Heaven's scales were a pale pink with pure white underscales and dark blue horns, like Silver's. She had the same dark blue tendrils on her chin and had the same pale green wings.

"I want blueberries," the twins said in absolute unison, and then burst out laughing.

"The odds," Sacrifice laughed. They both flew up to the balcony and went in the single wooden door. The walls were made of a white stuff and had log poles every 2 lining the outer walls and the roof was coated with dark grey shingles.

Inside the door, there was a small library with small bookshelves lining the walls. A portrait of Silver's family stood over the fireplace on the opposite side of the room from the door. On the left wall of the door, next to the fireplace, there was a staircase that led to another staircase that went the other way. They led to their bedrooms. The kitchen was connected to the library by a small hallway on the right side of the door on the other wall.

Their father, who Silver actually didn't know the name of, poked his head into the library and looked at them solemnly. His scales were dark purple with black underscales and wings with an ombré of black and dark purple. He placed his gaze on them with magical glowing pink eyes, and looked directly at Sacrifice.

"Hello," he said, then immediately walked away.

"Hi- oh, uh bye," Silver said awkwardly. "That's odd," she frowned at the doorway and looked to Sacrifice. She just shrugged and they went to get blueberries. Once they got the blueberries, they went to the balcony and shared them. Silver said that she didn't know if they were fruits or vegetables.

"Probably fruits," Sacrifice replied. "They grow on a vine." She looked quite sure about that, so Silver went with it. They heard something overhead, and they realized that it was Heaven and "father" talking about something in their room.

"Must've forgotten that their window doesn't close," Sacrifice said, looking up. They heard their parents talking about weird things a lot. Silver never understood. Mother taught Silver in private about sky spirits, but never let Sacrifice hear. Their father never let Silver hear about what her twin was learning. Their parents didn't make much sense to them, but they never let the twins hear anyway...

Well, never let them hear on purpose, of course. They didn't try hard enough to keep out the twins' curious ears.

"Sorry that Swirl's Lixora isn't good enough for you," Heaven snapped at him.

"I personally just think that Swirl is boring," father was saying. "If you assist in being fair, then why not hand over your abilities and get rid of them for overall fairness, not just the fairness of the past conflicts?"

"Are you SERIOUSLY comparing clouds to- whatever it is that you mages did?!" Heaven said firmly. "Your clan has done terrifying things to the progress of Swirl!"

"What are they talking about?" Silver whispered to Sacrifice. Her twin shrugged.

"Father told me about some of this 'evil shadow' stuff," Sacrifice told her. "Mother must know about it as well."

"If she knows about the shadows… then why won't she tell me?" Silver wondered out loud. This was a common issue. Nothing new learned for the twins here.

"Let's just ignore them," Sacrifice said to her. Silver nodded, but looked back as they flew away.

Forest of Sapphires

Jewelem didn't think anything was to be important or interesting about him. He didn't do anything important. He did go to school, just on a boat, he played with his brothers and did all the normal things that 17 year old dragons do. The only irregular thing was that he lived on a boat. Jewelem was deep, bright blue with paler blue underscales with a rainbow frill and pale green wings. His brother, Qwonzie, was dark turquoise and had crimson underscales with pale blue wings. And last, Emeraldite was, of course, emerald green with darker green underscales. His wings were an ombré of orange to blue-ish green. He didn't see his mother often, because she was second-in-command of their ship. Commander Garnet and General Gold were his parents. His father, Garnet, didn't really like Jewelem, but he didn't care. Jewelem loved his brothers and family. Although he didn't have many friends, Jewelem knew everyone on his ship.

"Salmon," Qwonzie said to him, grinning. He tossed his tiny salmon fish to Jewelem, who was deep in thought. It slapped Jewelem lightly on the face and he looked at him with a slightly shocked look. Qwonzie laughed, His brothers. Jewelem laughed along with them.

"That was a waste of a perfectly good salmon." Jewelem said. "How dare you waste it." His little brother grinned. Emeraldite, his other brother, flew in from the top of the cabin roof and landed next to them and asked, "Did you hear our dad?"

"He was yelling like a burning bobcat, how could I not hear him?" Jewelem pointed out.

"Yeah, but he was talking about an ocean spirit," Qwonzie said with a delighted look that made Jewelem curious. "He was saying he wanted to kill it."

"That got dark pretty quickly…" Jewelem muttered. "Why would he want to do that?" His brothers shrugged. They all glanced around the boat, and Jewelem spotted Obsidian, a boat guard, standing near a doorway into the boat's lower floors. She was admiring her spear with her friend, Ruby.

"We could just ask him…" Qwonzie said. Why wouldn't he just tell us?" Jewelem shrugged and agreed to ask Garnet. They went over to Obsidian and Ruby and they immediately stopped them.

"Nobody is allowed in the lower deck right now," Obsidian said. Her scales were a mysterious black and purple. She sounded bored, as though she'd said that a billion times today. However, even though Jewelem had only met her a bunch of times in the hall, the idea that her voice was always bored was a valid option. She was always serious but bored."Commander Garnet and General Gold's orders."

"We're his sons," Emeraldite protested with a short laugh. "We basically own this place." Obsidian sighed and snapped to Ruby.

"Go get the commander," she demanded. Her voice was cold now, and she was glaring at Emeraldite. She was slightly taller and a bit older than Emeraldite, but she wouldn't be getting much taller and Emeraldite would probably be taller than her some time next year.

"Y-yes, Obsidian," Ruby said, nervously. Her scales were ruby red, of course. She glanced at Emeraldite on her way into the deck, and he smiled and waved slightly. She blushed a bit and left.

"Did you notice that?" Qwonzie whispered very quietly to Jewelem. They both stood behind Emeraldite, and Qwonzie had clearly seen something worth telling him.

"What?" Jewelem asked, confused. He was more concerned at the look, no, more of a glare, that Obsidian was giving Emeraldite. She was glancing at him from her spear but the glances were glances of hatred.

"The way Ruby looked at Emeraldite," He whispered to Jewelem, "she probably likes him!" Jewelem only made a "hmm" sound, and then looked at Obsidian's expression. Finally, Ruby returned. She glanced around at them and shifted her red wings.

"He… uhm, the commander… He wanted-well he…" she stuttered.

"Spit it out," Obsidian hissed angrily but coldly. Ruby flinched, but carried on as Emeraldite glared at Obsidian. She hesitated before speaking.

"He's ok with seeing you 3," she finally said. Obsidian rolled her eyes and the 3 brothers smiled, "It's… He's in a difficult room to find, can I take you there?" Ruby said hurriedly. She said it mostly to Emeraldite, but Jewelem pretended not to notice.

"Alright," Emeraldite said. Jewelem knew his brother could read dragons easily, especially Ruby, and Jewelem was happy that Emeraldite could do that.

Because Jewelem sure couldn't.

They went down the halls after Obsidian's deathly glare and followed Ruby to Garnet's council room. Jewelem was nervous, as always. However, he'd walked down these halls before and there had never been this many guards. He counted them silently and once they reached Garnet and Amethyst's council room, he had counted 50 guards throughout the halls. He wondered if Garnet was afraid of something in the ship? Emeraldite knocked on the door of the room. The walls in the ship floor were made of marble and had crystals for lights, giving the room a rainbow glow based on the lights. The floors were a velvet carpet and there were some tables with potted plants. A dragon the colour of sunflowers opened the door and looked at Jewelem with a glare. She looked at Emeraldite and then Qwonzie, and then said something.

"What is it?" She asked. "This is a meeting." She glared at Ruby. "Why did you let them in here?" Ruby shrugged, but couldn't seem to speak.

"We kind of let ourselves in," answered Emeraldite. They heard a low growl. It came from a dragon inside the meeting room, and although Jewelem couldn't see him, he knew it came from a dark crimson dragon, one that sat in the far right corner, and one who was married to Gold.

"What do they want?" Garnet growled. "Actually, come with me." Garnet walked past them out the door and down the hall. They followed him down the hall a little ways away from the meeting room.

"Did we disturb something?" Qwonzie asked.

Garnet sighed. "No, it was just some war stuff. I wasn't really being used for anything. Quite boring, I must say," he grumbled.

"We heard something about a water spirit?" Jewelem asked anxiously.

"Yes," Garnet sighed. "I want it dead." Jewelem's head perked up at that.. So it was true? Why would he want to kill it?

"Why?" Qwonzie asked. "Dad, why would we get rid of it?"

"It's been at war with us for long enough. Remember Queen Zoka?" Garnet asked. Jewelem nodded. He did remember. He knew what the water spirit had done to the queen. "We want her gone." Garnet frowned at the floor then gave them a stern look.

"How would we kill it?" Emeraldite asked.

"We get our spears," Garnet hissed. "And we attack in the name of the Crystalians." He stalked down the hallway and opened the door to the armoury. He went inside and looked at the weapons. The brothers followed him. "These spears will be the ones with the ocean spirit's blood on them. I trust that you will help me in my goal." With that, Garnet left them and went back to his meeting.

"Alright, let's go to the decks and get another salmon," Qwonzie said.

"A bigger one," Emeraldite laughed, grinning. "C'mon, Jewelem!" Jewelem stood back and looked at the spears and weapons,

"Yeah, I'll be right there," he replied. His brothers nodded and left, but Jewelem couldn't help but think.

If he truly fought the ocean spirit with these weapons, then would it be its blood on them? And if he failed... then would it be his?

A Tide That Flows With The Moonlight, Not The Rivers

As bigger, wonderful things happened on the islands, the ocean was a calm and quiet place that offered both excitement, and imprisonment. This was how Princess Legend saw it. She wasn't allowed anywhere, because according to her mother, "Little whelps shouldn't be out alone and unsupervised." However, in her room, she wasn't supervised in the first place, so if she went anywhere and went with a jellyfish, she wouldn't be alone unsupervised. The note in her talon definitely concerned her, but it was more concerning the matter 'why are whelps forbidden from leaving the dang palace?' it basically read "bye, going on out to be stupid, from your mother. Don't forget that there is only a 100% chance I'm going to die, so make sure that naughty little whelp doesn't go anywhere, got it?". Legend looked out of her room and didn't see any guards watching, so she considered it safe. Legend swam down the hallway and carefully watched for the guards. Legend was blue-ish tinted with the littlest bit of purple. Her underscales were the same colour but a bit paler, and her wings were sea-foam green. Legend's horns were dark purple. She wandered down the hall and snuck out the doors. The hallway's walls were made of aquamarine and the floors were made of blue tiles. There were windows that showed the marvellous but kind of boring ocean. Blue blue blue. It was all blue. The ocean, the dragons there, a lot of the fish, the entire kingdom, 75% of the world. It was kind of boring.

The water dragons were called Poseidonite.

Legend was usually told to stay in her room, and unlike any other sea princess in, like, the ENTIRE world, she hadn't remembered any of the hallways in her own house. She was lonely. Legend was always in her room, leaning in her clamshell vanity, resting her head on her desk. She'd look into the mirror, trying to imagine the sunlight. But now, her mother had gone out to do some stuff and told Legend that she'd be home alone for a few days. Legend wanted freedom, excitement, adventures! She'd just leave…. Nobody was stopping her, and technically it was her mother's fault. She made Legend want to leave and, bonus, left her home in the first place.

I just hope I won't have to talk to anyone up there, Legend thought, going into stealth mode. *Also, what's so concerning and bad that she'd leave a note for her tragic neglected whelp that she treats like a houseplant?*

No, but actually. She would NOT be able to take care of a houseplant. She doesn't give me sunlight or anything, or pineapples or sushi or-

Wait, am I a houseplant? Not the point! ESCAPE. She crept around the corner and, unfortunately, a guard spotted her. He looked over, looking bored, and rolled his eyes.

"What is it now, kid?" He asked. Poseidonite communicated underwater with speaking, the way fish do. Legend didn't understand the logic as to how, but she knew she could do it. Legend blinked rapidly and her (metaphorical) words caught in her throat. She ducked her head and the guard chuckled. Legend was so bad at (metaphorically) talking to other Poseidonite. The language was called Axteian. He swam over to her, grabbed her wing and hauled her back to her room. Legend looked around her room. It was fine. Blue. Blue. Blue.

The walls were deep blue with paintings of green and blue and purple fish, some seaweed, a few sharks and a bunch of dolphins. The floor was tiled with pale blue and some multicoloured tiles the size of pebbles. There was some red, but it wasn't bright red. It was kind of grey-ish red that also seemed a little … Weird. Like the colour of her scales, it was unique, uncommon and special.

But also weird.

A huge clamshell vanity sat on the left wall of the circular room. In the middle was a huge stained glass window of seashells. It was easy to see through, but it wasn't red, so Legend didn't 100% love it to the fullest. On the right side of the room, there was a blue bed made of aquamarine and the pillows and blankets were just blue and white. Legend once saw a red fish, then decided that red was her favourite colour. She had never seen the colour red anywhere but there. She didn't have legs, only arms, so she was less of a serpent and more like a pterodactyl. But that was her magic. Some Poseidonite hatch with wings like wyverns, some hatch without legs or wings and rarely, some hatch normally. Legend didn't have back legs, meaning she swam amazingly fast, but would be helpless on land.

"And land is where I could see more red things," she thought (metaphorically) aloud sadly, staring at the blue carpets and walls all over her room. Her bed was made of comfortable rock, which she didn't even know was possible. She swam over to the window and glared at a blue fish. She heard a knock on the door and thumped her tail on the side of the desk, signalling that they could come in.

"Hello," a female guard 'said' to her. Legend considered speaking Axteian to be talking. They came in and Legend kept her eyes on the window. "I brought you sushi." Legend quietly (metaphorically . . kind of?) sighed angrily. Guards never brought her food unless she was stuck in her room. This guard didn't know she tried to leave, meaning she was supposed to be in her room until mother returned. 3 days. Only 3 to escape. Once the guard left, she opened the window and quietly swam outside. She'd gone this way before, and got caught by scouts. Their kingdom was obviously under the ocean, but whenever Legend swam up to the surface, she would just hit rock. She'd wondered if they were in a cave. She, and the other Poseidonite, didn't have night vision, meaning if they lived in a cave, it would be dark, but there were also many glowing fish, glowing coral, bioluminescent lights everywhere and some Poseidonite glowing in the dark. She saw a scout and went along the coral. Legend looked up and saw the stone barrier. A stone wall stood in front of her, blocking her way to the sun. The kingdom was the other way, so she just sat, or laid, by the wall. Legend 'sat down' by coiling up and putting her wings down beside her. She leaned on the stone wall and looked around at the blue ocean. She noticed a red fish and followed it through the coral. Orange and yellow fans danced in the currents, blue and purple tubes of coral surrounded underwater caves.

She tried to cover her weird purple scales with her wings, camouflaging into the abyss. Legend followed the fish down a cave and through the tunnels. She paused when she turned the corner, as she saw a guard.

"Hey!" She saw the guard flare to her.

"S-sorry," she tried to say back. She couldn't really speak like the others because she was young and didn't quite learn their language yet. *Well, I'm 16, I should know SOMETHING. But learning Axteian is for dragons 17 and older I guess. Or we've been learning it and I just don't listen..* The guard swam over to her and shook his head in disappointment. He took her by the wing and pulled her back through the ocean. Legend slumped and didn't bother to resist. She looked back at the stone wall behind her. In her mind, she pictured the sun and the clouds reflecting in the water. With that last thought, she saw the red fish, and felt a flash of sadness in her soul.

A Fire Burning on Nothing But Ashes

Fire. Power. Respect. Loyalty, allegedly. Most of all, strength. Heir to the throne of Fire dragons, the Ariash, was Princess Meteor. Meteor had a lot to say about her island's version of perfect. Because if Prince Volcanic, her brother, was considered perfect and her other brother was preferred dead, then the standards should probably change. Meteor glared through the fireproof wood at the 6 dragons below her. She was in the attic with her blind, 6 month old brother, Pyro. He snuggled up between her arm and her body and laid down between them. Meteor smiled down at him.

"What are you up to down there?" She asked affectionately. "You sleepy?" Pyro nodded a bit and leaned on her arm. Pyro was really small, and he could perfectly fit under Meteor's arm. He was yellow-orange with pitch black underscales. He also had small nubs which would one day be large black spikes down his back. Meteor was the exact same but with bright red scales and slightly larger spikes. But Pyro had been injured when he was little, and since then he had to wear a blindfold.

"Mmmm…" Pyro mumbled. Meteor chuckled and looked through the gap in the wood. As usual, really.

There were 6 dragons down there, but only 3 mattered. 3 of them were guards, 2 were princes and one was the queen. She sucks. Queen Magma, queen of the Ariash and mother of 4, once 5, whelps, Meteor's mother. The only thing the 2 could agree on was they hated calling each other mother and daughter. They were queen and princess. Nothing else. However, according to everyone else, it was queen and useless peasant. Meteor glared at them. She tensed her muscles slightly, and Pyro looked up at her. She could sense the confusion in his eyes, even though she couldn't see them. Prince Volcanic and Prince Incinerator were down there talking with the queen

"The war is continuing as you assigned," Volcanic said formally. "The guards have guarded the… " blah blah blah blah whatever. Just boring war stuff." Meteor didn't like it at all. He might as well have said "yak yak yak yak yak yak yak." Seriously, were there no other ways to say "Yes the war is going pretty good," then end it?! She put Pyro on her shoulder and flung open the window behind her. It opened into the dense, grey, smoky ugly island air. Ariash could breathe volcanic air easily, even if it was a bit unpleasant to see in. Her brother held onto her neck and wrapped his tail around her shoulder. He knew how this worked. Meteor smiled. They went down the ladder to the top floor of the palace after closing the window again. Meteor and Pyro both had scars on them, unfortunately. For Pyro, most were from the current war. But for Meteor, it was Volcanic. He was dangerous and scary.

Pyro had a long slash scar over his face and eyes, as it was something he got when he hatched. Meteor felt so guilty that she wasn't able to save her brother from Volcanic. Their oldest brother just didn't like his siblings. *Little rude, isn't it?* Meteor thought bitterly.

"You," An angry male voice snapped from behind them. Pyro whimpered and dug himself into Meteor's shoulder. She turned around to meet Volcanic's eyes. "What do you two think you're doing?" He growled. His scales were dark red, the colour of the volcano from the outside. His underscales were slightly darker and he had black spikes down his spine. Volcanic's wings were dark orange and black. He glared at them from down the hall. All three siblings had the same black spikes, with Volcanic being the largest by far. Meteor crossed her arms and it took a lot of courage to not bow down to him. She tried not to bow to Volcanic, because she hated making him feel like he had even more power. Pyro was terrified of him, and Meteor sort of was.

"Just wandering down the halls, why?" Meteor asked without a hint of warmth. Volcanic's glare deepened as he took a step closer. He arched his wings royally.

"The queen herself has summoned each of the royals to the arena immediately," he hissed to them. It took even more courage to not sigh. Meteor hated going to the arena. It mostly meant more fighting her siblings.

"Fine…" she grumbled. Volcanic looked to Pyro, who whimpered. The oldest prince stalked down the hallway behind them towards the arena.

"I don't want to…" Pyro whispered to her. He was so scared of the arena, and Meteor always protected him the best she could. Volcanic always went straight to Pyro, thinking that if he killed him, then Meteor would be weakened.

"It's alright," Meteor tried to assure him and she walked to the arena. She looked up ahead and saw Volcanic talking with Incinerator. They had nothing in common. Incinerator was 3 years younger than Volcanic, who was 21. So Incinerator was 18, Meteor was 16 and Pyro was 2 months old.

Incinerator was bright orange with bright red wings and bright yellow underscales. He was also exceptionally lazy and dumb. He didn't do much but laze around in his room. He didn't like fighting, he didn't like not fighting, he didn't care.

The only thing the two older princes had in common was their hatred towards Pyro and Meteor. The younger siblings would hide constantly from them. Meteor growled softly. Meteor has walked down these hallways countless times, every day of her life, and she was 16. At the arena, the walls were made of grey stone, something hard to come across on their island. It was a small room, about a large closet of fighting space. It wasn't like the colosseum. There was a small slope into a small square arena that the siblings were forced to fight in. No wait, it wasn't "fighting in," it was "formally training for battle while you kill your siblings." Near the doorway, a platform lit by torches was where Queen Magma sat and watched the fight. She gazed down into Meteor and Pyro as they entered the arena. Incinerator stood in the middle with Volcanic, talking about important stuff or whatever.

"Go on," Magma said in her chilling voice. Ah, go on. That was code for the older princes. Volcanic leaped at Meteor's shoulder where Pyro was hidden. He squeaked as Meteor shot out of the way. She ran to the corner, fearing what Volcanic could do to Pyro. She placed him in the corner of the arena and spun around to defend Incinerator's claws leaping at her. She spun so hard that she hit Volcanic with her tail and he stumbled backwards. Volcanic was to her right, reaching his claws to rake them across her throat. He growled and glared at her when he missed. He knocked her to the ground as Incinerator grabbed her horn. Incinerator leaped on top of her and raised his claws. Volcanic suddenly ran to Pyro, intending to kill him. Incinerator's claws were about to slash Meteor's throat when he paused. He stopped and looked down at her.

"Incinerator, you idiot!" Volcanic yelled to him. Meteor pushed him off of her, ran to Volcanic, pushed him back and got in between Pyro and Volcanic.

Magma glared from her platform. She turned and stalked out of the room, signalling that they could all leave. Meteor turned to Pyro and saw he had a bleeding wing. She picked him up and carried him to the attic where they always hid. She placed him in a far corner as she snuggled next to him. Meteor looked out the nearby window into the fire island kingdom. It was small, really small. Almost the entire island was just fiery plains. Meteor growled softly and winced at the pain she suddenly felt. She touched her horn with her talon and examined her claws. *Can someone tell me why this awful place exists in the first place?* They had some blood on them, and her horn was slightly bleeding near the base. *Probably from when that RAT Incinerator grabbed it.* She sighed and looked outside again. *For the love of Ignis Blaze, I hate this island.*

Chapter 2: Where Death and Fear Loom

Yin and Yang

Not a day goes by that Silver doesn't see her mother's lesson. She knew so much about the sky spirits and their history and their palace. Silver wanted to see it so badly.

"I've heard that it's made of white marble and lots of glass!" Silver told Sacrifice. She was sitting under the shade of a tree, reading a book on fantasy. "Also there are gardens, trees and lunar foxes and cool birds!"

"Father told me about the shadowlands," Sacrifice said. "It's quite bland. He probably hates it, really. He said it's bland, awful and food is scarce. Father also said that nobody is allowed to leave."

"Aww that's upsetting," Silver said sadly. "No wonder he seems grumpy all the time." The sun was slipping over the trees and the sunlight was fading. Eventually, Heaven came and let the twins in the house for some strawberries. She hugged Silver and let them into their art room. It was a large, spacious room with once-white walls that the twins had painted on over the years. The walls were colourful with splashes of colours, drawings of dragons in flight and flowers blooming.

"I've always wondered what shadowlands really looked like," Sacrifice thought aloud.

Silver flicked her wings as she drew on some paper. "Mother said that the Shadowland kingdom are bad guys that Aolites don't like!" She exclaimed. "In those words, I'm sure."

"According to the books, dark spirits are the enemy of light spirits," Sacrifice recalled. "Makes me wonder why mother married a Shadowling, after what happened."

"Makes *me* wonder what happened in the first place!" Silver said. "Like, why couldn't the two clans just be friends?" Before either of them could say another word, Heaven came in and told them that they had to go to sleep.

Silver's room was painted to have flowers reaching from the floors over the walls, with the floorboards being made of pale birch with a white carpet. Her bed had white sheets, blankets that looked like skies, lots of plushies and toys and her pillows were an ombré of purple and pale yellow. Her bed was pushed in the far left corner and a desk sat in two right corners. A large circular white rug was placed in the middle of the room. A door in the centre back of the room went to a small balcony with two outdoor white chairs. The left corner of the inside of her room was full of green blankets and leaf and flower stuffed animals that Silver called the nature corner. That was where Silver and Sacrifice painted and drew things when the art room wasn't comfy enough for them. Silver went to bed after her mother said goodnight. She snuggled into her bed and looked up at the ceiling, which she had painted to have black stars. Silver felt her eyes close and she soon drifted asleep.

Hours passed.

Time went by silently.

Until she awoke to the sound of scraping.

"Hm?" She said sleepily. She was pretty sure this was a dream, so she sat up and looked around. She was still in her room, but something was outside of the door, walking down the halls. Something black, purple, large and smoky stalked by her doorway to her sister's room. She squeaked and hid under the covers. Feeling silly for being scared of a dream, she carefully stood up and slowly walked to the door. She suddenly heard a loud scream of terror and jumped and gasped. *It was her sister!* Silver darted out the door to her sister's room and saw the most horrifying thing in the world. She was staring at her sister's dead body. Silver shrieked in fear and felt tears down her face. She whipped around to stare at a huge dark figure looming above her.

"What have you done to my sister!?!" Silver screamed at it. Two glowing purple eyes stared at her, and she heard something fall behind him. The figure moved slightly, just enough for Silver to look over and see what fell. It was her mother. There was a knife through her arm and she was staring at Silver,

"Go!" She yelled to her. "Leave here!" She looked panicked, and Silver couldn't move. Suddenly the creature darted at her and raked its claws along her underbelly. She turned back to her room and flew out the window, leaving her home behind. Seconds later, the wound that it left on her started to grow, and turned black. She felt faint, and her wings started to give up. She slowly sank to the ground and as soon as her claws touched the ground, her eyes closed. Silver's last memory before darkness was the blood of Sacrifice.

Forest of Sapphires

Jewelem should've seen this coming. He didn't want to come on the mission, but who was he to have a say in that?

"I want to see a dolphin again!" Qwonzie was saying. "They look like tiny whales." The two brothers were on the ship owned by their father, going on a mission to kill the ocean spirit, like Garnet had said.

"Oh yeah?" Jewelem said, half listening. "Do you think we'll see the ocean spirit? I hear there's only one in the world at a time." Qwonzie shrugged and Emeraldite came swooping down. He informed them that Commander Garnet (though he said "father") wants to see them all at the control room. The three went to the instructed room and saw Garnet speaking with a guard.

"The ocean spirit is a deadly foe," Garnet told him. "We must act with caution and appear in the dead of night, when it's asleep." Jewelem wasn't sure if ocean spirits slept or not, but he didn't dare argue with him. Jewelem was scared of the ocean spirit, and he didn't quite want to fight it. His family didn't seem scared at all.

"Hey, dad," Emeraldite said gleefully. "Do you need us?" Garnet looked over and smiled proudly at his oldest son.

"Yes, I want to make sure all of you know that we're fighting the ocean spirit *tonight*," Garnet informed them. Jewelem sat quietly from behind Qwonzie. "We arrive at midnight. We're nearing its lair, and it will rise to fight us when it's unprepared. I must consult the others." Garnet nodded approvingly to his oldest and youngest son and walked right by Jewelem. He gave Jewelem a certain *look* on his way out.

"When we kill the ocean spirit, the Aqua Tribe will be heroes!" Emeraldite said, not noticing Garnet's look at Jewelem. "Maybe father will reward us!"

"The ocean spirit must be powerful," Jewelem said skeptically. He shivered at what it might look like. He's heard it was a huge magic beast of the ocean, but that didn't quite narrow it down. *Sounds like another piece of delicious tuna, but bigger. A big, delicious tuna would be considered magical, wouldn't it?*

"Why do you think nobody has killed it before?" Qwonzie asked. "It's obviously the most dangerous thing in the ocean, but what about spirits? I mean, it is a spirit, but it's evil, right?" Jewelem shivered. He had a slight fear of the sea, and this ocean spirit mission wasn't quite helping. He spent the day wandering, thinking.

Hours later, night had fallen and midnight arrived. Garnet told them to meet at the main deck of the boat, the middle of the deck where the moonlight shines the most. The three brothers met there and waited for orders.

" Hey-what's that?" Jewelem asked, mildly startled. Something large was moving in the water.

"Ocean spirit?" Emeraldite asked, gripping his spear tightly. Jewelem looked down at it. He didn't want to hurt anyone, even the ocean spirit. His arms were shaking and his tail couldn't stay still. Suddenly a huge, towering serpent rose from the ocean. Jewelem's eyes widened and he only heard the loud shriek it let out. It sounded angry, furious, even. Emeraldite was by his side.

"Come on, Jewelem!" Emeraldite said next to him. Jewelem snapped out of the hypnotic trance and the hid next to the entrance to the lower decks. Jewelem moved just in time, as the ocean spirit slammed it's tail onto the deck, shattering part of the boat.

"NOW!"

Jewelem saw Garnet standing on the edge of the roof with half a dozen harpoons. Garnet glared at the ocean spirit, tightly gripping his spear. The ocean spirit rose up, and slashed her tail right through the middle of the boat. It made a huge cut in the centre of the boat, and Jewelem fell to the ground. His brothers stood next to him, glaring at the ocean spirit. Qwonzie stood at his brother's side and shook Jewelem's shoulder, maybe trying to wake him up. Jewelem knew it was Qwonzie because of the small talons.

Another furious roar pierced the sky, and they both looked up. The spirit used powerful oceans against the soldiers, sweeping them off the platform, some landing in the ocean. Jewelem stared helplessly at the dragons he knew being taken under the ocean, and felt like crying. The Poseidonite shrieked as harpoons struck her lower back, and swept the main part of the boat with her wing. Qwonzie and Jewelem were thrown against the walls of the lower deck.

Jewelem shook debris off his wings and searched for his little brother. "Qwonzie?" He called over the raging storms. He finally spotted a teal arm from under broken stones. He pulled Qwonzie behind something and examined him. "Are you alright?"

His brother didn't answer, but he was alive. Jewelem spotted Emeraldite throwing more spears directly at the ocean spirit. Emeraldite was a pretty strong dragon. He crouched down and narrowed his eyes at the spirit.

Jewelem didn't know how Emeraldite saw them, but he must've seen them out of the corner of his eye. Emeraldite looked between them and the spirit. His eyes said a thousand words. He dodged an attack and pointed to the door that led below deck. Jewelem had to throw his wings over his head to not cry from the sheer sound of the ocean spirit's shriek. Harpoons flew at the ocean spirit's throat, but just missed. The few that didn't bounced off her scales. Jewelem looked at the ocean spirit. For once, he saw something in her, not a beastly ocean spirit, but an injured serpent who doesn't want to die. Jewelem realized how similar they were, both scared, and both maybe don't really want to hurt anyone. He put Qwonzie in a fortified closet near the door to the deck, which had been designed for quick access and safety. Jewelem launched himself into the air and flew up to the spirit. It turned from Garnet and his army to look Jewelem straight in the eye.

"Stop!" Jewelem begged her. The spirit looked at him skeptically. Jewelem looked at his talon and then dropped his spear into the sea below him. The spirit's eyebrows raised in approval.

"I will let you all leave here alive if you never come to these waters again," the ocean spirit promised.

"Oh-uhm… I apologize, your majesty, for we didn't realize that…" Jewelem stammered. He paused as he looked up into her eyes, and tried again. "We didn't want to really hurt you, I guess," Jewelem tried. "We just thought that you killed Queen Zoka."

The ocean spirit closed her eyes, and Jewelem looked back at his father and brothers. They all stared at him, shocked.

"I killed your queen in a fair duel," the ocean spirit said. She looked Jewelem in the eye, directly. "You have the power and energy of his majesty," she said.

"What?" Jewelem asked, forgetting who he was talking to. She didn't quite seem to care though. He didn't know such a hated beast could talk to have feelings and he felt bad about thinking she was a beast as well.

"You must be related to royalty," the ocean spirit explained. "It must be directly," She replied.

"But … I'm just the son of a commander," Jewelem said, confused. His head was spinning. He wasn't anything special, right? He was just a random kid.

"Perhaps you were…?" The ocean spirit offered. "Although I never thought-" she was cut off. A huge harpoon was shot through her throat and she shrieked.

"No!" Jewelem protested. He looked back in panic and saw it was his father.

"*Monsters*!"

The ocean spirit rose the tides and slammed them down into the boat. Jewelem felt water surging everywhere, and he was thrown under. The last sight he had was a glowing symbol of a rose in his talon.

A Tide That Flows With The Moonlight, Not The Rivers.

Legend hated waiting. She wanted to leave and get answers, but had to wait. She had to follow a guard, not get caught, and then he would lead her to the surface. She had followed guards, but they mostly led her back inside the palace or she got caught. She also could rarely go 5 minutes without getting distracted. Finally, she found one. He was watching carefully, making sure nobody was around. Except she was! He swam quickly to the surface, but not through the roof. It was far to, what she was told was the east, and there was a crack in the walls. Legend's eyes widened. He quickly swam out and up, and Legend followed.

How dumb am I for not noticing this?

Legend thought about what it might look like. She paused and looked up. There wasn't any sunlight poking through, which slightly confused her. Then she remembered that thing about night and day, and she calmed down a bunch. Poseidonite sleep when the Lunar Pointer turns off, which is powered by zilo terminals. Basically the power source of the Poseidonite. She took her last breath of the water and shot into the moonlight. She gasped and felt the world go silent. The stars. There were so many!! She looked down and saw she was 'standing' (Legend didn't have enough legs to qualify herself for standing.) on top of the water.

"Woah," Legend said. She blinked. Talking felt weird without a bunch of water to interrupt her. It was interesting though. She slithered over to a nearby island and as she reached the shore, she felt the first dry thing she'd ever felt.

Legend had been told that fish can't breathe on the surface, or out of the water even. She thought she'd be the same. She looked over her shoulder and saw a huge wave in the distance, and then silence. Suddenly, clouds rolled in and lightning crashed above her. Legend took a deep breath and tried her best to fly. It was much colder than what she was used to underwater. The wind tried to bring her back to the sea or to random islands. It tried to catch her wings desperately like a starving shark. Legend tried to get to one of the islands. The Poseidonite territory was west of the Dark Isle but North of the Fire Isle in the corner of Anima. From there she could see the two isles, and far in the distance to the south-east, she saw the Southern Earth Island. She landed back down on the island and sighed. The warm sand wasn't exactly comfortable, but she was tempted to fall asleep under the perfect, beautiful moonlight. She couldn't believe she'd come this far already. Legend looked out into the water and thought about where her mother could be. She thought back to the things she always said. She recalled an old memory of the war council meeting that she once spied on.

"Are the Crystalians anywhere near the southern coast?" Oceanic asked. *The walls of the council room were pale blue, with the ceiling and floor the same shade of bright, sky blue.*

"No, Your Majesty," a guard answered. "However, the western coast was assumed to be the most vulnerable, along with the south-west." Oceanic shifted on her claws and glared at the door.

"No need to wait a year to finish this," she said. "In a few days, I'll take care of them myself."

Legend had left because she had no interest in the war council. But she couldn't help but wonder what the heck was going on. She settled into the sand, laying down to sleep. The sand dug itself between her scales, and she could almost feel the heartbeat of a few creatures sleeping below the sands. Legend curled into the pale yellow island, sleeping all her troubles away.

Fire Burning Away at Nothing But Ashes

Pyro and Meteor slipped into the royal kitchens, which was obviously a bad idea, because that's definitely not allowed. But you know what else isn't allowed? *Starving the royal whelps?* Which was exactly what they did.

No, that was allowed.

"What are you thinking?" Meteor asked the little whelp on her shoulder. The door was near a counter and the 2 whelps were hiding behind it. Even if the kitchen was empty, they couldn't risk someone walking in and seeing them.

Pyro looked around, although he was blind. "Fish," he said confidently, then snuggled back into her shoulder. Meteor smiled down at him. She reached up and stole some cooked fish off the counter and left. They both retreated to the attic, fearing the day.

"Today's the day, Pyro," Meteor said to him softly, making him wake up sleepily. She couldn't help but smile. Meteor was so easily angered at the princes, but Pyro's little future that she longed for so desperately made her remember the only goodness on the island.

"Hm?" He asked her sleepily. She explained what would happen that day, and how at the next sunset, they'd be different dragons.

"The fire spirit ceremony is today, which is when the next fire spirit is chosen and taken to the other island," Meteor explained. "Everyone knows it's going to be Volcanic, so when they take him to the island, we'll be free from him!" Pyro smiled and went back to sleep. He was quite tired because training had taken place in the middle of the night. He probably didn't understand that well, but Meteor did. She had been waiting for this day forever. Now it was here, and she couldn't screw this up.

Hours went past, which felt like eternity. Volcanic had hunted them down and informed them about what would happen at the ceremony that night. Yawn. Meteor had no interest in it. *My only interest is where they bring the chosen fire spirits, and how mad you're going to be about it*, Meteor thought. As soon as they arrived, Meteor could tell something was off. She didn't know what, just something was wrong. Too many dragons whispering to each other, not too many guards, which was definitely wrong. The ceremony took place in the huge arena attached to the back of the palace. It was huge, spacious, circular and cruel. Dark things happened there.

Whenever dragons are chosen, they are immediately taken away from the island. Banished. There was once a king named Firebrazer who was banished because he was a fire spirit. He, for some reason, stayed on the island. He didn't leave or anything. He just wandered the volcano plains. The island was long but quite thin. Therefore, it was quite easy to hide on the other side of the island from the rest of the Ariash.

The door on the other side of the arena was where they'd leave the arena.

Meteor turned and whispered to her brother. "Our lives will change when we go through that door." Pyro looked at the door with his blindfolded eyes. A blood red dragon stalked past them and glared at Pyro on his way to the arena. Meteor gave him a dirty look.

"See you on the other side," she whispered to Pyro.

The other side.

Meteor and Pyro went to the line of dragons in the middle of the arena. They all faced the queen, who stood on a platform overlooking the arena from the palace. She looked down on them with a dark, evil gaze. There hadn't been a ceremony in forty years, and they only occur when a fire spirit dies. The ceremony started, and an old guard holding a blazing scale stood in front of the line of dragons. He went to the first dragon and carefully handed him the scale. No reaction. They weren't a fire spirit, according to tradition. Same reaction from everyone. Once they got to Volcanic, everyone fell silent. Volcanic looked deep into the scale.

No reaction.

Volcanic's eyes widened, maybe in anger and shock. They tried it with a stranger, and no reaction.

Meteor was glad that her silent laughter was silent. Snicking at that catastrophic event sounded like a death penalty. Once it reached Meteor, every dragon in the world seemed to freeze. Even on the island of fire, she felt cold stares on her. She held the scale and looked deep into its fire. She stared into it, and saw two eyes arising to stare at her. The scale suddenly lit up in her claws, bright enough for her to flinch and everyone in the arena saw it. Meteor gasped.

"*Whaa?*"

Many dragons gasped and some turned to the queen. Meteor felt dragons tearing their claws along her back, dragging her somewhere. *The place where they take fire spirits?* Meteor thought. She looked back at her brother, Pyro, who was spinning around, trying to find her.

"What happened? Meteor?" He asked. She felt a stab of guilt, and decided to take him with her. She ripped herself free and ran to Pyro. Dragons were flying to flee the arena, and Meteor looked into her claws to see a shape appearing. She remembered that spirits get a constellation to represent their power. The shape of a dragon talon formed in her claws. She looked back to her brother in horror and before she could say anything, she was dragged into the sky. She looked back, tried to fight back. No use. Meteor felt cold pain in the back of her head, and her vision slowly faded. She was torn away from her brother, and forced to leave him in the claws of murderers.

Chapter 3: Arrival of Awaited Foresight

Princess of The Sunbird

Turns out that the sky spirit haven was both real and extremely populated. It wasn't just for sky spirits, but it was also a kingdom for the Aolite dragons. Silver soon found out that she wasn't just a white dragon, but also that she was a mix between an Aolite and a Shadowling. Which was a surprise, but it hadn't sunk in until then. When everything had faded to black when she escaped her home, her mother had found her and finally brought her to the sky spirit haven! However… Soon before they reached the borders of the sun kingdom, Heaven had made Silver wear an odd cloak.

"Child, you must wear these," Heaven said, *handing her a dark blue cloak and a brown pouch. The pouch could go around her neck and could fit about 4 books. The cloak, however, covered the mark on Silver's lower neck and had a gold button on the front. It didn't cover her legs or back, just the front.*

"Why do I have to wear this?" Silver asked, looking at it.

"Because we don't want anyone to know that you have that mark," Heaven replied. Silver reluctantly took the odd cloak and put it on.

"How many kingdoms are there?" Silver asked again. It was her fourth day in the sun kingdom and she was in a room called the storm chamber, and its name suited it pretty well. It was a huge spacious room with dark thunder clouds everywhere, making the walls invisible. The room was apparently made out of clouds and lightning, which was quite a surprise.

"There is the Fae kingdom, Ariash, Shadowling, Aolite, Poseidonite, Ghilist, Extivie, Crystalian, Earthin, Icelo, and a few unknown more," LightningRoar informed her. He was a huge storm dragon made of clouds and lightning. Silver thought the name was rather fitting. "There's also Olvin and a rumoured Azopholite, like Aolite but different."

"There are over 10?!" Silver exclaimed, flabbergasted. Just then, Princess Heaven popped her head into the room.

"Silver, dear, would you mind coming with me?" Silver bounded over to her mother.

"Ok!" She said happily. "Bye, LightningRoar!" Silver looked back as they left to see LightningRoar disappear into the storm clouds. Once they were down the hall from the storm chamber, Heaven turned to Silver with a strong look.

"Silver," she asked with full seriousness. Silver made a "hm?" noise and turned to her as well. Not with seriousness, no, Silver was never serious. "What may you have been in the storm chamber for?"

Silver blinked. "Just asking about the kingdoms, why?"

"You know you can't go to the kingdoms, remember?" Heaven reminded her with a sigh. "I don't want you knowing about those. They're bad places, they'll corrupt your mind."

"I know but-" Silver started. She stopped when a pair of huge wings descended, divine and white.

"There you are," Queen Shield said to them.

"Mother!" Heaven exclaimed with a small gasp. Silver remembered Heaven not quite liking Shield a lot. Silver giggled. Shield was almost pure white with next to no blue. She had pale purple feathery wings with pale blue diamonds. Shield wore a necklace made of ice that never melts.

"Hello, children," Shield said calmly to Silver and Heaven. Shield was Silver's grandmother, so she was allowed to say things like that and mess around with Heaven.

"Hi, grandma!" Silver said gleefully.

"I'll take it from here, my child," Shield said to Heaven. Silver didn't understand, but pieced it together as Heaven frowned and silently left the hall.

Shield led Silver through the gardens, along the clouds lining the kingdom, and into the great sky. There were no guards telling them what to do, no judgmental eyes of advisors looking at Silver and whispering about how useless such a small princess was. No dragons looking at them in awe of what they could do. Silver loved it so much. The two dragons met eyes and smiled at each other.

Shield sighed and cleared the clouds away. "Tell me, child. Are you happy here?" Silver's smile fell for a second, then returned.

She looked to the ground below the clouds. "I guess I wish my sister was here."

"Condolences," Shield nodded. She paused. "Your mother doesn't like your sister. She has her reasons. I spoke to her about it, and she wasn't pleased with it at all." Silver looked at her in confusion.

Silver said, "But what did my sister do?"

"It's nothing your sister did, child," Shield said thoughtfully. "It's something your mother had done many years ago."

They both hesitated and the sky clouds felt silent. Silver subconsciously leaned on her grandmother's side. She felt Shield carefully place her talon on Silver's shoulder. Shield waved her other talon, and the wind picked up, moving the clouds to clear their view to the ground below. They could both see the 6 islands against the blue ocean. She had to ask her grandmother something important. She had to.

"Grandma," Silver said, nervously. "When can I go to the islands?" Shield looked down at her and smiled.

"The islands are dangerous," Shield answered, but didn't sound like she meant it. "At least, that's what your mother says." Silver didn't understand why Heaven thought the islands were dangerous. She always said that other dragons could be evil at any moment, and that it was hard to find someone who was actually nice. She always said that Silver was too trusting of others.

"I wonder why mother thinks that others are evil," Silver thought aloud

Shield snorted. "Quite ironic, really."

"What?" Silver asked, turning to her. "What did you say?"

Shield looked at her. "I'm just saying that it would be good if I followed her own advice."

Just then, Heaven came over to them from the direction of the palace. "Shield, what are you telling her!?" She called. She landed near them, just a little bit away. Heaven looked at the hole in the clouds that looked onto the islands and gave Shield a dirty look.

"Just telling her about the islands, dear. Nothing to worry about," Shield said with a smug smile. Silver remembered something that Shield once said to Silver about Heaven.

"I'm her mother aren't I?" Shield had asked jokingly. *"I don't have to say anything about this."*

That was when she had taken Silver to the clouds for the first time, which was Silver's second day in the sun kingdom.

"Why were you showing her the islands?" Heaven demanded.

"Because she should know about them," Shield said as though it were obvious. "They're a part of her world as well, dear."

"Come with me, Silver," Heaven said. "We… have something to do." Silver reluctantly followed her mother to the sun kingdom as Shield watched her leave. Silver looked back, and was surprised to see her grandmother smiling at her.

They walked on the clouds for a few minutes before either of them spoke. It was Heaven first.

"Silver, the Aolite are your clan," Heaven reminded her.

"I know," Silver replied. "But I've always wanted to see the world, mother." It was true, Silver had always wanted to see the other kingdoms. She had never been allowed to leave, however. Heaven never let her.

Heaven spoke with an odd twist in her voice. "I want what's best for the future, the world, the kingdom, and" she suddenly stopped talking. Her wings dropped. "I want what's best for you, Silver. The world can be really dangerous, and I want you to be safe more than anything."

Silver looked down at the clouds, away from her mother. Then, after a moment, she looked back at her and smiled. "Thank you, mother." Silver said gratefully. Heaven and Silver both stopped to hug each other.

"I love you very much, dear," Heaven whispered in her ear. They both eventually got back to the sun kingdom and Silver went straight to her room. She gazed out the window and sighed.

"I do wonder where my sister is…" she thought aloud. She had seen her die, but she felt an odd presence in the air. One she had felt since she hatched.

One she had felt when two certain eyes were laid on her…

Princess of The MoonBird

Sacrifice awoke in a dark room. A slow ticking sound matched her heartbeat as she walked. She couldn't control her legs, she couldn't move her wings. She couldn't fly away. Did she exist? Where was she? Her mind didn't think about these questions, she only walked further. She couldn't see the walls or feel her legs moving. All was dark, but she felt like she was walking. Sacrifice didn't feel her legs moving but she sensed it instead.

"What is wrong with this one?" Someone asked. Sacrifice didn't hear them. Black and white flashed in her eyes, darkness engulfed her vision once more.

"She's… red?"

"Hm, seems more brown-ish."

"She's just walking."

"Following his command."

That last one hit her. She felt herself move differently as they gasped quietly.

"What did you do?"

"Can she see me?!"

"Is she going to die?"

"She's already dead."

She suddenly stopped. Sacrifice could open her eyes. She gazed up at the towering dragon in front of her. She couldn't speak, show anything in her expression or move. The clock she once heard had gone out. Sacrifice didn't feel herself breathing.

You have died.

A voice in her head told her.

Obey.

And with that, Sacrifice closed her eyes. She opened them into a blank world. Nothing around her, just straw fields. Forever.

For Eternity. But that isn't unsurprising, now is it?

The voice in her mind claimed. It felt like the voice was directly in front of her, beside her, behind her and above her. It was truly inside of her. It was strong, clear, loud, but not too loud, and sounded horrifyingly familiar. It was also a male voice.

Obey me. I am your king. I own you. Do you understand where you are?

Sacrifice realized that her eyes were open. Sacrifice didn't understand the voice, or what it was talking about. She had died, and this was death.

Was she talking to death?

I am not death.

The voice responded. Sacrifice couldn't control her mind, she could only think about what was in front of her.

You do not deserve will and freedom. You betrayed me, and the entire Shadowling kingdom. The Extivie, the Olvin, the Shadowling, they all depended on you and me.

Suddenly, Sacrifice gasped and opened her eyes. She could see, think, feel and move.

"Who-?" She started.

"Do not speak." A black smoke whirled around in front of her. Suddenly, she was in a long, dark hallway with brown-grey walls, black floors and ceiling and no light. She could see, barely, but something else was disturbing her. A dragon was standing in front of her, clear as the wind. She recognized him immediately as more than just her killer. She knew him very well.

"Hello, dear," her father said, looking down at her. He motioned to the hallway around them. "How do you like your prison?"

Sacrifice froze again and looked at him. "Where am I?"

He smiled and chuckled a little. "You are in the Blackzone, child," he explained. "A little space of mine to... *relax* in, one could say. Well, The god of Silence gave this part to me, but not all of it." Sacrifice stepped back in fear, trembling.

"Why did you bring me here?" She asked, panicked. He stopped smiling and stared at her with glowing purple eyes. His gaze pierced her like a knife, the one that could kill with more than a look.

Forest of Sapphires

Jewelem suddenly woke up from a deep sleep on an island in the middle of the ocean. He woke up coughing and injured. The moonlight was shining down on him from above, the ocean reflecting the stars, making them appear everywhere. He was on a completely remote island with some other islands around it. He felt a stab of pain in his head and right leg, so he sat there and waited for the pain to go down.

"Hello?" He tried to call out to anyone. "Help?" Speaking caused harsh pain in his throat, and he guessed he shouldn't quite do that. The island, from what Jewelem could see, was quite small with a small beach and approximately 40 trees with some grass. Not enough to be considered a forest, but not quite just some trees. Maybe a small hiding spot.

He suddenly heard a sound, a little splash and saw a small spray of sand.

"W-who's there?" Jewelem asked, trying not to sound panicked. He felt like his throat felt like it was filled with saltwater, and it honestly could be. He coughed more water out of his throat, pain welling inside of him. Suddenly, a beautiful dragon stepped out from behind a large rock. Jewelem stared at her and almost gasped.

Who stood before him was the most beautiful Poseidonite dragon with the most uniquely purple coloured scales. They were a grey-ish purple with the smallest hint of blue, all majestic and amazing and hard to describe. Her wings seemed to subtly change different shades of green in the moonlight and her eyes twinkled with all blues and purples in the world.

I don't even know this dragon, they could be deadly. Where's that natural fear response to strangers when you need it?

But as Jewelem looked at the dragon's innocent, curious eyes, he had a small feeling she wasn't going to kill him. He kept his weak guard up anyway.

"Hi," she said very nervously. She looked very anxious. Jewelem seemed stuck to the ground with his limbs all frozen. "I'm Legend.

"Jewelem," he replied weakly. She looked at him with mild confusion creeping slowly in the back of her eyes. "That's- uh, that's my name. I'm Jewelem." He added that last part hurriedly to his relief, she smiled at him

"Hi… Again," she said shyly. "I… I'm new to land. They both just stared at each other for a few seconds. Jewelem slowly examined her, trying not to just stare at her. She did the same.

"You're Poseidonite," Jewelem said finally. "I've never seen one on land before. I never thought that was possible."

"Honestly, I didn't think it was possible," Legend replied nervously. She only had two front arms, but seemed to be able to walk pretty well. Jewelem didn't quite know how to continue this conversation, so he tried small talk. He also didn't know how to "small-talk," so he tried.

"So, what brought you to the surface?" Jewelem attempted. Legend paused for a second, and then laughed under her breath.

"I guess mostly the fact that I'm not supposed to be here," she said. "Why are you here on the islands, Jewelem?"

"I seemed to have woken up here," he replied. "How'd that happen?" Legend looked away nervously. "Do you know something about that, maybe?"

She paused again and then spoke. "I found you injured in the sea, and brought you to the shore," Legend said, still looking away. "I mean, you're blue so I thought you were also Poseidonite. I thought-maybe that… I thought you were sleeping in the ocean, even thought sharks don't like eating dragons, they could still…." She looked back at him, only to see him smiling at her.

"Thank you, Legend," he said to her. She smiled.

He shifted lightly on his claws, but quickly sat down and grabbed his hurting head.

"Are you alright?" She asked, stepping forward to help him. Jewelem could barely keep his eyes open but Legend examined him closely. Before either of them could speak, they heard a splash from the ocean. They both looked to see it and saw another Poseidonite rising from the ocean. Legend looked at them curiously, but Jwelem tried to duck away from his view, trying to ignore the awful pain in his side. Legend ducked next to him and carefully put a green wing over him. Jewelem tried to see why he was hurting so much. He had marks and scratches on him, but he wasn't sure where they came from. The Poseidonite carefully inspected the beach. He tossed his head over his shoulder to look at the ocean. While he did that, Jewelem tried to take a closer look at him. He was a bright blue with darker blue underscales and all four arms and legs. He didn't have wings, meaning Legend and Jewelem could easily fly away if he tried to hurt them. The new dragon turned back to the shoreline and took a few steps onto the beach. He then motioned for someone to follow him, and another Poseidonite slipped out of the sea. She was deep blue and almost black, as though she were water from the darkest part of the sea.

"Why are we on this island?" The blue one snapped. "We're supposed to be looking for Queen Oceanic! She wouldn't be caught dead on this beach."

Snail shrugged. "Just thought we might find some Crystalians. If we can't do our regular posts, might as well hunt them and track down the queen." Jewelem flinched at the remark. Not *all* of them. Perhaps some Crystalians were bad, but Emeraldite and Qwonzie and his parents…

The other sighed. "The queen is powerful, she wouldn't have let any escape." She huffed and turned towards the ocean. "Come on, Snail. I'm in charge, so let's go."

Snail took another look at the island. Unfortunately, Jewelem accidentally moved his tail and made a sound. Both of them whipped around to look in their direction. Jewelem thought about using his magic to escape the situation. He carefully twirled his claws and sent 4 small crystals to splash into the ocean on the other side of the trees.

"Did you hear that?" Snail asked. "It sounded like there was something over there, in the water."

They both hesitated and waited before leaving.

"Let's go," the blue one said, turning back to the water. In a few moments, they were gone. It was just Legend and Jewelem. Both of them waited to make sure the guards were gone, and then stepped out from behind the boulder.

"Wow," Legend said, looking at him. "I didn't know Crystalians held magic!"

"Oh, uhm… Thanks," Jewelem attempted, feeling his throat hurt. "I mean, not all Crystalians can do this." He shook the remaining sand off his wings.

"Well I think that's amazing," Legend said gleefully. "Only thing I can do is splash fancy water." She flicked her tail and a small wave rose up from the ocean and splashed into Jewelem, drenching him.

"Hey!" Jewelem said affectionately as Legend burst into giggles. He smiled, but clutched his head from the pain. *What kind of sea elephant slammed into me?* he thought faintly. Legend must have noticed his pain.

"Are you ok?" She asked hurriedly. "Are you hurt? I don't know if I have anything…" she looked around. She lightly pulled him to the boulder for him to lean against. She rubbed cold, wet seaweed over his head.

He wasn't sure if he was awake for a moment. "Thanks," he whispered to her. For some reason, he immediately remembered his brothers and father. Maybe it was the colour of the ocean, and how they used to go fishing on islands like that one. Or maybe it was the way Legend laughed just like Emeraldite used to.

Or perhaps it was the Crystalian warship horn that sounded in the distance.

Both of their heads snapped up, Jewelem in fear and confusion and Legend in curiosity.

"Do we like them?" She whispered to him. "Are they friendly?"

"Not to you. They don't like Poseidonite," Jewelem informed her. "Maybe they haven't told you, but Poseidonite are at a small war with the Crystalians."

Legend's eyes went wide. "Why are they fighting? Is that where my mother went?" She asked, maybe to Jewelem or to herself.

"Who was she?" Jewelem asked. He immediately realized, however. He didn't even want her to answer, because then he would have to tell her. She looked at him.

"The ocean spirit, Queen Oceanic, is my mother," she said. Just then, the horn sounded again, and this time, the boat came into view. It was a small, scout boat. The smallest of the largest, however. It was still big, but small compared to the warships. It could hold about 50 dragons comfortably and was very, very strong.

"I-I have to go," Jewelem said to her. "I have to get back to the Crystalian kingdom." Legend's wings drooped a little and Jewelem felt a pain in his chest. He realized that he could easily be the only friend she had.

"But …" Legend started. She closed her eyes and then smiled, lifting her wings. She still looked a bit sad thought. "Alright, well, hopefully I can meet you again tonight. Right here." She smiled directly at him and Jewelem changed his mind.

"Actually, I'm looking for someone," he said. He wanted to find out what the ocean spirit had meant. She had said that he was the son of the Crystalian king, but he was the son of Garnet.

Wasn't he?

"I'll meet you here again tonight," He promised.

Legend and Jewelem said goodbye to each other and Legend disappeared into the sea. He smiled as he thought about the small ocean princess. He have to tell her about what Garnet had done, didn't he? Jewelem didn't want her to know that her mother was dead. He smiled anyway at the thought of his new friend. He went into the patch of trees and settles under a bush. He rubbed his head. It hurt less, but still kept cold seaweed on it just to be safe. He hoped it wasn't serious. Jewelem closed his eyes and drifted into a peaceful sleep.

A Tide That Flows With The Moonlight, Not The Rivers.

Legend couldn't believe it. She'd never seen a Crystalian before, but the one she'd seen was so… amazing. His scales twinkled with the star's reflection and seemed very… Well, something Legend couldn't describe. His name was Jewelem, and honestly, he seemed really cute. She liked his voice and the way he spoke about things.

He's adorable. Legend thought. *Jewelem is really cool! Crystalians are amazing. I wonder if he'll take me to see his magical kingdom… Lots of red things! His rainbow frill was so pretty.*

Legend hadn't wanted to leave. She wanted to stay with Jewelem for a while and talk to him about their kingdoms. She wanted to hear about his clan. Legend had known she couldn't stay, so she'd shot into the sea.

Down, down down. Into the dark, blue, lonely ocean. She missed them as soon as Jewelem's little island, the moonlight and the stars were out of sight. She felt a stab of sorrow for the longing. *I hope I can see them again.* As soon as she got back, she went straight to her chambers. However she was stopped in the hall by a guard.

"Princess Legend," he said, bowing to her. Legend has completely forgotten that she was royalty, and she forgot to tell Jewelem that.

"Yes?" She asked. "Is something… Wrong?" The guard looked up at her, and confusion and hesitation spread across his face.

"I regret to inform you that Queen Oceanic has been confirmed dead," he said, struggling to not tear his eyes away from her.

Legend almost crumpled to the ground. "W-what?!" She demanded.

"I'm sorry, but we found her body in the deep sea," the guard replied. He sounded scared.

She suddenly whipped around and shot down the hall to her room.

"*No!*"

The guard stumbled back at her sudden swing. Tears formed in her eyes, the ocean's waters taking them away. The guard stopped her quickly. She turned to look him in the eye, anger flaming below her eyes, behind her tears. She tried desperately to put on a calm, simple face. She buried her face in her talons and softly sank to the floor. She could sense the guard's judgement, but also his concern.

"Child…" He said, coming up next to her, brushing her wings with his. "Do you know what this means?" Legend momentarily tried to stop crying, but it was difficult. It died down after a few moments, and the guard led her down a hall. He brought her into the largest, scariest room in the palace.

The throne room.

He put his wings around Legend one more time and then left her alone. The more she thought about her duty, the more she wanted to beat her wings higher and higher until she would never see the ocean again. She just wanted to see Jewelem again and forget all this. Legend laid her claw on the throne, and silently prayed to her mother's spirit. Legend had been told never to go to the Great Mirror until she was queen, and now that she was, she had to. She hadn't ever gone there on her own, only with her mother. She picked up the crown that sat on the throne. It was made of perfect crystal silver and pearls with shimmering seashells. Legend carefully removed the largest seashell on the top of the crown and opened it. Inside, there was a silver key. It wasn't special in appearance, but it's purpose was the most important to Legend. She unlocked a secret keyhole near the back of the throne and opened it. She moved the throne, revealing a secret door. A long hallway led to a huge crystal cave. It was blue crystals and diamonds, glowing sapphires and lapis hung from the ceiling. It was less of a cave and more of a large chamber. Dragon-made, but cave-shaped. On the far wall hung a huge crystal mirror. Inside, it showed a regular reflection, an odd, purplish little Poseidonite. *That dragon was a princess yesterday*, Legend thought. *But now she is queen, staring at herself.* But if she laid her claw on it's glass, it could show a new world. She did so and the reflection changed.

This mirror was never made to show reflections; it was made to show the truth. As she looked inside, she could see the past of any recent royal member from the past 100 years. All of them were just regular Poseidonite royals, but one was Legend's greatest mystery, enemy and question.

Legend's father.

When she was little, her mother used to take her to this mirror. When she asked her why, her mother replied that she didn't want Legend to live in confusion of where her father went and why. Legend ran her claws over the mirror, reflecting the past.

"Oceanic, magic is a curse!" Riverstone roared. The walls of the palace rumbled as the dark storms above raged mercilessly. His deep blue scales reflected the glowing blue in Legend's claws. She looked up at him in confusion.

"So it's our fault that the spirits gifted us, but not you?" Oceanic snapped back. "Even so, how can you blame Legend and me for that?

"I don't want something that could destroy the world! I will never let dragons like you roam the world freely, shaping however you want it!" Riverstone hissed angrily. "Dragons like you have done awful things, and I will never respect someone who does those things." He turned to directly face the young child.

Oceanic stepped in his way. "If you want to leave, Riverstone, go right ahead."

He glared at her and scoffed. "I'll never forgive you, or any of them, for this."

As the past faded away, Legend turned to glare at her claws. *If it weren't for these, would father still love me?* This was a common thought. She always wondered if he'd love her if she was normal. But Oceanic had told her that she was perfect the way she was. Legend took her glare to her father's imagine on the mirror. *If you had stayed,* Legend thought. *Then how would you think of me now?* Legend went back to her room, thinking of her mother's death and the dark future that awaited. She guessed the entire palace didn't know yet, so she assumed she and Jewelem could see each other tomorrow. *Guess I can't run off with Jewelem. Someone has to rule the sea.* If she did run off him him, who would rule? She couldn't think of anyone for the job. Maybe if she hired a guard, or trusted adviser. Or maybe just someone smart, maybe, just maybe…

She and Jewelem could actually be together.

Fire Burning Away at Nothing But Ashes

That same, red talon in hers. Just looking at it appeared to make the flames burn brighter, hotter and higher. Meteor stared into the light of the fire, her blood boiling. She snapped her claw to the side, making the symbol disappear.

Just like him, she thought bitterly. The fires burning in the room around her would never go out, according to Firebrazer. He was a dragon who claimed she was the only mortal who could see her, until she told him she was a fire spirit. He then said that only fire spirits could see him. It sort of confused her how he had found her, even thought Meteor knew full well that he was dead. She growled and gazed at the door of the fire-filled cave. Meteor hissed and looked back at the flames.

"I'll show them all," Meteor said quietly to herself.

"Show them what?" Firebrazer asked, suddenly appearing out of nowhere.

"Revenge," she answered, growling.

Firebrazer shifted nervously on his claws. He glanced around at the burning room and sighed quietly.

"Are you sure revenge is a good idea?" He asked. For such a strong dragon, he seemed really nervous. He didn't look like the dragon to be scared of things, and she remember the story of when he died. Everyone said he had fought a long battle until he died at the claws of…

"What do you mean?" Meteor demanded. "That island is full of evil monsters who only care about making others suffer!"

"It's been that way forever!" Firebrazer protested. "They've always hated fire spirits! It's just the way the Ariash are."

Meteor didn't like the Ariash way of doing anything. They were all evil. All of them.

Not all of them, her mind reminded her. A flash of a small child in her talons snook into her mind. *Don't you remember? Even though he's dead, he was still a great dragon. He would've been the best dragon in the world if he hadn't been raised there.*

Meteor sighed and looked at the door again.

"I'm going to go outside," she told Firebrazer. He smiled at her as she left. She opened the door into the bright light.

The island they had put her on was a huge island in the middle of the sea with grass, trees, a small forest, a beach, a cave, a volcano and a small mountain. Part of the cliff jetted out from the island in the perfect spot full of sunlight, leaving a meadow where some flowers sprouted. Meteor had found a cave below the mountain where she could see the ocean from inside. Firebrazer had explained that fire spirits always found that cave, Meteor spread her wings and flew to the top of the volcano, doings flips in the air as she flew. She gazed at the huge island.

"Where are the other spirits?" She wondered aloud. She looked behind her at the infinite ocean. *My water spirit is in that ocean.* She thought. *They'll come to me. I won't be stuck here with Firebrazer and my own thoughts.* She glanced up at the sky. Only birds flew overhead, no dragons. Meteor glared down at her claws, the ones that held infinite power. As infinite as fire. Firebrazer had explained that she held the talon constellation and all her power was held in her claws. *Literally.* He'd said that his power came from his wings. She'd found out that she could use other fire spirits' constellation and that she could always use his to fly much faster.

"Is that all you're useful for?" She'd asked him.

"No, I'm also wonderfully smart and hilarious company," he had replied.

"The only hilarious thing about you is how wrong you are," she'd told him.

Meteor turned back to look into the volcano's hole. The fire inside glowed in the dark cave, despite what was left of the sunlight. The sun was creeping down the horizon, plunging into the sea, only to rise at dawn. With a stab of pain, she recalled something her little brother once said.

"Why do dragons say the sun is from an Ariash?" Pyro asked.

"Why wouldn't it be?" Meteor asked calmly. "Would it be a Furo?"

He shook his head. "Poseidonite!" He said. "It goes in water, come back soon."

The memory made Meteor's soul deflate. The fading sunlight shone on her scales, suddenly blazing into her eyes. She sank her claws into the volcano's edge and shot into the sky, a fiery haze blazing around the dragon's golden shape. The fire cleared and she admired the island from her new state. Meteor had found out that she had the ability to make herself much bigger. About as big as the volcano, which was just shorter than the mountain. She landed atop the volcano and crept down onto the ground below. She curled her tail around it's base and rested her claws on the top, leaving huge claw marks all over the volcano. She found a comfortable position and settled there. Meteor sighed and looked out to the ocean. *The others will be here soon.* She thought. *Soon. Maybe…*

I'll be happy with them.

Chapter 4: Hurricane

Princess of the Sunbird

Silver awoke the next day. The sun was shining slightly above the ocean, gleefully greeting the early birds. Silver yawned, stretched her wings and legs and leaped out of the room. She'd had a weird dream, that her sister was standing at the edge of someplace, waiting for her. She didn't want to think about all that though. Even if nobody realized it, Silver did think about her sister a lot. Everyone just thought she would get over it. But it wasn't that easy. Silver shook her head a little and just smiled. *Mother just wants me to be happy,* she thought. *I should make her happy that way.*

The throne room was empty when Silver walked in. Nobody else was there, other than her grandmother sitting on the throne. She had her talon over her forehead and looked as though she had a headache.

"Hi, grandma," Silver said, noticing her position. "Is something wrong?" Shield didn't reply for a moment, as though she didn't realize Sliver was there.

"Oh, nothing, dear," Shield replied, noticing the small whelp in the doorway. "Just a small issue, nothing to worry about."

Silver tilted her head at her, but knowing she wouldn't be getting any more information, she left. Silver wandered around and found closed doors that led into someplace she'd never seen. She walked down a long hallway, full of mirrors. Each wall had a pillar, and each pillar held a reflection. This was the only part of the palace that didn't have windows. It was dark, but still had some light from Silver's glow and the dim lamps. The pillars were made of quartz along with the ground. The walls were made of sapphire blue crystal and the floor was made of pale blue tiles. She remembered the few books her mother had brought her that showed pictures of the Poseidonite kingdom and how blue everything was. Silver heard a scraping sound and looked behind her.

"Hm?" Silver said. "Is anyone there?"

The reflections in the mirror started to change. Her pale blue scales turned a red so dark it almost pulled her inside. The scraping sounds started coming from behind her, but she couldn't look away. Her scales were still pale blue, but the reflection was much different. She looked deep inside and she swore she saw the reflection of her sister. Her eyes were closed, her scales were 3 times darker and her voice was broken.

And she a knife through her chest.

Well this is quite something to wake up to after a nightmare, she thought.

"Silver..." Her someone's soft voice hissed. It was cold and dead, nothing like her perfect, calm and silly sister.

"Sacrifice?" Silver called inside of the reflection. "Is that you? What happened?! What's wrong?! How are you-?!?" Silver stared at the knife through her sister.

Her sister opened her eyes and another cold, male voice slipped through her.

"Bring her back," the voice hissed. "She will disappear soon, Silver." Suddenly, the dragon inside the mirror, if it was Sacrifice or not, roared in agony and melted away into darkness.

"Eek!" Silver shrieked as the black dragon crumbled into dust. She looked back at the door as she heard talon steps running through the halls.

"Silver?"

A powerful glow raced through the hallway, calling Silver's name. She heard 2 familiar female voices talking about something quietly. She tried to hear as much as she could.

"Did she find the dark spirit?" Heaven asked, panicked.

"No doubt," a voice that sounded like Shield replied. "If anyone can find them, it's that little girl." Then Heaven came into view, a panicked look on her face. Behind her, Shield was looking rather unimpressed with her daughter.

"Hello dear," Shield said, suddenly smiling when she saw Silver. "What brings you into these ha-?"

Heaven interrupted her. "*Why are you in here?!*"

Silver was slightly surprised as to how they both wondered that. She was sure they never thought the same thing. Yet, now they both wondered why Silver was in the weird mirror hall. Silver looked around the room and then back at her mother and grandmother.

"I felt like I wanted to be here," Silver replied. She shrugged. "It seemed ... Peaceful."

"Alright, well please don't come in here," Heaven told her.

Shield looked back at the door and spoke quietly. "The last thing we need is more of them..."

"Alright," Silver said, stepping back. Her elders nodded and left out the door. Silver looked around at the dark, cold room. It seemed to go on for miles, stretching the darkness forever. She looked back at the mirror where her sister had been and almost gasped.

There was something different on the mirror.

Words.

The words spoke an ancient text that was written in the Shadowling language. All dragon clans spoke the same language, but back in ancient times, they all spoke different languages. Silver and her sister knew the Shadowling language from their father.

"Silver?" Heaven's voice called.

"Really, Heaven?" Shield said from down the hall.

"Ok, just a minute." Silver replied. She carefully read the text.

Bane of the day, Killer of Light
Prince of dark, Keeper of night.
Those who fight have come to fail
None have ever told the tale.
Torn between 3 worlds and despite his pain internally,
Never had he ever seen the true Prince of Eternity.

Silver read over the text a few times. What did it mean? Who was the prince of eternity? Silver couldn't understand, no matter how many times she read it. She remembered the text carefully and left the room. She met up with Heaven outside the door. She was whispering anxiously to Shield, probably about the weird mirror hall, but stopped when they noticed Silver.

"Hello, Silver," Shield greeted her.

Silver waved to her, but didn't say anything. Her mind was full of the text and what it could mean. Heaven opened her mouth to say something, but then closed it and stayed silent. When they thought Silver was out of earshot, she and Shield went back to whispering. Silver wandered through the bright halls, listening to the sounds of birds, cleaners, cooks and other palace sounds. The dark silence of the mirror room with the comfort of her sister had helped. She looked up and noticed she had stumbled into the library. Shield had told her about the library, but Silver hadn't had time to do anything there.

The huge, spacious room was made of white quartz, and the floor was made of white tiles. Each bookshelf was made of birch wood and had books of all colours. A huge stained glass window hung above an indoor balcony that had turquoise carpets and glass tables. Two large staircases lined the walls to get to the balcony area. Meanwhile, on the floor level, there was a large rug with bubbles and fish. All around it there were small toys for little whelps to play with. The different sections were all labelled above the bookshelves. A librarian desk sat below the balcony.

Inside it, a small, young, white dragon sat in the tall chair, organizing books. A stand on the desk had a name on it. *Gust.*

As soon as Silver walked in, he gave a small jump and smiled immediately. Silver walked up to the desk and smiled back.

"H-hello, Silver!" Gust said joyfully. Gust had pure white scales and pale yellow under scales with 6 purple horns. All Aolite except Silver and Heaven had 6 horns. Silver and her mother didn't because Silver was a mix, but she didn't know for her mother. "Do you need anything in particular?"

Silver laughed very, very quietly. He was a friendly little dragon. "Yes, do you by chance have anything on Shadowlings?"

He tilted his head at her. "Why do you need those? I don't want to sound rude, but those aren't quite. . Umm, popular among readers?"

"I need something on the art of Howler's gift," Silver whispered to him, remembering what she learned.

Gust froze and looked at her. "I'm not sure I'm allowed to-" he paused again. He looked at the books on his desk. Then nodded. He slid off his chair and searched through a drawer at the bottom of his desk.

"Are they not on the bookshelves?" Silver asked him, trying to see over the desk without looking rude.

Gust returned with a box of books labelled "*Shadowlings*" and put it on the desk. "They're mainly forbidden. But you're… you know, the princess. I thought maybe Heaven wouldn't mind…" He trailed off and looked up at her. He was much smaller than she was.

She sighed in relief.

"I didn't even know the palace had these," she said, relieved. "How much for them?"

Gust starred in a seemingly sorrowful way 'at the books in the box. "Just… Please don't tell Queen Heaven or Queen Shield. That's all the payment I need." He readjusted his wings and looked at the floor sadly. Silver looked in sorrow at the young child. She thought about how much trouble he could be in if her mother found out about this.

"Thank you, Gust," Silver said. She pulled out the small bag that Heaven had given her. Inside, she had put a few toys, food for her lunar fox, "some" money and tasty foods. (She was a princess, so her mother was rather generous with the money. She'd been given $100, but she'd spent $20 on some pastries and muffins.) . She retrieved a carrot muffin and $20 from her pouch and placed it on the desk, taking the books. Gust looked at the muffin and money with big, amazed eyes and smiled.

"My mommy needs this," he whispered to her, taking the money.

Gust's dad always worked, and his mom was the librarian. She had been injured and has been with the healers for a year. Gust had taken her job when he returned, but some dragons had stopped coming to the library after realizing the best librarian was gone. Everyone had liked his mother, and she did her job so nicely. Gust usually didn't have enough money to pay the healers, but Silver had always wanted to help him. Silver hugged him and left. She glanced back at him and saw him put the money in a small coloured box.

I should come here more often, Silver thought.

Once she left the library, she immediately remembered the odd text and why she had rented the books. She took them to her room. She read the title carefully and flipped the first open to a random page;

All dragons are clearly known to grieve when someone they love is lost. Most dragons just let it happen and don't try to prevent it once they're dead, but some Shadowling did so much more than just grieve. Shadowlings are a very old race, and they were known for their dark magic and spells. They could possess the underworld and the Darkest Worlds to their will. It is this power that led to their 'banishment.' Being 'banished' to the Shadowlands means they lost some of their connection to the night. They lost their full ability by the eternal barrier that blocked out the sky. Note; we can see the inside of the Dark Island through the barrier from the outside, but the inside acts as a transparent dome. They can't use the starlight from inside, and they can't escape. Without their full connection, they couldn't bring life back to their loved ones. However, before they lost it, it was a dark practice to bring back the dead. The practice slightly altered the zombie's appearance, and might make their body slightly colder. The main and most dangerous changes were in their personality. First, the zombie would perhaps feel more distant for their first moments. It isn't a pleasant experience to be brought back, but many of them would prefer it. I've personally found that zombies feel fine after a couple days. Though I've never been resurrected, plus I'm not a Shadowling, I lived around Shadowlings for the longest time. Very few Shadowlings had mastered this dark practice, along with Puppetmastery, a demonic practice allowing dragons to control dragons and

make voodoo dolls. More on that in later chapters. The way to conduct the spell was to tear a hole in reality and bring them back from the darkest world. The only way to do so was to follow these steps carefully. However, do so at your own risk. The spell was removed from any current spell book but this one.

Silver read the steps carefully. She wanted to bring her sister back right then and there, but knew how much trouble she'd be in if she was caught. Silver immediately took the spell book and threw it back in her bag. She flung open her balcony doors and leaped off, beating her wings faster than she ever had before. The sun was now higher in the sky. Silver's glowing shape in the sky was impossible to miss, but maybe she'd go unnoticed if everyone was elsewhere. Silver dived below the upper into the darker parts of the sky. The sun magic she possessed let her stand on the clouds. Silver ran across the grey clouds into a tall, old, abandoned building. It was dark and made of old wood, which was weird considering it was made in the sky. Inside, there was a small room and very little light. She opened the spell book and brought it to the page. She looked over the spell.

"Beware…" She read carefully. She looked at the author of the book.

NightChaser.

"Huh," Silver said. The book said a bazillion more warnings and how dangerous it is. *Can it, NightChaser.* Silver thought, feeling slightly bitter. *I want my sister back.*

She opened the page with the actual spell and looked at it. An odd symbol was written on the page. A spell was written on the page and she spoke the words.

"Spirit of Dark, Spirit of Light"

"One comes bearing gifts of might."
"Those who leave will live to see,"
"Those who don't will die with me."
"Bring the dead ones back to day,"
"Forever they will always stay."

Now I'm to ignore the slight immortality hint in the "forever they stay" line. Once she finished speaking the spell, the room lit up. Blue light filled the room and it swirled around her. It suddenly turned black and all Silver could see was the endless black abyss of the Darkest World.

Princess of The MoonBird

Death wasn't see-through or silent. It wasn't dead itself, and it was physical.

But if it wasn't *him*, then what was it?

If it wasn't real, she wouldn't be in this situation.

Sacrifice couldn't move. She could never move. She could listen and stare. No feeling, no life… No sister. Her sister had a new life. Sacrifice had stared at her from the mirror, unable to speak. He had her in the palm of this talon. She heard something from behind her. Just by memory, she knew it was the large black figure of her father. He walked in front of her and looked over at her with two glowing purple eyes.

"Hello, child," he said. The black nothingness around him and Sacrifice was suffocating. "Having fun?" He sat down, clapped his talons twice and the darkness swirled around them. It disappeared into the bright field, the huge black castle in the distance.

Sacrifice opened her mouth to speak, but no words came out. The evil dragon smiled again and chuckled a little. His deep, clear voice came from all angles. It felt like it was inside her head. The clock in the distance ticked. Sacrifice felt the presence of her father in her head. Each piece of her world is gone.

Forest of Sapphires

The next night, Legend appeared at the shore. She had a worried expression and seemed very nervous. Jewelem was out of sight behind a large rock. She sat on the shore, burying her tail and in the sand and then raising it. She pressed her front talon to her forehead and then placed it back in the sand, looking up at the twinkling stars. The moon shone down on her blue-ish scales.

"Hey,"Jewelem said, coming into view.

She turned around to look at him. "Oh-hello, Jewelem …" She seemed partially distracted.

"Is something wrong?" Jewelem asked. Why was she confused? She looked *scared*. "Did something happen?"

"I'm not sure how to say this, but…" She took a deep breath.

"Did you kill the ocean spirit?"

Jewelem froze. So she found out. Jewelem didn't quite know how to respond. He hadn't exactly killed her, but that was his father's intention. Though if he said no, it would seem like he was lying. He looked to the ground and nodded his head. Legend stared at him with large, confused eyes.

"I don't think you did…" She said. "You just…" She looked over him. Legend took a step towards him. Feeling nervous and a bit scared, Jewelem sighed and told her the pure, whole truth.

"It wasn't my idea," he explained. "My father took the Aquamarine Tribe out on a boat to fight and kill the ocean spirit. I had a choice to stay, but I didn't want to leave my brothers."

"Brothers?" Legend asked, intrigued.

"Emeraldite and Qwonzie," Jewelem replied. "They went on the mission, and I was told the ocean spirit was dangerous, so I couldn't let them go alone." He looked down at his claws, feeling guilty. "She destroyed our boats and now I don't know where either of my brothers are." Jewelem looked out to sea. He knew they could be dead, but he didn't want to think that until he saw the proof. He looked back at Legend, expecting her to explode in anger and hatred. He expected her to be upset, but she just looked sad.

"I have to be queen of the Poseidonite tomorrow," she muttered. "I'll never be able to come again." Jewelem's wings fell to the ground.

"Never?" He asked. Never again? Was he going to be lonely forever?

Suddenly, Legend's face changed to realization. "Not if we run away!" She whispered.

"Then who will lead your clan?"

"I have a cousin, it doesn't matter! We're fine to leave. My clan will be fine," Legend said. "Where should we run away to?"

They were both interrupted by the sound of a loud horn. It was a similar horn to the one they heard when they met, but this time, Jewelem felt a shock.

"Legend!" He whispered. "Come over here." He was hiding behind the large rock, motioning for her to come. She must not have heard him.

"Oh, do we like them?" She asked. "Are they nice?" The boat came and stationed itself about 2 islands away from shore. Three dragons flew off the ship, holding long spears and wearing armour.

They'd seen Legend.

"There!" One of the Crystalians called. "I've seen that Poseidonite before, on this very island."

From on the boat, another dragon called down to them with a horrifyingly familiar voice. "Give me a weapon. I'll deal with them myself." A large crimson Crystalian glided down from the boat and stood between Legend and the ocean. He had a long scar down his throat and across his snout.

This was for sure Garnet, Jewelem's father.

"H-hello," Legend said nervously, eyeing the spear in his claws.

"Tell me, sea dragon, if I am not being deceived, have you by chance ever gone to this island before?"

Legend hesitated. "Um, no." Jewelem almost sighed in relief, and then stopped himself. "I was just passing through. But if you need something from here, I can help you." Garnet swept his tail along the sand. Jewelem knew that was the sign to either attack, retreat, or capture, depending on the situation and the opponent. In this case, it meant *capture* or *attack*. Jewelem watched in horror as the Crystalian guards swooped down and dug their spears into the sand next to Legend's scales and the shape of a blue figure leaping out of the way. Jewelem barely had time to think. When his thoughts started working again, he knew he couldn't do anything. *But I have to do something! Legend needs me... But why is my father hurting her?!* Jewelem looked into his claws, and realized they were glowing...

And the symbol of a rose appeared in them. Jewelem knew what this meant.

He was one of *them*.

The symbol of a rose glowed brighter. Brighter.

I'm not brave like my brothers... But I am a spirit now.

A Tide That Flows With The Moonlight, Not The Rivers

Legend gasped as the crystal dragons dug their spears into the sand. They'd aimed for her scales, but she'd shot out of the way.

"Ow! Hey-why-?" Legend shrieked. She looked around desperately for Jewelem.

"Kill her."

She looked up to see the crimson dragon staring down at her, into her soul. He looked blankly down at her. Another spear came at her, this time she couldn't dodge. Instead, a huge crystal, green and blue got in the way of the spear and it bounced off of it. Legend looked around. The crystal suddenly shattered and Jewelem stood in between the crimson dragon and Legend. *He's so brave. I wish I was as brave as him.* Legend thought. The sight of Jewelem shook the crimson dragon, and he stumbled back. The other guards stopped and stared at him. The crimson dragon hissed.

"I always knew knew you were powerful, but I never expected you to be a traitor," the crimson dragon said.

"What do you mean you knew about my power?" Jewelem asked.

"Jewelem, who are they?" Legend pleaded. She didn't want him to leave yet, she wanted him to stay and be her friend. But if they were here to take him home, she wouldn't stop him. She couldn't understand the pain of wanting to go home.

But she could understand wanting to go to the past.

Another Crystalian shot at her from behind, but Jewelem, being awesome, got in the way.

"Get away from her!" He called, his eyes filling with light. The moon was directly behind him, giving him a perfect incredible glow. *He's so perfect*, she couldn't help but think. Jewelem summoned a gem wall and blocked the guard.

"Jewelem, what's happening!?" Legend shrieked again.

"I'll … Uh, explain later," He called to her. He spun and dug his claws into the sand. Sharp diamonds flew at the guards and pinned their wings to the ground.

"Jewelem, what's going on?" Legend asked. He looked down at her, his eyes filling with guilt. Just then, the crimson dragon leaped at Legend. He shot his spear at her and she couldn't move. Jewelem's head snapped up and she covered her eyes with her arms.

For an agonizing minute, a flurry of blue and crimson and blood red spilled around her half-closed eyes. The noise stopped. Then, Legend heard the most ear-piercing shriek she'd ever heard. She opened her eyes and gasped. Spears had been thrown into the ground right next to her and crystal walls were blocking the view of the trees behind them. But the worst thing;

The crimson dragon's spear had been thrown directly through Jewelem's back. The crimson dragon had ripped it out, and it was bleeding a lot. He hadn't completely impaled him, but he was fatally stabbed.

"Jewelem!" Legend screamed.

The crimson dragon and the guards had gotten back to the boat. Jewelem was hunched over and barely standing up, but he managed to look up at her. He collapsed into her arms as she pulled him closer to the sea.

"You… You don't have to help me," Jewelem tried to say, his words sounding odd and different.

"I'm going to help you, whether you like it or not," Legend replied firmly. Tears welled in her eyes as she tried to heal the severe wound. She lowered him close enough to the sea that his back was touching the cold waves. Jewelem yelped in pain from the cold water. *Please don't die.* Legend thought desperately. *I don't want to be alone anymore.* She could feel him slipping out of her claws. She remembered the necklace her mother had given her. It was supposed to heal any wound. Legend looked down at her dying friend. She didn't want him to leave, and she'd do anything to keep him alive. Finally, she saw him close his eyes, and she made her decision. She lifted it off her neck and carefully placed it around Jewelem's.

She remembered vividly her mother telling her that it would be ineffective for dead dragons, so she just hoped it worked. It felt like an eternity, waiting for the necklace to take effect. She wondered if he was dead already, and covered her mouth with her talons. Jewelem tightened his grip on her talon and softly opened his eyes. The wound on his back stitched itself together and the blood vanished

"Hi, Legend," Jewelem said, smiling.

"Jewelem!" She exclaimed happily. Legend helped him to his feet and after a few moments of awkward wobbling, they threw their wings over each other.

"So I am rather wondering…" Jewelem said. "By chance, how did you just magically fix me?" She smiled again and she showed him the necklace.

"Watch this." She took it off and placed it on the sand. She then picked up a spear and dragged the shorn end along her forearm, leaving a small but visible mark. She picked the necklace up again and put it over her head, and the wound healed itself immediately.

"Wow," Jewelem breathed, amazed. Just then, Legend's talons started to glow. Jewelem's head snapped up and looked at her claws. He stepped back. Legend looked down at her glowing talons in awe.

"What's happening now?" She asked him.

Jewelem looked her in the eye. He summoned a magic symbol of a rose in his talon and Legend gasped. "I'm one of them as well. So are you, Legend!"

She looked back into her talons.

The image of a magic star appeared.

"Is that good?!" She asked. Jewelem stepped forward, the symbols both vanished and he took her talons in his. "Legend," he started. "You and I, we're spirits."

Legend tilted her head at him. "What does that mean?"

"It means we can go to the spirit island and find the others," he explained. "Regular dragons can't go there, and it's not on any maps, but everyone knows it's real. There are supposed to be five. A light spirit, a dark spirit, a fire spirit, and we are the earth and water spirit, I guess. It means we can go to the island where the spirits are supposed to live and coexist."

"It's outside of Anima?!" Legend asked, flabbergasted. *Outside of Anima… There's nothing but ocean and oceans and more ocean out there! I've never even heard of an island! If we left, we'd have to go through… Him.*

She looked at her claws. "Ok, but, before we go… Jewelem… I think you're the king's son," Legend said with difficulty.

Jewelem stopped smiling, which effectively shattered her soul into a hundred pieces. "W-what do you mean?" He stammered. "What about Garnet and my brothers…"

"But only the king has the crystal magic, and it's genetic, isn't it? And if the crimson dragon is who you thought your father was, then didn't seem to like you very much. No offence."

Jewelem touched his forehead. "Alright," he said, smiling a little bit. "Let's go to the spirit island."

Legend smiled at him, and he smiled back once he saw. "Well then," she said. "Let's go meet the spirits."

Fire Burning Away at Nothing But Ashes

The sky spirit, the Aolite, birds and pigeons live there, Meteor thought as she looked at the sky. She didn't particularly know how to "birdwatch" so she was just watching everything in the sky. *Everything in the sky is either birds, dragons or clouds. Maybe smoke, though*. She was sitting on top of her stone cave. next to the volcano. Meteor had found a perfect place to watch the sky and the ocean. She heard wingbeats behind her and looked back. From the top of the volcano, Firebrazer was swerving down to her with his powerful wings. He landed a few meters behind her and she sat up.

"Do you need something?" Meteor asked.

"You said you wanted to meet the other fire spirits, right?" He asked. "Well, I brought them." He motioned to the top of the volcano.

"I didn't particularly say I wanted to meet them, I said I'd wondered who they were," Meteor replied.

"Well I think you'll like Cloud," Firebrazer said, grinning. The dragon on top of the volcano was but a silhouette of a weird creature, not quite a dragon. But as the thing slid down the volcano instead of flying, it hit Meteor like a rock.

Meteor couldn't believe that a human stood right there in front of her. And that it was a spirit, no less!

"This is Cloud?" Meteor asked. She then turned to him. "A human?"

"Now, I'm sure you're shocked," Firebrazer said formally. "But I've trained her to not bite."

"I don't need training, you lizard."

Meteor's head snapped back to Cloud. "She can *talk?*"

Cloud rolled her eyes at her, which was a good sign that she was interesting. She put her talons (which had no claws) above her head, but mystically, and a swirl of smoke appeared around her and blocked their sight of her. The smoke turned dark red and flecks of gold swirled around inside. Once it cleared, the human was gone. In its place was a large dark red dragon with a uniquely-shaped tiara. Her underscales were pale red, but her regular scales were a slightly dark red and her wings were orange. A weird tape-kind of rope was wound around both of her horns. They weren't connected to each other, but there were 2 long pieces of tape wound around her horns. The tape was red, brown, dirty yellow and a bit of grey, but it was an odd accessory, like her tiara. The dragon was bigger than Meteor by a smidge, but she was definitely shorter than Firebrazer, who was taller than both of them. She sat down casually as if humans turning into dragons was just a normal thing.

"Don't listen to Firebrazer, my name isn't just Cloud," the dragon said. "It's *CloudScraper*, and no, he didn't train me. I don't need training.

Meteor turned to Firebrazer with an impressed look. He laughed. "She's a human who can turn into a dragon, or vice versa. I'm not sure," he said. "Cloud has a magic Phoenix feather earring." Meteor looked at her again. Sure enough, the dragon had a feather hanging from a small string on her ear. She'd seen some dragons from her island who had earrings, but she never wanted any. She thought it looked painful to get a little hole in your ear just for some jewelry.

"So you're a fire spirit?" Meteor asked. "Like… A real fire spirit?"

Cloud nodded. "I was named CloudScraper because everyone thought I would be a sky spirit, but turned out to be a fire spirit. In case that's what you meant." Cloud seemed to have a calm, chill energy which was unnatural for any dragon from Meteor's island. She didn't know whether Cloud was a dragon turning into a human or a human turning into a dragon, but it confused her. *Pyro would like to see her*, Meteor thought without thinking. She immediately felt a stab of pain again.

"So, Cloud, this is Meteor. She's the new fire spirit!" Firebrazer exclaimed.

"How can I see you if you're dead?" Meteor asked. She definitely remembered his death. "Also, how old are you, Cloud?" She knew for a fact that fire spirits gain eternal life when their time is up. Then they have two lives; one for the real world, one for their next life when they're not as powerful. She'd heard of sky spirits getting another life in the spirit world again after their death in their second life, but she wasn't sure.

"As a current fire spirit, you're able to see the fire spirits of the past," Cloud explained. "You also get to use our powers and let anyone you want to see us."

"So nobody else can see you two?" Meteor asked.

Firebrazer nodded.

"Oh, cool," Meteor replied.

"And to answer your other question, Firebrazer is 46 and I'm about seven thousand years old."

"… That's… Normal, I guess."

"Where are your other spirits?" Cloud asked, looking around. "Aren't they supposed to be here with you?"

Meteor hesitated. Then Firebrazer jumped in. "She doesn't know, they aren't here yet."

"Let's hope her sky spirit isn't as bad as mine," Cloud growled.

"Are there any other fire spirits?" Meteor asked. "And if you gain eternal life, then how many are there?"

"There were many others. But sometimes, they erode, and die. Some of us like to keep ourselves in good condition. Less problems that way," Cloud explained again.

"The others are Final, Heatstroke, Phoenix, and Dusty," Firebrazer said. "You'll meet them soon."

Cloud turned back into a human form, this time less dramatic and more quickly. Just a little poof and she was a human. Now that Meteor saw her again, she could make out the little details. Her hair was short, choppy and blond. Cloud's skin was pale and she had a red top... Thing (Meteor didn't understand human things.) with short orange bottom things, along with a darker orange streak lining the bottom of her red one. Yellow lines ran through her clothes and her hair had a dark red streak in it. She had tall boots (some dragons wore boots for some stupid reason,) which were also dark red and gold. The human swiftly climbed up Firebrazer's leg, onto his shoulder and found a comfortable spot leaning on his neck.

Cloud crossed her legs and sat comfortably. Firebrazer was a huge dragon (about triple Meteor's size, and she wasn't small), so it was easy for her to sit on his shoulder.

"Where are the other fire spirits?" Meteor had to ask. "Are they hiding?"

Cloud snorted in laughter. Firebrazer laughed a bit and said, "Yeah, but so were we before we met you. I came back and met Cloud, then I followed her back into hiding. Then I heard that you got here and came over."

"How'd you find out?" Meteor asked.

"Talents," Cloud replied. "Also, I should probably go check in on the others. Dusty needs me."

"Why does she need you? You both seem pretty much fine on your own," Asked Meteor.

"We just have to," Firebrazer told her. "We need each other."

"Alright," Meteor said. "See you later… Probably." They both waved goodbye, Cloud turned back into a dragon and they flew off into the clouds and disappeared into flames. As Meteor watched her friends fly away, she gazed out to sea. *Somewhere. Sometime. Eventually they'll come. My spirits, they'll be here. But if they don't, then that's just fine. I don't need them to be happy, and I don't need them for anything.* She opened her claws. Blazing red flames burned in her claws. *If they don't come, I own this island.* She narrowed her eyes and glared into the fire. *If I want revenge to the Ariash, then I can burn the world down on my own.*

Chapter 5: Truly Chosen

Yin And Yang

Silver's vision cleared. She blinked rapidly and looked around.

"Hello?" She called. Silver was standing in the "darkest world," which sounded pleasant. It was dark; nothing but black walls, floors and apparently the ceiling. Was there a ceiling? Or was that the sky? "Anyone here?" Her voice echoed. She looked for an exit just in case she was in the wrong place. However, she only saw the dark abyss.

"I've always wondered how dragons end up here, whether it's on purpose or not."

Silver spun to find the voice, but didn't see anyone. The voice came again.

"Oh dear, you aren't very good at this game, are you?"

The voice sounded familiar, but she hadn't ever heard it in that level of glee. The voice had an accent, and was loud and booming. It seemed to come from all directions. Silver wondered if she was hearing voices.

"Who are you?" Silver called. "Where is my sister?!"

The voice sighed.

"You aren't my sister!"

The voice then chucked. "Of course not. But she is dead. You should go home to your perfect, beautiful kingdom." Silver stopped. The voice had spoke of her kingdom, but didn't sound angry. It sounded

a weird type of calm that Silver couldn't describe. It's like he was...
Mocking the Aolite kingdom.

"Who are you?" She asked. "*Where* are you?" Silver saw a purple light on the ground and looked behind her. She shrieked at the sight of 2 glowing purple eyes staring into her soul.

"Hello, Silver," the voice said. Silver recognized those two eyes, but didn't want to believe it. "How did you find yourself in the darkest world?"

Silver couldn't believe she had actually found it. Those two eyes had killed her sister. But they had raised them... What could she do? She didn't want to hurt him. But he had killed her...

"Father," Silver said firmly. "I know my sister is here. I could sense her."

Her father scoffed. "Your powers aren't that strong, child. Once you turn at least 8 is when they become that strong. You are useless to your sister. There is nothing you can do for her."

She didn't know why, but that last remark hit her really hard, and she stumbled back a little, putting her arm over her chest. Silver remembered the black mark and looked down at it.

It was glowing brighter.

It always glowed with a purple, evil energy, but now, it glowed with a red energy. The colour was dark red, the colour of her sister's scales. Behind the 2 eyes, a glowing blue light was shining brightly on the other side.

"Is that my sister?" Silver asked.

"Only if I want her to be."

Silver didn't understand his response. Of course that was her sister; she looked just like her... Just a little scarier and darker.

"Sacrifice, what happened?" Silver called to her sister. "Are...
You ok?"

Her sister didn't respond. But the voice did. "No. She's dead, and even a Shadowling's spell can't fix that. No matter what you do."

"You are nothing to her anymore, and she's nothing at all."

"GIVE HER BACK!!" Silver shrieked. Black and white pulsing lighting was fired at the 2 eyes. To her surprise, the eyes vanished and the lighting missed. Instead of 2 eyes, a huge dragon made of black smoke and purple energy stood in front of her. The same form her father had taken when he killed Sacrifice, just bigger. She was sitting in front of him, her eyes closed and wings fallen. Sacrifice didn't look injured, but she looked terribly sad.

"Answer me," her father said sternly. "How did you get here?"

Silver glared at him and hissed. "I used a Shadowling spell book to bring her back." She pointed at Sacrifice.

"The one written by... Nightchaser?" Her father said. He didn't sound angry or gleeful anymore. He sounded sad. *How do I feel about that? How do I feel about my sister's killer being sad? Who was Nightchaser? Why is he sad about him? Maybe he was someone important, and he died, or disappeared.*

"Who is Nightchaser?" Silver asked. "Was he important?"

Instead of answering, the Shadowling rose up and spread his wings, filling the Darkest World with a faint purple light. He looked down at Sacrifice, his purple eyes casting a glow onto her.

"Get rid of her, Sacrifice," he ordered. For once, her eyes opened. She looked at Silver with deep, lifeless eyes. She didn't attack, however. She only stood there and stared at Silver. "I said get rid of her!" The Shadowling growled. Sacrifice remained silent.

"She won't hurt me," Silver said. "She's my sister."

"No she isn't. This dragon is a shell, a corpse, a *zombie.* Your sister is gone. The dragon here has no soul left," their father said.

Silver looked at her sister. "Then why won't she attack me?"

"Because she's malfunctioning? How should I know?!" The Shadowling snapped.

If you're going to keep hurting both of us, then I'll return the favour. Silver thought. She didn't know why she was thinking these thoughts, but she wanted justice. *I will make you pay for this, Shadowling.* A thundering wind fired at the Shadowling. He noticed immediately, and was sent backwards, but he landed on his feet and he didn't look pleased.

"Why did I agree to have whelps?…" He growled. He let out an awful shriek that sounded like a call for something. Silver heard wingbeats around her. Hundreds of Shadowling were descending from the walls and ceiling of the Darkest World.

"Sacrifice! We have to get out of here!" Silver called to her sister. Sacrifice's eyes were closed as though she didn't notice the chaos around her. Two Shadowlings reached their claws onto Silver and ripped one of her wings. She shrieked and leaped forward. She waved her claws and manifested a powerful tornado to take away the army. Silver ran over and grabbed Sacrifice's talon. She opened her eyes, desperate and sad. Her sister looked like she'd given up.

"Go…" She quietly groaned. "It's… Not safe." Sacrifice exhaled, as though it was hard to breathe.

"Don't worry, I'm getting you out of here," Silver reassured her. She held onto her sister, fearing she would let go and give up. Silver looked up at the wall of Shadowlings falling down into the twins. She raised one of her claws and filled them with powerful energy. She remembered a spell called Light Sword, and hoped it worked. Silver raised it as high as she could reach and slammed it down into the Darkest World's floor. The blue light returned, and it swirled around the twins. Silver's vision fogged again, but she wasn't as scared as she was the first time. Because now, she had Sacrifice with her. Her grip on

Silver's talon was anything but firm, but she still was there. As the blue light turned whiter and paler, then brown, the abandoned wooden building came into view. She looked around at the building and smiled. *Home... I actually went to the Darkest World and came home!* Silver looked to her sister. Her eyes were closed, and her wings still drooped.

"Sacrifice?" Silver asked. "Are you alright?"

Her sister opened her eyes, which were lifeless and dead. "Silver, " she said. "He is following me for eternity."

"No, you're alright," Silver reassured her

She grabbed her sister's talons and held them tightly. She smiled to Sacrifice, but had to look at her talons.

They were *glowing*.

Blue and red, their talons glowed brightly in the dark room. As Silver released her sister, she opened her talons to see the glowing blue symbol of a feather.

She looked to her sister and saw a glowing dark red feather. Sacrifice looked at the symbol without any reflection in her eyes.

"Sacrifice?" Silver asked. "Are you alright?"

Sacrifice looked at her. "We're spirits."

Forest of Sapphires

Flying wasn't exactly a strong suit for either Poseidonite or Crystalian. Then again, nobody had ever tested to see which was faster. It was probably Legend, with her long scaly body and thin, skittish shape. Or it was Jewelem, who had large, powerful wings. Either way, they were both equally slow, and both of them asked the same question.

"Are we there yet?" Asked Legend.

Jewelem shrugged. "Probably."

About 15 minutes after that, they stopped at an island and took a rest.

Getting outside of Anima wasn't quite an easy task. It was surrounded by huge, eternal tempests, but there was a lot of water between the islands and the barrier. Anima itself consisted of six islands, two Earth Islands, one Fire Island, the Ice Mountains, The Sky Island and the Dark island. But the outside, nobody knew what was there. Everyone thought it was just the spirit island and nothing more than some small islands, which would be true. The Storm Guardian was the name of the barrier of storms. But for the last twenty-four years, some kind of dragon had been living there, patrolling the borders and making sure nobody left.

He didn't notice the two spirits sneaking out the side of it, however.

Night had fallen and the stars were twinkling above the deep blue sea. They were on a sandy beach island that was bigger than the one they first met on. It wasn't the biggest island Jewelem had ever seen, but it was good. The palm forest inside of it was large enough for them to find a clearing in the middle. The pathway to the clearing was only a few metres long and they could see the ocean through the bushes around their clearing. Not too big, and not too small. Jewelem wanted to sleep below the palm tree, which would shield him from the ominous storm clouds in the near distance. Legend, however, had other plans. She wanted to sleep in the middle of the beach and spread her wings, catching the raindrops and the starlight. She had eventually agreed to come into the clearing under the leaves when the distant lightning threatened to summon a downpour while she slept.

"Hey, Legend," Jewelem said, admiring the perfectly wonderful shape of the palm leaf in his claws. "What do you think the other spirits will be like? Do you think the sky spirit and dark spirit will hate each other like always?"

Legend shrugged. "Honestly, I kind of want to see them all."

Jewelem nodded. "I just want to meet the fire spirit. The other two seem a little chaotic."

"What do you mean?" Legend asked. "Do they always fight?"

"Dark and Light Spirits are known for their past troubles and undying hatred towards each other."

"Past troubles?"

Jewelem blinked in confusion. "I'm not completely sure, but it must be bad. What are the Water Spirits up to under the sea?"

Legend frowned at the ground and flicked a coconut with her tail. "Royalty, protection, securing the South-west and ONLY the south-west."

"What's the south-west?" Jewelem asked. She looked at him as though he was crazy.

"Have you been living under a rock?" She asked, half affectionately and half confused.

"Yeah, kinda," Jewelem replied, remembering his time at home split between a cave system and a boat.

Legend blinked in confusion. "Oh, alright. Well, the southwest is where the Crystalians usually come from." She stopped as her gaze scanned over Jewelem's shocked face.

"Should we continue the flight in the morning?" Jewelem asked, scanning the sky for... Anything. He had felt an odd presence when he looked east, and it was stronger now. Back on the first island near the Poseidonite kingdom, Jewelem had told Legend about it and she agreed that she felt it too. So they both decided it would be easier to fly east until they come from the west or until they found an island that made them say "oh yeah THIS seems like a good place for some gods to hang out, let's wait here." Legend smiled at him and nodded. She settled into a warm spot under the palm leaves in their clearing. Earlier, Jewelem had put up sticks between the trees to make a small canopy around the clearing for them to sleep and rest. He had gathered some coconuts that had fallen off the trees and found some berries that also fell off a plant and brought them to the camp to share. He had never felt good about hurting and hunting animals, along with taking berries and nuts off of trees. It felt disrespectful to the trees, but he was told that it didn't matter to anyone. He had still felt bad about it, however. He glanced over at the sleeping sea princess on the other side of the clearing. A comforting rain pattered against the trees around them as thunder and lightning soared over the clouds, scaring any nearby dragons out of the sky. Jewelem settled into the soft moss below the canopy and rested his wings in the small bed. The stars above him sparkled onto the ocean and reflected off the raindrops on Legend's scales. He closed his eyes and waited for the morning.

There was a long flight waiting for him. The night hadn't ended when Jewelem awoke. He wasn't sure why he was awake at midnight, but he just wanted to settle back into the moss and go back to bed. But he awoke again when he heard a rustling noise. It sounded like something or someone stepping over leaves. He looked up and saw the sleek shape of a blue dragon walking onto the beach from the clearing. He knew it was Legend, and even though he didn't want to bother her, he was rather curious. He smiled at the silhouette of the princess and stood up to follow.

He found her relaxing on the beach outside of the clearing. She sat down and admired the starlight above them.

"Hi," Jewelem lightly whispered to her. Legend didn't look at him, but he didn't mind.

"Those right there are called the Arol Noxia."

"Excuse me?" Jewelem asked.

Legend turned to him and smiled. "The stars there are called the Arol Noxia, that's the constellation. I heard that they come from a certain water spirit named SandClaw. She was a mix between Chia and Poseidonite, and gained her constellation for her solitude."

"Wow," Jewelem said. "I didn't realise you knew astrology. Or that you have a habit of waking up in the middle of the night for stargazing or snack breaks."

"Earthquake's constellation is Terro Knigyua, meaning stone king," Legend said. They talked about the constellations and stars for a long while, until the horizon started to turn a lighter shade of blue.

"Seems like it's almost morning," Jewelem mentioned. "My brother used to say that it meant the stars were going to visit the other side of the planet. Never had the heart to say 'no Qwonzie, that's actually- not what's happening.'"

Legend giggled and splashed him with her tail. Jewelem laughed and suddenly felt very tired. "We can just sleep here." He failed to avoid tuning out and softly leaned on the sand. Legend's wing brushed his and they both quietly fell asleep on the sands of the beach.

The next morning when Jewelem woke up, he immediately was greeted with a gallon of water landing on his head. He heard an uncontrollable laughter coming from the other side of the clearing. When his brain stopped thinking "Ack! The oceans are coming for me!" He realized it was just Legend. She had used magic to water down the leaf and drench Jewelem.

"Can I ask the thought process behind that?" Jewelem asked.

Legend laughed again and smiled at him. "Come on, Jewelem! We have to get to the island!"

The rain continued into the day when the two took off. It rained down onto their scales as though it was telling them to turn back. Just when they thought the storm would last forever, they saw the distant shape of mountains beyond the storm clouds. They exchanged a glance and powered on ahead, the storm following them. When they reached the end of the storm clouds, they were immediately greeted with the smell of ash and the sweltering heat of fire. Jewelem feared they had entered the fire island in the southwest, but soon realized that there were no mountains on the fire island.

"Where are we?" Legend asked him. In all honesty, he thought it was the fire island. He'd never been there, but he thought it didn't have mountains. What other option was there?

He shrugged. "I don't know."

He looked around, determined to find anyone. The fire island had a kingdom engraved into the volcano's unique, harsh landscape. But this island didn't only have a volcano, it also had a small forest and a meadow, along with a large pond and a mountain next to the volcano. The island was huge, as big as 10 of the biggest Crystalian ships. He'd never seen such a big place. Even the underground cave system of the Aquamarine land bases seemed small because of their tunnels. All the grass near their shore was set ablaze and covered in huge scratch marks, as thought a large Ariash had come and taken their anger out on the ground. *Not just any Ariash. A fire spirit*, Jewelem thought to himself. It seemed probable that this was the island they were looking for.

"Do you think this is the spirit island?" Jewelem asked. "Those seem like the claw marks and aftermath of a fire spirit's anger."

Legend nodded. "Hey, who's that up there?" Jewelem followed her gaze up to the top of the volcano. At the top, the silhouette of a dragon bigger than anyone Jewelem has ever seen stood at the rim. They stared at them from above, their scales a black against the light of fire from the volcano,

"That must be the fire spirit," Jewelem observed. He knew that was her. She didn't seem like he imagined; dramatic fiery terror. He imagined someone calm and friendly. The most common traits of a fire spirit were basically calm and fun. Sometimes, however, they can be…

Scary.

The Ariash leaped down from the volcano's rim. As she descended, Jewelem saw her body begin to turn golden orange. Smoke whirled around the shape and once the dragon landed, Jewelem leaped back in horror and Legend shrieked in fear. The dragon was well over 3 boats tall, had scales the colour of bright red rubies and dark black underscales, looked like she was going to kill them and didn't seem too happy.

"Hello," Legend said to her. She had a little shy smile as she looked at the dragon. Taking a closer look, Jewelem realized all the scars this dragon had. She was clearly an Ariash. He knew they were at war with the Shadowlings, and he knew that both of them were a strong clan.

"*Legend,*" Jewelem whispered to her. "*We shouldn't be talking to her. She's going to kill us. Like- it's written all over her.*"

"*Don't worry. She can't kill us; we're her spirits,*" she whispered back. He wanted to believe her, but looking up at the huge dragon, he just wanted to hide under a pillow forever.

"So, what's your name?" Legend tried to ask her. He could sense the effort, shyness, fear and nervousness in her voice as she asked.

The Ariash only stared, growled, hissed quietly and took a step back.

"What's you name?" Legend asked again.

The fire spirit said nothing.

She doesn't want to talk? Jewelem thought. *I wonder if she's introverted. But then she would've stayed away from us, right? What's her deal?*

The fire spirit looked from Legend to Jewelem with an unimpressed scowl. She finally sighed and spoke. "Meteor."

"Excuse me?" Legend asked politely.

"I am Meteor."

"Oh, well, nice to meet you, Meteor," Legend greeted cheerfully and quietly. The Ariash growled and flicked her tail. Meteor flung open her wings and launched herself into the air. Jewelem leaped back in alarm. She flew to the top of the volcano and vanished into it's rim.

A Tide That Flows With The Moonlight, Not The Rivers

"She seemed pleasant," Legend said thoughtfully. She thought about the dragon, and thought she seemed …

Different.

Meteor had seemed like a scary dragon. That was no surprise. But she had glared at Jewelem with a horrible expression. Did he notice?

"What do you mean?" Jewelem asked. "She was terrifying!"

"Yeah, but did you see the look she gave you?" Legend said. "It almost seemed like she thought you were familiar."

Jewelem shrugged. "I didn't notice. Also, I don't think that she remembered any Crystalian princes wandering through here."

Legend looked to the volcano's rim. *I know that dragon must be different.* She thought. *I don't want to believe she's just mean. What does she think of Jewelem?*

"What are you thinking?" Jewelem asked. Legend realized she was looking away and turned back to him. He studied her expression for a few moments, then his eyes widened.

"I'm gonna go after her," Legend said firmly. "She seemed a little bit sad."

"But she'll hurt you!"

"Only if I let her. I'll just fly out!" Legend said. Jewelem looked skeptical, but he nodded without further discussion. Legend smiled to him and leaped into the sky. She flew up to the top of the volcano and looked down into the rim. Carefully placing her tail on the rim to check it's heat, she landed on the warm stone after realizing it was ok to touch. The inside of the volcano was a brightly lit hole straight down into the unknown, plummeting down into the earth. The light from the magma in the sides lit the cavern, but it stopped glowing the deeper the cave went. The walls were dark red with cracks into the lava behind the walls. But strangely, the cracks stopped as the cave went on. Legend carefully swerved down the cave, keeping her wings from touching the infernal walls, even thought they were more than triple her wingspan wide in all directions. Legend saw light at the end and kept flying. After a minute or two, Legend found herself in a brightly lit cave with warm walls and floors. They were much warmer than the ones at the top, but still touchable. The cave was small, which was odd for such a huge dragon. Weird treasures lay in piles near the walls. Meteor didn't seem to have a system or a preference, or even a simple interest. It seemed as though when she found something, anything at all, she'd throw it into a pile nearby. The 'treasures' ranged from golden jewellery to little pieces of metal and broken wood, and she saw some old books and scrolls. There was an opening into another cave on the left side of the cave. Legend spotted a toy that looked like something that once belonged to a young child. It was a small stuffed bear with several burn marks on it's feet and other limbs, and it didn't seem of high quality. The toy was on it's own pedestal as though it was of great importance. Legend looked around for Meteor and saw the dragon perched on an odd stone structure across the room. She was looking down at something on a table-like thing on the platform of warm rock. Meteor had somehow become regular dragon sized and comfortably sat into the stone monument. Meteor's eyes were filled with an emotion Legend had seen somewhere before. They were slightly narrowed but widened at the same time. Meteor's eyes were tainted with small tears, and her wings trembled and her talons were clenched. It was all hard to describe.

Legend knocked softly on the wall next to her and Meteor's head snapped up. Her tears vanished as fury spread through her expression

"Hello, Meteor," Legend said calmly. She was slightly scared, but wanted to know this dragon. Meteor raised her shoulders, glaring at her. She clenched her claws even more and exhaled a small plume of fire through her nostrils.

"What do you want?" She growled softly. "You shouldn't be here."

"Where is this place?" Legend asked, admiring the 'treasures.' "Nice… Collection you have here. Where'd you find them?" Legend had never tried to 'small talk' anyone, but she tried anyway. Meteor looked like she wanted her to suddenly burst into flames and vanish before her eyes so she could be alone.

"I didn't find them. They came with the place," Meteor said, sighing as she flicked her tail towards a pile. "They all belong to Firebrazer, the other fire spirit before me." Legend felt bad for being relieved that those weird objects weren't hers, but then she felt worried for the sanity of whoever Firebrazer was.

"He certainly had... Talent. And interest in..." Legend trailed off.

Meteor shrugged. "I didn't know him in those days." The Ariash looked to the treasure pile and the small toy on the pedestal, and her scowl faded.

"Is that also his?" Legend asked, looking at the toy in confusion.

Meteor hesitated. Her head snapped to her looking away at the wall and her talons curled into a fist again. The heat in the cave was sweltering, and Legend could barely stand it.

"Should we go to the surface?" Legend asked. Her talons were in pain from the heat under the floor. She heard flickering fire and looked around for the flame. She realized the cracks in the walls went into a secret room filled with fire. Without saying anything, Meteor sighed *again* and leaped off the volcanic stone monument. Legend followed her out as Meteor shot up into the large cavern. Legend saw her red body swirl into red and gold smoke, soon emerging as a huge dragon almost as tall as the volcano. She stopped to stare at her impossibly huge shape in awe. She flew up to Meteor and saw her wings scrape the volcano's side. *That's what made the cracks in these walls.* She realized. Once they reached the surface, Legend took a breath of the cool air, a refreshing contrast to the boiling heat in the cavern. She also noticed all the fires that once burned the grass had vanished. She looked for Meteor and saw her perched in her regular sized form on the volcano's rim. Jewelem was pacing near the volcano's base. Seeing him and Meteor, she was struck with a realization. *Now Jewelem isn't my only friend in the world,* Legend thought happily. She looked to Meteor. *Maybe me and this dragon truly could be friends after all.*

Fire Burning Away at Nothing But Ashes

She doesn't get it. Meteor thought. No, the toy wasn't Firebrazer's. Maybe the Poseidonite should've minded her own business and stayed away from her. But now, standing here, there was no going back. She was stuck here with them.

Forever.

The sight of the blue Crystalian at the volcano's base seemed to hit Meteor hard. She couldn't do anything about the images of her little brother flashing through her mind and slamming themselves into the side of her head, giving her a headache. She didn't know if the island drove dragons to insanity, but she couldn't seem to control her thoughts anymore. *But… Pyro did look just like that whenever I took the blame for anything and spent a night in the dungeon… Without him,* Meteor thought. How lonely could that have been? She'd felt a horrible longing for her brother for every second she'd spent in those awful cells.

"Hey, Meteor! Come meet Jewelem!"

Meteor snapped out of her head and looked to the ground below where the Poseidonite had descended to the Crystalian. *Aren't they supposed to be enemies?* Meteor though. She didn't learn a lot on the island, but she wasn't oblivious to the Poseidonite and Crystalian battles. *Anyway, there isn't a lot of waiting with those two down there,* Meteor thought. Meteor opened her massive golden wings and leaped off the rim, soaring down to the waiting dragons. The wind whipped past her wings and sent cold wind all through her scales. Meteor missed the heat of her cave.

"Meteor, this is Jewelem," Legend said. "He helped bring me to this island." Looking at him, Meteor was engulfed by the thought of her brother. She didn't like looking at him…

Jewelem waved with a nervous smile to Meteor as though everything was normal. *He's never lost a sibling.*

"Nice to meet you, Meteor," Jewelem said to her. As she scowled at him, she realized something that shattered her soul into a thousand pieces. As much as she tried, she couldn't avoid the painful thought in her mind.

He and Pyro have the same pale blue eye colour, she thought. Even though he wore a blindfold, she'd still seen his eye colour when he opened them for the first time. That was how he probably knew what she looked like, or he didn't remember her. Before she could run away into the volcano and never return, Legend began going all out with the stupid questions.

"So what's the Ariash kingdom like? What's your constellation?" Legend asked. "Is everything red? What's it like there? Do you like it?"

Meteor frowned. "I hate it there. You can't imagine how bad it is." Images and memories of war and prison and fire and awful smoke fought over the main part of her head, battling the undying agony of Pyro's death.

Legend's face twisted into something Meteor had never seen before. Sympathy, confusion, sadness, shock? "Sorry, I didn't know it was that bad." Legend said. She turned to Jewelem. Meteor looked up to the volcano. "I noticed some islands outside the island! Let's go check them out!"

As the two dragons left for the other islands, Meteor took off towards the northern part of the main island where the volcano stood.

"Hey, Meteor, you coming?" Legend asked.

"No," Meteor snapped, winging away. She liked to map out the layout of the island. She was the first to get there, and she wanted it memorized before the others got there. *The volcano is on the north-west coast, the valley is in front of it and between the mountain and the beach across the south and west. The meadow is on the south-east coast...*

Meteor had mapped out the island a while ago, but still liked going over it. Alright, she hated going over it, but it was the only thing to do other than wait for Firebrazer and Cloud to come back. Sometimes they did, but she was usually lonely. *But now with Fishy and Rainbow over there, I'll have actual company other than dead fire spirits.* It took her a few moments of watching them wing away to realize how little they could care about her. *That's alright. I'm alright with being alone.* Meteor thought. She fought back against the tears in the back of her eyes and flew towards the volcano rim again, but swerved towards the base instead. The base of the nearby mountain snakes around the base of the volcano and made a cave into the volcano which Meteor made her home. There were two entrances; the volcano, and the secret door which Meteor entered. Two caves, two purposes, two doors. The one Legend had seen was Firebrazer's cave, but the mountain cave was Meteor's. As she entered the doorway to the mountain cave, she stopped. Firebrazer and Cloud, in her dragon form, were there, but three new dragons as well.

One was a tall dragon, taller than Cloud who was pale yellow with pale yellow underscales, the colour of sand. Meteor couldn't help but notice that they had a lot of jewellery. The yellow dragon next to Firebrazer had ruby earrings, a golden necklace with a diamond on it, armbands made of gold and emeralds and four golden rings on their front left talon. The sand-coloured dragon had... Hair? A trail of blonde fur ran down their head. *That's pretty typical actually. There was a prisoner who once had lime green hair. Weirdo. Cool hair, but the woman was a freak show.* The strangest thing of all, however, was that they didn't have one tail, but two! *Is two tails even possible?!* Meteor thought. They had two long leather pouches tied to their two front legs. *I wonder what's in there,* Meteor wondered.

The second dragon was dark crimson with brighter pink wings and darker crimson underscales and horns. Her eyes glowed the brightest and had the most colour. She also had an odd mane of, not fur, but some kind of flower with only one colour growing around her neck, as though her neck was a stem of a flower.

The third was the scariest out of them all. She was small, just smaller than Meteor, and had similar bright red scales to her. Her underscales were paler red. Her eyes were wild, didn't have pupils and faintly glowed yellow. Her horns were a unique shape that curved like a devil's horns. The dragon's expression was wild and uncontrolled, and Meteor could hear growls coming from her. Her wings… Perhaps the most noticeable thing about her was that her wings looked as though they'd been torn off. It was like someone just ripped them right off of her, making her unable to fly.

Firebrazer was talking to all of them quietly about something, but they stopped and turned to her when Meteor came in.

He laughed a little nervously as she came in. "Is this awkward?"

"I was just hoping you two would be around," Meteor said to him. She waved to Cloud and she waved back, smiling. "Uh, who are *they?*" Meteor motioned to the other dragons.

"Oh, right!" Firebrazer exclaimed as though he'd forgotten. "The rich yellow one is Heatstroke, who once lived in the desert of the husk island before it disappeared. The little crimson one is FinalFlame. Believe me, she's great!" As his gaze fell on the wingless devil dragon, his smile turned from a happy one to a sad but hopeful one. The odd dragon growled and hissed at him (or everyone, as it seemed) as he looked at her. "This one here is Dust Devil. She lost her wings aeons ago."

"Eons?" Meteor echoed. She remembered everything she knew about fire spirits. At least, she assumed they were fire spirits. She knew that when she died, they went to the spirit world and then they came back as dragons with powerful magic and lived forever until they died, but then another spirit could be chosen. Basically, when Firebrazer died, he came back and then Meteor was chosen. Now, he can be killed, but will live forever until someone kills him. "She's aeons old?"

"If it makes you feel better, I'm a few thousand years old myself," Cloud said proudly with a shrug.

Firebrazer started talking to the Heatstroke and Dust Devil. FinalFlame, from behind Cloud, peaked her head out at Meteor and pulled her claws closer to her chest. She ducked her head and made her wings appear to look smaller. She looked at Meteor with an odd interest, as though she'd seen her before. Meteor felt her scales start to numb for a few seconds, and as though Final could feel it, she looked away from Meteor. The others didn't seem to notice, but Meteor did. Even Cloud just smiled as she spoke with Firebrazer. Final's gaze deepened on Meteor, then it relaxed and turned to sadness, then something that Meteor had never seen. Next it turned to fear, then her wings dropped by her side, but Cloud still didn't notice. It was as though she was feeling a hundred things at once. Like someone was telling a story and she was feeling all the bad things that happened. Suddenly, her scales faded from crimson to something much more terrifying. Her underscales and wings changed from their original pink and crimson to black and yellow. Her scales turned to a yellow-orange colour. It all happened so fast, Meteor felt like she'd blinked and suddenly her little brother was standing right there in front of her, right behind Cloud.

Pyro, or Final, closed whoever's eyes those were and sighed. The scales snapped back to crimson, and Final was standing in front of her. Had she imagined it? *How is nobody noticing this?!? This has GOT to be real, right?* Final started turning all sorts of different dragons; Incinerator, Volcanic, Magma. *Oh no* Meteor thought. *Please don't turn into... Her. Please, please I'm begging you Final, don't-*

She did.

Her scales turned pale red, almost a weird pink, and her horns turned pale red-ish brown. Her wings turned orange and her eyes turned white with grey pupils. She flickered to the size of a watermelon, as after glancing at her claws, she immediately turned back. She stared at her now-crimson claws in horror, but her right talon was starting to turn pale red, similar to the young whelp's scales, but paler. She closed her eyes and took a deep breath, and the pale red scales turned to crimson. Meteor couldn't take Final anymore.

"Firebrazer," she asked. He looked over. "What's up with Final?"

Firebrazer looked to Final. Her scales rapidly changed from Incinerator to Volcanic to Magma to Pyro. She had her talons pressed to her forehead as though she had a headache. "Yeah, she'll do that with new dragons sometimes. Just don't worry about it."

Cloud finally looked behind her and smiled. She turned her body towards Final and put a wing around her.

"She just... Changes into different scales?" Meteor asked, confused. "I don't think dragons just do that. Is that something any fire spirit can do?"

"Nope, only Final. It's because of her Whitefox abilities," Heatstroke replied.

"...Whitefox?"

"The white around my neck," Final said, opening her eyes. "It's a curse. If I meet new dragons, sometimes I'll change into dragons they think about a lot. I can also turn into any dragon I want to, even some

103

that don't exist." She closed her eyes. Suddenly, Final's body became less small and shy and more sleek and long. Her scales shifted to a breathtaking blue that looked like the colour of the ocean surface, and her wings turned peach orange and sunlight yellow like the view from a sea cliff at sunset. Her tail and horns became twice their length. The white flower around her neck vanished as her form changed. Feathers appeared on the top of her head and resembled the feathers of a blue jay. Standing in front of Meteor, was a Veo dragon. It all happened so quickly, it wasn't like she faded into that dragon. It was like she suddenly snapped into a new dragon.

"Wow," Meteor breathed. "That's amazing."

"Hate to be that one, but Firebrazer, we gotta go. Phoenix needs us, probably," Heatstroke said from her side of the room. They stretched both their long tails.

"Oh, alright. Are we alright with that?" Firebrazer asked the others. He smiled when they all nodded. Except for Dust Devil, who glared and growled but followed when all of them left the cave. Firebrazer approached Dust Devil as if she were a stray cat, but she soon allowed him to lift her up and carry her. Meteor led them to the volcano rim and said goodbye to them. Cloud and Heatstroke reminded her that she'll see them later and maybe forever. *I mean, we are technically immortal, so yeah that checks out,* Meteor thought. She watched them wing away into the star-filled sky, little shooting stars filled with her only happiness and relaxation in this world. Meteor looked down off the rim at the two blue shapes by the shore.

Legend and Jewelem have returned, have they. Meteor thought bitterly. *Guess I'll have to wait for the others to come back to feel something besides that weird feeling I get from looking at Jewelem.* An image of Pyro poked its way into her thoughts again and she covered her head with her talons. She glared into the fiery cavern inside the volcano. She leaped down onto the cavern and hid below the earth. She settled onto her stone monument and looked at the toy on the shattered pillar. She sighed and closed her eyes, despite knowing she'd never find sleep with the death of being crushed by stone looming above her while she slept.

Chapter 6: Water Pressure

Yin and Yang

"So basically what you're saying is you went inside the Blackzone to retrieve your dead sister and bring her back to life and then you each obtained feather constellations?" Shield said slowly and skeptically. She had a noticeable hint of suspicion in both her voice and expression. It was the way she tilted her head at Silver.

"Yep!" Silver replied, beaming. Across the room, Heaven was carefully inspecting her undead daughter. She watched her with fearful, panicked eyes. They were all standing alone in Silver's bedroom. Shield stood by her large window, and Heaven sat near the door. Sacrifice sat on the other side of the door, staring at the ground with her eyes closed.

Silver's bedroom was made of azure sapphires and shimmering blue and white tiles. She had a potted plant on the left side and a bed in the far left corner. There was a huge window in the middle of the far wall. It was nearing the morning, and Sacrifice hadn't seemed to want to leave the palace, or the wooden building she came back in.

"Why did you bring her *here* of all places?" Heaven asked. Silver wasn't sure why Heaven didn't like her. That was her own daughter. Heaven turned to Shield with a look that said "am I wrong though?" But instead her true words were "She's a Shadowling, right?"

"But she's also my sister," Silver replied, feeling hurt.

Heaven looked to Silver and glanced at Sacrifice. Then she looked back to Shield, and her grandma only shrugged.

"Please let her stay here, mother," Silver begged. "She doesn't have a home, and she needs our help. Plus, she's my sister."

Heaven sighed. "I'm sorry, Silver… But this dragon isn't alive anymore. Sacrifice is gone, dear." The two princesses looked at each other in sorrow. Silver looked to Shield for something, anything, that could help her sister.

"I see no issue in keeping the Shadowling here," Shield said, as though she could sense Silver's desperation. "What's the problem, Heaven? Silver's got a point."

"But she's a Shadowling! And she's-" Heaven snapped.

"My granddaughter," Shield said coldly.

The room went silent. The clouds covered the sun, and rain started falling onto the window. Thunder and lightning lit up the sky and slammed onto the walls. *That's what happens when mother is worried or angry…* Silver thought. Shield turned to look out the window into the tempests. She closed her eyes and sighed.

Shield kept her eyes on the window as she spoke. "You can keep her. Just as long as she doesn't scare the entire kingdom into running away again. Last thing we need is another trip across Anima."

Silver wasn't sure what she meant by another trip, but she didn't know anything about Aolite history, so she thought she'd learn about it some other time from Shield. She smiled gratefully, went over to her sister, took her talon and escaped out the door. Sacrifice didn't want to stand up, but didn't seem to resist Silver's grasp. They escaped the bedroom and Silver brought her to LightningRoar for helpful advice.

The Aolite palace hallways relied mostly on sunlight to brighten the halls. But today, the most uncommon weather of a storm darkened the once-bright palace.

I wonder if Sacrifice likes it this way, or if she wants to see it with its full glory, Silver thought. The storm chamber was just down the hall, taking a left and then going straight. Then the Storm chamber was just on the right. Silver kept her right talon on Sacrifice's talon and used the left to knock on the door.

"Come in," a deep, wise, slightly muffled voice said from inside.

Silver opened the door and found herself greeted by the large dark grey storm clouds that plagued the outside sky. LightningRoar was sitting by his own window, one that was just a hole in the wall leading directly to outside because the room was just clouds. It was odd to see him in a regular size. He wasn't as huge today. LightningRoar was always twice Shield's height, but could change his height any time. With a limit, of course. There was a maximum.

"Hi, LightningRoar!" Silver called to him. If there was one dragon out there that wasn't in her family, and Silver could trust, it would almost definitely be LightningRoar.

"Silver?" He asked. "Is that you?"

"Yep, it's me!" Silver said cheerfully. "Also my sister. Ta-da!"

LightningRoar turned his head towards her. Once he laid eyes on her, he gave a little jump. He stood up, kept his eyes on Sacrifice and slowly walked towards them. He ducked his head and clouds swirled around him. He returned to a larger size and looked down at Sacrifice. Silver stood back in awe as Sacrifice opened her eyes to look at him.

"She looks like somebody I met once," LightningRoar said softly. He laid a careful claw on her dark shoulder. "What happened to her?"

Silver shrugged. "I'm not sure, honestly. I rescued her from the Darkest World and brought her here. I hoped I could see you for some advice. She isn't the same sister I knew, and I need to know why."

LightningRoar's eyes grew large and he stepped back. "All I can say for you is that you make sure she doesn't hurt anyone," LightningRoar said slowly. He turned to her with a serious look. "You and Sacrifice wield incredible power, child. As the daughter of the Sun Princess, Princess Heaven, and the granddaughter of The Rain Queen, Queen Shield, I hope you can use your power for good. Not everyone is as happy with their lives and family as you are. Many of your- of *our* clan and family are broken from the things your own relatives can do. I'm warning you; your sister will be questioned, but if you two continue your… Whatever you're doing, you can change something much bigger. Something that will be for more dragons than just the Aolite clan, but also all of Anima. Do you understand?"

Silver was silent because of the storm dragon's request. She wasn't even sure how to understand any of it at all. *Wait what?* She thought. "W-what??" She stammered. "How… What am I?" I'm just one of, what is it? *How many* princesses? I have 2 aunts and a sister, LightningRoar! Maybe even more!"

"But you are the daughter of a saint and a sin, child," LightningRoar pressed. "I suggest you keep Sacrifice away from the dragons of this clan."

Silver merely responded with hesitation and a nod. They parted ways and she immediately went to the mirror hallway. She'd been told not to go there, but how could she not? She had to find answers for her sister.

They entered the dark hallway and found all the mirrors blank. But as they walked further down the halls, Silver felt the subtle, noticeable presence she felt the first time. Suddenly, all the mirrors caught fire. But it wasn't orange and red fire.

It was bright pink fire.

Lightning and thunder crashed overhead. The pink fire didn't emit smoke or heat, and Silver swore she could hear a voice coming from it.

"Hello?" Silver called. The voice laughed. She almost gasped when she recognized it.

"Hello whelps," their father said gleefully, his voice coming from all angles. "What are your thoughts on the new lighting?" she kept whipping her head around in a panic, trying to find him. She heard a disappointed sound before the void again. "Give me some credit. At least appreciate the effort, Silver. This fire was hard to make without the help of a fire spirit, you know."

"What do you want with us?" Silver shrieked.

The fires paused, as though time had stopped for them. But they still made light, they just didn't move.

"I've been waiting a long time, and then you had to come and ruin it," the Shadowling's voice said again. "Everything was planned, you and Sacrifice had a role to play... I had a destiny, whelp." The voice sounded angry at them, but also desperate.

"What do you mean?" Silver asked, intrigued.

Instead of answering, he let the fire consume the space around the twins. She could see the ceiling, but it had made a ring of fire around them.

"Let me show you how cruel the 'amazing' Aolite clan can be," he growled.

The fire turned dark purple and took the form of dragons the size of her mother. The sound of the fire vanished and the dragon faded from sight. But now, the twins could hear the voice of Shield and Heaven from beyond the walls.

"If we're abiding by your grandfather's rules, then you might as well banish all four of us into Anima," Shield said. *She sounds mad and exhausted,* Silver thought. She couldn't see her Aolite relatives, but she could hear them through the walls of the creepy hallway. *Is this magic? Is Father letting me hear them?*

Why?

"Silver isn't a full Shadowling, she shouldn't be able to bring her back!" Heaven snapped.

"Well she managed it, and that's quite something," Shield said to her coldly.

"Her father had a skill… But I hoped she wouldn't inherit it," Heaven said. "Yet here we are."

"Nobody had to know anything. Though we could've told the twins, I feel like we should leave some parts out, perhaps?" Shield said slowly. "We couldn't have kept it a secret. It would just be easier to tell them now, and leave out Howler's part in it. I've got nothing but respect for the old guy, but he's got enough on his mind from the stars."

"I'm not hiding any more secrets from my daughter, Shield!"

"Irony."

"What do you mean 'irony'?!" Heaven yelled at her.

Shield sighed. "Heaven, you've hid the child from her own lineage. You've praised her about being an Aolite princess and nothing more. I know you, dear. You won't tell her anything but the perfection in her ancestors. But that's only *your* standard, not her's, and that means your view of perfection can hide her from so much potential. Some of her Shadowling ancestors may be… Who they are, but they aren't her and they held amazing talent and power. If she inherits any of it, we wouldn't know, because she'd feel like she isn't allowed to be a Shadowling heir."

Silver, Heaven and even the voice were all silent.

"I don't want my daughter to be banished for resurrection," Heaven said. If anyone else found out about her powers, they'd resent her existence. We already have dragons resenting *me* for what I did. Only some of them even know her father is a Shadowling, but if they found out his *real* identity…"

111

Suddenly, the pink flames around the twins vanished and the voices disappeared. Silver had to think about what she'd heard. What had her mother done to make dragons resent her?

What really was her father's true identity?

"Who are you?" Silver asked. She wasn't even sure if she was asking herself that or her father that.

"You've missed the point, you idiot," her father snapped from wherever he was. "Your mother made a mistake and they hate her. You've made a mistake and they're gonna hate you. Your grandmother, you know, married a Poseidonite and they killed him." He paused. "You give life, the thing they all value, you exist, you're my daughter and they fear you. They are bad dragons, Silver. Don't let them take advantage of your abilities."

Silver's head shot up. Even if she didn't know where he was, she felt like she could feel the dragon's voice in front of her. "They... Killed... My grandfather?" She stammered.

"Coral," her father said solemnly. "He... Was a good dragon. He did nothing wrong. I wasn't alive then, as I remember. But he was reasonable from what the books told."

"I'm related to a Poseidonite?" Silver asked. She looked at her claws, the dark blue padding on them that she almost never noticed. She gently rubbed her chin. "Is that why I have tendrils on my chin?" It was true, she had 2 long, dark blue diamond-shaped things on the end of her chin. She also had only 2 horns, like most of her family. Other Aolite had 6 horns. Her tail was also a little longer than the other's. Silver never understood why she had those strange features. "Because he was a Poseidonite. What about my horns and tail?"

She heard the voice sigh. "Your other grandfather was a Veo Icelo mix. You're related to Icelo, Poseidonite, Aolite and Shadowling.

112

You'd be all the elements if you had any Fire or Bitu in you, but unfortunately, your stuck with nyx, umbra, water, earth and caelum."

"What are Bitu, Nyx, caelum and umbra?" Silver asked. "Aren't Nyx and Umbral ice and dark?"

"Bitu and caelum are slime and sky, the worst elements," he muttered.

"Is there a Bitu god?"

"Jeez, I'd rather not think about that, haha."

"I have other family, don't I?" Silver asked, although she was getting tired of the shock. Her father was quiet for a moment. "This may shock you, but my brother Brightleaf had antlers."

"That's kind of cool- wait why are you willingly telling me this?" Silver demanded. "You're evil. You killed my sister and tried to kill me, you dirty rat!!" She whipped her head around, hoping to catch a glimpse of the horrible monster of a dragon.

He hesitated.

"Anyone ever told you that you're wonderful at insults? You really are my daughter. Also, I needed you two to kill each other," he said

There was dead silence.

"*WHAT!?!*" Silver screamed.

He sighed again. "If you had won, then I could leave your mother and find my son. I could also make the lie that the Aolite clan princess murdered a child, so dirt on them. If your twin had won, which she probably would've, I would tell Sacrifice not to kill you and take you hostage while blackmailing Heaven to do what I want. Simple and smart, eh?"

"FIRST OF ALL," Silver demanded, internally and externally screaming. She glared as she looked around with the most angry and mean eyes she could muster "I have a BROTHER? SECOND, I would never *ever* hurt my family. But I would GLADLY hurt you!! And third…" She stopped and felt her anger burn and melt into a bit of sadness. "I thought you loved all of us. Mother, Sacrifice, *me*. I thought.. I thought it was real."

He stopped. "Do you want to know what happened in those days?" he asked.

"What days?" Silver asked, her voice trembling. *What is going on?*

She heard a small sigh. She couldn't understand this dragon.

"Firebrazer was only 30 when he died," her father began. *Firebrazer?* She thought. *King Firebrazer, banished Ariash king.. He died 16 years ago, when Legend hatched. King Riverstone vanished, never to be seen again after that.*

"Firebrazer didn't have anyone with him. I don't either, but that's none of my business. I'd love to continue, but someone is looking for y-"

"*SILVER?!*"

"How the heck did she find me here?" Silver squeaked.

"Kid you can't just scream and not expect your over-paranoid mother to not come screaming," her father said casually. "Well, frankly, I hope you all die and I'll be back for you. Bye!" The voice fell silent and she felt the presence of being watched fade away. She looked to her twin, who Silver had forgotten about. *Just breezing past the last things he said, huh?* She thought angrily.

"Silver! Why are you here again?" Heaven demanded when she got to Silver.

"Just looking at the mirrors, nothing much," Silver lied.

"Heaven, leave the kid alone. She's fine and this hallway is fine," Shield called from behind her. "Go do what you have to do, dear."

She tapped Heaven on the snout teasingly. To both of their surprise, Heaven went running out of the hallway without another word.

"Well that was surprising," Shield said, looking at where Heaven had once been. "Anyway, what's going on in this hallway?"

"Why do you keep trying to take me away from it?" Silver snapped. Shield's face melted from her regular, smug half smile to a blank, solemn stare.

She sighed. "Your mother won't be happy if she knows about this. Do you really want to know?"

"Yes. Why can I feel the presence of someone here?" Silver asked. She didn't go into details because she didn't want to be questioned that much, but she needed answers *now*.

Shield looked around the hallway as though someone was watching her. "I know you've heard someone. Now, I'm not gonna stop you. Do what you want, kid. Whatever they're telling you, do what you want to do." She bent her neck down to look Silver in the eye. "The voices you heard can tell you anything they want. If it's somebody else, then I may know what they're saying. Our clan has done some... Bad things in the past, and we've made some enemies. The Shadowlings are a gifted clan, and they possess powerful magic. But they're stronger in the mind, and could be trying to convince you of something. Be wary of those dragons."

"But..." Silver started.

"Go on," Shield said.

"The voice wasn't trying to convince me or deceive me. It told me things I couldn't imagine. It said our clan was evil, and that we hurt dragons and made them miserable. He said someone killed my grandfather..."

"Coral..." Shield whispered. Sadness spread into her eyes. "Your great grandfather did that. He got rid of Coral because he was a

Poseidonite. I killed your great grandfather and took the throne from him. " she paused. Silver looked up at her with huge, wide eyes.

"That's why Heaven hates me. But once I told her why I killed him, she understood. They were close, though. She and my father were close. All of my children were, except for Aurora. Aolite have always been perfectionists, and they don't like imperfections. Your mother married a Shadowling, and I married a Poseidonite, so we weren't that popular among them. But this is a new era, and you and Sacrifice can prove that."

Silver was speechless. She didn't know what to say. "Who- who actually is my father really?" She stammered.

Shield looked away for a moment. She closed her eyes and rose back up to her full, tall and elegant shape. Shield opened her eyes and she looked down at Silver. Her eyes glowed like crystal glaciers in the sunlight.

"Your father has murdered hundreds of dragons in his time," she hissed. "The enemy of the Aolite. I don't know what Heaven was thinking. "

"Silver, your father is someone known as the Eternity Prince."

Forest of Sapphires

Jewelem and Legend soon returned to the main spirit island around sunset. The islands they found had a lot of crabs, seashells and coconuts. It was prettier than the island they met on, but not as big or memorable.

Once they returned, they found Meteor flying around the tip of the mountain's summit. *Fire spirits are terrifying, wonder if Firebrazer seemed like her,* Jewelem thought. He didn't know anything about King Firebrazer; he just thought that someone only named Firebrazer would do something like that. Glancing around, he noticed the fires that burned when he arrived had reappeared in a few places.

"Hey look, some fire," Jewelem pointed out to Legend. "Why has Meteor summoned them again?"

As though she'd heard him, Meteor turned and faced them. He could see her flap over to the volcano and once again, disappear inside of it.

"Oh, hey there, dragons."

"Huh?" Jewelem and Legend said at the same time. They turned around to see a dragon they'd both never seen before. They were about the size of Garnet with pale yellow scales. The new dragon had beautiful blonde-ish hair and fiery orange eyes. They had their wings raised in a majestically royal way and their neck was craned a little so they could look at them better. They had a lot of unique jewelry, including rings, earrings, two horn rings and a necklace. But instead of having only one tail, the new dragon had 2 tails, both whip thin and extremely strange. They had two long pouches strapped to their front legs. Hair wasn't *too* rare among dragons, but most of them didn't have it. He remember Qwonzie asking a Crystalian if her bright purple hair was her 'natural colour.'

"Who are you, and where did you come from?" Legend asked with a small laugh. "Um... Welcome to the island!" *Legend. Too brave, far too trusting and much too awkward for someone who loves to talk,* Jewelem thought. *Also, are we just ignoring the fact that this dragon has a literal* tattoo?

"My name is Heatstroke," the yellow dragon said, sitting down and tipping their head back. "Anyone seen Meteor? Tall, red, black, has cool spikes?"

"Uh- yeah, she's over there…" Jewelem mumbled, trailing off. He hated the feeling of Heatstroke's bright, powerful eyes being laid on him.

"But she isn't happy, like, at all," Legend said, jumping in for him. "She doesn't want to talk to anyone right now."

Heatstroke raised their eyebrows a little and glanced up at the volcano rim. "Well that sucks. What are you two doing on this island? I thought it was only for-" Heatstroke stopped and their eyes widened a little. "Ohhh you must be the earth spirit and water spirit."

"Yeah, that's us!" Legend said, smiling. "I am Legend, and my friend here is Jewelem."

He wasn't sure why, but Heatstroke looked quite pleased with that and laughed a little under their breath. They had a funny half smile and their eyes were lazy.

"Well, that's fun. Your island isn't anything like mine was, no, not at all. And this one has a cool mountain, grass and a volcano." Heatstroke looked around with a pleased look.

"Oh!" Legend suddenly said. "You must be a fire spirit! I read about those! I heard that any fire spirit can talk to fire spirits from the past, and other dragons can't see the fire spirits from the past."

Heatstroke nodded and looked quite impressed. "I can let you see me. The others are a little shy with mortals and regular spirits. Not me, though."

"Where would your island be if you didn't have any grass or trees?" Jewelem asked.

"Eh, don't worry about it," Heatstroke replied, laughing a little.

A couple minutes later, the three went to the beach, and Legend and Jewelem were growing a liking to them. They told them about her time as a spirit.

"I lived in the underground kingdom of the desert. Honestly a terrible place. My dad went to prison and I fought Queen Sphinx. I left the city and travelled the island in a spirit form, which was fun. I met Firebrazer, and Cloud, who took me to Ashen, the fire kingdom. I met Phoenix, Final and Dust Devil there."

"Wait. . Desert," Legend said. "Do you mean the sunken Chia island? I read about that. Poseidonite aren't allowed to go into those waters, believing they're haunted by Chia ghosts. Only mountains and a small archipelago remain. You must've lived there right?"

Eventually, after a little convincing from Legend, Heatstroke told us where their island was. They said it was the Husk island that mysteriously disappeared somehow. Legend said it was because of an ancient water spirit that was fighting against some other spirit.

"Not an uncommon issue, I must say," Heatstroke said. "Probably the earth spirit. A bunch enemy clans all cooped up on an island can lead to some issues."

"Wait what?" Jewelem asked, suddenly. "They were fighting? I mean, the clans were, of course. But the spirits?" He glanced at Legend. *Are you gonna fight me because we're Poseidonite and Crystalian?*

"The war between the two is old," Heatstroke replied with a laugh. "And besides, Shadowling, Aolite and Ariash; enemies. Now, no offence, but Poseidonite and Crystalian, also enemies. I wonder who's idea it was to put a bunch of powerful enemies on an island and not expect something to go wrong." They snorted a laugh and shook their head a little, smiling. "Anyway, what's life here been like?"

"We've only been here for about a day and a half," Jewelem said, taking a lot of his courage not to squirm under the eyes of Heatstroke and Legend. He glanced between Legend and Heatstroke.

"Huh, what's it with you two?" Heatstroke asked with a suspicious half smile. "You two in love?" They asked casually, but with a hint of mischief in their voice.

"W-what?" Jewelem stammered. His eyes flew to Legend, who was looking at Heatstroke with a pale, nervous smile.

They laughed nervously, and scratched the back of their neck lightly. She glanced at Jewelem, and the two made eye contact for a split second.

"Ah, I see how it is. Have you met Meteor?" Heatstroke inquired with a lazy, mischievous half smile. "Don't wanna sound like a weird parent."

Legend nervously stretched her wings a little. "She... didn't really want to talk, but I'm not sure why."

For the first time in Jewelem's few memories of her, Heatstroke's smile fell and the cool energy in their eyes faded and they looked to the ground. "Meteor's lost a lot of dragons in her life, and she lost the last dragon she cared about not long before she got here," Heatstroke said, nodding slowly. "I don't wanna share too much of her business, but her little brother, Pyro. . . Yeah, she isn't very cool with everything right now."

"Oh, that's horrible!" Legend said

"I'm an only-child, but I can't imagine the pain of losing a loved one," Legend said, sorrowfully.

Jewelem nodded slowly. "I don't know for sure, but I think my brothers and mother died in the recent shipwreck."

Legend put a supportive wing around him and leaned lightly on his shoulder. The sun reflected into Heatstroke's eyes, turning them into flaming opals. Anger burned lightly into those opals. Dark silence fell over the group as they thought about everything they said. *But I wonder if my mother, Emeraldite and Qwonzie had survived.* Jewelem thought.

If they did, what would they think of me with a dragon from the clan who almost killed them? What would they think of me with a Poseidonite?

"Anyway, I have to go. My friends need me," Heatstroke said, interrupting the silence. "I'll be back to talk with Meteor tomorrow, maybe. I'll be back here soon!" Legend and Jewelem smiled and Legend got off his shoulder to stand up so she could wave goodbye to the cool dragon. Jewelem looked at the dazzling shape of the mysterious fire dragon winging away into the sunlight. Legend had a funny look on her face as she watched her. Her eyes turned to Jewelem and she suddenly broke into giggles and nudged his shoulder so hard he almost fell over.

"Did you hear what she said about us?" She laughed. "Is that how you feel? Because if so, then Heatstroke just completely-"

"No- uhm, wait a minute-" Jewelem stammered. "I mean- yes, but I didn't …"

"Oh it's perfectly fine, I don't care how it is. Just as long as you're still cool and all," Legend smiled at him and gave a little hop, which was easily the cutest thing he'd ever seen in his life.

"Yeah, ok alright, " Jewelem tried. *Honesty, this is a little awkward. I hope she doesn't think too much of it.*

"I know it's early, but I want to go check out that little cliff over there. I thought I saw a little lagoon that's worth checking out," Legend said, breaking Jewelem out of his trance. "There was a *biiiiiiiig* stone cliff with a little cave and I thought I saw a coral reef!"

Jewelem just laughed a little under his breath and smiled at her. He nodded a little and waved to her as she left. They were both up really late last night, flying to the island. He watched the beautiful blue shape against the green, pale red, pink, orange and blue sky wing away and soon disappear below the mountain. He started towards the cave on the south-west side of the volcano. The volcano was raised up over a plateau that overlooked the ocean. The cliff face held a little cave he figured must be the earth spirit cave. He looked inside and immediately had to stop and realize he wasn't hallucinating. The first thing he noted was all of the glowing diamonds and rubies and emeralds littering the walls and ceiling of the magnificent cavern. He walked forward and had to stop himself before walking off the huge cliff into the giant cavern. Water fell from waterfalls that he didn't even understand where the water was coming from, and glowing lime moths wrapped their wings around the spectacular crystals.

This is kind of my home now, he thought. *I could always go and see my brothers, if they're alive. But I want to be here for a while. This is amazing.*

He settled himself into the stone and watched the beautiful view in awe. All he could think before he drifted into sleep, was how amazed his brothers would be if they met Legend.

A Tide That Flows With The Moonlight, Not The Rivers

Heatstroke was one of those dragons that Legend really liked. And she only knew 3 dragons like that. Jewelem, Meteor (kind of,) and now Heatstroke. They were really cool, and so beautifully unique! Their scales were the colour of sand!

As she flew closer to the lagoon, she wondered where the other two spirits were. Well, she also wondered where the third one, the fire spirit was. Meteor was probably moping around in the volcano, as always. But her head seemed to just be in the clouds all the time. She'd only seen the lagoon when she and Jewelem had flown over the island to map out what it looked like. She was super happy to be a spirit. The island was just a beautiful paradise for spirits to become close friends and be happy together. *Don't forget what Heatstroke and Jewelem said, though*, she reminded herself. *The sky and dark spirit were always at each other's throats. The water and earth spirit seem really happy with each other, so at least we're cool with one pair.*

She could only imagine how much Meteor must dislike them. Legend decided she didn't think Meteor was mean, she thought of her as a territorial Ariash who didn't like them invading her personal space. As she approached her destination, she got a good look at her new home. On the side of the stone mountain was a smaller one. It was tall and narrow, much like the bigger one. But big enough for a little cave to be near the bottom. A waterfall fell from 2 smaller twinning holes in the mountain above and on either sides of the small, jagged mountain. Parts of the brown mountain circled around the lagoon, and opened up in the middle for other Poseidonite to swim inside. The water was so clear that Legend could see the rainbow coral at the bottom of the lagoon. Rainbow fish swam below the surface, jumping up to show off their beauty to all the dragons nearby.

"Woooahh," Legend awed at the beautiful magic below her. She sighed deeply and smiled as she dove into the glimmering sea. She didn't swim along with the fish. It's been a while since she'd dove into the cold water. A few hours, maybe? The last time was when she and Jewelem had swam around the islands outside the barriers. She smiled as she remember those moments.

Legend watched the clouds floating around the open sky. She turned her gaze back to the water around her. The island wasn't too far away. She dove back down into the water and saw Jewelem swimming in a circle near her. He swam up to the surface, and Legend followed him. They reached the island and Legend helped pull him onto the sand.

He smiled and breathed in the warm sea breeze air. Bundles of yellow and purple flowers danced through the wind with palm trees flowing peacefully.

"You ok?" Legend asked him with a small laugh. "Come on, I found a coconut tree!" Closer to the middle of the island, a large tree swayed in the breeze with coconuts at its base. Legend shook water off her wings as Jewelem sat down where he was. She wanted to tell him how great he was, but she stopped herself. We're friends, right?, she thought.

"Have you ever had a coconut?" He asked. She shook his head.

She sighed under the water as she thought about him. Legend lay in the tide, her tail curled around pieces of coral. She opened her eyes and saw the sunlight coming into the underwater museum of the sea and spiralled up to the surface. She flew into the air, shaking water droplets everywhere as she went. Flying up to the mountain cave, Legend shook the remaining water droplets off her tail and peered inside. It was dark, very dark. But as she walked inside, the walls started glowing, and she soon realized that they were made with glowing fish carved into the stone. It was so fascinating how they somehow carved *glowing fish* into the walls. They had white outlines with all the scales and the insides were glowing with purple and blue. Glowing moss patches in the shapes of stars covered the ceiling and helped to illuminate the dark cave. Wandering into the mystical cave, she saw a drop into the mountain through a long tunnel. The fish on the walls were carved into a beautiful spiral, letting her see all the way to the end. At the drop into the mountain, the walls around the circular room were made of glass and had real glowing fish inside them. Legend flew down through the long tunnel, skipping the staircase. Once she reached the bottom, she gasped and looked around the new chamber. She landed on a small, sapphire island in the back of a massive crystal chamber. The walls were seeming made of ice and sapphires, but somehow the water was still… Water. It wasn't even cold in the cave. She wondered how they could possibly be made of ice. The water went over 100 feet deep, and even though it was clear, she couldn't see the bottom. A little bridge made of the same enchanting crystals went to a bigger sapphire island in the middle of the chamber. Little waterfalls fell from the ceiling into the lakes, and lily pads floated on the surface of the water. On the middle of the larger platform was a huge, diamond mirror. Legend walked towards the mirror, across the bridge and sat in front of it. Her reflection stared back at her, and she smiled to herself.

She realized that the mirror was exactly the same as the one in the Poseidonite palace. She looked up at the twinkling diamonds and seashells all over the mirror. She laid her talon on it; yep. There, the ripple over the surface of it as though it was made of water from the deepest sea. Legend thought about who she wanted to see, and she didn't have to think for very long.

"RiverStone," Legend whispered. She loved coming to the mirror at home and checking to see who her dad was. Usually after doing something great. He left because she had magic, but she made sure that she didn't use it so that she could someday look at him and say, "Look at what I've done. Anyone could do this, but you were too stubborn to care."

As soon as she spoke his name, the mirror rippled and the face of a green Poseidonite appeared on its surface. His tendrils were dark green, and the webbing between his wings and frill were all green-ish turquoise and his scales were dark green. Legend set it to showing where he was right that second.

Her father was wearing a dark green cloak with less dark green on the edges. He was at a room in the Poseidonite palace, clearly trying to hide himself. *Or his identity,* Legend thought. *He probably has a bad reputation for abandoning the queen and her daughter.*

RiverStone was surrounded by a crowd of dragons. Dragons lining the balconies, dragons all around him, dragons on a stage above the ballroom.

"Today we mourn the death of our fair queen," she heard someone say in the Poseidonite language, Axteian. "She fought a fair battle and defended our kingdom for 20 prosperous years. Now, we allow her to rest peacefully. We witness her depart from this world and ascend to the next."

Legend watched in awe as her father smiled, scoffed quietly and turned and left the room, without looking back. She glared at the image of the awful king.

She set it to show the past, hoping to find herself in the time when he loved her, if he ever did.

She found herself looking at a scene of RiverStone, Oceanic and a small dragon egg. The egg had swirls of bright sky blue and flecks of turquoise that looked like embers from a teal fire. It was shocking to see RiverStone the way he was then. The same dragon who abandoned and hated his own daughter, the same dragon who laughed at the death of his own wife, sitting there and loving them both.

"This is our future princess, RiverStone!" Oceanic exclaimed excitedly, holding Legend's egg in her talons "Or a prince. They're going to rule one day!"

RiverStone laughed under his breath and ran his claws softly over the shell of the egg. He smiled down at his future daughter.

Legend touched the surface of the mirror and remembered the reason he left her. Her magic. It wasn't that rare, it was just uncommon. About an eighth of the kingdom had it. She felt tears forming the back of her eyes as she wondered a chilling thought. *What if my mother didn't want me either?* She thought. She imagined being thrown into a cavern of sharks, or into the deepest abyss of the sea, never to be seen again. Legend softly cried to herself and as she went to the scene of her mother's funeral. She tried to see one of her only friends, one of her cousins who never noticed her. She only knew that his name was Bubble. She felt like she lost herself in the sea of silence as the waters from the mirror pulled her inside of the scene. It felt all to real, even if she knew it was happening. It felt like she was right there, and she kind of was. All Legend did was stare as she watched the funeral of the one dragon who wanted her, the dragon who died to her friend's father.

Fire Burning Away at Nothing But Ashes

Meteor watched the entire conversation between Legend, Jewelem and Heatstroke from the flat area on top of her mountain side of the volcano cave. She didn't hear them, but she saw them. She didn't quite know what to think of her new best friend getting along so well with dragons she didn't quite like. But she didn't try to stop her. It just bothered her so much. Meteor wasn't used to attention. She didn't get the power or love that she wanted, but she would have had either. Now she finally had both, though. She wasn't sure how she felt about Heatstroke going around and just liking everyone. *But then again, Dust Devil is terrifying, I somehow someone feel like Cloud is anti-social to some dragons, and Final is the most shy dragon I've ever met. Heatstroke and Firebrazer seem popular, friendly and really chill. Honestly quite likeable.*

She decided not to think about it, not like she had a choice. FinalFlame had chosen to come that day. She recently arrived in her cave, but Meteor had pretended not to notice. Final creeped her out, but she didn't want to admit it. *She always changed her scales to look like dragons I don't want to see.*

"Many dragons see it that way."

Meteor spun to see the small crimson dragon standing a couple feet behind her. Final had her eyes closed and was sitting there. Final had concentration and frustration on her face. Meteor didn't know how long Final had been sitting there, and neither of them had said anything.

"What?" Meteor asked. "I didn't say anything!" She frowned at her.

"But you thought about it," Final said quietly. "I see all thoughts of everyone." Her scales flickered from Final to Jewelem, then to Legend and then to a little white dragon with a turquoise cloak, and then back to herself. She inhaled and exhaled deeply, then opened her eyes. She looked to the ground in sadness.

"Huh," Meteor replied.

"I see all odds and all thoughts. They will not leave you for a while... I-I think," Final said, frowning and touching her forehead with her left talon. Her face twisted in a spring of fear and pain for a brief second before she looked to Meteor with panic in her eyes.

"Alright, good to know," Meteor said, cautiously. "So why did you try to stay with me?"

"I always try to be friends with other spirits, but it doesn't work out to well..." Final trailed off sadly. She looked away again. "I have been told I am a listener, though at the same time, I am someone who is important to listen to." Final looked Meteor directly in the eye and tilted her head at her.

"Interesting," Meteor replied, slowly and skeptically. She waited for Final to say something, mainly because she didn't know how to continue this conversation. The two dragons watched each other closely and silently.

Final looked down to the tiny forest across the island. Only about 30 trees, pretty small. Final mumbled something to herself.

"Did you say something?" Meteor asked, immediately curious.

"I-I was just asking if you-" Final started. She shivered, for some reason. "Ah, never mind.."

They both hesitated. Meteor was the first to speak again. "Do you have any idea where my sky and dark spirits are?"

Final shook her head.

Meteor could've sworn that she waited a hundred years for Final to say anything. Forgetting that she could see her mind, Meteor thought some *bitter* thoughts about the peculiar dragon. *Do you just not understand that there is a conversation that I'm trying to expand? You're making this conversation quite impossible, Final.*

Final winced. She looked to Meteor suddenly. For the first time she'd ever seen, Final had a small, happy smile and held her wings ever so slightly more confidently. *That smile could be fake.*

"Do you … want to talk about something? What's with the other fire spirits?" Meteor asked, trying to talk to her. Final nodded.

They actually had a functional talk with each other. Meteor smiled and laughed when Final told a joke, and she was surprisingly funny. They talked about the other islands and clans, and Final mentioned that she'd been alive in a time called the Golden Era. She said that it was when the Husk Island was still above the surface. Meteor didn't understand what she meant, then Final said that it had been sunken under the sea by a water spirit.

They finally got to the part about the other fire spirits.

"So what's with… Dust Devil?" Meteor asked.

"I can sense much hesitation as you ask," Final noticed, nodding slowly. "She is a mix between an Ariash and an Aza, an old breed of Ariash that were less of dragons and more of creatures." Final closed her eyes, concentrated, and then her scales slowly flickered to a bright, slightly fogged red, similar to Dust Devil's scales. Final's horns curved like a literal devil's. Her wings disappeared, but didn't looked cut off like Dust Devil's, and she opened her eyes slowly. Then she returned to her crimson colour, but Meteor was still impressed.

"She was banished to the Aza territory for being half Aza," Final continued. "She was also hated there for being half dragon. Her entire race was controlled by their king, and the Ariash killed almost all of them, leaving Dust Devil as the last Aza. Her king cut off her wings and left her to die there, alone. The cave trapped her for thousands of years before Firebrazer, me and Cloud found her."

"Wow," Meteor breathed. She narrowed her eyes into a glare and clenched her talon. Why did they have to hate Dust Devil? What did she even do? "Why did they hurt her? Just because she was an Aza!?"

"All of us, including I, know a thing or two about evil dragons," Final said solemnly. Her right talon slowly turned white and she hid it behind her other talon.

"Even Cloud?" Meteor said. She wanted to learn more about the cool dragon, or human.

"Cloud lived on an island called the Ocean Harbour," Final recited. It seemed to calm her down a bit, so Meteor listened very intently. "But before that, she lived on a regular islands, but not in Anima. She was born a human, and many dragons came and burned her island down. She didn't want revenge, she wanted trust and peace. That's one of the reasons that Firebrazer likes her. She got her powers from a magic dragon who wanted peace with humans. She wished to become a dragon, and he granted her wish. They decided to create an island kingdom for dragons and humans, and with her experiences, Cloud agreed. A couple years later, she asked to become a human again. Before the dragon passed away, he let her switch between dragon and human. The islands they made, it isn't on one of the islands in Anima. It's a completely different island that's now known has The Islands of Crimson Tempests. It got it's new name when King Takulon, an evil sky spirit, turned the island into a prison for its inhabitants. He had to fight against Cloud to get control over the islands, to which he won. That's how Cloud died and got her eternal life, by dying in a challenge."

Meteor decided not to point out the fact that Final seemed to know a little too much, but she probably saw it in her mind, so she just didn't say anything. Meteor just stared at the crimson dragon in shock of what she just heard. *Do all of my new, amazing friends have terrible trauma or is it just Cloud and Dust Devil?*

"Someone is chosen as a fire spirit for a list of reasons, one of them being the strength to continue through bad situations, yes," Final said slowly. "If a dragon is suffering, sometimes they'll be given a constellation. Usually it's those who are unique and different and have strong passion, but it can also be a sign of suffering."

"I'm gonna pretend you didn't take that question from inside my head," Meteor said. "Is there something about... You?"

Final froze and her small smile faded. Her front left talon started to turn white-ish red and unlike the other times, it didn't stop at her wing. It slithered up her wing, across the back of her neck and down her tail.

"Final?" Meteor asked, concerned. Final suddenly gave a small jump and blinked rapidly, wrapping her wings around her back. Meteor didn't know how to help, but she still grabbed Final's white talon, not knowing if it was hurt or not. Final shuddered and the white slowly disappeared.

"T-thank you," Final whispered.

"What the-?" Meteor started quietly.

Final took a deep breath. "No, it just happens. Just... When I'm a little stressed, or feel... Emotion. I'm sorry." She managed to stand up on her own, but sat back down for Meteor to put her wing around her.

"So, you're fine?" Meteor had to ask. "What... Was that?"

"Fire spirits always ask me, and I always have to avoid the question, answer the question, or just do what I did right here." Final put her left talon over her chest and sighed. "It's a curse. I can't feel emotion, or to much of it, as least."

Meteor felt a surge of sympathy for the crimson dragon. They both heard wingbeats overhead and saw Jewelem hovering midair above them. He wasn't too low in the air, and they couldn't see him very well, but he was there. Final lightly gasped and she suddenly vanished or turned invisible. *I wonder if she went back to the Fire Kingdom*, Meteor thought.

She looked up at the Crystalian and growled. "What do you want?"

"I was just exploring the island..." Jewelem said, trailing off a little and looking away. He turned and smiled to her. *He looks just like Pyro when he does that...* Meteor thought. "Alright." She turned and flew to the volcano to sit on the rim and wait for the sky spirit and dark spirit to come. She sighed as she felt the rain slowly patter onto her wings. She'd found herself feeling happier with Final, Firebrazer or Cloud around. They all seemed amazing. As the rain fell harshly onto the spirit island, Meteor felt a sudden longing for Final, or any fire spirit to come back for her.

Chapter 7: Princess of the Sunbird

Ah, the explaining and calming it took to get Silver to shut up and not explode. Shield had taken her back to where they could see the islands of Anima and explained everything. Silver's father, the Eternity Prince, also known as E.T, is a well-known criminal who has committed murder, slavery and many other crimes. Shield mentioned that he was "infamous," but Silver didn't know what that meant. A hard truth that felt like swallowing a rock to hear was that E.T had killed her mother's best friend, Firebrazer, a banished Ariash king. All she remembered of Ariash was that they hated spirits, and that they always banish them immediately. Apparently, her father had only married her mother to get out of prison and hopefully carn Shield's trust, along with the trust of the entire Aolite clan. Several times did Silver have to remind herself and her grandmother that this was her father they were talking about her *father* and not some murderer, but Shield said that they were unfortunately one in the same. Shield somehow knew a lot about his plan, and relayed it to Silver. He'd wanted Silver and Sacrifice to kill each other so if Silver had won, he could get the Aolite to get the other clans against them. If Sacrifice won, he could use Silver as a bargaining chip to bend the Aolite to his will. He'd killed Sacrifice because she didn't fight Silver. Shield theorized that his next idea could be either to wait for another opportunity, frame Silver for the murder, or hunt down the next fire spirit. Silver had asked why he hated fire spirits, and her grandmother didn't know, however, she said that his brother came by and said that an Aolite assassin had killed their father, but that Shield didn't know anything about it, so it couldn't have been her that sent it.

"Wait wait wait," Silver interjected. She was looking at the islands with her brow furrowed and confused. "I have an *uncle?!*"

"According to this dragon, you used to have 2 uncles, but I didn't inquire much further," Shield replied, looking sad. "He clearly didn't want to talk about it. He seemed scared and alone, but he worked through it and still lives here."

Silver's ears perked up and she looked to her grandmother. "What's his name? I need to ask him questions! If he's ok with it, of course."

Shield chuckled a little and raised an eyebrow, looking at Silver with a skeptical, mischievous smile.

"His name is LightningRoar."

Silver froze and her jaw dropped. Shield tossed back her head and laughed. "Go on, child. Go talk to him if you need to." She shooed her granddaughter lightly with her claws and yawned. She flew really fast to the Aolite palace and found herself at the front gates in a matter of minutes. She scrambled inside and traced the hallways back to the Storm Chamber, not bothering to use her map. Silver arrived at the front door of the special room, and was suddenly hit with a realization. *Grandma said that you* used *to have two uncles, meaning one of them... He's my* UNCLE *and nobody ever told me? I wonder if he knew I was his niece.*

Silver took a deep breath and softly knocked on the door. She heard a voice say to come inside, and she peeked her head into the room.

The chamber was always full of clouds, and they were always dark storm clouds, for some reason, and today was no different. She found her uncle laying down in the middle of the room, and he sat up to welcome the Aolite princess. The two smiled at each other.

"Hi, LightningRoar," Silver said, feeling a little awkward. "I... I have something to ask you."

"Anything," he replied firmly.

Silver sighed and closed the door as she walked inside. "So... I don't know how to say this... How many siblings do you have?"

Silver tensed every muscle and nerve in her body, expecting him to explode into a bunch of emotions and confusion, but he stayed just as ever. A little surprised, but mostly normal. His eyes went slightly wider, and he blinked in confusion, but he took Silver's talon and examined it, and then smiled and laughed a little.

"Maybe... Somehow, Brightleaf's daughter?" He said, hopefully. His smile faded a little when she shook her head. She looked him deep in the eye, her bright pink eyes reflecting in his bright, turquoise eyes. He slowly backed away and stared.

"Yeah, do you remember any *other* siblings you had?" Silver asked, feeling extremely nervous and guilty. "Shadowling ones?"

"His name was rarely spoken..." LightningRoar said faintly. "20 years. Brightleaf-" he stopped abruptly. "I thought your mother married a Shadowling. What was his name?"

Silver's shoulders fell. "As crazy as it sounds, I never knew his name. My grandma said that you might know something about what I'm looking for. I need to know who killed my granddad and why."

LightningRoar froze. He stared at Silver in a weird, confused way, as though he had to look after a hundred rabid monkeys.

"I'm sorry, I didn't mean to-" she started.

LightningRoar laid down in front of her to explain himself. "It's alright, Silver. I don't mind it." Silver smiled and felt slightly better.

"Our father, your grandfather, was a mix between Earthin, Icelo and Aolite. That's why I have-"

Their conversation was interrupted when an Aolite guard burst into the room without knocking. (Something that always effectively bugged her mother, Heaven.)

"Princess Silver! Sir LightningRoar!" The guard called to them. He sounded panicked and out of breath, and he'd probably been looking for her. "The Shadowling are attacking the Aolite palace! Come with me!" Another guard came from behind him and lightly grabbed Silver's forearm and gently ushered her out of the room, but she pulled back for a moment.

"Is LightningRoar coming? Will he be safe?" She looked towards where her uncle had been a moment ago just to see him darting out the walls of the Storm Chamber, gone into the evening sky to fight for his kingdom. *He'll be alright though, won't he?*

"He'll be alright, I promise," the guard said. "Come, quickly, I know your mother."

That's one way to kidnap me. She and the two guards arrived at the balcony of the throne room.

The walls of the magnificent hall were beautiful open balconies to let any kind of wind, air, rain and storm into the shimmering palace. It was stormy outside, but the sky was turning dark purple and orange. She could see faint stars against the colourful sky. The whole place was lit up with glowing orange and purple from the unique array, making the entire thing a golden diamond of a kingdom.

"Silver!" Heaven and Shield said at the same time when they saw her. Silver ran over to greet them. She noticed a small white whelp about her age hiding behind her the guard that had brought Silver there. She had pure white scales, pale blue wings, pink spots going down her scales and bright, vibrant blue eyes. Strangely enough, this little dragon had the same dark blue tendrils that Silver had, along with the two horns. Other Aolite dragons had 6 horns, so it was strange. But Silver was a mix, so it was understandable. The young whelp looked shy and scared. The guard smiled to Silver nudged the little whelp next to him.

"I'm Sir Kye, Heaven's brother," he said, lightly bowing his head to her. "This is my daughter, Polka." Another dragon, who was a comfortable shade of brown with flecks of gold came over and nudged Kye's snout. He was taller than Kye, and he had larger wings than him. Kye had the same tendrils and green wings that Silver had, along with a small Poseidonite frill. Silver remember that her grandfather was a Poseidonite, which would explain that. Kye had grey scales and white underscales with blue lines along him.

The new dragon also turned to Silver and smiled the same way at her. "I am Mountain." He bowed to her as well. *Wait... He's a Crystalian.* After some subtle inspection, Silver saw 2 horns, crystals and stones on his back and strong scales. He was a Calx Nation dragon.

"I sent my brother to find you," Heaven suddenly interjected.

"Mother, grandma, um, what's going on?" Silver asked. She could hear distant noises down the halls, and she feared for what could come their way. Polka flinched and buried her head between Mountain's wings. Her fathers each put a wing over her protectively.

Before her mother could say anything, one of the regular guards pulled her off to the side and discussed something with her.

Silver turned to her grandmother. "What's happening?"

Shield grabbed her talons and looked deep into her eyes. "You need to get your sister and escape this place, go to the spirit island and find the others."

Silver didn't have time to say anything when a huge crash interrupted them all. Everyone looked down the hallway to see a huge shadowy figure had stepped into the throne room, with Sacrifice following him with her eyes shut tightly.

"Go, Silver!" Heaven screamed to her. Silver watched in fear as her grandmother bent the storms to battle the Shadowling. It wasn't until Silver got a good look at his eyes that she realized that was the Eternity Prince, her father. While Shield fought him off, she ran over to her twin and pulled her to come with her.

"Come on Sacrifice! We gotta go!" Silver urged her. Sacrifice opened her eyes and she pulled Sacrifice to the balcony. It was a couple moments later that they were flying west towards the spirit island. She didn't know how to find it, but she felt as though it was west.

She had absolutely zero evidence of this.

Silver had to keep stopping to check on Sacrifice. Her sister had always been the faster flier, due to her larger wings. Silver was a small Aolite, and they flew faster than other clans, but Sacrifice was still bigger. But now, she fell behind and couldn't seem to keep up. She looked like she was in a trance, staring at the ground. Every time Silver looked around, she has to stop for her sister to catch up, and she wouldn't answer when Silver asked if she was ok. They finally stopped at an island around midnight. Silver wasn't tired, and Sacrifice didn't seem to care, but both of them were scared of the dark.

Silver wanted to set up a little campsite, but someone had already done it. There was a little canopy along with a nice moss carpet for sleeping. After inspecting the setup, she theorized that someone of the Calx Nation must've lived there. Silver remembered her and Sacrifice learning that the Calx Nation consisted of four clans, Veo, Crystalian, Earthin and Fae.

She knew it wasn't Ariash because there was no fire pit or scorched grass. A Poseidonite would've been in the water, not on the island. Shadowlings or Extivie wouldn't go this far, they're known to stay in their kingdom. She just didn't think that one of the elegant, mystical Icelo or Aolite would've built something like the camp.

"Sacrifice?" Silver whispered to her sister. She smiled to her. "You alright?"

Sacrifice didn't reply. She just sat there with her eyes closed.

"Goodnight, Sacrifice."

Hours passed, and Silver didn't want to wake up when she heard the noises. She just laid on the moss carpet. But remembering what happened last time she woke up in the middle of the night, she looked up and saw her sister leaving the clearing. Silver yawned and followed her. But to surprise, she saw her sister take flight and start flying in the direction they were going in the morning.

"Sacrifice?" Silver called to her, but as usual, she didn't reply. Silver sighed, tired, and followed her sister. Another exhausting hour passed, and they found themselves at a larger island. She saw the outline of two mountain-shaped things somewhere nearby, and she could see a volcano as one of them on the western side. She and Sacrifice were in a valley of sorts, but it was small. She could see a meadow overlooking the sea, and a tall mountain with a sharp summit.

This has to be the spirit island, Silver thought, awestruck by the amazing island. *I wonder if the others have arrived yet.* As if they heard her thoughts, two blue shapes started winging towards them. They were different shades of blue, but still really pretty. One of them had a rainbow down their back, and the other was probably a Poseidonite with having no back legs, that Silver could see, at least. Sacrifice sat down with her eyes dreary and tired again.

"Oh-hi!" One of the blue dragons called to them. The brightest, deepest blue one landed in front of Silver and he didn't even have to help her. The one with two legs had no trouble landing, and probably taking off as well. She seemed to stabilize and walk quite easily. Silver knew from looking at them that they were Crystalian and Poseidonite.

The deepest one smiled and waved nervously.

"Hi," Silver said, smiling. "I'm Silver. This is my sister, Sacrifice!"

"I'm Legend, and this is my friend, Jewelem," the Poseidonite introduced them as. "If I'm not mistaken, you're the dark spirit and sky spirit?" She looked so hopeful, and Silver guessed that they'd been waiting on them for quite some time.

"I think so. I have this." Silver showed them her feather constellation, but to her surprise, it was glowing even more. Even if it was nighttime, it was noticeably brighter. Legend and Jewelem brought their constellations out. Legend held out both her talons gleefully, showing a blue crystal star shape, kind of like a magic sparkle. She smiled happily at the sight of her magic shape.

Jewelem kept his right talon close to his chest and lightly held up a green rose symbol, quickly closing it after a couple seconds.

"Woah," Silver breathed. "Do we have a fire spirit?"

Legend and Jewelem exchanged nervous glances. They looked up to the volcano.

"She's in there," Legend said, looking back at Silver. "She said she didn't like the fire island, so I know she isn't homesick. I don't know why she didn't seem to like me… Was it something I said?" Legend kind of looked to the ground in a confused hopefulness. Jewelem looked back at her in concern at put his arm the back of her neck.

"Should I gw up to see her?" Silver asked.

"You can," Jewelem said. "Just fly through the volcano's tunnel."

Silver did a little jump on her talons. She glanced at her sister, and realized that she didn't want to bring her into the Ariash's lair.

"Uhm," Silver hesitated. "This is probably awkward, but can you guys… Maybe watch Sacrifice, my sister? She hasn't been acting normally and I don't want to bring her into a volcano."

"Alright!" Legend said gleefully.

Silver sighed in relief and thanked her new friends. She set off towards the volcano of the Great Fire Spirit.

Forest of Sapphires

Jewelem watched the little dragon fly towards the volcano, fearing for her safety. *She seemed really nice,* he thought. *Silver could maybe be good friends with Legend.* He turned to Sacrifice.

"So," Legend said in the silence. "Sacrifice, was it?" When the dragon didn't answer, she for some reason kept trying. "It's quite late, I think every spirit gets a place on this island. Let's go find yours, or if we don't find it, you can stay with me or Jewelem. Or you'd want to stay with your sist-" Sacrifice suddenly stood up and stepped past Legend and Jewelem. The two glanced at each other in confusion. They watched Sacrifice take flight and disappear into the dark sky. The two followed her, barely keeping their eyes on her. She suddenly descended into a dive near the base of the mountain. She flew down a dark, dark tunnel until Jewelem wasn't able to see anymore. He stopped and landed on the ground, but he could still hear wingbeats.

"Legend?" He called.

He wasn't sure if he imagined it, or if it was all a dream, but he seemed to realize himself in a large cavern with dark stone and red streaks on the walls. Legend was next to him, looking just as confused as he felt. Sacrifice wait in front of them, looking more regal than usual. For the first time, they heard her first words out of her.

"You shouldn't be here," she whispered to them in a creepy voice. "Go back to the Sunworld."

"But what about you?" Legend asked, reaching towards her. "What are we supposed to tell Silver?"

"I'm here. Tell her I'm here."

Jewelem looked up and saw a large hole in the ceiling, dim moonlight shining through it. "Alright." *A little weird, I mean she just got here and is already sitting in giant holes.*

He started towards the hole in the ceiling, taking off towards it with Legend behind him. They reached the surface in a matter of moments, and Jewelem felt the cold moonlight on his scales. He looked back at Legend to see her rise from the hole in the ground again.

The sun was already rising in the distance, and they could see the orange rays on the sky.

"Is this the same hole we came in through?" Legend asked. "It was hard to see in the darkness."

Jewelem shrugged and rubbed his eyes tiredly. "I may go back to my cave. I didn't sleep much."

"Alright." Legend smiled to him. They parted ways for then and Jewelem went straight to his cave under the volcano. It was surprisingly cool down there, especially when the volcano was right above it. He flew across the early sky and dove down into his cave, swooping in and almost hitting the ceiling of it.

The glowworms and emeralds embedded in the top of the cave lightly reflected the sunlight. He looked up at them, they looked like little green stars all over the ceiling. Whenever he tried to sleep or take a nap, he noticed how uncomfortable the rock was. The layout of the cave was shocking. There was a large platform where he entered with a small wall so nothing fell off. Then it was an enormous cavern with platforms, stalactites, glow worms and diamonds. He rubbed one of his eyes and leaped off the stone balcony into the large cavern. Soaring through the underground tunnel, he noticed the first dirt he'd seen. He flew down the unique cave and found himself in a smaller, but more colourful area.

The walls there were made of brown stone and had much more colourful ores. He saw sparkling gold, shimmering diamonds, glittering rubies and every other colour. There were small words engraved on the far wall of the room.

"This cave reminded me of the mine I had back home. Although Firebrazer never got to see it, I used to believe we would bring Oceanic, E.T and Heaven here … But E.T ruined it. I wonder if it wasn't real… He said he was NightChaser, but I don't know what to believe anymore. I still see it every night, he's watching me. If he wasn't haunting me, I would've thought it was a bad dream. If I didn't wake up to Oceanic and Heaven's arguments, I would've pretended it didn't happen. They told me it was alright, and that he was gone now, and that nothing is going to be wrong anymore. But I wasn't there to help Firebrazer, and I couldn't save him. And now he's gone and Oceanic is leaving and Heaven went home. I'm alone, and even though we weren't too close, it feels wrong to be one of five without the rest, or that they hate each other. I wasn't able to save Zoka either, and I thought this was a second chance. I thought they chose me, not because I was royalty, but because I could have another chance. But no, they chose me for my royalty; something I'm supposed to wear proudly. I shouldn't have the throne. I shouldn't have this opportunity. I shouldn't have a friend as perfect as Oceanic. I don't deserve anything. I shouldn't be given any more chances. My son doesn't deserve me; I don't want to fail anyone

anymore. I'm already going to die to him, and I just wanted to make everyone happy."

"-Earthquake."

Jewelem stood at the message, shocked by Earthquake's last words. He knew immediately this was his father. Zoka's official title was Queen Zoka, and the only dragon to call her otherwise must have been her own husband. He gave away his son to someone else in *guilt,* but since hearing he wasn't Garnet's son, he'd been wondering why he'd been given up. He was killed by someone named E.T, and he'd heard of someone called the Eternity Prince. Were they the same dragon? Everyone said that King Earthquake had died of a strange illness… But nobody knew what the infamous Eternity Prince was capable of. *How could they do that to him? Why was he friends with Oceanic if she killed my mother? The other spirits… Heaven, Firebrazer, Queen Oceanic and E.T… If E.T is the Eternity Prince, then he is a past spirit. Then how does he have his powers?! Past spirits are half as powerful, aren't they? Is he a past spirit, or is Sacrifice lying somehow? Silver must know if she said she's her sister.*

He took one last look at the message before leaving the cave.

He didn't care about the uncomfortable hard stone, he didn't think about the creepy sister living with him, he didn't see the emeralds the same anymore. He could see them as something that could easily be taken. Jewelem lay on the stone, his scales going numb. He had nightmares of spirits battling over a scorched paradise.

A Tide that Flows With the Moonlight, Not the Rivers

Legend paced in front of her mirror in confusion. She tried ten, a hundred, a thousand times, trying to understand everything.

"So... What were their names?" She asked.

"Firebrazer, Heaven, Oceanic, E.T and Earthquake," Jewelem said. It was bright in the morning, and Jewelem had come down to her cave to tell her about what happened. He said that he explored his cave for somewhere to sleep, and found a colourful cave with words engraved on the wall.

"Oceanic was my mother," Legend whispered, just loud enough for Jewelem to hear. "I can imagine her telling King Earthquake that everything would be fine. She tells the entire kingdom that sometimes."

Jewelem nodded. "Do you think E.T is the Eternity Prince?"

"Who's that?"

"How do you not know him? He's the most wanted dragon in Anima!"

"I didn't get much *exposure,* Jewelem."

Jewelem made a "hm" sound. "E.T is a past dark spirit that's infamous for killing the Ariash King and kidnapping hundreds of dragons from their kingdoms and clans. Nobody knows his full power, his whereabouts, or even his name."

"What about his family?" Legend asked, wide-eyed.

For the first time in her memory, Jewelem's bright, nervous eyes deeper into a solemn glare at the crystal floor.

"The stories said he killed his family in a fit of rage, but the true story is unknown. He had two brothers and some say he had a sister, and no one knows their names. If they're alive, they're probably concealing their identities, in fear of being hunted for their knowledge of the Eternity Prince. The kidnapped dragons were never seen again once the Eternity Prince has them, none of them ever escaped him.

Reports say whenever he shows his face, it's to kill, and he travels with an army of strange black dragons."

An eerie silence fell over the two. Legend thought about the story, adding it to her list of concerns. *Surely it can't be real, right?* She thought. *Sounds like another ghost story… But if reports and the few survivors said so, it must be true.* Legend shivered at the thought of black dragon claws shooting up from the ground and plunging into kingdoms.

"That's horrifying," Legend said. "Why do you think Sliver is involved?"

"His appearance was described as a huge, black, Smokey figure with bright pink lightning, along with pure pink eyes," Jewelem replied. "Silver's eyes are the same colour, but The Eternity Prince's eyes are *completely* pink. It could just be a coincidence, but her sister looks like a strange red Shadowling. Those don't normally exist."

"What are you suggesting?" Legend asked. *I already think I know what he's going to say…*

"I think she's The Eternity Prince's daughter," Jewelem said firmly. "Or his sister, but considering her age, maybe just a thought."

"No way!" Legend said suddenly. "She's an Aolite, and they're the enemies of the Shadowlings. I mean, you and me, we met by chance. Even though our clans are- you know, Shadowling and Aolite's war is much more serious. Sacrifice may be a Shadowling, but maybe- maybe she's adopted? An Aolite wouldn't marry a Shadowling!"

"It's all proven with Heaven, Firebrazer and the Eternity Prince's actions. W-which I have no idea what they were. But they probably did something to each other! We know the Eternity Prince killed Firebrazer, but that's about it."

"Should we go check on Silver?" Jewelem asked.

Legend nodded and followed him out the tunnel. Once they reached the valley, they found Meteor, Silver and Sacrifice in the middle of the valley. Legend and Jewelem stopped near a boulder and listened to them.

"I didn't see it happen," Silver said. She sounded sad as she explained the memory. "I just remember the dark dragon in our hallway, seeing her body, and fleeing the cottage."

Meteor was in her regular sized form, but she was still a dragon much bigger than Legend or Jewelem. "I remember dragons like that from the battles the Ariash had with the Shadowlings," she hissed.

"Hi!" Legend called to them, a bit too enthusiastically. Meteor looked up at them and scowled, and Silver looked over her shoulder with a smile.

Jewelem waved a little to the three.

"Hey, Legend," Silver said as the two walked up to them. "We were just talking about our lives before we came here. I lived on the southern earth island, or at least, that's what they told me once I got to the Sky Spirit Haven."

"Oh, interesting," Jewelem said to her.

"I lived under a rock," Jewelem said. "I mean. .. Sometimes,"

Silver giggled. Meteor just sighed and shook her head. Sacrifice just sat there silently.

"Idiots" Meteor muttered, unimpressed.

"Of course," Legend said, smiling.

"So did you guys need something?" Silver asked.

Legend glanced at Meteor. *Are we able to ask Silver all our questions with Meteor around? Shadowlings and Ariash are at war. Is she going to hate Silver if she finds out she could be a Shadowling?*

"So, Silver, are we… able to talk?" Legend asked. She saw Jewelem glance at her with wide eyes, as though she'd just embarrassed him.

"Um, ok" Silver replied with little hesitation. "Can Sacrifice come?"

Legend looked to Jewelem, and he nodded. It wasn't like Sacrifice was going to stop Silver from saying anything.

"What are you little worms hiding?" Meteor growled. She rose up and her body slowly grew to a slightly larger size. It was that, or Legend was just very, *very* threatened by her tone of voice. Meteor's sharp eyes looked from Silver to Sacrifice to Jewelem to Legend.

"Nothing, we just want to talk," Legend said to her.

"It's alright Meteor," Silver reassured her, turning to face the fire spirit. "We'll be quick. You can go meet your fire spirit besties. I'll meet you later. Come on Sacrifice." She lightly tugged on her sister's talon, and the Shadowling eventually stood up and followed, but kept her eyes closed.

They went back to Silver's cave inside the mountain, entering through the base of it. It was a beautiful, long cavern in the mountain, turned into that of a library. Like Meteor's volcano and Legend's cave, almost the entire mountain was turned into her domain. It was made of golden, diamond and quartz walls with countless books lining it's walls. When she was exploring her cave, she found that she had an enormous library of books, files, scrolls and papers.

She remembered being told that the Poseidonite Clan was the Clan of knowledge. They were the oldest clan of them all, the wisest creatures of the sea. They entered Silver's cave and sat in the circular room at the bottom. They could see a blinding light from above them and glowing on the shimmering walls of the library. The four sat down on the glowing white floors.

"So, what did you want to ask me?" Silver asked, smiling. Legend stopped looking at the incredible room and looked to the young Aolite. She couldn't imagine this little dragon being the daughter of a nefarious villain. Maybe they shouldn't have done this. But Silver's bright pink eyes were so vibrant and beautiful, it was hard to imagine an evil dragon having such a gorgeous eye colour.

"So, are you aware of someone called the Eternity Prince?" Legend started.

Silver tilted her head, and a moment later her eyes slightly widened. "I... I *have* heard of someone like that. Why do you ask?"

"I'm not sure how to ask this," Legend said. Why did it feel so awful? Why did she feel hurt just asking this young child this harsh question. "But can we ask you something?"

A Fire Burning Away at Nothing but Ashes

Ok, there is no chance, no chance *they are coming back.* Meteor watched the four dragons leave, and she had so many questions. She left towards the volcano, beating her wings heavily. The fire spirits had just left, they weren't coming for her any time soon. As for the other spirits, they were probably leaving to plan revenge on her for existing. *What are they hiding?* She glanced over to Sacrifice's hole in the ground, wondering how she never noticed it before she arrived. *I bet it showed up when that angsty worm got here,* Meteor thought

She shot into the sky and dove into the mysterious cave. Meteor engulfed her body in flames to light the way in the darkness. Cracks appeared in the black stone around her, but she didn't care. There must have been red lava behind the walls, because the cracks were bright red and she didn't need to make her own light. She spiralled down to the dark floor and landed on the middle of a huge cave. It was *enormous*. Meteor thought she could use her giant form and still be able to not crush the cave. Still, she refrained.

As she walked through the red and black cave, she thought about the spirits on the surface. *How could they just abandon me like that?* She thought, bitterly. She saw a small, raised platform of smooth stone and flew up onto it. Meteor ran her claws over the stone. She saw a huge tunnel and swooped down to it, continuing her walk through the cave. *Then again, there isn't much I'd do for them anyway.*

She walked down the large tunnel slowly, glaring at the ground as she went. The cracks lightly turned purple, but she didn't care to look at them.

"Jewelem… He seemed like Pyro," she thought aloud. Her voice echoed in the cavern.

"It's frustrating, isn't it?" A male voice told her.

"Yeah…" She grumbled. "I-" she froze. Meteor spun around to face the large black figure with glowing pink eyes and pink lightning beneath the black smoke covering his scales.

"Hello, Meteor. Nice to meet you. My name is E.T," The voice said to her, calmly. She stared at him and dug her claws into the earth before leaping at the figure. Meteor tried to rake her claws across his face, but she went right through him instead. She felt a whoosh of wind and he appeared in front of her as he slammed his claws into her throat.

But she didn't die.

She woke up very shaken, but not at all hurt. She looked around desperately, thinking about waking up in some sort of prison, or black world. But she was still in the cave, and it was still red. Meteor was laying on the raised stone platform. She wasn't dead yet. She touched her throat; not bleeding at all.

She left the cave in a hurry, afraid of the dragon coming for her. *It was a dream,* she thought. *But I know that I don't dream about things like that. If I had a nightmare, it would be of Magma. I don't dream of scary Shadowlings.* Once she escaped the cave, she wanted to go straight to her volcano immediately. As she reached the top, she froze. There was a sloth sitting at the top.

"Why?-" Meteor started.

"Ah, apologies," the sloth said. Meteor hovered in the air around the sloth, rather confused.

"Final!?"

The sloth's fur suddenly turned to crimson dragon scales as Final flickered out of that form. "S-sorry. I like sloths... So fuzzy."

"... Ok?" Meteor said.

"I like sloths" Final said quietly. "They're so fuzzy, and I love the animals."

Meteor nodded skeptically. "Alright. Can I help you?"

"I've come to tell you about some Shadowling," Final said. "He's coming for you."

"Well good timing," Meteor snapped. "He already came."

"No ..." Final whispered. "I meant behind you."

Meteor's eyes widened and she spun around to look behind her. Sure enough, an enormous black figure with bright pink eyes stood on the horizon. The smoke ran from his scales in the wind, and it would be an amazing sight if she didn't know what it was.

"I should go now," Final started. She suddenly faded from her spot and disappeared. Meteor reached for the fading dragon, but her claws didn't touch anything by the time she was gone. She looked between Legend's cove and the dragon on the horizon, wondering if she should get the other spirits or fight the dragon herself. The dragon started running towards the island, and she leaped into her huge spirit

151

form and flew towards them. He leaped into the air and swirled around her for a few moments before striking her wing with dark energy. She roared in fury and shot blazing fire around her at the dragon. The dragon didn't dodge, but it was useless, *the fire went right through them!*

She landed on the sand, and the dragon vanished from sight. "Fight me like a real dragon," she hissed. "Come on. If you're so strong then come really fight me.

She spun and found him coming to strike her from the back like he did in the cave. She tried to lift her claws up from the water. But they wouldn't move. Meteor looked down at the water she was standing in, deep, but only ankle deep for her powerful size. Black vines and chains wrapped around her claws and talons, locking them into the water. The dragon rose into the air, his huge wings wrapped in black smoke. *Does he even* have *scales?* She wondered. She tried to breathe fire at him, but the black vines and chains wrapped around her snout. Meteor narrowed her eyes, ready to be killed easily by this dragon. But she was quickly thinking about how to kill him. Just as he was about to strike her, Meteor stretched to bash her head into his throat. He seemed to effortlessly dodge her attack, and he raised his claws to kill her. But before he could kill her, there was a blinding flash of red light. *What was that?!* Meteor thought, panicked, as her eyes were filled with bright red. Once the light cleared, she saw Sacrifice standing on the ground in front of her. The water swirled around the dragon as she held the black dragon's claws and neck with blood coloured chains. Meteor looked up and saw Jewelem, Legend and Silver on the shore. Silver started flying rapidly towards her sister, but before she could reach her, the black figure turned to a puff of smoke and flew towards the island. He seemed to be going right to Silver. Sacrifice vanished and Meteor flew towards the shore, trying to dig her claws into the black dragon's back. *How are my claws going right through him?*

"Meteor!" All three of the dragons called to her. Silver was scared and seemingly genuine. *I wonder if she actually cares about me.* Once the black dragon vanished and she reached the beach, she looked around desperately for Sacrifice.

Only to find her sitting with her eyes closed next to Silver.

They all looked to sea and saw the dragon descend from the sky into the water next to the shore. Meteor landed and shrank to her smaller size. He let out an ear-piercing shriek that sent chills down Meteor's spine. The pink lightning under the black smoke flashed brightly and coloured the sky the same dark and bright colours. After looking closer they realized that the sky was full of dragons just like the powerful one standing in front of them, just much smaller.

"Silver?" Legend asked the Aolite.

"I didn't think he would- I thought it was impossible!" She replied in a panicked voice.

Meteor turned to her with an angry and hurt expression. "What do you know about this dragon?" She demanded. *What is she hiding from me? How could she hide* this guy *from me and I didn't notice?*

She didn't get a chance to answer before he slammed his tail down on them. Meteor dodged to the left, while the other's flailed to the right. Her eyes were filled with black, dark purple and white light. When she opened her eyes, she saw the dark dragons attacking a white barrier around the five. Silver's scales glowed brighter when using her power. Meteor glanced at the huge dragon across the water, who's pink lightning was glowing brighter. *And they have the same colour eyes?*

"Silver, what is going on here?" Meteor asked again.

"Uhm, there's a lot to explain," she said.

Meteor narrowed her eyes. "What do you mean?"

"**These wonderful puppets are my daughters.**"

They all spun to look at Sacrifice, whose eyes were now glowing bright pink. She stood up and strolled over to Silver's side. She went behind her Aolite sister and appeared on her other side. Her eyes flickered to Meteor, then Legend and then Jewelem.

"**Didn't think I had this much time to play with her,**" a familiar male voice said through her. "**But I can't make dragons eternal. If I could, this wouldn't be happening, now would it?**" Even in her shock, Meteor managed to tear her eyes away from the dragon. She looked to the dragon across the sea, who now had sat on the water with his eyes closed. Sacrifice threw her head back and laughed.

"**Meteor, kid, you can't have two consciences. That's ridiculous.**"

"Sacrifice?" Silver asked her sister. Meteor could tell that Silver was on the verge of tears. "W-what's going on?"

"**I already told you, dummy,**" she laughed. The voice was clearly male, and had no sign of Sacrifice herself behind it. Or that was just her voice, but considering Silver's tone, that seemed very unlikely. "**Sacrifice is long dead. I just use her body for some errands now.**" She smiled and shrugged.

"What is going on here, you murderous rat?!" Meteor demanded.

Sacrifice smiled devilishly to her. "**This little puppet here and her pathetic twin are two of my children. Honestly, speaking as a spirit, why summon life when you can live your own just fine? But frankly, I prefer my oldest daughter over these two.**" Sacrifice's eyes narrowed into a murderously happy look and she lunged at Silver. Jewelem leaped in the way to protect Silver and Meteor flung herself onto Sacrifice's back.

"If only I could kill this one again," he said, clearly trying to hide the struggle behind his happy voice. **"Wonder how badly that would help me. Guess I can just let her go for a bit."** Her eyes closed and she seemed to pass out. The huge Shadowling's eyes opened. He started running towards the island and he slammed his tail into Silver's shield. Meteor shot strong fire at the dragon, but he didn't even flinch. The shield shattered and the dark dragons fell onto the island.

Meteor swung her head around to see the other side of the island. *If I can't fight those dragons, then none of us can.* She thought about hiding in the volcano, but she didn't want them seeing the inside of her room.

"Follow me!"

Meteor looked behind her to see Jewelem and Silver following Legend. They stopped and waited for her. When Meteor caught up to them, she saw them flying to the mountain lagoon. They quickly got inside and flew to the bottom of a long, long cavern. Before they reached the bottom, however, Legend took them into a larger cave made of sapphires. The large room shimmered with smooth, blue walls and floors with many dark wood bookshelves lining the walls. Small waterfalls fell from the ceiling, and it was oddly calming for a cave with so much water, especially for an Ariash.

Silver and Legend met in the middle of the library to talk quietly. Meteor saw that Jewelem was carrying Sacrifice, who he laid on a pile of cushions carefully. He looked slightly concerned and laid his talon on her chest. He looked shocked and pulled back.

"Jewelem, I think that's a zombie," Legend said to him.

"She isn't breathing, so that makes sense." Jewelem played with his claws. "So can anyone explain to me what's going on here?" Meteor demanded, spreading her wings. "Why is that thing on our island?"

The other three glanced between each other. Silver was the first to step forward and speak. "That *thing* is my father," she said to her.

Chapter 8: Prince of Eternity

Princess of the Sunbird

Silver could tell from the start that Meteor was quite mad. She wondered how many secrets this dragon had been kept from that she was she immediately furious after realizing Silver's secrets.

"You two are his daughters?!" She snapped, appalled. "That's impossible."

"It isn't!" Silver promised. "My grandma told me that he married Princess Heaven to get out of prison! He only had heirs to convince her that he loved her to get her trust!"

Jewelem lightly grabbed Silver's arm and whispered something to her. *"Silver... Your sister, I think she's... I think E.T killed her."*

"He killed her when we were back home," she whispered back. *"I brought her back. It's a long story."*

Jewelem stepped back and nodded, then looked to Meteor.

"What are you two talking about?" Meteor snapped. "More secrets?"

Silver smiled nervously. "I have a lot to explain, Meteor." Silver explained how her sister had been murdered in her sleep by someone she didn't know, and brought her back with a spell book written by NightChaser. She said she entered the realm known as the Blackzone to take her sister back and had to fight Sacrifice's killer. Turns out that he was her father and he is E.T.

Then she told her about his plans, or what she knew about them. Silver explained how he married Heaven to get out of prison. He needed Silver and Sacrifice to fight each other and had different plans depending on who won. She told her that if Silver won, then he would use the death of Sacrifice to get dirt on the Aolite. If Sacrifice won, she'd be ordered to keep Silver alive and use the Aolite to his own benefit.

By the end, Meteor looked cold and angry at the same time. She seemed mostly confused though. Her eyes were slightly narrowed, and she rose to a slightly larger form.

"While I was escaping the cottage when she was killed, I got this scar." Silver open the one flap of her robe and showed Meteor the dark spot on her neck.

"That's... Not what I was expecting," Meteor said.

Silver played with her claws. "It's very confusing, I know. I didn't know anything about this until like, two weeks ago." Sacrifice now sat behind Silver with her eyes closed, and nobody noticed when she woke up.

"So the Eternity Prince is E.T?" Jewelem clarified. "Also he's your dad?"

Silver nodded. "As I understand it." They all heard a loud crash from above them. *He won't stop until he finds us*, Silver thought, *And then what?*

"I'm all for ideas, for, you know, *getting the evil dark spirit out of our island*." Jewelem muttered. Legend put a soothing wing over him.

"Can we just go fight him?" Meteor demanded. Silver went over to one of the bookshelves near the wall next to the door of the library. She sat down and sighed sadly. *I don't want this*, she thought. *I just want to have a sleepover with Sacrifice again*. She felt her eyes getting heavy. She hadn't slept peacefully since arriving. All night, Silver had been worrying about Sacrifice. Her mother had always made sure Silver's mental health was alright, but she felt a bit lost.

"Respectfully, Meteor," Legend said. "I don't think anyone has the power to beat him."

She glanced over to the door. Jewelem walked over to the large tunnel door and peered up, but Silver was the only dragon who seemed to notice.

"Do you think he's more powerful than I am?" Meteor challenged Legend. Silver had her eyes on Jewelem, who kept glancing up and around the tunnel and occasionally back at the other three. He looked at Legend for a moment with big, hopeful eyes. His wings drooped and the light faded from his eyes when she didn't notice him.

"No, I'm really just saying that nobody can do anything to him," Legend was saying.

Jewelem's eyes went to Silver, and he silently spoke to her with his eyes, but she couldn't quite figure out what he was saying. Not before he launched himself out of the tunnel and up into the Prince's destruction.

Forest of Sapphires

Why did I think this was a good idea? Jewelem swiftly flew through the tunnel and up into the dark hallway. He landed slowly, the sunlight behind something in the tunnel. Midway, he saw the giant, unmistakable figure of the Eternity Prince. He was reaching his dark, powerful tendrils of black magic into Legend's tunnel to where they were hiding. He paused to look at Jewelem.

"Oh, hello there, Calx Prince," he said to him, gleefully.

Jewelem stared in shock. He couldn't believe what he was seeing. The dragon that had killed hundreds of Crystalians, Earthin, Veos and Faes. *He's the one who killed my father…* Jewelem thought once he got control of his mind again.

"H-how did you find us?!" Jewelem stammered. "And how do you know me?"

"You look just like Earthquake," E.T replied. "Same scales, wit, courage and gullibility." Jewelem shrank back to the edge of the tunnel, folding his wings closer to his body. He glanced down the long cave. *They're going to come after me,* he realized with a jolt of remorse. *I don't want to hurt anyone, or cause any more trouble.* He gathered the little power he knew how to use and a strong, impenetrable diamond wall blocked the library doors. He felt bad, locking them up. But he would release them when it was safe. *That is… If I survive this.*

Suddenly, without warning, the smoke surrounding E.T vanished, revealing a large, purple and black dragon standing in front of him. He had bright, glowing pink eyes and deep purple wings. Small trails of smoke radiated from the corners of his eyes and from his wings, but now Jewelem was able to see his body.

He wasn't sure what to say that wouldn't make the dragon want to kill him, but E.T had something to say. "You know, I'm honestly quite impressed with your father's abilities," he said, swirling a hovering black diamond in his claws, and he spoke so casually. Jewelem could never be so calm in the presence of a powerful spirit.

He struggled to answer. "What do you mean?"

The black diamond turned bright blue, flickered, and vanished as he clenched his talon. He smiled before turning to Jewelem. "You and your father have this… *Something* inside you that gives you a strange fearlessness." He paused and his smile grew the smallest bit. "I can sense fear, and you are scared of me. But you still try and fight me."

Jewelem's eyes widened. How did he know? *He can literally smell my fear...* Jewelem thought. He paused to think about E.T's question. "I don't know," he finally answered with.

E.T tilted his head and looked at him. "Then why did you come for me?"

"I wanted to protect my friends. Do you ever feel any kind of longing to protect anyone?"

He offered a small, sad chuckle. "I don't have friends. Nobody loves me anymore. Everyone who was supposed to doesn't understand." E.T shrugged and sighed, his playful smile now disappointed and sorrowful.

"Oh," Jewelem said sympathetically, forgetting that E.T had done so much to so many dragons. "I'm sorry."

"At least my son loves me," he replied. "I think. But he... Doesn't quite count." Black tendrils of dark smoke coiled themselves around Jewelem's talons, claws and legs. He looked to down at them, the back to E.T in mild panic and confusion.

"Why-?" He started.

"I need earth and crystal magic to free my clan," he replied, standing up and eyeing him with cold, blank eyes. "I need a lot of magic, really. The Aolite and Ariash combined aren't strong enough, but against all of Anima, I need more dragons to go against them. Clans like the Extivie, Veo, Fae and perhaps the Crystalian will be difficult." He laughed a little. "Your clans were the strongest, Calx Prince."

"But now the Shadowlings must prevail."

With a sudden thrust of dark magic, Jewelem was thrown against the far wall of the cave by the black tendrils and fell down the long tunnel. He felt a burning pain through his body as he hit the wall. His bones felt weak and shattered. It was a long way down, so he had time to throw his wings open and not fall to his death completely, although they stung with pain. He saw the enormous creature that the Eternity Prince was famous for. He climbed down the long shaft and pinned Jewelem to the floor with his talon, injuring his back again. He hovered over him in a huge black storm of pink lightning.

Jewelem tried to get out from under the powerful force, but it didn't work. *I wonder if Meteor could take this guy down…* he thought. But looking at the huge, towering figure, he suddenly agreed with Legend; he didn't think *anyone* could get rid of him. It was hurting him to feel the pressure on his scales. Jewelem felt a creeping sensation in between his scales and wings. Black marks appeared around him and he tried to break the wall he put to keep his friends inside. He hadn't had much, if any at all practice with his magic, but he knew how to summon diamonds at his will. Concentrating on the essence of the nearby stones he made earlier, he tried to make them combust. He didn't hear them shatter, but definitely heard something that let him know Legend got out.

"*JEWELEM"* Legend screamed. Jewelem's body burned from the heavy weight on him, but and he longed to go tell Legend he was alright. He struggled under E.T's talons.

He looked down at Jewelem. "I'm not here to kill," he said in a cold, soulless voice. "I need *you,* Silver and Sacrifice." he continued to stare at him. He felt like he was going to pass out.

"I need everyone except the Poseidonite, but you came after me. You're one of my only threats. You're one of *our* only threats." He curled his huge wings in. He closed his eyes for a moment, then opened them and gave Jewelem a sad, sorrowful look. "I'm sorry, Jewelem." He raised his other talon and slammed it down onto Jewelem, and his vision faded to black as the Eternity Prince disappeared into the top of the tunnel.

A Tide That Flows Among Moonlight

"JEWELEM!" Legend screamed as a diamond barricade appeared where Jewelem had just vanished. "Come back!"

"Why did he-?" Meteor started, but stopped herself. Legend tried to shake the walls and break them, but it didn't work. *Why did he leave? Where is he going?*

"What now?" Silver asked. Legend tried to smash the walls with her shoulder, but with only two legs, it didn't work. All she did was hurt her shoulder and fall over. Silver came and put her wing around her back once she got up. Legend looked to Meteor, who was standing on her other side, glaring up at the wall. The library door was tall and wide, but if Meteor spread her wings, she would be able to put her wing across it. After a few minutes of trying to break the wall (by Silver throwing various books at it) Meteor finally had an idea.

"What if I try to smash it?" She asked, eyeing it threateningly.

"Why didn't you ask to do that five minutes ago?" Legend asked.

Without warning, the Ariash suddenly lunged at the walls and raked her claws across it's surface, her scales glowing orange. Silver and Legend both gasped and stared in awe when burning orange streaks appeared on the wall's surface. The wall suddenly combusted before their eyes as if the force keeping it together vanished.

Meteor stepped back. "I didn't think I did *that* much," she said, shocked by her own claws.

Legend barely heard her. "JEWELEM?!" she screamed down the tunnel.

They peered outside and saw the huge black creature controlling the long tunnel. The black smoke wasn't hot, and it wasn't cold. It wasn't smoke from any fire, or any normal fire. Jewelem had to have been right; even if legend didn't know he existed, this was the Eternity Prince himself. *The Prince of Eternity*, her mind echoed.

"What is that?!" Silver cried.

Pink lightning and black mist flew by the doorway as he flew back up the tunnel and disappeared.

"Where's he going?" Meteor asked, looking up. But that was the least of Legend's concerns. She leaped off of the ledge and flew down the spiralling staircase, not bothering to go down the stairs. She reached the bottom and froze.

Laying on his side, Jewelem had dark purple cracks throughout his unconscious body, black smoke pouring out of the wounds. The tips of his wings were slowly turning dark purple. His back was turned to her, covered in black and red marks. She felt tears in the back of her eyes as she ran over to help him. She pulled her necklace over her head and draped it over Jewelem's neck. To her surprise, all it did was heal a few wounds in his back.

Legend leaned on the back of her tail to pick him up and carry him to the surface. She beat her wings harder than she had before, and once she reached the top of the cave, she immediately went to valley where Silver and Meteor were. It was extremely hard to land with Jewelem in her talons, but she put him on the grass and landed next to him.

"Oh no…" Silver whispered, laying a concerned talon on his side. The dark shades of purple were bleeding through his scales, smoking black and purple.

"Why is it spreading?? Legend asked in a panicked voice. *No, please, please don't turn into one of E.T's little shadow monsters.* She didn't want to admit it, but he was turning the exact same colours, it was horrible to watch. She sat down to put her claw under his neck. Meteor stood further behind Silver, eyeing her volcano.

"I'm not sure," Silver replied. She didn't have her normal cheer and smile. Her scales glowed a bit brighter. They all looked up as a huge shadow fell over the land. E.T was flying above them, his huge, powerful wings practically controlling the wind. He stared at them with glowing eyes. Everyone stood there, frozen by the creepy sight, until he finally turned and vanished into the sky. Legend curled her free talon into a fist. She looked down at Jewelem, his face lightly twisted in a form of pain.

Legend whipped her head around to stare at where the Eternity Prince had just been. She felt like going after him and killing him herself, but knew she couldn't do that.

"What do we do?" Legend asked Silver. The Aolite examined him closely.

"I could try to heal him," she answered. But she didn't sound really confident.

Legend tore her gaze away from Jewelem to look into Silver's fearful eyes. Legend finally noticed the tiredness and fear under her eyes. She put her wing around her.

"Silver, are you alright?" She asked, glancing at the sky. The sun was starting to fall over the horizon. She didn't realize the day had gone by so quickly.

"Yeah," Silver answered. "I'm fine."

Legend squeezed her talon. "You seem tired. Let's bring Jewelem to your cave, and you can go to sleep." Silver smiled to her and they flew back. Legend carried Jewelem and Silver flew by her side. Silver showed her a room that looked like a hospital in her mountain. Pale yellow walls looked like they're made of gold and quartz. Windows spread moonlight into the room. Piles of pillows and blankets lining the walls as crystal lanterns made of fiery crystals lit the room from golden pillars around the room. The room wasn't very big, but it was beautiful. They put Jewelem in one of the blankets and Legend carried Silver to the top of the mountain. Her bedroom was astonishing. She had azure blue tiles across her ceiling and a rainbow window of stained glass showing the entire island. Sacrifice was laying next to her bed, her eyes shut tightly. She didn't notice the Shadowling had left the library or woken up. Legend placed the young whelp in her pile of blue pillows and blankets. She rubbed her back and left her. Legend went back down to the hospital room and sat next to Jewelem all night.

A Fire Burning Away at Nothing but Ashes

Meteor frowned after the two dragons leaving to the mountain. Later that night, Meteor went to her room. She'd been wandering the island for the last hours of the day. Remembering Final's power of seeing all thoughts, she tried to tell her something. *Hey, Final*, Meteor thought. *I gotta tell you something.*

I'm coming with the others, Meteor heard coming through her mind. ***We'll be there quickly.***

As she reached the top of the volcano, she dove into it with full power and swooped into the stone cave tunnel when she reached the bottom. Near the next morning, when she thought they'd never get there, Meteor saw Cloud, Firebrazer, Heatstroke and Final coming in from the sky through the doorway.

"So I told her we'd be there pretty soon," Final was telling Firebrazer in a quiet voice.

"I'm sure it couldn't be that bad," Cloud assured them.

Firebrazer smiled and waved to her as he entered first. "Hey, Meteor," he said. "Final told us to come quickly. Is the a problem?"

With a small puff of greyish red smoke, Cloud turned into her human form. Firebrazer put Dust Devil, who he was carrying, down and she stalked over to a corner.

"There kind of was a problem," Meteor told them.

She explained how there was a huge Shadowling at the island who seemed to manipulate extreme power. She wasn't able to burn or scratch him, and he could posses Sacrifice. She also had to explain that Sacrifice had died and been brought back as a strange and lifeless dragon. Through the entire explanation, Final kept her eyes closed and held her wrists tightly. She sat near the wall away from Dust Devil. Firebrazer and Heatstroke kept sort of glancing at Cloud who had a serious, intent look. Despite her clear interest in the topic of the evil dark spirit, she did occasionally glance at Firebrazer.

"Then he just left," Meteor finished.

"Sound familiar?" Firebrazer asked Cloud.

What would she know? Meteor thought. Cloud had lived for a long time, but she couldn't have known much about the spirits of Meteor's time.

"A dark spirit, clearly," she said, looking at the ground. "I was taught they were powerful, deep and mysterious. They're chosen by fear, danger, sadness, wisdom, or being… Insane. Usually, a broken difference between them and other clans is what gives them an Umbral Constellation. I was told how to deal with a powerful and evil one, but I can't really do that now. There used to be a secret art of exorcism that the people of the Ocean Harbour knew." She paused to look at Meteor. "We'll need your sky spirit."

"What?"

Meteor spun around to see the small blue Aolite standing in the doorway to the volcano. Firebrazer suddenly smiled, straightened up and waved, which for some reasons gave Meteor a stab of guilt.

Silver tilted her head at them all and smiled.

"Oh no, a whelp," she heard Final whisper.

Meteor took a step towards Silver. "What are you doing in here?"

"I wanted to see if you were alright," Silver said, smiling. Meteor would've cried if she saw Pyro smile that way. "The Shadowling that came scared Legend, and I wanted to see how you were doing." She glanced around at the strange Ariash around her. "Who are they?"

Meteor looked behind her at Firebrazer's warm smile, Cloud's cool look, Dust Devil's... Whatever she had.

"I'm Firebrazer," he replied with a small wave, stepping in front of Meteor. *He can sense my feelings towards Silver,* Meteor realized. *Almost as good as Final can.*

"This is Cloud, Dust Devil, Heatstroke and Final," he said to Silver. "They're all awesome." Meteor glanced at Cloud when he said the last part, and she noticed Heatstroke and Cloud whispering, both with a small grin.

"Hello," Silver said, smiling. "I'm Princess Silver." Meteor's head jerked back to her. *Princess?!* Her mind shrieked. *Would've been something to mention when we were talking with the other spirits. She did say her mother was the Aolite Princess, and I probably should've guessed that E.T was royal.*

"So, you're the sky spirit?" Cloud asked. Silver's eyes lit up as Cloud walked towards her.

"Aw, a human!" She said, clapping as her eyes lit up in an adorable way that Meteor couldn't explain.

Firebrazer and Heatstroke laughed a little when Cloud blinked in confusion at the Aolite'a reaction. Even Final and Meteor smiled.

"Oh- sorry, was that offensive?" Silver asked, taking a small step back.

"No, just nobody has said anything about my human form for many years," Cloud replied with a small laugh.

"Alright," Silver said. "Yeah, I'm the sky spirit."

Meteor saw Cloud look to Final, who then looked at Meteor, opening her eyes. She gave her a certain look, looking between Silver and Meteor with significance in her eyes.

Oh, she wants me to tell her. I-I think that's what she meant.

"We think Cloud found out how to get rid of E.T," Meteor said to Silver. She stared at Meteor with wide, scared eyes.

"Exorcism," Cloud interjected.

Silver played with her claws nervously. "I-I don't want to kill him, he's my dad," she whispered loud enough for them to hear. Firebrazer's eyes widened and he stumbled a bit. Cloud put her hand on his talon and leaned on his shoulder.

"Kid, why don't you want to stop this guy?" Heatstroke asked, walking over to her. They'd been uncharacteristically quiet, and they sounded sincere when they talked to Silver.

"I know he's done bad things," she replied with her eyes on the ground. Heatstroke crouched down and put their talon on her back. "But he's my dad anyway, but I love my sister as well." Heatstroke moved their talon to the back of her neck and pulled her closer into a small hug.

"But we do have to do something," Silver said. "I just don't want to… Like, end him."

"Exorcism is mostly painless," Cloud replied. "It makes them weaker, but it doesn't hurt too much." She shrugged and smiled nervously. "Mainly, it's their ego that's in the most pain. Believe me, I've seen exorcism take place, it's not that bad."

Silver returned Cloud's smile. "Then I'm alright with it." She hesitated. "Um…What do I have to do, exactly?"

Chapter 9: Flourish

Princess of the Sunbird

Cloud had taken Silver back to the mountain, after revealing she could turn into a *dragon*! It shouldn't have shocked Silver as much as it did, but it was amazing to see something like it. Once they reached the mountain, Silver brought her to the golden healer, which was what she called the golden room of blankets and comfy pillows. Cloud asked if she had any questions, and said she was willing to answer anything. If Silver didn't have any questions, then she would teach her magic.

"Wait, so this may be pointless," Silver started.

"There are no pointless questions, only pointless answers," Cloud replied with a smirk.

"How can you turn into a human?" Silver asked quickly.

"My feather," the fire spirit said. She pointed to the bird feather in her earring which Silver thought was just an accessory. "A very powerful dragon gave it to me."

"Wow," Silver said, her eyes shining. "Why aren't you able to do the exorcism? Because you said to Meteor that you needed me to do it. Can only sky spirits do it? And if so, then who taught you and why? Why not teach the sky spirit instead of a fire spirit?" Silver got a hint to herself that she was probably asking too many questions, but she wanted the answers.

"I come from the Ocean Harbour," Cloud started. "Everyone thought I'd be a sky spirit for their unique culture, but I became a fire spirit, so it was a little confusing. I had to learn all the fire spirit etiquette for my island, which was interesting."

Silver asked a couple more questions, with Cloud being happy and glad to answer her questions. Silver asked a little about the Ocean Harbour, a little about being a fire spirit and where they've lived. She only seemed reluctant to answer exactly where they live, but she mentioned they live in a kingdom called Ashen.

Until finally, after about 10 questions, they moved to the valley to use sky magic.

"Alright, I've never taught anyone anything, other than teaching Firebrazer that grilling cheese doesn't really work on a sidewalk without a pan," Cloud began with a laugh. "What do you know how to do?"

Silver lit up her claws, her eyes sparkling in the light. She spun and beat her wings to lift three meters into the air. Her arms opened wide and she created a little cloud of blue and white sparkles.

"I'm impressed," Cloud said after a moment, awestruck.

"Really?" Silver asked. *I barely knew what I did*, Silver thought. She had just tried to make something, but she didn't know what would really happen.

"Yeah, it was pretty," Cloud said with a confident nod. "For the exorcism, you don't just need to use sky magic, but you also need pure white magic, which a couple sky spirits have managed to not have." She vanished for a moment to turn into a dragon. "The dark spirit we're dealing with, from my calculations, he's able to take pure white magic away, so we gotta be careful of that."

"Exorcism should be easy for you, as you seem to have the right magic, along with a hint of shadow magic."

Cloud taught Silver how to do what she called "drawing magic," which Cloud said was summoning rune spells. Silver drew a certain shape in the air and cast it, drawing lightning to her claws.

"The most I know how to teach little idio- less experienced pupils," Cloud said after a couple minutes. "How much experience have you had?"

"I was taught for a while by my mother and grandmother," Silver replied.

"They seem like perfect teachers," Cloud replied, "I think I can teach you the actual, direct technique instead of random spells."

Silver agreed to that and practiced the Ariash's instructions with one thought in her head; *I will protect this island.*

Forest of Sapphires

Jewelem stumbled as he woke up. He was already standing when he realized where he was. An infinite stretch of land in every direction, holding nothing but a castle on the horizon with long, yellow grass up to his shoulders. The field was peaccful, but at the same time, it felt like he wasn't alone.

"Hello?" Jewelem called. He gazed at the far, faded castle. It was a generic castle, big towers, huge base. It looked small from where he was, but he knew it was probably big. The only strange thing was the towers looked oddly sharp and the entire thing looked taller and thinner. There was no sound. He couldn't near the rushing wind, the scurry of usual mice in tall grass, nothing. He didn't even see any grass moving, or any life. The grass and land was all there was.

Except, when he turned around, on the near horizon, near where he was standing, a tall rock ledge jutted up from the ground. A dragon stood on top of it. Jewelem wasn't close enough to see his face, and even if he was, the dragon wore a large mask. It seemed to be made of the bones of a ram.

"Jewelem?"

Jewelem looked over his shoulder to see a familiar dragon standing behind him, wearing a worried face. (She definitely wasn't there before. The field was so strange.) Her voice was so different from the creepy whisper he'd imagined her with.

"Sacrifice?" He said to her. "Where are we? What's going on?" He felt calm. It was obviously a bad place, but he didn't feel too panicked, which warned further thinking. Of his brother's, he'd always been the worrier, which had gotten them out of some situations. Mainly ones where it was a bad idea in the first place.

"We're in the Blackzone," Sacrifice said. Now that Jewelem got a better look at her, she had brighter red scales, still dark red though, and she had more light in her eyes. She looked more like a normal dragon instead of the weird creature she was in the regular world. "It's a world created by some kind of god. Once he killed me, I was trapped here. He told me after a while that I didn't die because I take after him, in the logic that I have the same eternity as he does."

"So... You're going to live forever?"

"I've been trapped here for thousands of years, alone." Sacrifice said. "I won't really 'live' forever, but I guess I'll exist forever."

Jewelem couldn't believe what he was hearing. "Sacrifice, . . What do you mean? You've only been here a few days." She stared at him, awestruck. "Silver told me that once you died, she went to to Aolite kingdom and used a spell book to bring you back. After that, you never acted the same. You never spoke or opened your eyes, and seemed much stiffer."

"W-what?!" She stuttered, stumbling back. "No- it's been hundreds of years-" she was cut off as a shadow appeared, cast over both of them. The palace Jewelem had seen in the distance was suddenly there, in front of him. It just suddenly flickered into view.

Where is the light coming from? He thought. The shadow over them clearly blocked the view of some kind of light. Before he could look behind the palace, the ground under his talons shook and broke apart. Sacrifice shrieked, but didn't start towards the castle, which had no crumbling ground. Jewelem's feeling of warm calmness slowly faded. The air became colder, and he felt like his scales were wet with cold wind against him.

"Sacrifice?" He called to the Shadowling, who had shot into the air. "Shouldn't we go in the castle?"

She stared at him like he was insane. "No! We can't go in there! The warden will catch us!"

The grass vanished into black flames, revealing cracked, brown stone. Between the cracks, black light shone from a hidden light source. Jewelem saw a large creature rising from below the ground. He felt like he was going to faint; he'd seen that dark black right before he awoke in the field. Suddenly, all the wounds the Eternity Prince had given him before tore open and he felt extreme pain all over his body. Loud crashes came from the ground. He trembled, pain welling in his chest.

"Jewelem?"

He closed his eyes for a moment, and when he opened them, the world fell dark and silent. Sacrifice was next to him, bewildered but scared. Suddenly, the world dropped away. They were in a large cave, stone walls so dark they were almost black. Small, ruined stone buildings covered some small ledges, while some sat on the ground. Cages hung from the ceilings and large stone spikes hung from the ceiling.

"Where are we?" He asked Sacrifice, hardly keeping his eyes open. There was no answer. When Jewelem looked behind him, he saw her sitting quietly, engulfed in a thin layer of black fire.

"Quite nice," a voice said from inside of her. Jewelem was distracted from his pain by the shock and leaped back. **"She's a wonderful asset, yes."** Sacrifice turned her gaze to the ground and opened her eyes. They were sad, and the words didn't sound happy or murderously gleeful like they had before.

"Why are you doing this? Where am I?" Jewelem asked, trembling and stepping back slowly. She turned her head all around to stare at Jewelem. Sacrifice's eyes suddenly flew open and a large creepy grin appeared on her face, revealing incredibly sharp teeth. Her eyes were pitch black with just white slits in the middle. She flung herself towards Jewelem and locked her sharp claws onto his chest, pinning him to the ground. Sacrifice raised her claws and dug them into his chest, and Jewelem's vision faded again.

A Tide that Flows Amongst Moonlight

The next morning, Legend flew down the shaft from Silver's room in the healer room. She found Jewelem still asleep there. She ran her talons lightly over the back of his neck. *He'll be alright,* she thought to herself. Legend soon went out to find Silver. Of course, first she took her shell necklace. From the sky, Legend saw the Aolite princess with an unfamiliar Ariash. She flew down and landed nearby. Silver was using stranger magic, and the Ariash used a similar technique. Not wanting to disturb them, she flew towards the volcano to see if Meteor had any idea of who the new Ariash was.

"Hello?" She called into the volcano as she reached the bottom. The molten room was bright and still messy, but empty of dragons. No one was there.

Looking around, Legend spotted a hidden tunnel she didn't notice before. Inside, there was a much, *much* larger cave. It was dark, but there was a glimmer of light from the ceiling where molten stones covered the ceiling. It looked like big mounds of dark red stones covered the floor, but she couldn't see. In the beam of light, there was a dragon sitting there, leaning on a large rock. Legend walked closer to him while trying not to disturb him.

Suddenly, something large and red tackled her and threw her into a nearby mound of stones. It barely hurt, of course; her necklace healed all injuries. The dragon from the light didn't move. Legend saw the silhouette of her attacker.

"Who are you?" She asked. A devil-like creature leaped towards her and pinned her quickly, but she sent a waterspout to knock the dragon over.

"Hey, stop!" She yelled. She looked over to the dragon on the light. He looked up, tired eyes and exhausted sadness consuming him. He looked much older than Legend, maybe 20, while Legend was sixteen.

He looked up at her, and suddenly smiled and straightened up, but he still looked tired. "Hey, Dusty!" He called. For a moment, Legend thought he was talking to her. But the dragon who attacked her ran up to him and he patted the back of her neck with a smile. Legend went up to him and smiled back.

"Oh, sorry about her," he said to Legend. "This is Dust Devil, she's pretty protective. I'm Firebrazer." He had bright orange and yellow scales and bright, colourful eyes.

Dust Devil was smaller than Legend, she had bright red scales and large devil horns. Her eyes had a certain feel to them, large, yellow and bright, but extremely terrifying and sharp. Dust Devil didn't have wings... They looked like they had been ripped off.

"I'm Legend," she said to them with a small bow. *He's tired, something just happened to him,* Legend thought. "I'm assuming you're one of the fire spirits?"

"I am," he said. "You're Meteor's water spirit?"

I'm not her *water spirit,* Legend thought. "I guess so. I-I mean, I'm not *Meteor's* water spirit, I'm just the water spirit."

FireBrazer looked away for a moment. "Oh, sorry. Everyone always told me I was *Oceanic's* fire spirit. Sometimes it was Earthquake or Heaven, but usually Oceanic."

"You- You know Oceanic?"

"Of course, she was the water spirit in my time. Or my phase? Whatever it's called, we were spirits together. How do you know her?"

"Yeah, she's my mother," Legend told him. "What was she like? Was she always so..." She tried to think of something she thought her mother wouldn't be as a whelp, or however old she was. Legend considered that her mother was a water spirit when she was little, but she once told Legend when she was 9. She couldn't imagine her serious, terrifying mother being on an island with FireBrazer.

FireBrazer laughed. "She was incredible. Once Ni- our dark spirit attacked us, Oceanic was the one to fight. Me, Heaven and Earthquake all hid on the island. I went back to the Fire Island to find my brothers and father, but the dark spirit found me. I never saw Heaven or Earthquake after that."

"Heaven!" Legend said suddenly. "That's Silver's mother, Earthquake was Jewelem's father and Oceanic is my mother. Sacrifice is E.T's daughter, that's your dark spirit! I Wonder if all spirits are somehow related." She realized the slightly shocked look on FireBrazer's face at the last part.

"I assure you, Meteor and I aren't related," He laughed nervously. "Also, not all fire spirits are Ariash. Just like how there have been Icelo water spirits, Earthin dark spirits, Furo sky spirits. I think there was once an Icelo fire spirit."

"Spirits, magic, a ridiculous amount of spaghetti dreams at night…" Legend murmured.

"Is there something up with these spirits?" FireBrazer asked. "Cloud told me there was a big mystery, or a problem? I didn't catch all of it."

"Ok, so basically, Jewelem was hit with powerful dark magic, and hasn't woken up from it," Legend explained.

"An Ariash was with Silver, using some sort of light magic. E.T attacked us; he was the dark spirit that hurt Jewelem.

We didn't know how to stop him, but he left eventually. As we understand it, there's an evil dark spirit and 5 younger, royal whelps as spirits."

"Sacrifice was killed by E.T, but Silver brought her back, and now she's an entirely different dragon. We're all the whelps of royals, probably why we were chosen. I think that only royals are chosen."

"Actually," FireBrazer replied. "None of us fire spirits are really royal. Cloud was an adopted leader, Heatstroke is just an outcast. Final and Dusty are just unique, not royal."

"You're a king, aren't you?" Legend asked. She definitely remembered the book she read about royalty. It wasn't a recent book, as it was written in the last 36 years. FireBrazer, banished king of the Ariash. About 20 years was how long it had been since the Eternity Prince became a rumour in the Poseidonite palace.

"I. . . Uhm…" FireBrazer looked away for a moment. They heard a growl and some talon steps from the cave entrance. They both looked over to see Meteor standing in the entranceway. Firebrazer's face lit up and he smiled, waving to the Ariash. Meteor had a solemn, slightly angry expression, her eyes dark and menacing.

"Final has something to tell you, princess," Meteor snapped to Legend. "Well, most of us." She turned and continued down the hall.

Legend turned to Firebrazer, who stared at the doorway with a puzzled, concerned expression. "Seems like we should go," he said to her. Firebrazer lead Legend down the hall into a cave made of normal stone. It was a colder alternative to the warmer molten stone below the volcano. There were already a couple dragons gathered inside, mostly Ariash, but Silver and Heatstroke were there as well. A taller, slightly darker red Ariash sat next to Silver with a beautiful feather earring and a unique tiara. An unfamiliar crimson dragon with a strange fluffy cloud type thing around her neck. It seemed like it a part of her, not a piece of jewellery. Meteor had perched herself on a stone platform near the doorway. She scowled as Legend entered the room.

"Final, is something going on?" Firebrazer asked. The crimson dragon looked up.

"I saw some weird things," she whispered.

"Who are these dragons?" Legend whispered to Firebrazer. She wondered if they would ask her any questions. She didn't know too much. Legend was just about as confused as they were.

He sat next to her in the other side of the doorway and whispered to her. "The crimson one is Final, she's shy but is super fun. That darker red one is CloudScraper. She can turn into a human, so don't freak out when that happens. Her feather is magic, let's her transform."

Legend nodded as she observed them all. Cloud looked
threatening; she didn't want to answer *her* questions. Overall, there
were six dragons in the room. Cloud, Final, Legend, Firebrazer, Meteor
and Silver.

"Did you figure out how to get rid of that dark spirit pest?"
Meteor hissed to Silver.

The Aolite flinched. "Yep. The spell takes 5 days to fully work,
so we'll start it now."

Cloud brought them outside to begin the ritual. The valley was
wet from soft rain that pattered lightly on the island. Morning birds flew
through the sky despite the weather.

"He's coming now," Final murmured.

Meteor whipped her head around to stare at her. Final pointed to
the ocean, and there was a large black creature with pink lightning
through its scales charging at the spirit island.

Legend turned to Silver anxiously, wondering if the spell would
somehow work right then. The little Aolite leaped up on her two back
legs for a moment, then a large circle of light appeared around her when
she landed. Legend and the other dragons stood back, glancing at the
Eternity Prince coming closer. Silver's scales glowed brighter and so
did the circle around her. Suddenly, E.T vanished from sight. For a
silent moment, everyone but Silver looked around to find him. Silver
stood in the centre with her eyes closed. Without warning, E.T dropped
from the sky on top of them, his army of Shadowlings following him.
Meteor hissed with alarm, Firebrazer and Final shrieked. Before he
landed to crush them all, everyone was blinded by a bright light. When
Legend could see again, she saw the Eternity Prince flying above them,
his huge wings causing lots of wind. Silver seemed unbothered and kept
concentrating. *Is she going to stand there for five days?* Legend
worried. *I'll protect her regardless.* The light rain soon turned into

powerful winds, darker skies and raging thunderstorms. Meteor roared loudly to the powerful dark spirit and launched herself into the air, coils of golden flames circling around her until she reached her full size, a mountain sized fire spirit. Cloud looked at Silver, concerned.

"What do we do now?" Legend asked Firebrazer. She tried to find any confidence in his eyes, but he looked as panicked as she was, maybe even more. He turned to her

"Take Final, and hide her. " They heard a loud crash and looked up. E.T's claws raked Meteor's side and slammed her into the base of the mountain. Meteor flung herself back into the sky and breathed bright fire at the dark spirit. "Or protect her, either is fine." Firebrazer leaped into the air and tried to fight off the black dragons who followed him.

Legend nodded to Firebrazer and ran over to Final, who was crouched frozen in fear. Legend took one of her talons and urged her to follow her. She knew Final wouldn't hear whatever she had to say over the roaring thunder and battling spirits. Legend brought her inside the cave and found a place behind the stone platform where she wouldn't be seen if E.T were to look in the cave.

Legend ran back outside just in time to almost be struck with dark magic. She stumbled back just as it hit the ground in front of her. In the sky, Meteor kept flinging herself towards the Eternity Prince, but he kept dodging her fire and claws. She had large, bloody scratches all over her body. Between the fire, lightning and thundering roars, it was strangely beautiful. But it made Legend wonder why dragon clans fought. The Eternity Prince readied a powerful force of energy, and aimed it at the island. Not knowing what to do, Legend stood there in shock as Cloud grabbed her talon and brought her closer to her and Silver. Legend looked away just as the strike was about to hit the island, but heard the sound of shattering diamonds. She opened her eyes, and there in front of her, were Jewelem and Sacrifice.

A Fire Burning Away at Nothing but Ashes

The dark marks covering Meteor's body felt awful in the cold rain. The dark spirit in front of her continued to fire dark energy towards her. She attempted to dodge, barely doing so while sending more fire his way. With a bloodcurdling shriek, more Shadowlings flung themselves onto her wings and weighed them down greatly, digging their many talons into them. Golden fire covered the annoying little creatures and flew around their wings, dragging them into the ocean. The large dark spirit grappled onto her shoulders and threw her onto the volcano again. She hit him with more fire, but it didn't do anything. Firebrazer came up behind him and burned a large hole through his eyes. The Eternity Prince whipped around swiftly, flinging his black tail over Firebrazer's face, leaving a bloody scratch. Suddenly, two large dark red shadowlings came up from the ground and fought off the darker army. Meteor looked over to Firebrazer and noticed that, although he had a large scratch on his face, he wore the same confusion on his face that she felt. Lightning struck the sky and ground around them. Something in the back of Meteor's mind told her to look back at the other spirits. She looked down at them and saw Jewelem and Sacrifice had then appeared, somehow. *Wasn't the Crystalian dead?* She thought. Meteor came down from the sky and went back to her smaller size, landing next to Cloud, Legend and Silver. Firebrazer soon landed slightly behind her.

"Where did those come from?" Cloud asked, pointing at a group of the red shadowlings. "Did E.T summon them as well?"

"It was me."

Sacrifice stepped forward. Silver, who had left her magic circle, did a little jump and threw her wings around Sacrifice. "I didn't know you could do that!"

"I couldn't before,' she said. "I got a couple powers after leaving the Blackzone, somehow."

"I didn't get powers, probably because I wasn't dead," Jewelem said.

"I didn't want to freak her out," Silver nodded at Legend. "But there was a *liiiiiittle, tiny chance* you were dead. Probably not."

"WHAT," Legend said.

"Sacrifice wasn't a spirit when she died, meaning she was dead," Silver explained. "Jewelem half-died as a spirit, meaning he transferred to the spirit world before returning to this world, but that didn't happen. Sacrifice got new powers because... Well, actually I don't know how."

"And what do we do about the war going on above us?" Meteor demanded. As much as she *loved* the whole 'dramatic reunion,' they were in quite a killable position out in the open.

They all turned to CloudScraper, who stared at the dark spirit and Sacrifice's army, shocked. "What?" She asked when they turned to her. Meteor heard a piercing shriek and whipped her head around to look up at the fighting.

The Eternity Prince had called more of his warriors, who were being quickly defeated. When killed, the Shadowlings' bodies just vanished into thin air. Meteor couldn't see them land, and some of them just turned into ashes before hitting the ground.

Although she was ready to go back up and fight him, he flew back a couple wingbeats and examined the situation before turning and leaving. As the skies cleared, the shadowlings slowly followed their master, who slowly faded into the sky. They all saw him shoot into the clouds and suddenly dive into a portal and disappeared. They all stared at the sky where he'd been before, then Meteor turned to stare at the others.

"You," she growled and pointed to Silver. "Explain."

Blazing Watcher of Passion

FinalFlame stared into her visions. Standing next to her, Quorteze stared at the white creeping up her legs. *It shocks me that this is a thing*, she thought to herself. She played with her claws and watched the changing shapes. They all glowed red, white rectangle screens of differing sizes shifted around her. Careful not to open her third eye, she pulled the brightest vision closer to her, examining it closely. It was Meteor, she was surrounded by pink, black and red eyes. A red light shone on the Ariash princess, and black chains covered her wings. No surprise, the visions are always vague.

She jumped as she heard another piercing roar from outside. She shuddered at the thought of a huge dark spirit clawing his way through the cave. A few moments later, Meteor, Silver, Legend, Jewelem, Sacrifice and CloudScraper rushed into the cave. Cloud let FireBrazer lean on her back, as he had a huge scratch across his head. It might scar, which Final knew he wouldn't like.

She quickly closed her visions and made Quorteze disappear. Firebrazer sat in a corner in the farthest wall from the entrance, and Cloud lay down next to him.

"Oh- Hello, Final," Legend said to her. She and Jewelem came in behind Meteor.

"What's going on?" Final asked the group.

"A dark spirit, NightChaser, I think. Came for us," Firebrazer said. "Not fun, he's quite powerful." He laughed a bit, but Final knew he was laughing through an awful pain.

"The spell circle is working right now," Silver said. "After five days, it will do something or other, and I will be able to banish E.T to the spirit realm."

"Can you not just kill him?" Meteor snapped. Her mind wasn't happy about Silver being a coward. Well, a friendly coward. *Does she dislike Silver?* Final thought to herself. *Silver doesn't seem like Meteor's type, to be fair. But I think she's really sweet. I see no evil in her, mostly friendliness in her, only a bit of confusion and sadness to her parents.*

"Is there a way to make it go faster?" Jewelem asked. Final couldn't see any anger, hate or evil in Jewelem, so she couldn't understand why Meteor didn't like them. It was almost impossible to see into just one dragon in a room full of them, so she kept quiet.

"What should we do for the next 5 days?" He asked.

"Research, planning, trying to understand where the heck the Shadowling clan went?" Legend suggested. "Something makes me doubt the Shadowlings all followed E.T with no regrets. He had to have enslaved them or something."

"I think they're all just evil," Meteor argued.

"Not all of them," Silver said.

"Can I just ask; what's his name?" Jewelem asked them all.

Everyone fell silent.

"Dragons think his name is NightChaser," Cloud said. "The Shadowling King."

"King NightChaser died!" Firebrazer exclaimed. "He was assassinated by an Aolite, and the killer was never caught."

Cloud thought for a moment. "Then who is E.T?"

Final knew. She always knew. But she wasn't 100% sure, so she'd stayed quiet. But she spoke anyway.

"It's his son."

Sacrifice suddenly whipped her head to look at her. "He told me in the Blackzone. That realm is created by the God of Silence. He wanted access, but he had to give some kind of information, so my father gave him a riddle." Sacrifice went silent to remember it.

"To steal the truth of a bloody night,
To slaughter the sun, and kill the light.
To take and destroy, to steal serenity,
Is to birth the form of the Prince of Eternity."

Oh, now it was easy to read the room. Literally, she read them easily. They were just thinking the same thing.

"The first two seem… Concerning," Cloud said uneasily.

"What does serenity mean?" Silver asked.

"Peace of mind, sanity," Firebrazer said, he sounded slightly shaken. He winced and pressed his talons to his bleeding face.

Cloud turned to him with a worried expression. "Even if we find a way to stop him, he has an entire army, and the dragons of the Calx Nation in his dungeons. If he wanted to, he could demand our lives for theirs. He has blackmail material."

"He has Calx Nation dragons?" Jewelem asked.

Cloud nodded. "Unfortunately so. Earthquake was killed and shortly after, the Eternity Prince attacked. Many Crystalians vanished into his claws, assumed dead, while others flat out died. Almost the entire Veo Clan was taken, along with the Maple Furo, who hid alongside them. Some Squirrel Crystalians were also taken."

"Any ideas, Final?" Legend asked.

She jumped as they turned to her. She examined the room closely; Firebrazer was hurt and scared, Cloud felt worried, and Silver was just confused and didn't understand what was happening. Sacrifice was slightly scared, but Final was impressed with her understanding, formality, and calmness.

"He's going for the Fire Island next," she said. Final wanted to reveal his plans to them… *But then Meteor might - will - go running off, which will definitely get her killed.* She sighed. "And I think Meteor and Silver are his next targets. But I think-"

"Then I'm going to find him," Meteor said. Final almost slapped herself in the head.

"What?" Legend gasped.

"No, Meteor you can't do that," Silver told her.

She whipped around to glare at the whelp. "Why not? He's just another enemy!" Final could see that Silver didn't disagree with that to the fullest, she did understand that he was dangerous. *Silver knows he's her father, she feels guilty,* Final noticed. It was difficult to see specifically, but she could sense guilt. Strangely enough, she didn't see remorse, which was similar to guilt. She didn't have any decisions she wished to change. *Much unlike me.*

"Meteor, it isn't safe to go there alone," Firebrazer reasoned. "We haven't figured out how to actually fight him, and every encounter turns out bad. it wouldn't do us any good to go after him now, and I think-"

"It doesn't do us any good staying here and doing nothing!!" She snapped at him. Final was bombarded with visions of the pain in Firebrazer's heart. She understood that. *He's almost impossible to see. Looking into him is looking into a flakey beach, much unlike the razor-sharp minds that dragons seem to brag about.*

"I know you want to fight him, but what will you do when you get there anyway?" Firebrazer asked. Meteor looked at her claws for a long moment. The room fell silent. Legend glanced at Jewelem's worried face, Cloud was concerned for Firebrazer, knowing he was in a dangerous zone with Meteor's temper. Final wanted to look inside Meteor, but she enjoyed the usual minor headache compared to the raging explosion of burning paper smell she got from the average Ariash mind. Meteor looked up and gave the room one last dirty look, before turning and storming out the cave and taking flight, far to the edges of Anima's corners. Everyone was more silent than before, even Silver's usual brightness was dimmed for a brief moment. In that moment, she felt something pressing at the sides of her head. There was a voice. She recognized it.

Do stop her, I would recommend.

What do you want now?

She will die, and I do not want to kill her. But I will.

Why... Why would you kill her then? Why be evil?

...Answer me this. Do you trust the God of Silence?

Part two

Chapter 10: Hidden in the Wind and Earth

Yin and Yang

Silver can understand when she is wanted in a place. But now, as she paced in her bedroom at the top of the mountain, she couldn't understand whether she was needed there anymore.

"I-I don't understand why she would just leave!" Silver squeaked. She paced back and forth in front of the window, just like her mother did when she was stressed. Sacrifice sat near her bed, quiet and not moving much. Ever since her arrival in the fight with their father, she'd been more mobile, being able to talk and finally being more open. But not by much, as she was still not her sister.

"It is odd," Sacrifice said. And left it at that.

"I think I should go warn someone in the Aolite kingdom," Silver said, lightly panicking. She wanted Sacrifice to say something that would keep her there on the island with her, something to convince her not to leave Legend and Jewelem. But her sister remained quiet.

Silver went over what happened with Meteor. She wanted to go back to her island and fight her father, but she couldn't, and she knew that, didn't she? Silver narrowed her eyes and thought harder about it, still confused her.

"I think I'm going to find Legend," She told her sister. "You can stay here if you want." She started towards the shaft down the mountain, but paused to look back at her sister. "Be careful here, Sacrifice," Silver said. "This place is dangerous right now." She smiled and leaped down the tunnel.

She floated carefully through the air currents until she reached Legend's cave. Silver saw the Poseidonite curled up on the ledge nearing her cave, watching the sunlight pour over her waters. Legend smiled softly to the Aolite approaching her.

"Hey, Silver," Legend said. Silver landed next to her, watching her carefully. *She's obviously shaken from what happened*, Silver thought. *Is now the right time to ask if I should go to the Aolite kingdom? Either way, I have to tell them that my father is coming for them, probably right after the Fire Island, where Meteor is going to get attacked...*

"So... " Silver started. "What are you going to do now?"

Legend paused and looked out over the ledge. The sunlight shone gleefully over the blue-ish purple and white scales, reflecting the waters and casting itself over the island. No clouds floated over the spirit island that day. Silver would have to travel back through the Storm Barrier, over the ocean and then find the Aolite palace. But she could do it.

"I think I might go back to the ocean for a while," Legend said with a smile after hesitating. "Never thought I would go back willingly, but someone has to look out for it." She looked into the waters below them. "They need a water spirit to defend against Crystalians."

The two princesses shared a bittersweet smile smile for a moment before looking out into the ocean again.

"When should we leave?" Silver asked. "Do you think Jewelem and Sacrifice are going back?"

"I haven't had the chance to ask Jewelem yet," Legend replied. "But I'm not sure. When I go back, I have to take the crown - not looking forward to it, - and I think Jewelem has to as well. I can't really imagine that he'd be excited for that type of thing, but it's his choice."

Silver felt bad for the two of them. They had to go back, separated, and rule kingdoms at war. She knew they would try to make peace, but although Silver didn't understand the war, peace wasn't that simple. Although, if it did work, she might be able to use that with her and Sacrifice to solve the Aolite Shadowing war. *The shadowlings being able to shape shift into other dragons of other clans made everyone try killing each other, but that didn't work, now did it, Queen Lioness?*

Queen Lioness was the queen of the Veo clan. She had her entire clan go into hiding, not being able to get attacked. That was, until the Eternity Prince found them there anyway. Nobody really heard anything out of the Veo clan after that. Some dragons assumed they were extinct, others understood the secrets powers of the colourful jungle-dwelling vipers. Her father couldn't see camouflaged dragons, but wherever someone is, he will find them. An entire clan can't hide from the rest of Anima, hidden or not.

"You can go find your family, Silver," Legend told her. "I can ask Jewelem what his plan is, and we can go back together. I don't know what we'll do from there, but- I mean, we'll think of something."

Silver thought about that, and smiled. "If I go, I'll be gone for three days," she said. "I'll return for the last two days of the ritual."

"Ok," Legend replied. "You think you'll leave now?"

Silver nodded. "I have to be fast, or I might not get there in time. I think- I think sky spirits are slightly stronger in the daylight."

The two looked to each other, knowing it could very well be their last time. Legend stood up and put her wings around the small Aolite, and Silver did the same. They released each other.

"Goodbye, Silver," Legend said, a sweet smile coming across her face. Silver matched it with a polite nod and a gleeful smile before shooting into the light sky. Silver couldn't see hints of orange in the sky anymore. Meteor left some time in the morning, so Silver had a while to find her or the Aolite kingdom.

She went over the map of Anima in her head over and over again. The Aolite kingdom sits over a bunch of floating clouds. Usually the clouds never move, but sometimes, quite rarely, they do. The sky islands don't usually move unless Queen Shield makes them move. She floated along the vast, blue skies, drifting towards the swirling tempest far in front of her. It took about two hours of flying to get to the Storm Barrier. She landed on a small island near the base of it, and felt her stomach drop. She didn't realize how big the Storm Barrier was until she saw it up close. When she was going to the spirit island for the first time, it had just opened and let her through. But as she stared at it from the bottom … words couldn't describe the size of it. She felt like a grain of salt in the saltwater ocean. She couldn't see the other sides of it, she couldn't see over top of it, and Silver couldn't imagine swimming under it. Maybe a Poseidonite could, but she most certainly couldn't.

Well, my grandfather was a Poseidonite, maybe I could go under it without dying. Silver weighed her options. Inside the storm barrier was just the islands of Anima, wasn't it? What was stopping her from going right inside of it?

She looked between the ocean and the barrier, and made her choice, but had to test it. She took a deep breath and dove into the cold ocean. It felt like breathing through smoke-filled air, so she went fast. *Well, that's a surprise,* she thought. *I don't have gills, how can I kinda breathe under water?* Silver felt something big and fast rush past her underwater. She didn't want to freeze and see what it was, so she went even faster. About three minutes into her journey, she could barely take the cold water and lack of air. Silver quickly brought herself onto a small island inside the Barrier. She shivered and caught her breath, then finally looked up.

"Ohhhh," She said. "So *that's* why dragons don't come here."

Surrounding the Storm Barrier cove, mountains outlined the barrier's edge, and some jutted out from the ocean. Very few small islands were scattered around the place, as though someone had set up the islands just to sink them under, drowning anyone trying to enter Anima.

She shivered.

As she looked up more, she saw a huge grey and blue storm dragon above the cove. He stood on the clouds and spread his mighty wings, blaring blue electricity through the shadowed cove. *Wait, is that. . ?* Before Silver could finish her thought-question, it was answered as the powerful dragon swooped down to land in the water in front of the island, standing between Silver and Anima.

"LightningRoar?" She asked. The dragon stepped back to examine her, and soon jumped a bit and vanished to a smaller size.

"Silver?" He called to her. It was *definitely* LightningRoar. "Why are you in the Storm Barrier?"

"I was trying to get back into Anima," she said nervously. "I have to warn my mother and Shield about the Eternity Prince. He's coming soon."

LightningRoar's bright blue eyes widened and he nodded. "Then follow. I know the easiest way into the Aolite kingdom from here." He motioned with his head for her to follow. They leaped into the dark sky and Silver followed the storm dragon to the top of the clouds. She wanted to ask about why *he* was in the Storm Barrier, but there was no way he could hear her over the howling winds. When they reached the top of the barrier, she finally saw light pouring through the layers of clouds. As an Aolite, she could choose to fly through clouds, or stand on top of them. But she couldn't go inside the clouds while on top of them, that just sounded quite dangerous. Silver could see white clouds and blue sky when she went above the black clouds, along with some Aolite in the distance, flying along the bright sky.

"Wow," Silver said, astonished with the beautiful sight.

"Aolite are a mostly peaceful clan, despite the war," LightningRoar said. "They live above the Storm Barrier in peace, with few disturbances." Silver looked around the Aolite village and LightningRoar nodded in a direction. "That way is the main palace, you can find the Queen and the Rain Princess there. I have to stay here for business, so good luck."

Silver smiled and waved to him as he leaped back into the barrier. When he was gone, she quickly flew all the way to the palace. On her way, she caught a glimpse of the islands of Anima below. Most of them looked normal, but one stuck out to her.

The Fire Island.

There was a speck of black and pink on the south-west coast, not moving much and barely visible, but there. She had to hurry.

It was the afternoon when she reached the palace. She quickly ran inside to find Shield. Silver found her grandmother in the council room. Nobody else was there, so Silver let herself in. Shield had her face twisted in a fit of frustration, light confusion, and not the calm, genius leader she always was. Shield heard the door creak and she looked up. She raised her eyebrows lightly to see her granddaughter.

"Ah, welcome back, child," she said. Silver could tell she put on a fake facade of that dragon she knew, but Shield was up to something, she knew it. "What brings you back?"

Silver told her grandmother some of the events in the past couple days, Sacrifice's return, E.T's destruction on the island and

Meteor's sudden departure. She also mentioned the fire spirits, how nice they all were, and that Legend was the Poseidonite princess, along with Jewelem and Meteor's royalty. By the end of it, Shield looked as calm as ever, which Silver half-expected.

"Should I alert your mother, or handle things myself?" Shield asked.

Silver blinked in confusion. "What do you mean, *handle it?*"

Her grandmother smiled. "I have a way of removing important pieces." She flicked a small figure off the table that showed Anima with her tail, disturbing Silver. Even with her granddaughter's mild shock, Shield's playful, sinister smile remained. *What is she playing at?* Silver wondered.

"I guess we should get my mother in on this," Silver decided. She wasn't sure how she felt about making decisions when her grandmother was in this state of power. Silver was told once by LightningRoar that she couldn't yet understand the sheer power of Queen Shield, which she kind of agreed with. Although, despite her high role in power, Silver didn't like the idea of everyone in her family having some sort of *second life* behind her back.

Shield made some sort of face that Silver questioned, but didn't say anything. "I guess Heaven should know something about this, yes," Shield said, exasperated. "She was a good friend of the Ariash king, Firebrazer. She would want to know what to do for the island."

"My mother was friends with the Ariash king?" Silver asked, raising her eyebrows. *Jewelem said something about Heaven and FireBrazer being friends, or at least spirits together.*

"They were almost inseparable," Shield sighed. "She was devastated to hear of his death. I'll never understand how she forgave E.T for his actions." Shield shifted uncomfortably. "She isn't one to forgive and forget, take it from me. Her Shadowing choice certainly gave me questions, but an Ariash wouldn't raise as much suspicion or uproar if it were to be exposed. I do suppose that's why she didn't tell the public, and only rumours filled our dragons' ears."

There was a short silence. "What should I do until we go to the Fire Island?" Silver asked.

"Well, how long did you say you have here?" Shield asked.

"Three and a half days. I did something at the spirit island that takes five days, and I want to be there for a day and a half at the end."

"Three days... You could meet your uncles, your aunts are questionable, but some are almost normal. You have a cousin, Polka. She might want to meet you, but she's rather shy."
Shield continued. "If you want to be productive, you could convince your mother to help you, as I may not be able to."

Silver weighed her options before choosing. *I can ask about Hea- my mother more with my uncle. I don't think Shield is going to give me too much information, but maybe she shared her plans with her brother instead of her mother first?* "I'd like to meet my cousin, Polka," she said.

Chapter 10 Part 2: Yin and Yang

It took most of the day to get to the Aolite kingdom, so Silver stayed in the Aolite palace until dawn, where her mother would take her to her uncles, Kye and Mountain. The next morning, Silver was escorted to the throne room, and noticed Heaven speaking in a panicked tone with the two dragons she saw before leaving the kingdom the first time. She saw her daughter enter the room and jumped, startled for some reason. Silver recognized them as Kye, Mountain and Polka from when her father attacked the palace before. Although this time, she noticed how dark, really dark Kye's eyes were.

"Hey," Kye said to her with a warm smile.

"Hello, Princess Silver," Mountain greeted her with a slight bow.

Polka sat between her fathers, and she looked at Silver with fear in her eyes. She looked terrified. Heaven looked between Silver and her relatives, including Shield.

"Are you sure this is a good idea?" She whispered to Shield. Silver overheard them, but she didn't think Kye or Mountain did, however Polka seemed to. "Sending our targeted princess away to someone else when we could protect her here?"

"She'll be fine, Kye's my whelp, he'll tell me if something bad happens," Shield waved her off.

Shield smiled to Silver before turning back towards the halls behind the throne room. Heaven stared worriedly at Silver for a moment, but Kye gave her a look, and she smiled before following her mother.

"Can me and Kye discuss something?" Mountain asked Silver politely. She nodded and he smiled, stepping away with Kye to talk.

Silver turned to Polka. "Hi!" She said warmly.

The young whelp winced and watched her closely. *She seems scared...* Silver noticed. She tried a more delicate approach.

"My name is Silver," she said softly. "You're Polka, right?"

Her cousin nodded a little and stepped a bit closer to her. "N-Nice to meet you," she said hurriedly.

Kye and Mountain stepped back over to them and they set off to their place in the Aolite Kingdom. Silver followed them through the hallways, they all followed Kye. He seemed to know the palace as though he built the place. *Well he lived her for, what? 16 years?* She thought. He brought them outside through one of the many doors and lead them to a place in the kingdom. She hadn't seen many floating islands around the Aolite Kingdom, but she knew they were there. When she asked Shield how they moved, Shield replied that it was slow, slow process to move the Aolite kingdom anywhere. Despite it being on clouds, everything moves at a pathetic pace. Silver's grandmother described it to her as "half of the pace of a snail made of potatoes."

Silver saw many windows, golden pillars near the front door and quartz walls. It seemed like a rather wealthy place to live, which was understandable for a prince and his family. Plants hung from baskets around the front, the windows on the side of the house, but it wasn't very big. Her uncles lead her inside. To the left, she found many blankets and pillows on the floor near a small table, which had paper, pencils and crayons. On the other side of the room, a large cooking stand sat in a corner with a place for fire below a medium, golden cooking pot. The stairs had golden railings, but the walls were marble-seeming along with sunlight simmering through the windows. Another door leading to the backyard was between the two rooms, and to the right of it was a staircase upstairs. It was overall a cheerful environment to be in, and it reminded Silver of the nice cottage she used to live in.

"I hope the place is to your liking," Kye said, fidgeting with his claws.

"I love it," Silver said, nodding politely. "So I have to be somewhere in about two days. It took me most of a day to get here, then I stayed for the rest of the day. I have to be back for the last two days, and I leave in two days."

Mountain and Kye nodded, while Polka darted through her father's legs over to the table near the living room. She fiddled with some of the dolls under the table before examining the paper on it. Kye and Mountain exchanged a look.

"Polka might have some things to show you," Mountain said to her. "She was very excited to meet her cousin."

Polka didn't look up from the paper in her claws. She fiddled with the paper a little and her eyes darted around the various items on the table.

Kye and Mountain whispered something to each other, and Silver went over to see what Polka was looking at. She overheard what the two were talking about as well.

"Why did Heaven send her here, exactly?" Mountain whispered.

"...Is there a problem with her?" Kye asked nervously.

"Heaven asked me, and I told her it was alright, just if you don't-"

"I'm fully on board!" Mountain clarified with a slight laugh. *"Just, I think it's not the best place for a hunted princess. I would love for Polka to have someone to play with, or for you to have a piece of family in the house, but if your.. uhm, 'father'-in-law, attacks us, what are we supposed to do? Aolite soldiers coming to break our door down to find her? How am I supposed to know?"*

"I don't know…"

"You know what?" Mountain whispered. *"Let's just lay low. Silver is very sweet, and despite her social state, so to speak, I think this can be easy. Your family might be powerful, but so are you."*

Silver knew what they meant. She couldn't be an easy task. *Am I burdening them with too much?* She wondered. *Maybe they're too stressed with Polka to deal with me?* Silver didn't say anything.

Polka noticed her watching her work. She looked up at Silver with big, curious eyes. Silver smiled to her.

"What are you working on, Polka?" She asked.

Polka picked up and showed her one of the books she had on the table. "I'm trying to write books," she said. Polka seemed to struggle on some words, but Silver was shocked flipping through her book. They were written with beautiful penmanship, and the art was gorgeous. Most books were relatively small, but amazingly written. They seemed like books for whelps.

"These are amazing," she said to her cousin. Polka smiled.

"Thank you," she whispered.

"Want to see how I draw?" Silver asked. Polka grinned lightly and slid a piece of paper and some crayons over to her. The two painted and drew and wrote for a long time. Most of the day was spent on the art table. Kye and Mountain cooked carrots and potatoes.

Near the end of the day, Polka showed Silver her room. She shared a room with Polka for the night, which Silver absolutely loved. Although there was only one bed, Kye and Mountain made Silver her own pile of pillows. Next to it was a small bedside table with more papers on it. Silver didn't want to look nosey, searching through Polka's works, but she noticed something under a pile that caught her eye for some reason. She read it over carefully;

"MY TEACER SAYS I HAVE GOOD SPELLING AND TALONRITING. SHE SIAD FOR A 2 YEAR OLD, I AM GOOD. SHE SAID THAT WHELPS ARE SUPPOSED TO HAVE THIS KIND OF TALONRITING WHEN THEY ARE AROWND 5. BUT SHE SAID I HAVE TO WORK ON PUTING TO LETTERS TO MAKE SOUNDS, LIKE GH BUT I DO NOT KNOW WHAT THAT IS. SHE ALSO SAID TO COMBINE WORDS LIKE 'DO' AND 'NOT' TO MAKE A WORD THAT SOUNDS LIKE DONT, BUT THAT LOOKS FUNNY. TODAY IN SCOOL, OUR TEACER ASKED US TO HAVE 'PRINCESSES' ON ONE SIDE AND 'PRINCES' ON THE OTHER. I WENT WITH MY FRIENDS, ON THE PRINCES SIDE. IT FELT VERY RITE, BUT SHE TOLD ME TO GO ON THE PRINCESSES SIDE. I DONT KNOW, IT FELT NOT RITE. I WISH I WENT ON THE PRINCES LINE. THE PRINCES ASKED ME A LOT, LIKE WHY I WAS NOT WITH THE PRINCESSES. I SIAD I LIKED THE PRINCES LINE, BUT I WAS SENT TO THE PRINCESSES. THEY ALL LAFED AT ME."

Silver immediately knew what Polka meant. It was very surprising, but she didn't ask her about it. She just smiled at the little whelp, drawing princes and butterflies in her drawing book.

The view from Silver's window was a sight of the shimmering Aolite kingdom in the moonlight. Silver couldn't sleep well that night, perhaps due to the terrifying thunderstorm that kept shaking the entire planet. The walls were much like the ones in the rest of the house, and the floors were made of nice birch wood. A couple windows sat on Silver's side of the room, allowing her to see the Aolite kingdom at night. Silver usually wasn't afraid of thunderstorms, but this one was particularly bad. She got out of bed and wandered the halls for a moment. As she passed the balcony door, she found Kye standing on the balcony, leaning his arms on the railing. He looked tired, but not sleepy. She paused in the doorway, puzzled for a moment, but pretty soon realized; it was probably about her. She knocked quietly on the side of the doorway, and he looked over his shoulder to see her. He smiled and welcomed her on the baloney.

"Hey, Silver,' he greeted her.

"Hello," she said, smiling. *He's not really smiling,* she thought grimly.

"I'm… I'm so sorry," he said. He looked off the balcony into the cloudy, night sky. They could see some of the stars, but most were hidden by a dense layer of storm clouds.

"What are you sorry for?" She asked.

He hesitated. "I don't know, I just think I should be better, or something." Silver was about half his size, and she looked up at him, puzzled.

"I'm pretty sure you're doing just fine," Silver told him.

They both fell silent for a moment. A bright crescent moon lit up the sky, dodging the clouds' darkness.

"I think I understand why Mountain and Heaven were kind of hesitant to bring you here," Kye said. "Mountain was thinking of how your father might come looking for you, and he wants to keep you, Polka and I safe. Heaven was concerned for a similar reason, but also is hiding things from you, and she knows I can tell you."

The last one caught Silver's attention immediately. Her eyes widened a little and she stared at the floor. She closed her eyes and sighed. Silver looked back at him. "What's she hiding this time?"

He hesitated again and fiddled with his talons. "Our past together, I assume."

"Your past?" Silver asked.

Kye nodded. "If you want to hear it… I can tell you."

Silver paused before nodding slightly.

He shifted on his talons and started. "I have 6 sisters. Oldest to youngest, Snowy, Lightbeam, Sunshine, Heaven, Rainbow and Aurora. Snowy was about 20 at the time, I think I was 18, and Aurora was 10. Since we're the children of a Poseidonite, we all had some unique features, except for Lightbeam and Sunshine, who were twins. Our father, Coral, was murdered by our grandfather, Depth. Nobody told us, and the 7 of us were all infuriated with Shield when she killed Depth, but it made sense to me eventually."

"We were all super close to Depth, and when Shield killed him for the throne, we all hated her. Snowy, our oldest sister, wanted the throne to honour him. Shield left Aurora in charge while she left the Aolite kingdom for business. Snowy had plans, but she needed support. She ordered me to kill our sister, Sunshine, and blame it on Lightbeam. At this time, I was just dating Mountain, and Sunshine was always returning home later than us. It was odd to me, and I didn't want to do it, but she threatened to …end Mountain if I didn't. I was ordered to kill Rainbow, Sunshine and Aurora. I was super close to Aurora. But I was terrified for Mountain, and I went after Lightbeam first. I wasn't able to… ki-kill her, and I soon found out that it wasn't Lightbeam, it was Sunshine. I asked what was going on, and we were both confused. Lightbeam told me that she and her twin were going to a secret fighting lesson, and not to tell anybody else."

Silver's eyes widened. *A secret fighting lesson? Must have been why Kye couldn't kill her. I bet she never told anyone. I wonder if she had her sister cover for her while she went, and Lightbeam made sure nobody got suspicious when her sister was there. Impressive.*

"I then went to find Rainbow, but never found her. I left a note by her bed and told her that she had to escape the palace. Lightbeam and Sunshine left the palace, and Rainbow moved in with her friend. Aurora lived with us for a while, but soon vanished and was never seen. Snowy was put into prison for attempted murder, and left. Heaven still holds the fury because she never forgave Shield for killing Depth. Heaven and I never saw each other again. Shield returned and Aurora told her what happened. She vanished after that, while Shield and her only remaining daughter stayed at the palace."

Silver was shocked. She had no words.

"That … went a bit over my head," she said. Silver blinked in confusion and shock. "I didn't catch why Shield killed Depth."

"She married a Poseidonite, and the Aolite didn't like that," Kye said. "Shield eventually changed the law. Mountain told me he was a Crystalian, and I'm grateful that my mother changed the law." Silver felt bad for the prince. She couldn't imagine what he would've gone through in that time, dealing with the Aolite not wanting a Crystalian in their kingdom. Not to mention the things that Snowy made him do. Even if he didn't go through with it, Silver felt guilty for him.

"I don't understand why the Aolite would hate other clans," Silver thought aloud. "They're just like them, aren't they?" *I remember Firebrazer saying something about something or other happening between Oceanic, Heaven, Firebrazer, Earthquake and E.T. I should ask about that sometime.*

Kye hesitated. "Dragons, especially those in power, fear what they cannot control." He looked outside to the storms. "Polka wouldn't be afraid of storms if she could make them go away." He stopped to look out into the dark, clouded sky. A thin layer of moonlight shone onto the balcony, illuminating Silver's pale teal scales. "Did something happen between the spirits before us, my mother, Firebrazer, E.T, Oceanic and King Earthquake?"

Kye titled his head back and his eyes widened. "That was the most terrifying reign, in my opinion. It's a bit of a long story."

"I'm willing to hear it," Silver said confidently. "I need to find out the truth. But only if you're feeling, you know, ok with it. I don't want to hurt you."

"No, no it's ok." Kye told her. It all started when Firebrazer went back to the Fire Island, E.T killed him there, and the other 3 spirits showed up eventually. Heaven was furious and awfully upset to see her friend … uh, dead. Oceanic put him in prison with absolutely no warmth or care, the right choice personally. Earthquake went back to the spirit island alone, hoping Heaven would be there, but she went back to the Aolite. Earthquake passed away alone of an illness later in the Royal Crystalian Tribe palace. He was supposedly hiding the illness from his friends.The Aolite Princess retreated in guilt to the prisons to yell at E.T. He eventually persuaded her to marry him for some reason. The two vanished and Oceanic went back to the Poseidonite Kingdom with her husband, King Riverstone who left due to her being magic."

"Wow," Silver breathed. "You really know a lot about this."

"I overheard a lot of my mother and sister's conversations." he laughed nervously. "I honestly should've said something about my sister marrying a… serial killer, but I didn't. Mountain said I shouldn't be acquainted with the drama until the past wounds were healed. I should've said something, but I wasn't even sure at the time. I… uh, I think I am now." Silver stepped back and smiled at him. He smiled back.

"I can use this information to help stop the Aolite Shadowing war," she promised. "Trust me; this is going to be amazing." He smiled brighter and laughed a bit.

"You are certainly a special little dragon," he said. Kye leaned his head on his talons and took a deep breath, and actually showing a real smile, not the totally exhausted smile she'd seen for the entire conversation. Once Silver noticed he was mildly shaking, she flew up onto the balcony railing and put her talon on his shoulder.

"Kye…" she whispered to him, feeling awful for the dragon. He had too much that he was going through, and although Silver was probably making him worse, she tried to help him anyway.

"I'm ok," he said to her. "Just… I don't know. I'm blessed by HighWish to have met Mountain, and I can't imagine my life if I lose him."

"You're going to be ok," Silver reminded him. "I'm going to make sure you're ok. Now, you look like you haven't slept in three days, so please go to sleep."

Kye laughed. "Thank you, Silver. I love you."

"I love you too, Kye!!" Silver said to him. "Oh- also, I don't know if you know this, but I think you should always be open to whatever Polka wants for now," Silver told him, thinking about what she had read from her notes. "She seems really unique, and don't force her to be… I mean, let her be whatever she wants."

Kye sighed into the moonlit night. "Oh, we know. I mean- we aren't sure, we're all just waiting for Polka to… I don't know, just to figure it all out. We won't make her be her teacher's princess if she doesn't feel like that, and we won't make her figure it all out herself."

They both paused for a moment. "Goodnight, Kye," Silver said. "You're the only one of my nieces that I would trust with my life," Kye replied. Then, Silver returned to her room.

The first time Silver was awoken by bad noises, her sister was murdered. What a thought to have. The second time, her zombie sister ran off. Pleasant? The third time, she didn't even try. Silver probably would've just turned over in her pile of pillows and gone back to bed if there wasn't a squeaky whelp under her wing. Polka had snuggled up next to Silver to sleep away from the storms. Polka was like a little kitten, curled under Silver's wings and snuggling between her. But now

Polka was *shaking*. She was terrified of something. Silver got out of bed (always an unpleasant experience) and went over to the window.

Black smoke poured into the sky, the sunrise barely over the clouded horizon.

The Prince had found the Fire Island. She turned to Polka. She watched the smoke with horrified eyes. She looked to Silver. Polka must've woken her up. She motioned with her head for Polka to follow as she bolted downstairs. Mountain stood by the front window, watching the smoke. He whipped his head around and relaxed a slight bit when he saw them coming downstairs.

"What's going on now?" Silver asked.

"Well, as I understand it, your father is at the Fire Island now," Mountain replied. "Kye went off to fight him, but told me to stay here with you."

Polka ran over to her father and threw herself onto his talons, scared for her life. Mountain tried to soothe his daughter, and Silver went through some things in her head. *Took me one day to get here, and I slept at the palace that night. One day. Came here, slept here, it's my second day away. I have one more day, then I have to get back. Why would my father go for the Fire Island now? Is Meteor there?!* She ran over to the door to get to the island fast. *What if... what if he wants fire spirits? Is that why he... g-got rid of Firebrazer?* She felt uneasy.

"Got a plan?" Mountain asked. He sounded confident in her.

She nodded.

He gave her a firm nod.

She ran out the door and over to the edge where she could see the islands. From there, she could see where he was actually attacking.

The Southern Earth Island. The Ice Island was the furthest north, the Southern Earth Island was the second furthest south, the first being the Fire Island much farther west and below the Dark

Island.. Above the Northern Earth Island was the Dark Island, the second most north.

She tried to think of a decent plan. Go to the Fire Island and find Meteor? Risk her anger, which meant death. Also risk her father seeing her, also equaling death, very much death. Going to investigate the earth island?

"Good enough," she mumbled. Her tired brain didn't have this kind of energy yet.

In a matter of minutes, she was above the Southern Earth Island. She knew that it was just trees and some ponds, maybe a couple rivers and four parts of the jungle. The trail, the thorn, the Maple and the Wood. The wood is for the few Earthin there. The Thorn is for the Veo Clan. The Maple held the Furo, and the Trail is for the Fae. The black smoke was from the Thorn, a place where the jungle was dark and fewer light poured through the deep leaves.

Silver followed the smoke to the top of the Thorn and tried to see through the smoke and leaves. She couldn't see much, but there were flashes of colourful Veo Dragons below. *Maybe they're trying to fight for their forest,* she thought, panicked. *The Veo don't stand a chance, do they?* Queen Lioness had the Veo Clan hide, but they'd been caught and forced to imprison any other dragons to enter the Thorn. Queen Lioness had allegedly said to an Earthin newspaper reporter (because Earthin are pretty famous for that, or infamous for being nosey) that she feared that the Shadowlings could turn into dragons of any clan, and so she hid her dragons away. These must be the survivors. She landed on a particularly large tree that stuck out and waved the leaves away with the wind.

The forest below looked as though it had been struck by a black wildfire. Dark flames stroked the trees, Veo dragons flew panicked around the burning forest. Silver could see the river below covered in the blood of dragons. It was an awful sight for Silver. She hid herself behind the leaves from the big, crashing creature coming through the forest. It was her father, of course it was. He looked around at the forest for a moment before vanishing. The fire disappeared and she could see dragons hiding in the forest. She dove off the tree and swept into the woods, searching for her uncle.

"Kye?" She called into the forest around her. Fallen trees covered the ground, and some Veo dragons helping each other. Some injured dragons were leaning on others for help, and others seemed alone, in pain. Silver went up to one of them, getting some odd looks from Veo as she went, but she was the least of their concerns.

"Hey," she whispered softly to the Veo. He didn't answer. He was older than Silver, about thirteen. She ran her glowing talon over his wound, and it slowly faded and healed. He stared at where his wound was, shocked. She smiled and went to help the next dragon.

Silver healed as many Veo as she could find, hoping to find Kye somewhere. Silver heard rustling in the trees around her and glanced around. Behind her in the trees, a tall purple and green Veo dragon sat on the branches. She had swirls of colourful pinks with dots of blue along her. She also had two emerald bracelets with gold edges. Silver thought they were very pretty.

She watched Silver with big, curious eyes, despite being obviously three times her age.

"Um hi," Silver waved to her. She was getting tired of greeting these dragons, but didn't say anything about that.

"Tiger," the Veo said. Silver remembered Veo culture was to lightly nod their head when they were respected. *She could be a princess, or an important guard. But... what does she mean?*

"Excuse me?" Silver asked. The Veo slightly reeled back, surprised. She blinked in confusion before her ears perked up in realisation.

"M-my name," she stuttered. "My name is Tiger."

"Oh, I'm Silver," she replied, nodding the way she did. "I'm looking for my uncle, his name is Kye. He looks like a grey Aolite Poseidonite mix, have you seen him?"

Tiger glanced around.

"I saw him with a troop," she replied. "They said they were taking him back to the Aolite kingdom soon. If you want to find him, I can take you-" she paused and looked up behind Silver in surprise. She saw a small green creature standing near some roots in front of a trail that Silver probably wouldn't have noticed on her own. The creature stared at her with its huge green eyes.

Chapter 10 Part 3

"It seems the forest takes an interest in you. It wants an audience, I believe," Tiger whispered to Silver.

"Wait- bring me to my uncle please?" she asked. "I just want to see him."

Tiger glanced over at the 'forest,' but motioned for Silver to follow her anyway. She brought Silver down a path and into an open clearing, dark wooden bridges and camps hung over the trees, and large walls surrounded what Silver thought was the Veo kingdom in the Thorn's centre. Tiger and Silver found the camp where Kye was brought to in the trees.

"Is that him?" Tiger asked, pointing at one of the dragons laying on the bridge. Tents and carts covered the many platforms in the trees, and there were also ramps for several carts. Kye was lying asleep on the floor of the bridge, black scratches over his body. Silver went up and nudged his head, but no response came from her uncle.

"What happened to him?" Silver asked a Veo who stepped out of the tent.

"He was hit by the Eternity Prince," the young Veo whelp said. "I'm really sorry. My name is Mango, Queen Lioness's royal healer." She showed the two her emerald bracelets, just like the ones Tiger had. Mango pulled Tiger into the tent to talk, but Silver stayed by her uncle.

He opened his eyes and smiled at her. "Hey Silver," he said.

"Are you ok?" she asked him. "These... don't look like normal scratches."

"Yeah, the Prince is pretty strong," he replied weakly. "I honestly didn't think you'd stay at the house. I knew you'd go and find him yourself, but I had some Veo friends that I wanted to find."

"I'm going to try and fix this." Silver ran her glowing talon over his injuries, but her healing abilities had no effect on them. She remembered how Legend's healing necklace had no effect on Jewelem when the Eternity Prince hurt him. *The only difference was that Jewelem was half-killed... Kye seems alright, but the Prince's abilities have never been examined. Anything could happen to him.*

"Have you something out?" Kye inquired. Silver loved how well he could read her face. "You look like something really weird just happened and I feel kinda threatened."

"I-I can't heal you," Silver stammered. "I've never seen- actually, I have seen something like this. I'm so sorry though, I can't even DO anything!"

"I'll be ok, Silver." Kye brushed the side of her neck. "Don't worry, just go find... I don't know, whatever you need to find. Mountain and Polka are together, and the Veo are going to fix this."

"I'm going to save the world when I find my friends," Silver promised him. "Don't worry, your Veo friends will never have to worry again after we fix everything."

She vanished into the trees.

The 'forest,' as Tiger called it, stared at her for a moment. "Hello?" She called. She went after it as it ran through the forest. She hopped over the roots and chased after the small thing. Silver heard birds chirping overheard, a canopy of summery leaves shimmering with the dewdrops dripping onto the cool grass. Verdant flowery vines hung around each tree and hung from the high branches. Overall, it was a beautiful sight to see, especially with the dark, dense leaves fading into a more cheerful, spring forest. In the morning light, flashes of grass were painted in a fiery orange from the sunlight. Silver paused and glanced around, losing sight of the green creature. She realized where she was in the Trail, the Fae part of the rainforest. Silver noticed the creature again, this time on a higher branch above her. They both looked around when they heard a voice. It called a word that Silver didn't recognize, perhaps something in another clan language. *But they all speak the same language now,* Silver remembered. *Most of the other languages have been forgotten.* Silver didn't know any of the Calx Nation clan languages, but she figured this must've been one of them. The voice called something loud and graceful, like a song. It sounded like a call for someone. It called something like "nalu" but longer.

"*naaaaaaa-luuuuuuu*" the voice called again. The green creature looked up, then pointed to the forest. Silver looked around, confused.

"What?" She asked.

"*naaaaaaa-luuuuuuu*"

The creature pointed all around. The voice came from all around. *What does "nalu" mean, though?* Silver wondered. The creature pointed to itself, as the voice called again.

"Are you Nalu?" Silver asked. It nodded. It hopped off the branch and landed on a log in front of her. It had a bright, pale green glow around it, streaks of green through its body. It didn't just look like a dragon, it really looked like a past earth spirit or something. The only earth spirit she ever met was Jewelem, and he didn't tell her much about the other earth spirits.

Nalu didn't speak, but he hopped around her for a moment before leaping into the forest again. He looked behind him a couple times to make sure she was still following. *Well, if Kye is safe with the Veo, Polka is with Mountain and I have 1 more day, I have some time to spare.* Silver followed Nalu through the dazzling morning light. The rain from the storm the previous night had draped the forest under a sheet of moisture. The green forest was a nice sight for Silver. Just as she was starting to question the navigation skills of the creature in front of her, he brought her to a clearing. It didn't take another look to realize why Nalu brought her here.

"Is this… my home?" She asked him, confused. "Why would you bring me here?" Although she couldn't see his face clearly from the glow of his scales, she could've sworn he smiled at her before leaping back into the forest. Silver tried to turn around and follow him, but a green barrier prevented her from going far. She thought she was trapped before she realized that she could go through it, but Nalu appeared next to her and pointed back.

She could tell he didn't want her to leave there until she found something. Silver was on the south side of the cottage. The door was on the north-east side, she knew this. She saw the pond with the bridge and the tree she used to sit by with her sister, Sacrifice. Silver remembered all the times she played outside here, the yard still had the toys she used to play with still sat in the long grass. *I wonder if Sacrifice's body is still here,* she thought grimly and shivered, looking up at the windows of her late sister's room. She flew up to them and glanced inside.

The body was gone.

Must have disappeared when I resurrected her, Silver thought. It felt like being stuck in sticky mud, thinking about the situation she was in. She considered staying in the cabin for the next day before returning to the spirit island. *What if my father comes back here, though?* Maybe he'll see her and remember his daughters. Part of her wanted it to go back to normal when he was her father. *But he isn't. I'd never feel safe, Sacrifice wouldn't even be here anyway, she would never come back to him. Mother would never come back either.*

Would I?

She went up to her parents' bedroom. *Should I try to find something to put me on the right track?* Silver wanted to know what really happened from Heaven's perspective. The bedroom was exactly the same as before. The birch room and the blankets and pillows were still the same. She searched through her mother's bedside table. *It's not stealing if she doesn't live here anymore right?* She thought as she found a book in the bottom of a drawer. It was a white book with pink details and colourful feathers in the pages for bookmarks. It had sketches of feathers in the corners of each page as Silver flipped through it. *Oh, I think, it's a diary, or a journal of some sort. I wouldn't be surprised if she wrote about the times in her life at that point.* She opened to a random page near the late middle.

"Earthquake is gone now. I make only mistakes on this journey, but I mustn't go crawling back to my mother. She will only lead me astray. It has been so long since I spoke with any other spirits. I miss Firebrazer so much. If only he was here to help me. The world would be much more bearable with my dear friend here. He was on his second life, in the spirit realm and then came back. So he is dead. I did not believe I would forgive him for this, and I do not. I will never understand myself for why I married him. I do not understand why I feel this way. I was the one giving him food and water in prison... we had some kind of understanding. It did not feel right. It still feels so strange to imaging marrying this monster. But he is pleasant now. I just hope my dear friend, Firebrazer, his soul, forgives me for this sin."

Silver went to another page, one closer to the start. *Mother, what were you thinking? Why the heck did you marry this guy!?*

"I can not stay with Shield anymore. I seriously can not. It is impossible, everything is unbearable without Firebrazer. I need him here, but I cannot seem to get over it. I feel a strange feeling when around E.T, I do hope it will go away. I do not feel right around him, but

I do not understand this feeling. I like it, but it does not feel right to like it. If it is love, then I will not have to live with Shield anymore. That will be good for me, yes. Firebrazer would want me to forget him and marry whoever I want. Yes, I understand. Besides, we are both spirits. Shield can no longer ruin this for me."

Silver couldn't 100% understand her actions. *What did Shield really do to her? She killed her grandfather, but it was because he killed Heaven's father. I would forgive anyone for killing E.T, but-*

No, I don't want anyone to kill him.

But I do! she argued with herself. *If he dies, the world will be at peace!*

I should find a page that explains a time when they were all friends.

"I have never had any true friends before. But I was blessed by HighWish herself to have found Firebrazer and Prince Earthquake. They are both amazingly sweet, and Oceanic is so smart. E.T is rather playful; I have truly never found any other dragons like them. I am fortunate to have these dragons. Especially FireBrazer. E.T is a little strange, and a Shadowling, by the holy divinity. But he is rather amazing, and I am pleased to have them with me."

It was strange for Silver to see how happy her mother was with her friends. She didn't know how badly things would go, how badly Earthquake would feel, how Firebrazer would die and what would happen to her life. She found a note written in a much different manner than Heaven's notes. After a quick inspection, she noticed something quite significant. *These aren't just notes; these are messages from Earthquake.*

*"**Princess Heaven**

I assume Oceanic has given you the news already. Although if she hasn't, I hate to be the bearer of bad news, but I don't think I'm

going to be able to see you much longer. Firebrazer never truly got a proper funeral of any sort, but I don't think I'll live long enough to do anything with you. You see, I've fallen with a strange illness, something of a disease, although not a plague. Dragons have been told to stay away from me in order to stay clear of the illness, but I know inside that it's not contagious. We all know earth spirits don't live forever. We aren't the immovable mountains that we're painted as. We're just dragons with a bit of rock magic. As you always said, you can paint a coal to look like a diamond, but it will never change its worth. I was born a simple and faithful dragon, but I failed. You are a beautiful piece of the sky, a perfect and shining star from beyond the clouds. I know how you feel about your mother, and I'm sorry for everything. I wish I could be there with you right now to help you. I said the same thing to Oceanic. You know what happened to her poor whelp and family, it's understandable to believe she'd be desperate to return. Anyway, I'm messaging you now to say these things. I'm becoming much weaker, as I'm writing to you first, I pray I will be alive long enough to even write anything to the others. Now, regarding the prince, I see how everything is. You may feel whatever you want, and I'm allowing you to forgive him, but please don't ever be blinded by anyone. The world is really complicated, but I know you're the best of us so far. Firebrazer was, is, and always will be our king. Sending my soul for us all, Heaven. Make your own decisions. You are a talented and intelligent dragon, I hope you know that."

Silver had never seen someone respect her mother that much. It made her wonder why she didn't marry Earthquake instead. Depending on when Zoka died, which was a long while, seventeen years ago, he could have married Heaven. *Wait, no, no NO NO NO she was like seventeen, and he was around 40, aaaaaaabsolutely not.* He seemed like such a loving dragon. Silver flew up to the roof where she and her sister used to play when their parents weren't looking. They had some toys and books in case they would have to stay for a while, like if their parents were fighting. It was late morning, and Silver didn't have much to do alone. Silver didn't have anything to eat for a while, and considered going back to her uncles' home. They wouldn't be too surprised if she didn't come back, or they might be concerned, but Polka would be lonely.

Maybe we can hang out when all this is over, she thought. Silver looked up into the blue skies. The Aolite kingdom hid behind clouds, mostly hidden from dragons. She thought about the place of Anima right now.

King Nightchaser was assassinated by an unknown Aolite, she relayed to herself. *Queen Shield never sent them, but the king's vengeful son killed the Ariash king to show his fury, as the Aolite, Shadowling and Ariash clans are at war due to an unknown cause.*

Why is everything in Anima unknown?

He showed the Aolite his power. The prince's name was unknown, (of course it is) and was called the Eternity Prince. He tricked my mo- Princess Heaven into letting him out of prison and marrying him, knowing her relationship with her mother, and how Queen Shield was hardly able to stop her. The prince hoped his Aolite daughter would kill the Shadowling twin, hoping to make them look guilty. If the Shadowling won, he'd use the Aolite as treasure and things to bargain with. He killed one of his daughters, the Shadowling, hoping to get dirt on the Aolite himself, but once that becomes known, everyone will know it was him and not the Aolite. When Sacrifice tells the world what really happened, he'll go back to prison and we'll all live happily ever after.

Silver kept going through the information over and over again, making more questions and getting less answers. Why wouldn't he just kill Shield? If she's stronger, why doesn't Shield kill him?

"But I don't *want* anyone to kill anyone," she fought with herself. "I want everyone to be happy." She dug around in the pouch her mother gave her. Silver rubbed the black scar on her neck, almost forgetting it was there. At the bottom of the bag, she found a strange circular object made of crystals and diamonds. She looked at it curiously as it sparked for a moment. She jumped from the light shock. Two dark symbols formed on it like a clock. One was blue and the other was pale white. They were long and had symbols on the front of them. The dark blue one had a tall triangle on the front. The paler one had a diamond sort of shape. she soon realized that it was a compass to the Aolite kingdom. The other was pointing to the spirit island.

She put them back in her bag and decided to look for Nalu again. She wanted to ask if he knew anything about the Eternity Prince. So Silver spent the rest of the day looking under rocks and logs to find the green dragon. Vines sprinkled morning water on her and the rainforest was wet from the rain that had started to sprinkle. It wasn't hard rain, it was nice. She eventually heard noises from around her, and saw him standing behind her on a log, tilting his head at Silver.

"Hi, Nalu," she called to him. He hopped down into the wet grass and looked up at her. He was a bit smaller than Silver, which was surprising considering she was 6 years old. "I was just looking for you!" He smiled to her, or at least she though he did. He didn't really seem to show much expression. She told him everything about the Eternity Prince, her father, her story and her sister. After everything, he went over to a small river that had formed from the rain and took a stick from nearby. He started to draw something in the mud. Silver watched intently.

He drew an H at the top, three lines going down and out from it, and then three letters below them. L, D and E. D and l were then crossed out, while E got four lines coming off of it like he did with H. LR, BL, BT, and ET were drawn below them. Silver felt one of them was *definitely* familiar. He continued. Nalu drew two lines coming from ET, and put S at the bottom of each. He then went back up to H and put two lines going from its side horizontally. He then put A and HW on the end of them. He gave them each another horizontal line, and a line down. There was W and B. W got a line down, and so did B. A's line down was S, HW got WS, B got F, W got N and H got L, B and E.

Nalu stepped back to admire it. Silver examined it closely. H, A, HW, B and W. Was there a secret acronym with those letters? Was it a code? Did it mean something in a certain language? They all had a line down. H got three lines, L, B and E. HW got WS. B got F. A got S and W got N. E got four lines down. BT, LR, BL, and ET. ET got two lines down, S and S.

"I don't understand," she said. Nalu pointed to S, and then pointed to Silver. He pointed to N, and pointed to himself. She started to get it. He pointed to the sky, in the direction of the Aolite kingdom, and pointed to WS and HW.

"This is a family tree, isn't it?" She asked him. He nodded. "The ET is my father, LR is LightningRoar. . me and my sister are the next two. Who are the-?" She paused. Nalu was gone. Thunder sounded overhead. Silver looked at the ET in Nail's drawing. *Soon,* she thought. *Soon we will be safe from you.* Silver remembered what he did to everyone, to her mother, to *her.* She took the stick and crossed out his symbol.

Chapter 11: Sea of Stone and Royals

Forest of Sapphires

Jewelem was shocked. When Meteor left, Silver had gone to her cave with Sacrifice, while Legend had gone after Meteor a bit, returning after not finding her. He'd spent the rest of the morning wandering his cave, trying to distract himself from the events. But as he watched Silver fly away into the sky… it was just him and Legend. He laid on the edge of his cave platform, just thinking. *I bet Legend will go back, and rule the Poseidonite. I have to lead the Crystalians, the second in command of the Calx Nation after Queen Nutrients, the Earthin ruler. If I don't go back . . who will lead? What if we both stay here? Can we stay friends that way?*

Legend swooped into his cave suddenly, almost making Jewelem fall off the ledge. She sat next to him.

He smiled at her. "Hey," he said. She smiled back. Legend must've noticed his feelings. He felt unsure, nervous and scared about Meteor. Legend laid down next to him and put her wing on his back.

"Silver left just now," she told him. His ears perked up.

"Left?" He asked. "Where? Why?"

"She went to the Aolite kingdom," Legend answered. "She said her father might go there next, so she's warning them. Silver said she'll return when the ritual takes place."

Jewelem hesitated. "Are y- are *we* going anywhere?"

She fell silent. "I may have to take the throne of the Poseidonite kingdom," she said quietly. *Oh, right,* he realized. *The Crystalian clan... Do they have a ruler? Oh dear, that's going to be me, isn't it?*

"We should make peace between the clans," he said. He didn't have any confidence in that plan. How could years of war and violence be solved with a simple friendship between rulers? If he and Legend were actually friends, that still wouldn't be enough to stop a war. Even still, he was way too old for her. She looked about fourteen, but he wasn't sure. Legend seemed willing to try. "I think we can," she said. "We have 3 days, then we should be back here. Silver will return in three days."

"Wait, where's Sacrifice? Did she go with Silver?"

"I didn't see her," Legend replied. "I'm sure she followed Silver."

Jewelem took one more look at the Crystal cave. Earthquake wanted the other spirits to come see it. *But he was left with guilt instead,* Jewelem thought sorrowfully. *All he wanted was to make everyone happy. But Firebrazer was killed by his friend, Oceanic and Heaven left and his friend was a killer. He was left feeling like his wishes were foolish...*

That's awful.

It put a strange feeling in Jewelem's chest to imagine that feeling. Helpless, forgotten, betrayed, feeling guilty of a crime you didn't commit. Legend could tell something was off.

"Earthquake would want you to end the war," she said nervously. "We can do this." He smiled to her and stood up.

"Should we go to the mainlands now?" Jewelem asked. "What's the plan?"

"I think we should go together now," Legend replied. "We should get there quickly. We only have three days, probably not enough to end a 400 year long war, but enough to say we're trying to do so."

They stepped out of the cave and leaped into the sky. It was almost mid day, the blue sky almost cloudless.

"So, without the pretty metaphors and poetry, how, logically, would we end the war?" He asked.

"Well, let's think," Legend started. They soared over the beach and onto the open ocean. "The war started how?"

Jewelem thought for a moment. "Wasn't it for land, fishing and Calx Dragons' locations on the Husk Isle? I think the Crystalians wanted the Husk Isle, but the Poseidonite claimed it as their own due to the Chia clan living there already. The Chia hadn't officially joined the Calx Nation despite the other two tribes joining. The Dune Crystalians and the Desert Furo. The Diaknya didn't join because they're a solo clan. The Poseidonite considered the Chia an alliance, while the Crystalians wanted the island due to their dragons living there."

"At the time, the Diaknya were claiming themselves as an independent clan and they weren't Chia, but the Crystalians called them Chia, making them mad. The Poseidonite fought for the Chia, while the Diaknya, Dune Crystalians and Desert Furo still stayed out of it. Then the water spirit, SandClaw, sunk the island. The two clans still fight over over it. Whoever wins gets the territory. The Aqua Crystalians probably need more ship docks, while Poseidonite just want the ocean place to build more castles."

"… What?" Legend asked, blinking in confusion. "That was a lot."

"basically, there was an island that Calx Nation dragons lived on, but it wasn't Calx nation land. Crystalians thought it was, but

Poseidonite didn't think so. Crystalians accidentally made the Diaknya mad as well."

"How do we end that debacle?!" Legend panicked. "Do we just say 'share the land'?!"

Jewelem hesitated. "Maybe we do. If the Crystalians want the territory for ships, and the Poseidonite want it for the ocean floor, it can work. The Poseidonite get the bottom, while the Crystalians get the surface."

Legend nodded. Something in her eyes made Jewelem uneasy. "How old are you?" She asked.

That wasn't what Jewelem expected. "Um… seventeen?"

Legend nodded. "I'm sixteen. We aren't old enough to rule kingdoms. You have to rule like, four clans! The Fae, the Crystalian, the Earthin and the Veo."

She's sixteen?? I thought she was like, thirteen. Then again, Poseidonite always look naturally young.

"I never really thought about it like that," he said. "Earthquake became king at fourteen, but he had a lot of help."

"Do you think you'll be ok?" She asked.

Jewelem hesitated. "I'm scared… But, I'll manage."

Legend gave him a sad look. "I'm sorry."

He smiled, but was still nervous.

"My mother was queen when she was 12. She had her friend, King Riverstone," Legend said, nodding slowly.

"Do you. .. mind telling me what happened to Riverstone?" Jewelem asked nervously. *She probably wouldn't like taking about tha-*

"Oh *that* stupid worm," Legend laughed. "Yeah, he's pretty bad. He left the Poseidonite kingdom and was never seen again. Some dragons say he's really evil, or dead, and that his spirit is haunting the

Poseidonite kingdom. I really think he just disappeared and lives as an outlaw."

Jewelem pretended to laugh, but Legend is a bad liar.

A couple tiring hours later, they reached the storm barrier. The sky was beautiful, but the Storm Barrier was a bunch of dark clouds. The first time they passed through, it had just opened and let them through, but for some reason, it stayed closed.

"Uh, what do we do now?" Jewelem asked. "Can we go through it?"

Legend flew up to the barrier carefully and put her talon in its clouds and jumped back. "We can't go through, it's full of electricity, I think."

"Can we go under it?" Jewelem called to her. They looked down and both soared down to a platform made of emerald Jewelem made for them.

Legend put her tail in the water for a moment. "I think I should try it. It's cold, but I'm a Poseidonite. We're used to cold water."

"Uh- Careful," he said. She smiled to him and leaped in the water. Some water splashed onto his claws, and he felt how cold it was. Jewelem watched the water carefully for a while, waiting for her to come back. *I wonder what we'll do when we get to our kingdoms,* his mind wandered.

I'll go back and see who's in charge. I'll find my brothers, talk to the council, and see how everything has been. Maybe Legend and I- a-and our council could meet up somewhere.

He heard a loud splash and a scream from somewhere, and it sounded like Legend. His head snapped up. "Legend?!"

Jewelem dove into the ocean immediately. He spun and turned to find her. He saw a pale-purple-blue figure and sped towards it. Jewelem felt a huge creature shoot by below them. The ocean where they were was super dark, almost black, and nothing was around them at all.

Except for something below them, which had long and terrifying blue tentacles that grabbed his tail.

He almost shrieked and shot various sharp crystals at it. *I'm going to die,* his mind said. Jewelem heard a loud roar, or a shriek. He couldn't think about anything, just the idea of drowning there alone and the tentacle dragging him down into the ocean. He felt a talon grab his arm. The tentacle, which seemed to go down forever, let go for a second and he then realized he was on a small island. He looked up and saw Legend next to him, but a moment went by and everything changed. Thunder roared above him suddenly, he felt freezing cold, a shrieking demon appeared from the ocean and Legend disappeared. Jewelem made a shielding orb of emerald glass around him. He weakly stood up and looked around from inside his shield. Then he saw what had almost killed them.

Can someone tell me why that exists?

Jewelem had always wondered why demonic creatures existed. Like that. Like the fact that an actual sea monster stood in front of him. He couldn't see it clearly, but it was much bigger than any ships he'd ever seen, it had crab-like legs and some type of shell. 2 heads shot piercing shrieks all over the cove. White and teal lines spiralled over its body and the demon had 4 eyes. It had a bunch of slimy tentacles from its tail. The creature slammed its tail down on Jewelem's dome, but he escaped before he was killed. He saw Legend hiding behind a couple trees on the small island they were on. Jewelem built up power in his left talon and waited for the right moment to hit it. *What am I even thinking? I have negative fighting experience, and the first time I tried, I ended up losing miserably. I didn't stand a chance against an ocean spirit, but this creature isn't a spirit.*

I hope.

The roaring thunder above them sent chills down his spine and the shooting array of lightning behind the demon cast a brief light onto it, showing its demented, twisted face. The demon leaped up on two legs and dug its sharp crab-legs into the sand next to Jewelem as he dodged. He then struck its tendrils with his energy-filled talon and it shrieked in pain before vanishing into the ocean.

Moments went by. There was a quiet silence, only the thunder and rain made any sound. Jewelem breathed heavily and heard Legend run up to him.

"What the heck was that?!?" Legend called.

"Water demon," he gasped. "I didn't know I could do that."

"Are you ok?" She asked. Not waiting for an answer, Legend suddenly took off her healing pearl necklace and put it over Jewelem's neck. He didn't realize the blood from his arm, but he saw it fix itself with the necklace's power. She put her talon where the wound was for a moment.

"What… Happened, exactly?" He asked. He rubbed his forehead softly.

"Uh-" Legend was cut off.

They heard large flapping wingbeats, seemingly from a giant dragon. They looked around, but couldn't see it.

"Oh, what now?" Jewelem whimpered. Legend stepped in front of him protectively. The storm clouds parted and a large part of them stepped around the clouds, circling over them from the storms, watching them like a hawk. It had enormous wings, and teal lightning glowed from its body.

That's a dragon, Jewelem thought and almost fainted. *That's an enormous storm dragon that's going to crush both of us and Silver is going to be devastated and we're going to die.*

"Spirits," the dragon said almost curiously. His voice was pleasant, yet commanding, but not menacing. "Your sky spirit, Silver came through here, and I believe Meteor was a fire spirit as well. She did not stay long though."

"We're sorry for entering your cove," Legend yelled to him over the waves, thunder and howling wind. "We tried to go under it, but a demon attacked us and I had to make sure my friend was ok. My name is Legend, and um- h-he's Jewelem"

"My name is LightningRoar," he said. He looked to Jewelem. "It is against my oath to allow you to stay, but I can lead you to the other side if you're able to get there." He waved his talon at the other side of the barrier and it opened on command. "The Aolite kingdom is where Silver went, if you're looking for her. However, it's not the best place for other clans."

"So, are we free to go?" Legend asked him. LightningRoar nodded. "I wish you good luck on your journey, spirits." He stepped out of their way. Legend and Jewelem hurried out of the storming cove.

They found a place on the north side of the Southern Earth island with a cliff overseeing Anima. It was nearing the afternoon, and they had a nice view of everything. The Southern Earth Island had a part of it called the Maple for the Furo, and they stayed there. The cliff was a nice spot. It was a bit of flying to get there, but it was worth it for a good spot. The stars were almost invisible, but they were a little bit there.

"That was an adventure," Legend said. Jewelem laid down and rested his tired body. He'd been flying for hours, then swam in a freezing ocean with a demon. He sighed.

"Are you ok, Jewelem?" Legend asked.

"I'm fine," he muttered.

"I think we should stay here for the night," she said. "We should go to the kingdoms in the morning, and try to think from there."

Jewelem didn't even nod before he closed his eyes and slept.

The next morning, Legend and Jewelem watched the sunrise and tried to come up with a strategy for the war. In the end, they came to see how the war was and make the new orders to stop the war. Jewelem didn't tell her, but he wasn't sure he completely believed in their plan. Well, he certainly didn't have the same enthusiasm or confidence that Legend had.

"So, we're ready to go?" Legend asked him. She had her wings held differently, more regal than before, as if she was preparing to become queen and had to look like it.

"I guess so," He replied. He wasn't really. He was scared, and he didn't want to do it alone.

"Is this goodbye for a while?" She said, "Are we going to see each other again?"

Jewelem hadn't thought about that. *What if my dragons kill her? Or they kill me and we don't get to be together and oh dear that's very likely isn't it?* "Let's... Hope that we do?"

She laughed a bit. "If we do come back one day, where would we meet each other?"

"The island where we first met," Jewelem said confidently. "I think that's best." She nodded.

They looked out onto the ocean, the islands of Anima. "Jewelem," Legend whispered in a sad way, "we're going to rule kingdoms."

He nodded. Jewelem wasn't confident, and he couldn't be brave, but he could smile and try to be positive. He went up next to her. "We can try to do good," he said.

She laughed again. Legend brushed Jewelem's tail with her's. "I don't even know how long it's been," she said. "But it's been great, this time." Jewelem knew it may be their last time they ever saw each other and built up power in his talon. He laid a claw on her talon and made a pearly-glass bracelet with a glistening ruby stone, knowing red was her favourite colour.

"Bye, Legend," Jewelem said. She nodded.

"Thank you. Bye!" She hopped into the air and soared for a moment then dived into the blue ocean. He waited for a moment.

Jewelem took a deep breath and started flying towards the Northern Earth Island, the home of the Crystalians.

Specifically the Royal Crystalian Tribe. It's the main source of art, commerce and trade in the Calx Nation. The other clans also traded there, and it's one of the biggest caves in the world, along with being the biggest tribe considering all 4 tribes have a large population. Royal Crystalians are rich, and their tribe is in the centre of the Northern Earth Island. Their cave is shaped like the ribcage of an enormous beast. It's filled with housing caves, markets, stores and other forms of commerce.

The other 4 tribes were Ox, Dune, Squirrel and Aquamarine, shortened to Aqua Tribe. The Squirrel Tribe lives somewhere in the forests surrounding the mountains on the Northern Earth Island. The Ox Tribe is known for creating tunnels underground and they used to travel in a savannah, but there aren't any savannahs in Anima, so that always confused Jewelem. Dune used to live on the Husk Isle, also home to Chia, Diaknya and Desert Furo. They disappeared or died when the island sank though. He'd read a lot of legends about them. They lived in the Crystal Port on the island. There was also OakHorn, the Chia village, Oasis, for the Furo, and the Diaknya Mountains for the Diaknya. The books didn't have much on those, just their names and inhabitants.

Then there's Aqua. They don't live on islands, they instead travel around in boats and ships. Occasionally they trade cargo and fish in the Royalty Tribe, but they normally just travel, fish and sail. Main talents they have that most dragons don't learn are how to make bait, way-finding and navigation. Jewelem had a pretty bad sense of navigation, but he could use stars as a way of location sometimes and made pretty good bait. *It's strange though,* he thought. *You can't see the Storm barrier until you get close, then it's right in front of you.*

Jewelem flew until he was right above the Crystalian kingdom. The Royalty Clan's cave had huge stone 'claws' around it called the 'Royal Spires.' The spires casted a slightly eerie shadow onto the clan's kingdom. The tribe was a bunch of markets, stalls, caves and the palace on the eastern side. The palace doors, at least. The palace lead into the mountains and mostly went down into cave systems. *I should hide my identity,* he thought. *I'll find something in the palace.* Jewelem dived down and landed on the castle steps.

The guards didn't stop him.

They just stared at him, and he looked between them.

"Hi?" He said nervously. The guards exchanged a glance and allowed him to open the doors.

Inside the main room, a throne made of various rare ores sat atop a raised platform. The walls were made of quartz and mostly stone with many hallways leading to different parts of the palace. He didn't know the palace very well at all, but followed the signs above the doors to find the armoury, hoping for something to hide himself with. He went down one of the first halls on the left side.

Since all the halls and doors and walls looked the same, he just wandered until he found something. The first thing he found was another Crystalian. But this one was… funny.

Jewelem half-turned a corner and saw her walking down the hall looking just as confused as he was. Her ears perked up and she looked at him.

"Huh?" She said. *Holy- her eyes are so bright!* She had the most unique eyes he'd ever seen. First, her eyes were *huge,* so he could see them clearly. The whites of her eyes were black, and her pupils white with teal outlines. They also had flecks of green and gold. Her scales had various shades of really dark purple. The dragon's wings also had diamond patterns on them, a unique thing that he hadn't seen on a lot of dragons.

"Um. . hi," Jewelem waved awkwardly.

She hopped over to him. She looked about his age. "I'm Crystalexite. Who are you?" She looked close. " Wow, you look a lot like King Earthquake, if that's not rude."

Should I tell her the truth? She seems just as confused as I am. "Jewelem… uh- Earthquake's son," he replied quickly. "I was just looking for the armoury, or something."

She gave him a look like he was lying, and she could tell. "Well, then. I'm a messenger from the Ox tribe," she said. "I was told to tell the king some boring stuff, but that's a bit confusing considering nobody is actually, like. . the king I guess?"

"I think I'm… the king, or something," he mumbled. "Where is the armoury, may I ask?" Crystalexite nodded. She motioned for him to follow. She led him down the hall a couple ways and seemed to half-understand the palace. She eventually brought him to a room full of armour, some weapons and a couple of shields.

"Welp, this is it," Crystalexite said. "I gotta talk to your council. Queen Crimson and King Cobalt sent me to talk to, and I quote, 'someone in charge,' so I'll find them. If you need anything, messengers have a spot in the lower parts of the castle. Bye-bye!" Crystalexite spun and darted down the hall like he was chasing her. *Who the heck are Queen Crimson and King Cobalt?* He thought. He didn't have time for any of that. Jewelem went into the armoury and selected a dark, almost black, navy blue robe that covered his rainbow frill and his wings. It could also cover most of his bright royal blue scales, which would obviously give him away as Earthquake's whelp.

He ventured through the castle until he found the throne room again a while later. But instead of the throne being empty, a tall purple Crystalian with angry eyes and a lot of jewellery sat on top. She looked *mad*. More importantly, she was going to kill him.

No, not that.

It was the crown she was wearing, and the guard that called her Queen Amethyst.

"Well then?" She snapped. "Where is he?" The guard got up and a new dragon entered the room. Jewelem was standing in the hallway he came through the first time he was in that room. Off to the side, he could still see what was happening, and had to look super close to see him. *Garnet!?*

Commander Garnet stepped into the room, displeased and furious. Many guards were behind him.

"Your majesty," he bowed to her. "I've been informed that Prince Jewelem has entered the palace."

"Find him!" She hissed. "I will have none of my brother's descendants, relatives or *acquaintances* get in my way. Zoka was already a desperate fool. Is Irid here yet?"

Ohh, now Garnet was *furious*. Even Jewelem agreed with him then; Queen Zoka wasn't a *desperate fool,* she was a strategic mastermind who led the war proudly, and only died in a duel with the Ocean Queen. *Wait- did she say her* brother's *relatives? Is she my aunt? I definitely hope not, I do NOT want to converse with her.*

Garnet swallowed his words of displeasure. "Yes, Irid is outside. I'll fetch her at your command."

"No, I want my nephew," she yawned. "Our little plaything Irid can wait." She looked around a bit. "Where's Crimson's new toy?" Garnet flicked his tail at the door. Jewelem almost gasped when they dragged Crystalexite inside. Her wings, tail and claws were chained and she struggled against the guards around her.

"This is her," Garnet said. Jewelem could tell he was sick of Amethyst, but had to respect her. "We could take her to the dungeo-"

Amethyst stood up and leaped off the throne in a second and grabbed Crystalexite's chin. "Find Jewelem or I *will* cut out your tongue!" She roared.

Crystalexite flinched. She looked around and spotted him, but didn't say anything. Amethyst kept her eyes on her, but Garnet and his guards looked around with her. Crystalexite looked back to the vicious queen. "He's not here anymore," she lied. "He must've already left."

Amethyst moved her talon from her head to her throat. Crystalexite's large eyes were filled with horror as the queen stared into them. "Then tell me where he is," she growled calmly. When Crystalexite didn't speak, she tightened her grip on the young dragon's throat. Every moment she didn't tell her, Amethyst held her even more tightly. Jewelem didn't know what to do, but he couldn't watch her be killed. He tried to impale Amethyst with sharp shards. He sent them flying quickly her way, but she looked over sharply and moved her head out of the way. She stared at where they landed on the wall on the other side of the throne room. Then she dropped Crystalexite, who fainted, and turned towards him. Jewelem was stuck staring between the powerful queen, and poor Crystalexite who just wanted to do her job. He hoped she was alive. Garnet saw him and narrowed his eyes. Jewelem slammed his claws on the stone floors and made sharp mounds of crystals attack the dragons. He didn't want to kill them, he just wanted them to go away. He saw guards try to spear the crystal mounds, but it knocked their spears away. Amethyst chased after him, smashing the mounds with her strong horns as she chased him. He stopped in front of Crystalexite and made stronger walls surrounding them made of glamouring gold.

"Crystalexite?" He said. Jewelem knew he might have to run away from Amethyst, but he couldn't leave her. Jewelem put two claws on her neck. He felt a steady pulse under her scales. *She's alive for now.* He thought. He heard the violent queen clawing on the gold. Jewelem could see her glowing purple eyes through it, horrifying him. Jewelem heard soft coughing and looked down at Crystalexite. Her bright, chaotic eyes were dimmed and weaker than before, but still bright. He gently put her down.

"Sorry," he said.

"Jewelem?" She called weakly. "What's happening? WHY IS THERE A DEMON!?" She pointed to Amethyst.

"We're dead," he said nervously.

'Open the floor," she said."

"What?"

"Just do it."

Jewelem shrugged and commanded the stone in the floors to open, revealing a lower floor.

"I can't go with you," he said. "They'll follow me, but you can still get out safely." She paused, but nodded.

"You'll be alright, right?"

Amethyst roared and smashed her talon through the gold, opening a hole to hear the screaming of the guards behind her. "Can't promise that," he laughed nervously. "Um, you should go, like, now."

"Thanks Jewelem." She hopped into the hole and Jewelem filled it again. He busted out the other side of the golden walls. Amethyst chased after him and Garnet suddenly appeared out of what Jewelem thought to be absolute *thin air.* Garnet reached towards him but Amethyst shoved him out of the way and leaped on him from the side, slamming him into a wall. Jewelem tried desperately to escape her claws, but they pinned him to the floor. He saw Garnet come up behind them, holding his bleeding shoulder.

"Sir," one of the guards said. She examined her commander's shoulder. "We should-"

"He'll be fine," Amethyst growled. The guard fell silent. "Golden, take this one to the dungeons. I'll deal with that from there. Then we hand him off to Irid." Jewelem never really felt bad for Garnet after hearing about his lies, but he could honestly see the pain he was in. Serving a queen who hated his former rulers, the one he respected. Garnet just seemed miserable with his position. "Also, it's Garnet, not Golden."

"I don't care, worm!" She snapped. Amethyst turned to him "Take this one away!" Her piercing, evil gaze turned back to Jewelem. She brought her face close to his so she could look him in the eye. "I don't want to see him again for 4 days. Until then. . " She turned back to stare at the place in the ground where Crystalexite disappeared. "I have to find a little traitor." Amethyst left, leaving the scene confused.

The guard looked awfully concerned. "Are you sure-?" "Don't worry," he replied. "You're... Agate, right?" She nodded. "I'll be fine, you and the others can go rest somewhere."

Agate seemed to hesitate for a moment, but she smiled and left with the others. Garnet seemed upset still, but he continued his job with Jewelem.

Garnet didn't speak as he walked Jewelem through the dungeons. He didn't talk about what happened with Amethyst, how she got in power, why he served her or anything. He just kept his strong talon locked on Jewelem's forearm and didn't wait for him as he was slowing down due to being tired. But Jewelem could tell Garnet was also tired. He didn't have his wings raised in the uncomfortable-looking way they always looked. His shoulders weren't constantly tense, and he just seemed more exhausted than normal, making Jewelem wonder what Amethyst had done to the poor dragon.

"Garnet?" He called to the empty dragon. He opened a cell with a key locked on his armour and tried to throw Jewelem inside, but ended up just kind of pushing him in a bit.

"Get. .. *in"* he growled. Jewelem stood in the doorway of the cell, staring at him, awestruck by the change. Garnet was always a confident, regal dragon who held himself with status. He even seemed like a decent dragon to be around when talking with other commanders. He was fun when around the dragons he liked, but now, he just seemed empty. *What did Amethyst do to you?*

"What happened to the Royalty tribe? What happened to you?" Jewelem asked.

Garnet spun and successfully threw him against the wall of the cell, growling at him before locking it. Jewelem was shocked, maybe from the sudden stabbing pain in his body. Garnet was so different. It was terrifying what Amethyst could do to a dragon in less than one moon cycle.

A couple moments of silence passed.

"He used to be able to do that, but stronger, with half the effort. It wouldn't have taken so much out of him. Now he feels like he's going to pass out."

Jewelem spun to see Crystalexite nearby outside the cell. She had a lot of bleeding marks and bruises all over her. She was clearly good at hiding in dark places.

"Crystalexite! Are you ok?" He called.

"Yeah, it looks worse than it is." she waved it off. "I can help you, by the way." She pulled a long, thin sword off the wall and used one of the torches nearby to melt and then sliced through the bars like butter. She cut open a large enough space for Jewelem to get through.

"Thanks," he said once he got out. The dungeons were made of moist stone bricks, dark and impenetrable. There were two rooms of the dungeons, and they were long hallways full of cells. There were cages lining the walls and some on the ceiling. It seemed like some of the walls were new, as there were a couple platforms and the swords Crystalexite used all looked very fresh and new.

"So, I've been wondering for a while," Jewelem started curiously. "They knew you knew something about me. How? Did you tell them?"

She hesitated and fiddled with her claws nervously. "I …talk to myself, a lot," she said. "I'm… *very* lonely here." Crystalexite looked around. "This place got so much worse when Amethyst became queen," Crystalexite whimpered as she looked around. "It used to be. . well, not *pleasant,* but certainly not this gloomy."

"What?" Jewelem asked. "What did Amethyst do?"

"Well, when Earthquake was in charge, this dungeon, first it was called a 'confinement system,' it used to have less cells and no SWORDS. Why did she add these?" She looked at the sword in her talon. Next, oh dear, the things she did to her poor commanders and guards."

"Is that why Garnet is so tired and miserable?"

'Once she found out he was a King Earthquake supporter, she was pretty mad. She had a lot of his followers tortured, some banished, and a few protesters were executed. It's awful. I actually used to have a part-time life here, as King Earthquake thought I was really nice and good at my job, so we were acquaintances. Sure; I was two at the time, but I was still a good messenger."

'*Tortured?!*" Jewelem yelped. "She *tortured* Garnet?!" *That's awful!! He didn't even do anything bad! All he did was support his king, and Amethyst TORTURED him!?*

"Yep. I hate her," Crystalexite growled. "We should assassinate her."

"I'm here to take the throne and stop the Crystalian Poseidonite war," Jewelem said confidently. "I'm all for getting rid of her. But first, I have to find my brothers and tell them what I'm doing. I have to explain every-" Jewelem suddenly remembered something. Something very important.

Wait. .. What did Amethyst do to my mother?

"Crystalexite, do you know General Gold?" Jewelem asked desperately.

Crystalexite looked anxious and looked to the ground. Jewelem feared the worst. "Amethyst is holding her hostage," she said grimly. "If Garnet doesn't obey her, she'll kill Gold."

Jewelem almost fainted. "W-what?" He stammered. "Where is she!?"

"I don't know," Crystalexite said. "What should we do now?"

"I want to see Amethyst's plans," Jewelem replied. "Where's the council room?"

Crystalexite motioned for him to follow and she darted out of the confinement system and up to the main floors. Eventually she led him to a room with a bunch of counters, tables and maps. Bookshelves were filled with books along with a huge map of Anima on the far wall. Jewelem examined the tables with maps and the pins on the locations. Crystalexite looked closely from behind him.

A moment later, he found out what she was doing.

"Crystalexite…" he started. "I think she's trying to wipe out the Poseidonite."

"WHAT," Crystalexite yelped.

"Look," Jewelem showed her the map. "She has these labels for each symbol. This right here is a bomb." He pointed to the yellow circle with purple outlines. "Look how they're placed all over this area?" Above the Poseidonite kingdom, there were almost a hundred of the circles.

"How did she find the Poseidonite kingdom?" Crystalexite asked. "Wait, how do *you* know where it is?"

"Their new queen, Legend, is my best friend," Jewelem replied, feeling odd calling Legend a 'friend.' "I do wonder how she found the Poseidonite kingdo-"

"May I ask why you're here?"

The two spun to hear Amethyst coming down the hall. *She saw us,* he panicked. Jewelem pulled Crystalexite behind a couple of crates near the corner of the room.

"I'm sorry, your majesty," Garnet's voice said. "But we have new messages from our alliance."

Alliance? Jewelem thought. *Garnet wouldn't call any dragon of the Calx Nation that. Well, Amethyst might've made him, but I don't think he would do that on his own. Garnet was always offended when a dragon in power dismissed any dragon as anything less than a dragon, not just any guard or 'alliance.' Unless it was a group of dragons, he would've called them by their name. He'd told someone to find a guard to do a certain task, but would always specifically address someone by their name. Maybe it* is *a group?*

"Well?" Amethyst snapped. "What did he say?"

"He said he's coming for an audience here," Garnet replied.

Amethyst yawned. "Who is he again?"

Garnet hesitated. "We… don't know, your majesty."

"Why does he matter?"

"…He tends to meet in secret with the ruler. He met with King Earthquake a lot-"

Amethyst spun and pinned him to the wall by his throat on the opposite side from where Jewelem and Crystalexite were hiding. "Earthquake is not a *king,* fool!" She looked around and snatched a dagger off a nearby shelf. "When he gets here," she growled calmly yet threateningly. *"Find him."*

Amethyst held him there for a few moments. Jewelem could see how Garnet didn't dare fight against her grip. *She isn't going to kill him, is she?* Jewelem panicked, but couldn't move. Garnet looked as though he was going to die, and Amethyst showed no mercy to him. Jewelem was trembling until Amethyst let him go. He was starting to worry she was *actually* going to kill him, but she dropped him and he gasped. He laid down for a few moments and Amethyst turned to the table with the map.

"While you're at it, we need more bombs." Jewelem was horrified at how she spoke so… simply. She was so calm and dismissive of how she hurt her commander. He wanted to kill her with his magic, but he didn't want to risk hurting Garnet or Crystalexite. "Also, can you by chance find your little whelps? I need to speak with them."

Amethyst turned and left the room. Jewelem was starting to worry that his adopted father had died or fainted, but Garnet stood up and went over to the table. He had to hold onto it so he didn't collapse, and he just looked tired. Garnet stood over the table, he put one talon over his eyes, breathing heavily from the pain. He looked around the room, and Jewelem swore he and Garnet locked eyes. The commander's ears perked up, and he looked a bit surprised to see his son there.

Jewelem wasn't expecting the smile he got from Garnet. He sighed and left the room, following Amethyst.

"That was awful," Jewelem whispered. "I can imagine her trying to wipe out an entire clan." he couldn't get the image of Garnet and Amethyst out of his head.

"Is he like, your friend?" Crystalexite asked.

"Yeah, adopted father. I never knew I was King Earthquake's son until a few days ago."

"By Wilder's name, I had no idea," she said in shock. "I'm so sorry you had to witness that. Are you alright?"

"I'm fine," he told her, but he wasn't sure.

"You've got to get in control," Crystalexite said. "I have to get back to Queen Crimson and King Cobalt."

"I'll try," he said. "Should I escape the palace? I have a disguise."

"I think you should find the alliance," she replied. "You're powerful, and in control. And besides, maybe they'd respect you considering your rightful position. Maybe they'd even help you take out Amethyst!"

"That's probably unlikely," Jewelem said. "They wouldn't have supported King Earthquake if they suddenly decided to work for another queen. The only way they'd be trustworthy is if they're doing it to trick her and are coming to kill her. If this audience isn't what Amethyst expects, and Garnet seems to think he's important."

"The audience room is near the throne room. You can read, so you'll figure it out," Crystalexite said. "Good luck Jewelem!" She ran out the room the opposite way Garnet and Amethyst left.

After Crystalexite left, Jewelem searched for the audience room. Through the throne room, he found a hallway that said "Meeting room," and thought it was the same as an 'audience room." Inside, Amethyst waited on a platform slightly raised above the ground. A dragon in a black robe sat in front of her. They faced each other, with Amethyst facing the door. The room was big and mostly empty without anything. Just the portraits on the wall and the platform. Jewelem hid behind the wall and listened in.

"So," Amethyst started. "I've been told you're supposed to be important."

Jewelem didn't hear the other dragon talk, but he probably nodded.

"Well?!" She roared. "What do you have to say? I don't got all day, so-"

"The boss has informed me of a new lead," the dragon said. "He said he'd examined the Keystone Mirror. Princess Legend knows more than we thought."

"And?!" Amethyst yawned. "So a little princess thinks she's so smart, big deal. Your little gang thinks they're all on top of the world, don't you? Well, I rule the four Calx nation clans! I'm the most powerful ruler in Anima!"

"You're a fool if you think you can rule this kingdom."

There was dead silence. *Wrong move, whoever you are,* Jewelem thought.

"*DO YOU UNDERSTAND-*"

"I don't think *you* understand how to run a war. My plans are simple and they've always worked for your brother," a male voice slithered. He spoke simply and sounded honest. "Prince Jewelem has a more strategic mind. I'd rather speak with him, if you don't mind."

Jewelem had to think about that. *Why would I be the best dragon to talk to?* He thought. *I'm probably more strategic and a better thinker than Amethyst, that's probably true. She has nothing but rocks in her head.*

"PRINCE JEWELEM WILL DIE WITH YOU BEFORE YOU EVER SPEAK WITH HIM!" Amethyst roared. "TELL ME HOW TO WIN THIS WAR AND WIPE OUT THE POSEIDONITE OR I WILL CUT OUT YOUR TONGUE!"

"I'll help you kill Queen Legend," the dragon said. "As long as we can keep a secret between the two of us."

Jewelem heard Amethyst growl something, but he wasn't sure what.

"We can't talk here," he said. "But I can tell you're too unstable to hear the truth. So I'll find Jewelem myself. Luckily, I have dragons on it."

Jewelem looked behind him to see two dragons, both Poseidonite standing a little bit down the hall from him. The first was tall and deep azure blue. She also had paler underscales and white-blue wings. The other was more sky blue and he had navy wings. She leaped over and pinned him to the wall in a quick, agonising flash. He heard the dragon inside speak something else to Amethyst.

"Sounds like my dragons are here." He came out the door and saw him against the Poseidonite's talons. He smiled and Jewelem got a glimpse of his glowing green eyes. He felt a slicing pain on the back of his head.

When Jewelem woke up, he was back in his cell. He pretended to still be unconscious to hear the dragons outside.

"He didn't tell us we'd have to deal with him!" A snappy female voice said. "Riverstone told us he'd figure it out once we had him! Here we are, and he goes right back to the Erosion kingdom!"

"Azure, we can't call him that here," a male voice whispered. "We have to call him 'The Ally."

247

"So what does that make you then, Tide?" Azure hissed. "Am I supposed to call you 'The Assassin,' when clearly I'm the one doing all the hunting and killing? What does that make me? The Receptionist?"

"I'm the assassin, he's the ally, and you're the mastermind," Tide said.

"I don't make plans! The boss makes the plans!" Azure hissed.

"Realistically, Seaweed is the Mastermind, you're the assassin and I'm… I don't even remember. Anyway, we have to get out of here before Queen Amethyst finds us."

"Amethyst can eat my tail," Azure muttered as they left. "And what are these stupid names the boss gave us? I should make a note that no matter how high the pay is, stupid names stain more than gold coins are worth."

RIVERSTONE!?? Jewelem thought. *No no no, that doesn't make any-*

But then he thought about it more. That's the thing, it doesn't make sense. Because it made perfect sense. *Nobody would be suspicious of a secret alliance with the Crystallians, it would only be suspicious if they weren't in the Calx Nation. Riverstone must have plotted against the Poseidonite after leaving his wife and daughter for their magic. He's probably been helping the Calx Nation win the war from the shadows, concealing his identity so he could still be known as RiverStone someplace else. Where though? And why? What does he want? If he's just not being Riverstone for the Calx Nation, then he may not have a secret identity as himself anywhere else. If he's helping wipe out the Poseidonite, what does he want from them? And if he hates magic, what does he think of the spirits? Oh dear, too many questions.*

Jewelem got up and looked around. The cell wasn't locked, so he could just open it and leave. He wandered through the confinement system for a moment and noticed there weren't any other prisoners in there. It was just him. Except for one other cell, where there were two dragons in there. Jewelem, still wearing his disguise (that frankly hadn't worked in the brightly lit castle) walked up to the cell carefully and looked inside. There was a young dragon, not quite a whelp, in there with emerald coloured scales and bright aquamarine wings. The other one was smaller and younger with foggy grey-teal scales and paler underscales. Both looked tired and starved, with the youngest one lying motionlessly in the corner of the dark cell. The emerald one had some kind of notebook and was writing in it vigorously. Jewelem walked up and glanced inside. Once he got a closer look, he was shocked.

Qwonzie and Emeraldite.

"Em-Emeraldite?!" Jewelem called. As soon as Emeraldite looked over, his ears perked up and his face twisted in anger. In that same moment, he threw a blinding-fast knife at Jewelem's head that almost impaled his eye. Jewelem ducked out of the way just in time.

"What was that for?" He protested. "Emeraldite, it's me, Jewelem."

He paused and looked at Jewelem closely. *"Liar!!"* Emeraldite suddenly yelled. "Jewelem is dead! You're a liar!"

The brothers stood there and stared at each other for a long moment. *What did Amethyst do to you now?* He thought sorrowfully. Jewelem took off his hood, revealing his bright scales and rainbow frill.

"Impossible…" Emeraldite gasped. "That-that's impossible! She- They all told me you were dead!"

"Amethyst lied to you, and everyone must've thought I drowned," he said to him. "Emeraldite, what happened to… Everything? I know Amethyst has changed a lot, but what happened to you?"

Emeraldite hesitated. "King Earthquake died 16 years ago, and we were ruled by council and King Cobalt of the Ox Crystalians from

249

the shadows. He wasn't a bad ruler, but certainly not qualified for the main Royalty Tribe of the Crystalians. Recently, when she heard of your existence, Amethyst came and took the throne. Garnet told her that the actual rightful prince, *you,* had died in the shipwreck. The kingdom believes she's the only living royal, but now there's you. I think they'll believe you're an actual prince considering how similar you look to King Earthquake."

"Recently, Amethyst had all of King Earthquake's supporters killed and some lucky ones were banished," Emeraldite continued. "She's hunting down her last relatives so nobody can take the throne from her. She wants you dead." He turned to him.

Jewelem knew some of that, but it still terrified him. "What happened to Qwonzie? Is he ok?"

Emeraldite turned to their little brother. He went over and touched his neck carefully. His back was turned to them so Jewelem couldn't see his face.

"He's basically starving to death," Emeraldite said in a sorrowful tone. "He needs to get out of here, but we can't get out. If the queen finds us, she'll kill us both." Jewelem looked around. The fires were out now, so he couldn't use a sword to get them out.

"What can I do for you?" He asked. "What do I do?"

"I don't know," Emeraldite replied. He stepped into the light.

Jewelem's eyes widened. His eyes were bloodshot and he was in a much worse condition than when he left. "What happened to both of you?" He asked.

"Amethyst had us both taken to her new torture chamber and interrogated," he said. "She threatened us with our parents' lives. We had to tell her everything we knew about you, which wasn't much. All we said was that we knew you and that you drowned in the shipwreck. That's all-" Emeraldite paused and clutched his head. Jewelem quickly summoned some kind of silver tool to pick the lock on the door and get it open.

"Emeraldite?" He held his brother's shoulder tightly and examined him. His brother laid down. "What-?" *My brothers are starved, wounded, trapped and one of them is sick or something. They have to get out of here. But I can't carry both of them, and Emeraldite couldn't get Qwonzie out on his own.*

I'm certainly not leaving them here.

And I'm DEFINITELY not leaving Qwonzie alone. He can't survive alone here.

Emeraldite closed his eyes for a moment. He breathed deeply for a few moments and opened his eyes again.

"How do I get you both out of here?" Jewelem asked.

"You can't," Emeraldite said. 'But you can get Qwonzie somewhere."

"No," Jewelem said. "No, I'm not leaving you here. He whipped his head around, not sure what he was even looking for.

"I'll find a way out," Emeraldite said. "And besides, you can't stay here while Amethyst is in charge, we have to find someplace safe to take Qwonzie, and I'll find my way there eventually." Jewelem didn't want to, but he didn't have many other options. He could either leave them both here or take Qwonzie and hope Emeraldite could make it out. He sighed and went over to Qwonzie.

"I can't believe she's done this," he whispered. "He's a whelp, he doesn't deserve this." Jewelem slid his claws under his brother and pulled him up so his head was on Jewelem's shoulder. "Where should I take him?"

"There's a rebellion camp somewhere near the Ox Tribe tunnels," Emeraldite said. "They knew he's a part of it. We joined shortly before getting captured. They found us on an island near the shoreline. When the ship sank, I went out to find Qwonzie. They found us on the island."

"You managed to find him in a broken shipwreck?" Jewelem couldn't help but ask. "I'm impressed."

"Found him in a safety closet as I call it near the door," Emeraldite said back. "Almost drowning, but he was alive."

Jewelem nodded. "Alright. This isn't goodbye, I'll see you in a few days- maybe less." Emeraldite smiled and closed his eyes. "Just- Hang on, Emeraldite. I'm coming back for you."

Jewelem took Qwonzie to the place Emeraldite told him. He looked at the map his brother had given him. In the main cave, there was a certain cavern that the resistance worked in. He followed the map there and found a place guarded by two dragons. Jewelem wasn't sure they were guards, but he remembered that Amethyst wouldn't give anyone else any armour or weapons.

The first dragon looked up. He recognized them immediately. He knew these dragons pretty well.

"Hey, Obsidian, Ruby," he said to them.

The two glanced at each other. "Who are you?" Obsidian demanded suspiciously.

"Jewelem," he replied.

Ruby's ears perked up. *She's probably wondering about Emeraldite,* he thought with a stab of guilt. *She won't like what's happened to him. Maybe I could go get him after I leave Qwonzie here.*

"You're delusional," Obsidian growled. "We heard that his brothers were the only others that survived the- "

Jewelem took off his hood. "I'm taking my brother to the resistance because I'm going to kill Amethyst." Obsidian and Ruby stared at him for a moment.

"How?" Ruby asked with her eyes wide.

"With this," Jewelem said, holding up his rose constellation. He hadn't really brought it up since Silver arrived, but now, he showed them the glowing rose floating above his talons. It glowed so much brighter now though.

"*Shh!*" Obsidian whispered and slapped his talons with her tail. "You can't just bring that up here! Amethyst will have you killed!"

Jewelem was struck with an idea. It was stupid, obviously, but it might work. *If she tries to kill me, I can get close to her. She seems to have no good ideas in her, so she'll try to kill me herself.*

No wait, that's stupid. Just kill her in her throne room.

"So, did you guys join the resistance?"

"We joined when my father was banished for supporting King Earthquake," Obsidian said. "Ruby's older sister was also banished. She got into the school she wanted and wrote her essay on his reign and why it was one of the most unique."

"Are you able to help Qwonzie?" He asked, showing them his wounded brother. "He needs help." Ruby reached forward and took him in her talons. He was smaller than her, and she helped raise him a lot. *She would be a great older sister for him,* Jewelem thought. *She's very sweet. I wonder if Emeraldite really likes her as well.*

"What's your *mighty* plan then?" Obsidian asked.

"I think I'll use earth spirit magic," he replied. He remembered a line from a book he once read from an old earth spirit. *"Nobody has ever deflected a shard made of the will of a thousand dragons."*

The two stared at him, Ruby awestruck and even Obsidian a bit surprised.

"You won't believe me when I say this," Obsidian started. "You'll think I'm trying to get on your good side, but I don't think I ever personally disliked you."

Jewelem laughed nervously. "I'd honestly be surprised if you disliked me. Just a feeling I guess."

"Please free this kingdom,' Ruby asked quietly. "Amethyst is awful." She pulled Qwonzie close and rubbed the back of his neck carefully.

Jewelem nodded. He smiled and took flight towards the palace once again. He hovered in the air and heard wingbeats below him.

"Wait," Ruby called softly to him. "What happened to Emeraldite? I-I saw the guards taking him to the torture chamber- is he alive?"

"He's in the dungeons right now," Jewelem said. "I wouldn't say he's alright, but I saved Qwonzie from the same place. When Amethyst is dead, I'll free him and bring him here. Just take care of my brother until- well, until he's ok."

Ruby smiled at him. "I will. If I'm completely honest, I-" she paused. She looked away for a moment, back to Obsidian. The cave of the resistance. "I want to see him again."

"I promise I'll bring him here," Jewelem promised. They shared a smile and Jewelem continued towards the palace. *The plan is still the same. Kill Amethyst, take the throne, free your family and stop the war. Simple. Now I have Crystalexite and perhaps the resistance on my side, I have acquaintances all over the Crystalian Kingdom. If- ONCE I get the throne, I can ask Crystalexite to send a message to the Poseidonite kingdom to ask their queen for an audience. A bit messy and quite political, but it should work.*

Once Jewelem reached the palace, he dove in and landed on the steps again, still wearing his disguise. He thought about it for a moment for the 80th time. *Do I assassinate her or just kill her? And how do I get RiverStone and his group out of the kingdom? I'll worry about that later.*

Jewelem opened the doors and saw Amethyst on her throne, speaking with a guard. She looked up and her bored gaze turned into a vicious glare. She smiled at him. She leaped off her throne and threw the guard aside.

"You have the nerves of my brother coming back here," Amethyst growled. "Not like either of you to announce your arrival though."

"I've come for the throne," Jewelem challenged. "Your reign has caused nothing but suffering and pain to the dragons you're supposed to respect. You are not a queen. You are an idiot with a crown and devices."

Amethyst leaped at him and clawed at his throat. Jewelem leaped to the side and jumped on her back. She slid and threw him off. He spun and slid his back talon the the floor, summoning various sharp crystals at the queen. Amethyst dodged to the side, but they circled around and struck her back. She roared in pain and Jewelem stepped back. She charged towards him and slammed her horns into his chest. He was thrown against a wall and felt like he couldn't breathe for a moment. He coughed and weakly got up.

"You are unfit to fight me, or rule this place," Amethyst hissed. "You *will* die here. I will not allow my nephew to surrender."

Amethyst charged again. Jewelem made a diamond wall between her raised claws and him. He jetted sharp emeralds out at her, stabbing her sides. Jewelem sent the wall flying towards her, slamming her into the ground in the middle of the throne room. He leaped on top of her and dug his claws into her underscales, but she wrapped her strong, impenetrable talons around his throat and pushed him into the wall below the raised platform. Jewelem tried to break free of her powerful grasp. *Ahh, why does she love strangling everyone?* He thought.

"Jewelem!"

Crystalexite? He looked over Amethyst's shoulder to see Crystalexite, Ruby, Obsidian and some unfamiliar dragons behind them standing near the doorway.

He knew they were counting on him. They needed him to kill Amethyst. He was the only dragon who could rightfully kill her, and nobody else was allowed to. Jewelem was the last living relative of King Earthquake, and he could die from Amethyst. He looked up at the platform above him and Amethyst. He manipulated the stone and sent it down on them both. Amethyst roared in pain as the throne came down on her, while Jewelem encased himself in gold. When there was silence he moved the stone and got rid of the gold. He stood up and saw the dead queen lying lifelessly on the floor. He looked down at his bleeding neck and throat.

"Jewelem!" Crystalexite called to him. She came up next to him. He closed his eyes for a second. She put a talon on his back. "Are you alright?"

"I'm fine," he whispered.

"It's over now," she assured him. "You're ok. Breathe"

"Now what do we do?" Obsidian asked. "Ruby, where are you-?"

Ruby darted down the hall to the dungeons, probably to find Emeraldite.

"Topaz, explain to the others what happened," Crystalexite said to someone in the doorway. The various dragons followed Topaz and whispered among each other.

"Jewelem, come with me," Crystalexite said. She put his arm over her back and helped him through the palace. A few minutes later, she'd lead him to some kind of bedroom.

"Are you ok?" She asked again. "Because I don't believe you."

Jewelem laid down on something and closed his eyes. "Thanks," he said to her.

"I feel bad," she said. "You shouldn't have had to do that alone."

"What did you see?" He asked, opening his eyes.

"When I walked in, she had you on a wall," she said. "It was scary, I thought you were dead and we were too late."

He nodded. "I was terrified. I'm not brave or anything. It was just something that I felt had to be done."

"I get that," she replied. "I should eventually tell Queen Crimson and King Cobalt about this."

"Wait- If you're going, are you able to send messages to Poseidonite?"

"Umm, I don't think so, with the whole war going on? I'll try, but no promises," She said nervously.

"Alright," Jewelem said. "I'll tell Legend when I get there."

"I'll let you rest now," Crystalexite said. She smiled and left the room. Jewelem stood up and looked around the room. There was a pile of blankets and pillows near the corner with a vanity made of gold and silver near it. The walls were made of quartz with emerald markings all over it. It wasn't very lit without the window open, but when he pulled the curtains, it opened into the sky. *I thought we were in a cave. This must be an exception. Perhaps a tower of some sort.*

He opened a drawer on the vanity and found some bandages. He wrapped something around his bleeding injuries and saw something on the desk that made him sad.

In a golden frame, there was a painting that was in some places embedded with jewels. There was a young white dragon with pink spots on her. The dragon was a mostly white mix of some sort with blue tendrils. She had rose quartz on her eyes, spots and along her wings. A much taller, more fiery coloured Ariash with orange-yellow scales had a bunch of topaz, rubies and gold along his wings, eyes and scales. Then there was a small little Poseidonite with a strange white flower-cloud thing around her neck that looked a bit like a lion's mane. She might've been one of the prettiest, having layers of sapphires, diamonds and crystals all over her. Next it had a bright navy blue dragon with paler blue underscales and a rainbow frill. He looked the oldest. He had much less ores or crystals on him. Last, it had a black dragon layered with obsidian, black diamonds and purple crystals. He also had bright pink stones throughout his body.

The Ariash was in the middle with his wings over the other four. The black one was in the bottom right corner, the white mix was next to him, the blue sapphire dragon and the navy one were in the other corner. It took a moment for Jewelem to realize who they were. It was Heaven, Earthquake, Oceanic, Firebrazer and E.T. The look E.T and Heaven had while looking at each other made Jewelem sick. Heaven loved him, and he tricked her. Firebrazer loved all of them, but they either died or left. Earthquake was devastated to hear of everything. He wasn't sure how they all got their constellations, but he thought about what he knew.

Firebrazer and E.T were best friends. When Firebrazer met Heaven, they also became friends. Firebrazer just seemed to be friends with everyone. *It seems like they were all friends at a time. Why did E.T truly kill him though? What was the real motive? Why specifically Firebrazer? Was there a bigger picture? Or was it all something traced back to the death of King Nightchaser? Wasn't it the Aolite? How did he trace it to Firebrazer, and if it was the Ariash king, what's his motive? Is it something that happened a long time ago, or recently? There's something tied between Heaven, E.T and Firebrazer. E.T killed him, but why?*

And where did Riverstone come in? Who are Tide and Azure? Who's the boss she was talking about? Are they connected, or does Riverstone just want power?

I know Oceanic is related. She was one of the spirits alongside E.T, Heaven, Firebrazer and King Earthquake. Maybe Riverstone gathered his crew and went after her, helping the Crystalians wipe out the Poseidonite. Why would he wipe out his own clan though?

King Earthquake died when I was one and the same year Legend hatched, he tried to decipher it all. *He was about 34 when he died of the illness. A little while before, Firebrazer was killed by E.T. Oceanic and Heaven were left on the island. Oceanic returned to her home. Was Riverstone with her the entire time? Was she with him when King Earthquake died, or did he leave her after his death? Did Earthquake know about Riverstone and then betray her along the way? Did Oceanic betray him and secretly send Riverstone? Maybe Heaven sent the assassin after Nighrchaser to trigger E.T into killing Firebrazer... but the Eternity prince knew it was Aolite, so why target Ariash? DID he know it was Aolite? It's a common fact, how would he not know? Did he just kill Firebrazer for the fun of it?*

"This is so weird…" he thought aloud. So many questions and so few answers. He had two more days after that one, and even still it was nearing night. Jewelem settled into the pile of blankets and pillows and sighed.

The next morning, Jewelem heard whispering from outside his room. He listened in from behind the closed door.

"Is Irid ready?" A nervous voice asked.

"Who cares?" A voice hissed. "Jewelem will never agree to it."

"Nobody in their right mind would agree to it!" The first voice said. "It's stupid. We should've done something else."

"Irid is pretty stubborn, she probably doesn't even want to do it," the second dragon said.

Suddenly, someone grabbed Jewelem's back.

"hey-!" He started. Three guards came in from the window and caught him. "I don't think you have the authority to do this!"

Jewelem was brought through the halls to the throne room. Qwonzie and Emeraldite were chained and held by guards. Qwonzie still didn't look great, he wasn't conscious yet. A very beautiful dragon with shimmering blue wings and azure-sapphire scales stood there, confused. *Why are so many Crystalians blue?*

Jewelem saw other dragons of the resistance being guarded. A large group of them stood in the doorway and around the corner on the opposite side of the room from him. Guards stood all around them, but didn't directly attack. Crystalexite was among the resistance dragons. Along with Obsidian, Ruby, her little sister, Topaz and surprisingly, Agate. "

"What's going on?!" Emeraldite demanded. "Let my brothers go!"

"Lady Iridescence," a commander said from somewhere. *Oh, Irid, Iridescence. I see,* Jewelem thought. "This is Jewelem."

"He's the prince?" She asked, delighted. *Why are you so excited?*

"Well, he's supposed to be the king now, but we can't really do that," the commander said.

"What?" Jewelem asked.

"Our ally said you work for Poseidonite, so it's not right for you to be king," the commander said. He glared at the prince.

Jewelem froze. *That's fair. But how did he know that?*

Oh, Riverstone thinks he's so smart.

He probably is smart... he said something about a Keystone mirror.

He said his boss looked through the "KeyStone mirror.' Is that the mirror that they use to see past Royal Poseidonite? Then they must know about me and Legend.

"You can't do this!" Emeraldite yelled. The guards held him back. "You can't just get rid of him!"

"Yes, we can," the commander growled, barely glancing at Emeraldite. "We're sending him off with Irid."

"What??" Jewelem asked.

"It's an arranged marriage," the commander yawned. "We did it to your father and mother, Garnet and Gold. They got used to it, you'll be fine."

A guard pulled him up next to Irid.

"Just send him out to her place," the commander whispered to the guard.

"YOU CAN'T DO THIS!" Emeraldite fought against the guards holding him back. He managed to get one of them off of his right side, but the other held him with an iron grip. One of them smashed the back of Emeraldite's head with a strong metal bar, instantly knocking him out. From across the room, Ruby shrieked and tried to push her way through the guards to get to him.

Emeraldite... Jewelem thought sorrowfully.

About 4 guards took Irid and Jewelem back to a place in the Crystalian kingdom. It was clearly a wealthy place. Someplace high up and made of marble. It had a balcony with a lot of pillars, a bunch of windows and looked fancy.

"Thank you!" Irid sang. "Welcome!!"

"Um, hi?" Jewelem said. "What's happening?"

"My dad told me I was getting married. I'm going to have a daughter!"

"What?" Jewelem asked.

"My dad said it was a PRINCE! An actual prince wants to marry ME, can you believe it!?"

"I'm a prince…" Jewelem muttered. He shouldn't have said that.

"Then I guess I'm marrying you!"

The doors were locked it seemed. Everything he wanted to do, find Legend, stop the war, it was all impossible without being either free or the king. It's impossible. He was stuck here, and woke up to being forced to marry whoever this was. His brother was probably out cold for a while and soon would be killed or tortured.

He blinked in confusion and fear. "… what?"

Chapter 12: To Oceans and Bounty

A Tide That Flows With Moonlight, not Rivers.

Legend flew away into the sunrise after she parted with Jewelem. She'd slept one night, and so she had two more days before returning to Jewelem and the others. She swam through the ocean, just simple parts with a bit of coral and fish. *I've got to send Jewelem a message somehow. They probably have messengers somewhere, but will they even send to Crystalians? Hopefully they will.*

Legend was lucky enough to find the deep hole in the ocean floor where she emerged from. She dove down into the cavern and the glowing little fish illuminated the way. It was much more peaceful than she realized the first time. She was so intent on leaving that she didn't realize how pretty the fish were. She soon found the entrance to the Poseidonite kingdom for real. Legend adventured into the enormous cavern and saw the pretty kingdom. Poseidonite dragons were swimming all through the caves, carrying barrels of fish and doing normal stuff. The Poseidonite kingdom was a large cavern made of rich marble, quartz and cavestone houses. Green sea lamps covered a lot of the kingdom to illuminate the mystical place. Even though nothing really suited her preferences, she always knew it was a gorgeous place. *I wonder if dragons would consider it irresponsible to put any colours other than blue in this place. Nobody else has ever done it except for the absolute genius who made green sea lamps.*

She followed the path down to the central cave where the palace was. The Poseidonite castle was never really interesting to Legend. She always thought it was a prison. She felt embarrassed by her past self. Then again, it wasn't even one moon cycle ago. She felt like an older dragon looking at a stubborn little whelp. But now she was able to look at it in a new light. Seeing the palace from the outside and knowing it wasn't there to keep her inside, Legend was happier with it. It was a tall temple-like building with a bunch of narrow windows and a couple balconies. The towers were sharp and tall, and the doors sat at the foot of the dazzling palace. She went into the doors and found the throne room. Legend never explored the palace, as she rarely left her room. Inside, it was beautiful. The main room had balconies around the edges and it was a sapphire crystal ballroom. A chandelier made of diamonds hung from the ceiling over a blue glass floor showing water underneath. Cleaners and guards went throughout the palace and the ballroom doing various tasks. Legend wasn't about to tell anyone to do anything for her; she wasn't that kind of dragon. They all seemed happy with their jobs. *I may have had a bad time here, but these dragons are proud to work for their queen.*

W-which is me. I think.

A circular pool in the middle of the throne room had twinkling lights below it. She flew off the baloney and looked down into it, with some of the other dragons watching her curiously with others minding their own business.

"Are you new to the palace?" One of them asked.

"Um- y-yes, I am," Legend said politely.

The dragon smiled. "That's the way to another part of the palace," she said. "I'm not sure what it's called, but you can investigate it." She smiled and went back to work. Legend looked back to the pool and dove down into it. *Should I have been worried she might've been lying and I could've looked like a fool? That wouldn't have been good for me. I'd announce that I'm queen and they would say "isn't that the dragon who tried to swim down the fountain?"*

The pool led to an entirely different place than what she'd expected. Legend found herself in another large room, but this one had 4 waterfalls coming through each wall, and the walls were made of light brown stone. The floors were still crystal, as was the ceiling. It was also empty. The pool waterfall was long, straight and clear with a small pool at the bottom.

Legend stepped out of it and marvelled at the room. Although the room didn't have a clear purpose, it was still pretty.

"It's beautiful, isn't it?"

Legend heard the voice and replied before she even saw them. "I know- wait, what?" She turned to find the dragon, but couldn't see him. She jumped as a dragon materialized out of nothing beside her. He was a tall, older Poseidonite with pretty sky blue scales. He had a long, graceful tail and frill that just seemed unnatural. He didn't look 100% like a normal Poseidonite.

"Who are you and where did you come from?" Legend asked, tilting her head.

"My name is Syntha," he replied with a nod. "You're Princess Legend, correct?" She nodded.

"Right," Legend said back. "What's this room for?"

"You know, magic. This is going to be super random, but wanna see something kinda cool?" Syntha asked. He didn't wait for an answer. He took a step, and where his talon landed, the floor seemed to ripple like a large lake. In his other talon, a long sapphire spear-like thing appeared and he touched the floor with it. Right where the sapphire touched the ground, it turned the floor into a much darker colour, almost the colour of the night sky. He slowly lifted his sapphire object and the night-mark on the floor covered the entire room, even the stone walls. The waterfalls started *glowing* with teal water and stars appeared all over the room. When it was finished, a nebula covered the ceiling with shooting stars covering all of it. A gorgeous sky was summoned by Syntha's own talons right there, in front of her.

He wasn't normal. She knew what he was.

"You're a past water spirit, aren't you?" She asked, awestruck. He smiled

"You could say that," he replied. "You'll notice that my powers don't really suit the other's though."

"Others?" Legend squeaked. "You're saying the other past water spirits can do that?"

"They're special alright," he said slowly. "But they're more knowledgeable and less mystical. I'm the main one who makes all this." He waved his claws around at the enchanting sky. "Oceanic is always asking about you."

Legend was surprised to hear her mother's name."My mother? You talk to her?"

Syntha sighed. "She's interesting. Oceanic is trying to get back here. I'm just a scout for her. She's in the spirit realm, but she's coming back somehow. She said she has a plan, but I don't exactly believe that."

"So, what did you come to me for?" Legend asked. "Did you just want to show your cool powers?"

"Oceanic told me to answer your questions about ruling a kingdom," Syntha laughed. "Not sure what she thinks I know about that, but Queen's orders."

"I have no idea how to stop a war," she started. "I also don't know how to ask for anything, demand anything, imprison anyone without feeling bad for them or solving problems."

"I know how to start a war," He offered. "All it takes is a bit of murder and some trespassing."

"I have to stop the Crystalian Poseidonite war," she clarified.

"Crystalians… Poseidonite…" he mumbled. "Who's their king now?"

"My best friend, Jewelem," Legend replied. "He's my best most amazing friend in the world so far."

"That could make it easy," Syntha said with his eyes lighting up. He summoned a map of Anima and zoomed in on the Poseidonite territory. "If King Jewelem bans the Calx Nation from this Area for a while like cancelling Aqua Tribe's routes and Veo's scouting, Poseidonite can rule that area. But if you're trying to STOP the war and not WIN it, then that's a different story. If you command your dragons to stop killing each other and he does the same, that should cool the heat for a bit. The clans won't be at peace, they'll just be standing there with their weapons raised. It would take something to unite them. Oceanic told me of this eternity prince fellow, no? Forming an alliance could perhaps work, but that's also risky. I say just call off all kinds of attacks or ambushes and tell King Jewelem to do the same. The best way to communicate would be to either meet up somewhere with high councils or send trusted messengers."

Legend was shocked. "Have you stopped a war before?" She asked.

"No, but I've seen what causes one," he replied with a laugh. "Just don't do that and it should be ok."

"Well, I have to get back to do some stuff, so you should probably leave before someone sees you," Legend said to him.

Syntha rubbed his neck nervously. "Yeah, I wouldn't want my mother finding out I'm here. She wouldn't be happy. Bye." Syntha disappeared into the water and the nebula sky vanished along with him.

He *was pleasant,* Legend thought. *But he's a past water spirit, how would his mother find him? The spirit before my mother- who were they? Even still, how old would Syntha's mother be? Could've been a joke, I can't tell.*

Legend explored the palace a bit and was rather tired by the end. She hadn't had much food that day other than some fish she'd found outside the sea gardens. Legend went to find the kitchens and instead found her mother's old bedroom. The crystal vanity was still there along with the moss blankets and the huge stained glass window. *Why would that have been moved or changed though?*

She'd wasn't often in her mother's room, but she found something on her vanity that surprised her.

A little sapphire-coloured dragon made of crystals sat on the corner of her desk. It looked like Jewelem but older and the underscales were darker blue. *King Earthquake,* she realized. Inside the top drawer, there was an old letter buried beneath documents and old jewellery. Legend read it carefully.

"*Dear Oceanic.*

It's almost been a year since everyone left. Heaven is broken from FireBrazer's death and E.T is in prison. I know we both have responsibilities, but I need help. I've been told I'm dying of a strange illness and I'm all alone. I don't know how you feel about Zoka, but I need you to know that I forgive you… In fact, I wasn't ever really upset. It was her decision, and I know you didn't want to. I'm the earth spirit, strong and supposedly indestructible. But I want to confess. I've been lonely for so long. I sent a message to Firebrazer before he died. I told him I was sorry and I wanted to help him. He couldn't come to me in time and was killed. I arrived at the Fire Island to see him die, shortly before you arrived. Heaven and I made it there first, too late. I sent something to Heaven and told her I hope she's well and reminded her that she can be independent of his choices. She wasn't able to get to me before E.T had her with him. She's not coming back. I can barely breathe and it hurts so bad. Now I'm sending something to you. I have a lot to say, and not much time to write. I just want to tell you that I'm sorry, and that I'm awfully guilty about what I put you through. It was awful, and you shouldn't have had to bear that burden alone. If you need something, anything, in the next 2 days, please come to me. Even if you don't need anything, just send me a message, and I'll see it in the spirit realm.

I'm sorry for everything. I tried, but I know that's not good enough. I couldn't save Firebrazer, or stop E.T, or help Heaven and I couldn't help you. I can't do anything but this now. All I'm truly asking is that you send me some kind of letter. I want to die knowing how you feel about me.

Goodbye, Oceanic."

Legend read it over a bunch of times. She was awfully devastated to hear of King Earthquake's tragedy. All he wanted was someone to talk to in his dying moments. *I'll never forgive Oceanic if she didn't send him something back.* Legend dug through the vanity and found a secret compartment in the side. She opened it and unrolled a rolled up paper tied in a blue ribbon. She opened it and read it.

"Dear Earthquake.

I am truly devastated for you. Heaven is lost, E.T is gone, Firebrazer has indeed died and I am at fault for leaving you. I should've stayed to give you someone, anyone for comfort. You didn't deserve that and I'm truly sorry. You said in your last moments, you wanted to know how I felt. I want you to know that I'm ok. I'm feeling

alright. It wasn't a burden I carried alone. It was the guilt, the anger of
E.T's sudden betrayal. I was angry, and I said things I shouldn't have
said. I didn't know that would cut you deeply, and I wish I could be
there to apologize. I was blinded by another grief I suffered recently…
But I can't, and this is what I can do. I'm sorry, my friend.

If any other earth spirit finds this, please tell Earthquake this.
Please let him know that he can rest in peace."

There were some other words crossed out. It seemed the two
were super close before she left.

What did he put her through? What kind of pain was she in
before she left? Why did she leave him? Was it to go back to Riverstone
before his departure? Or was it to rule the Poseidonite kingdom? Maybe
both? Why didn't she send the message if it's still here? *If he died 16*
years ago, that's the year I hatched. That means Riverstone was still
with her because he left when I hatched. King Earthquake died 16 years
ago at age 34, Riverstone left 16 years ago, and Oceanic is currently
46, that means Oceanic was alone for a while. If she left before I
hatched, that is. I bet Earthquake was sad for Oceanic as Riverstone
left her. She must've forgotten to send this message, or thought he
wouldn't accept her apology. What was the 'grief that blinded her'
though? Was it losing Riverstone? That happened a full year before
King Earthquake died. She wouldn't have felt devastating grief over her
awful husband leaving, would she? And would it have been so bad that
she would've forgotten about her dying friend who stayed with her
through everything? When did Firebrazer die though? It must've been
before Oceanic's husband left if that's the grief. She left after Firebrazer
died, knowing E.T and Heaven were gone. But in-between Heaven and
E.T's disappearance together, she left then. Why didn't she stay with
Earthquake? Unless there was something else that pulled her back.

So E.T killed Firebrazer, then Oceanic and Earthquake went back to the island while Heaven went back to the Aolite. Soon she disappeared with E.T. Oceanic returned to the Posiedonite and then Earthquake died days later alone in his clan. Somewhere in between Firebrazer's death and Oceanic's return, Riverstone left. The timeline is so confusing...

I haven't announced myself as the queen yet. I should try to find somewhere with more information.

The secret compartment also had another scroll. It was a map. It had rough sketches of a place Legend hadn't ever seen before. It was a place with many waterfalls and fish. Honestly a nice place, but Legend wondered what her mother had hidden there that was so important. She looked at the text on the back of the map.

"I told my mother I wanted to see magic when I was younger. She never showed me. She was always against the idea of having a magic princess. Riverstone showed me these caves. Here's a map to and around them.

If only Firebrazer, Heaven and Earthquake could see them."

Legend pitied her mother's loneliness at the end. *Those caves probably have clues of the past. Should I first try the Diamond Mirror?*

Legend went back to the throne room and behind the throne to the Sapphire Cove where the Diamond Mirror sat. There wasn't any water in that cave other than the pools around the mirror. It all went through the drain in the hallway to get there. Through its glass, anyone could see any royal Poseidonite or Crystalian from the past 100 years. She searched for Oceanic 16 years ago, when Earthquake died.

"Firebrazer!" A young Aolite called. She flapped towards the Fire Island quickly. A small Poseidonite with a white thing around her neck followed next to her. Oceanic?

"Is he here?" Earthquake called, scanning the volcanic plains. "I don't see him."

"There!!" Heaven pointed to a place on the island where there was a large crater and two dragons, one black and another orange. The three spirits dived towards the fight to help him. Oceanic watched in fury as E.T dug his claws into Firebrazer's scales as the Ariash yelped in pain. She pulled water from the nearby ocean to attack her former Shadowling friend. He noticed them and shot powerful black energy through Firebrazer's chest.

"NO!!" Heaven screamed and ran to Firebrazer's side. The Ariash fell to his smaller form and shivered in agony. Heaven ran up to him and shook his shoulder, but Oceanic was focused on the Shadowling.

E.T pretended to feel weak and tired from the fight, but Oceanic secretly knew he was fine, and it took no effort to beat the Ariash king.

Legend stopped the mirror, as she'd seen all she needed to see. *So,* she thought. *The three spirits tried to save Firebrazer before his death, but he was impaled and died in Heaven's arms. That's awful. Oceanic didn't have her diamond ring on there. That meant that Riverstone was gone.* But that still didn't explain the timeline. She had to find someone who was there and alive the whole time. *If only King Earthquake or Firebrazer were here. I could check for Riverstone, but I have no idea when he was planning his ideas.*

"But Firebrazer is still alive," she suddenly remembered. She knew the whole time, but got wrapped up in the idea of his death. Legend felt embarrassed that the dragon she was reading into the death of she had been talking to a couple days ago. But she wasn't able to talk to Firebrazer from there. She didn't have time to go back anyway. Were there any other dragons involved?

272

"Firebrazer, Earthquake, some Aolite royals, probably Riverstone himself and perhaps some of Oceanic's friends," She said to herself.

Follow the map and find someone there, she thought. Good plan.

It took Legend many long hours of searching to find out what the map meant. She thought it was a location, and that she had to find it in the ocean somewhere. So she'd searched for many MANY hours before realizing.

"I don't think this map leads anywhere," Legend said to herself as she wandered the palace halls. "I *really* think my mother was delusional when she wrote this."

Then she looked at the wall.

"You've got to be kidding me." *So it's a painting, very clever of you, mother.*

It wasn't a map. It was a giant coral painting that frankly wasn't very detailed and worn out as though it were from the Storm Ages. It was a drawing of a huge coral block, and the awful sketch matched the painting on the wall in the hallways.

And when Legend moved the painting. What do you know, a secret hallway behind the mysterious painting. Legend hopped into the tunnel and closed it behind her carefully. Still a nice painting, but a nicer map- well, a map drawn much worse, but more valuable to her.

Through the tunnel, she saw many little peep-holes through the walls into the palace. Legend was able to see all through the underwater palace around the secret tunnel. It was small, but she was able to stand up if she ducked. It didn't seem like something her mother would allow. In fact, Legend couldn't imagine her mother sneaking off into the palace walls to go to a secret place. She followed the tunnels to a light at the end where it opened into the ocean. There was light shining from above, but they were in a cave. *How did my mother make light so far down?*

The open area was a much brighter, sunnier place than the other parts of the ocean. Legend wandered around, trying to find what her mother had put there. A few large rocky stage-like platforms sat near the sides of the place, along with dragon-made carvings all over them. A few caves had nicely shaped tunnels, and Legend went into one of them curiously.

"Hello?" She called in Axteian. She heard a bit of shuffling from down the tunnel, but there was a soft voice behind her.

"You're... Not Oceanic, are you?"

Legend turned to see a Poseidonite-but-not behind her. She looked very young, maybe Silver's age, and had cheerful teal scales. The little whelp had a bright magenta frill and wings, but didn't have the tendrils or anything of a Poseidonite. *If she's not a Poseidonite, she must be a mix to be underwater...*

Right?

"Where did you come from?" Legend asked.

"My name is Koko," she replied. Koko was kind of hovering in the water behind Legend. Koko tilted her head at Legend. "I'm from the Condricala."

"Condricala- What's that?"

That definitely shocked Koko. "... You're *definitely* not Oceanic, are you?"

"No, I'm her daughter, Legend," she replied. "I followed my mother's map here, but I didn't think I'd find a whelp. No offence, of course."

"You must be looking for answers," Koko said as though she'd just figured something out, her eyes widening a little. "You must come to the Condricala Clan, then."

"Condricala *clan?*" Legend gasped. "There's an entire CLAN?!"

"Of course," Koko said like she was surprised Legend didn't know. "They live on underwater islands to hide from the Araish, Aolite and Shadowling war. It became pretty chaotic."

"Wow," Legend said as she thought about that. "That's incredible." an entire clan being able to easily hide from a war.

Koko beamed with pride for her clan. "I'll show you, Legend." Koko turned and swam down behind the stage rocks, and Legend followed. Legend followed the whelp into a cavern below the flat stones where the ocean was slightly less cheery, but the greenery and fish were brighter and more colourful. Through the cavern was a large tunnel going through the ocean and perhaps under some island.

Koko eventually brought them up and into a huge open area. The entrance was more regal, a bluestone archway into a gorgeous place. It was a huge sapphire square platform with water on the sides in a cinnamon brown stone cave. It wasn't filled with water, allowing the two to not speak Axteian. Palm trees were scattered around the place, and sunlight seemed to shine from a bright light in the ceiling. Legend saw fire burning inside a large crystal, shining onto the many plants and flowers around the magnificent sight. It was almost exactly like the large room she met Syntha in, but this one had more detail and seemed a bit more populated.

"The Condricala Ocean Kingdom," Koko said, clearly still blown away by the place.

"It's beautiful," Legend agreed. "Do they all live here?"

"Most of them live on islands," Koko clarified. "They live on small tropical islands, usually outside the Storm Barrier on the north-East side to avoid spirits crossing over."

"The Storm barrier?" Legend asked. "Like, *outside* of it? There's only one island out there, the spirit island."

Koko smiled and shook her head. "Nope, there are Condricala islands as well."

Legend looked back to the platform. A glass part in the floor showed a view into the ocean, but on the far wall from the entrance, there was a stained glass picture against an ocean through the window. The image was a large, lime green dragon with teal hair hovering above the oceans with swirling water around her. She had two teal braids and large glowing mint green eyes.

"Who is that?" Legend asked, astonished.

"Azela Nexo Flora," Koko smiled. "Goddess of Bounty. The first Condricala to become a god. She used to be a powerful earth spirit protector. There's a story that said Azela's lixora was made of sunlight reflected off of her dear oceans."

"Incredible," Legend said. A lixora is a symbol of a god's power. It can be placed into an object or just the default as a crystal ball. "My mother had a map leading here. Do you know what she might've been looking for?"

"No, what's the situation right now?" Koko asked. Legend told Koko what she knew; King Riverstone and Queen Oceanic got together and had 1 egg. When they found out the whelp had magic, they fought, and Riverstone left and vanished. During their fights before he left, Oceanic's friend, Earthquake, had died. She went into detail about Oceanic and Earthquake's relationship and what happened with Heaven and Firebrazer as well.

"That would explain why King Imniomni had an audience with her every so often," Koko discovered. "She must've had a lot going on, but there was a tragedy that he never told anyone about. It was super suspicious though."

"I take it King Imniom-something is the Condricala ruler," Legend said.

Koko giggled. "so… what's your plan then?" Koko asked, motioning for Legend to follow her.

"Well, I have to leave tomorrow. Really important." Legend followed Koko through the cavern. Legend tried to explain everything as best as could, but it was a lot for Koko to understand.

Am I able to tell Koko that I'm a water spirit? Legend thought. *What if she turns me over to the Condricala clan? Would she do that?*

"So if Oceanic has a map coming here, then there's something she either wants, or something she can't lose," Koko said. Koko had brought Legend to a small cave in the underwater kingdom. It was a pleasant place to live with a few rooms and glowing sea lights. Moss carpets covered the floor and coral rocks lined parts of the walls.

"Maybe she was looking for the Condricala Clan?" Legend thought out loud. "Maybe she never found it, or they never found her."

"Oceanic was a water spirit, right?" Koko asked.

"I think so." Legend played with her claws. "There was a chance she was just a refined fish, but that's none of my business."

Koko thought about that. She had a frustrated look as if she was piecing something together. She nodded like she figured something out. "She was looking for Azela."

"You mean the goddess?" Legend asked. "I don't mean to be disrespectful, but isn't she…?"

"She's a past earth spirit," Koko told her. "Although she's a god, she never really left her kingdom. You should be able to connect with her from the shrines. Condricala are water element dragons, but Azela is earth which means she connects with memories instead of knowledge like water dragons."

"Not going to ask what shrines are, just where can I find them?" Legend asked, now curious.

"The closest one is nearby, I'll show you." Legend followed Koko again through the village. She noticed a lot of other caves around, many looking like Koko's. Legend also wondered where Koko's parents were. Did she live alone? Was the Condricala clan so safe that a lone whelp could survive alone? *Maybe this place is so safe that her parents are always working?* She wanted to ask, but it would be rude and she was too shy. Koko went into some kind of smaller cavern, and Legend was *slightly* hesitant to follow her. Inside, the cave was mostly dark except for the bioluminescent pearls that lined the walls and the glow-in-the-dark stones all over the ceiling. A winding path leads to a larger area, still small, with a tiny island in the middle. The path had gone up, and so the area wasn't filled with water. Lily pads sat around the tiny island, the little pond filled with simmering rock from the lights.

"Here we are," Koko said as she arrived at the top. "This is Azela's shrine."

On the island, Legend saw a stone statue of a dragon on a pedestal platform. It was slightly taller than her, and had the same shape and eyes as Azela Nexo Flora.

"Great!' Legend exclaimed. "Now... how do I use it?"

Koko shrugged. "I guess I'll leave you to it." Before Legend could say or protest anything, Koko was gone. She looked back to the statue. Azela didn't magically appear, so she tried a different, more *social* approach. "Umm, Azela? Hello? I can call you Nexo, or Flora, whichever you-"

"Azela is ok for me."

A larger lime green dragon appeared on top of the statue, looking down at Legend. She was the striking image of the god, Legend knew it was her. Although this one had slightly paler and slightly translucent scales, as if she was a ghost. Little white dots flew off of her body as she moved.

"Hi Azela!" Legend greeted. *Oh wait, she's a god, I should bow, right?* Legend bowed her head to the mysterious dragon, and heard a small laugh.

"I heard that someone named Oceanic was looking for me," Azela said. "Are you Oceanic?"

Why in Abyss's name does everyone think I'm my mother? "No, I'm Legend, her daughter. Oceanic had a map here, so I followed it and met Koko."

"*Oohhhh,* Koko," Azela said. Legend noticed that the god had a childlike memory, a cheerful manor and a warm aura around her at all times. "I remember her. She used to come to my shrine and ask that I heal her family." She looked away sadly. Her head then snapped up and she stepped off the statue.

"So, did my mother ever come find you?" Legend asked curiously.

"Mmm, Oceanic, I think so," Azela thought out loud. "She used to ask me for something, but I can't really remember. It had something to do with Crystalians, a sickness and a lot of royalty. Oh, right! There was also a prince… and a king- a couple kings, actually.. I think I remember! She came and asked for me to heal a sickness in a Crystalian, and save some kind of prince, and then find another king." Azela nodded confidently, clearly proud with her answer.

"She must've asked you to heal King Earthquake, find King Riverstone, and… who's the prince?" Legend reasoned. "She wouldn't ask to save the Eternity Prince, would she?"

"Wait, what are you asking?" Azela asked cluelessly. She summoned and peeled a ghost-banana, something Legend immediately felt jealous of. "Should I take you into my realm?"

"Uh, what?" The water around them swirled and rose about them until Legend couldn't see the cave anymore. Azela stood there so calmly and smiled at Legend's shocked face. The water fell and vanished, showing a vibrant green forest. Legend heard birds chirping around them and some water flowing from a nearby stream. Flowers and fruits grew on everything, low hanging vines held colourful orchids, and it was overall a pleasant sight. Azela claimed onto a tree of some sort, motioning for Legend to follow her. She and Azela flew and climbed up the tree and into a gorgeous treehouse. Nicely coloured oak wood held together with wooden nails and baskets of fruit around the room they were in. It was like a treehouse palace.

"I made this place for me to live in," Azela said, brighting Legend onto the large balcony.

"This is *incredible*," Legend said, awestruck. "Why is the sky purple?"

"I'm not allowed to bring dragons here," Azela laughed nervously. "But this is like.. a half god realm? You're a spirit, so I can tell Howler, Verii and Wystora that I didn't know anything."

Legend's head snapped up. "You're kidding," she accused. "You can't talk to Howler." *Tri-God of Time, Death and wishes. Eternal overseer of the stars, the original summoner of the Dark Element, Master of.. What title was it again?*

"You're right, he'd never listen to me," Azela laughed. "Anyway, what is it you were saying? Something about royalty and such?"

"Do you know of someone called the Eternity Prince?" Legend asked. She was disappointed when Azela shook her head and blinked curiously.

"My mother had a map here, and she was looking for you," she replied. "I'm just wondering if she ever tried to find you, or if she said anything to your shine."

"I do remember something she left here." Azela pulled something off of a desk in the treehouse. "She left this, and I took a phantom of it. T-That means I took it, and left a physical copy, but I have one for myself as well."

"Thanks, Azela," Legend replied. The god smiled and took a step back. She faded into lime wisps of twinkling lights and flew into the forest. Legend read over the note.

"*Azela Nexo Flora.*

I am Queen Oceanic, the current leader of the neighbouring clan, the Poseidonite. It has come to my attention that you, a god, are powerful and omnipresent to your clan. A great tragedy has befallen our clan, for I personally have suffered 3 losses in the past 4 years. King Riverstone has recently left the kingdom, outlawed. A dear friend, King Earthquake, has passed away due to illness. The last will remain silent. I have come in need of answers. I must know if Earthquake can forgive me, if Heaven will be safe, and what to do next. My daughter hatched a few years ago, and I fear for her safety. I don't wish to ruin her by keeping her in the palace at all times; thus I wish to end the war with haste to allow a safe surface for my daughter. Zoka's death is tragic, and I will always regret winning the duel. But I couldn't leave my whelps without a family. Earthquake died, my daughter hatched and my husband is gone, I already lost 2 of my family, I cannot allow myself to lose my daughter as well. I am certain Earthquake died hating me. He knows of my losses and has sent me his condolences, I only wish to have sent him more.

— Queen Oceanic."

Legend read over the part about Oceanic's daughter. *Her.* She just wanted to keep her daughter safe. She just wanted to keep Legend safe from Riverstone and the Crystalians and the rest of the world. It wasn't fair that Oceanic and her friends had to suffer so much. Despite all that, she didn't learn too much from that, but she definitely didn't know of the *losses.* Who did she lose that 'remained silent?' *Time to find Jewelem,* she told herself. She'd forgot to mention to him that they'd meet earlier on the third day due to the long flight, but she'd go there and wait for him until they returned. She found a strange looking terminal type thing and when she touched it, she reappeared in the cavern where she'd left. Koko wasn't there, but Legend found her outside the tunnel. They parted ways and Legend quickly sped to the island. She wasn't sure which one it was, but she darted out of the Condricala cave, into the open ocean and onto the sky. She went back the way she came the first time and found the right place.

"Jewelem?" She called. But nobody was there. She waited for a few minutes.

Then a few hours.

Night came, and he wasn't there.

He's not coming, is he? She realized with a pit in her stomach. The next morning, he wasn't there. *Silver would be there by now.* Legend thought for a long, long moment. Should she go to find him, or should she stay there and wait? She glared at the Northern Earth Island across the ocean, realizing where she should go.

I have to go get him.

Chapter 13: Flaming Farewell

A Fire Burning at Nothing but Ashes

Stupid, stupid idiots. Across the open sky, Meteor had her eyes set on the Fire Island. She had a plan. She'd go in, kill Magma, kill the Eternity Prince, kill Volcanic, kill EVERYONE WHO STOOD IN HER WAY, and maybe send an entire tsunami over to destroy a few things. That wasn't evil, was it? It wasn't evil if they were *all* evil, right? Meteor beat her wings to soar higher into the air and circle the island, watching it closely. It hadn't taken her a long time to get there. She used Firebrazer's constellation to increase her wing speed, allowing her to get there in under two hours. *Do I just become huge and then dive into the kingdom demanding I fight Magma, or do I make them all feel terrified and charge in from the volcanic plains? Charging in makes them feel intimidated, giving Magma more time to prepare, making a better fight. But going in from the sky lets me see her stupid face right as I get there!* She would've charged right in right there if she didn't see something strange in the plains first. Instead of going in the middle of the kingdom, she turned and flew up a bit higher before descending right onto the volcanic plains.

When she thumped onto the rocky ground, Meteor saw what she was looking at before. In the middle of a large crater, there was a stick stabbed into the ground. A sign on it read a message;

King Firebrazer. Died at the talon of the Eternity Prince. Let this be a warning.

Meteor read it over a few times. She was half expecting Firebrazer to materialize out of the air next to her.

And he did.

"What happened that day?" She asked. "I was wondering why you didn't stop me from going after him too much. You told me not to; but you never tried too hard."

"I trusted him," Firebrazer muttered, looking to the ground. "He was my best and only friend, other than Heaven. Me and Earthquake were close as well, but he was friends with Oceanic. The five of us were all together though. When he did this, I felt so awful for the others, having to abandon E.T, and being split up. They didn't know it was my first life, and they probably think I'm dead." He let out a light sigh and could barely stand to look at the sign. Part of Meteor hoped he just set it on fire and helped her fight the Ariash. But he didn't do that.

"Meteor, you don't need revenge," he said in an almost desperate voice. "You don't need to do this to the Araish. The Ariash can't continue like this for much longer, and if you get rid of them, they'll just hate fire spirits even more. Please, think of the possibilities, we can fix the clan without-"

"*I DONT CARE!*" Meteor roared. *"You've lived in Ashen forever! They took my brother- They took EVERYTHING away from me! You weren't raised like I was!* Don't pretend that you know how it feels to live here! The Araish are evil!" She paused. *Look at me... I'm going to kill my own family.*

Firebrazer went still for a chilling moment. His wings fell by his side and he stared at her directly, a terrified light in his eyes. Meteor could see an obvious hint of something like surprise.

"I..." he started. "I'm sorry," he said finally, looking away. "I remember my mother died in the Shadowling war. The last thing she said to me was, 'the harm does not stem from one's impurity, just someone else's lack of understanding.' I didn't understand it until I found the other fire spirits."

"The Ariash deserve to fall," Meteor hisses through her teeth. *That probably wasn't the right thing to say. But he should hate that clan. Their war killed his mother, but Ariash parents are awful.*

284

Aren't they?

"Your brother must've been a good dragon," Firebrazer said. She could feel his voice breaking, and she could see small tears in his eyes. "I know how you felt when he died, but the Ariash clan doesn't deserve to be completely wiped out. What about the other dragons like your brother? If any other fire spirit had done this before you, he would be dead, and so would you. What about the other good dragons?"

Meteor had to pause to think about that. *He's right… but there isn't anyone else like Pyro. No other Araish has a heart like his.*

"Nobody else in the world is like Pyro," Meteor said firmly. She looked him in the eyes, staring him down with a glare. *I can't let him stop me from doing this.* "Sorry, Firebrazer." She saw his eyes widen for a moment as she rose to a higher size and flung him aside with her massive claws into the nearby ocean. She turned and sharpened her gaze, charging towards the Ariash kingdom.

When the guard posts came into view, she felt herself smile in a strange way. A way that promised victory in her mother's death. Meteor stepped into the middle of the kingdom, a circle holding a stone statue of their queen in the centre. Meteor swept it aside with her tail. Magma stood on the platform on the volcano, about 3/4 of the way up with a doorway inside. Dragons were watching her now; many, no, all of them. Almost the entire Ariash clan was about to die there. A malicious smile crossed Magma's stupid face, and Meteor knew something was off. *She can't kill me, though,* she thought bitterly. She tried to raise her claws to slash Magma in half, but for some reason, she couldn't move her talon. She looked down and saw black, glowing pink vines and chains rising from the stony ground. They wrapped around her talons, then her legs and up her body until a wave of black smoke filled the area around her. She couldn't see the ugly grey sky anymore, or the Ariash clan, or the ground. It looked as if the world was engulfed in black smoke.

"COME OUT, ETERNITY PRINCE!" She roared. "I KNOW THIS IS YOU!" She wasn't surprised to see two bright pink eyes staring at her from beyond the smoke. Suddenly everything turned dark.

The prince stood in front of her, casually laying down and drinking some kind of fancy-looking drink with a stupid smirk on his face.

"Well that was beautiful," he said, his drink vanishing into black smoke. "Ah, 'Eternity Prince,' is an *outstanding* name I've made for myself. Oh- but do I have to change it to 'Eternity Overseer' when I ascend? HA! Just kidding, Howler wouldn't give me a Lixora." He started listing things off as if he was about to do them right away. "So next I should find Heaven, my daughters should be dying sometime around here, maybe five more minutes… Firebrazer should drown soon, adorable thing can't swim." He chuckled. "As for- oh, no wait, I want to see it." he flicked his tail and a part in the black void opened as some kind of window. Inside, there was a lifeless fire spirit in the ocean. His eyes were closed and he didn't move. Meteor had never hated herself more than she did at that moment.

The prince smiled. "As for you, well you seem a bit occupied right now, but if you're not, I'm sure Gano needs another reason to hate his life. You should do the trick pretty well."

If it weren't for the chains wrapped tightly around her snout, Meteor would've bit his throat off and then set his bleeding body on fire.

He sighed happily. "The smell of another fire spirit. Really, it works wonders for the mind. Try it sometime." He smiled and turned away, fading into smoke. The vines tightened their grip all over her and she roared as loud as she could through them. But she knew there was no escaping the Prince of Eternity then.

One day, her mind growled. *I'm going to tear him apart.*

Chapter 14: Prince

Princess of the Moonbird

It wouldn't have made sense for him to kill Heaven. But it would for Sacrifice, so of course he did. She sighed and looked at the night sky. It was the fifth day, meaning Silver and her friends should be there. But of course not, the two had been delayed.

But here comes Silver, oh dear.

Sacrifice didn't dislike Silver, perhaps only the opposite. She admired her perseverance and dedication to her friends, something Sacrifice never had the time to practice. It was just her overall reckless and overbearing energy. But that was ok.

The ritual circle was glowing. She'd spent the last few days doing nothing but circling the island.

"Sacrifice!" Silver squeaked. "Where are the others? Jewelem and Legend aren't here yet."

Sacrifice shrugged.

"I guess we'll have to do it without them." Silver seemed much less enthusiastic about that. *Silver wants her friends to do this with her,* Sacrifice thought. She enhanced the circle with her power, and Sacrifice stepped back to avoid messing it up. E.T's infamous black smoke swirling in front of them for a moment. The middle of the valley was engulfed in it and soon, the dragon stood in front of them. He was in a regular sized form, just a normal looking smoke-dragon. He looked at them with a murderous glee in his eyes. He looked over Silver's shoulder at the ritual circle and smiled.

"Oh no, sky spirit magic," he sneered. "It's not like I've prepared to fight *every single one of them.*" Sacrifice couldn't think of anything worse than that yawn, and then the wine he had in his talon.

Silver manipulated the ritual circle to fly at the prince, encasing him in white coils. He stared at Silver and Sacrifice, slowly turning the mild frustration on his face back into a smile. "It may take an eternity to return, but as all our favourite dragons say, you haven't seen the last of me. Bye-bye now!" He allowed the magic to take over him and he vanished into a black and white explosion along with purple and blue. Sacrifice threw her wings around Silver to protect her before it went off. She heard crashing and burning for a moment, but she didn't dare look up. When the sound cleared, Sacrifice opened her wings a bit, but Silver must've been injured or knocked out, as she didn't wake up. She put her sister down carefully on the grass and looked around. The prince was gone, and so was the ritual circle. The island would disappear and reform itself for the next spirits coming, or it would stay the same.

Eternity, A voice in her head said. **Even if it takes an *eternity.***

What do you want now? Sacrifice snapped back. *Just want to ruin me and Silver's lives?*

You truly keep giving me reasons as to why your brother was a better serial killer.

He hesitated and the cheeriness vanished, making way for a haunting whisper.

Let me tell you this, princess, the prince hissed. **If you're so smart, you should understand.**

A black note with pink writing appeared in front of her. She already knew what it said, he said it to her directly. But she read it anyway.

"The rise of Fire, be the fall of Eternity,"
"The rise of Sky, be the storm to set them free."
"The rise of Dark, be the eyes to protect the three."
"The rise of Time, be the one to let them see."

Epilogue

Wings of Gentle Blazing Flight

F irebrazer always knew there'd be a reason to bring Final along.

"I'm sorry, there was just a lot of yelling," Final mumbled. "It was really scary, so I just came after you and I didn't..."

"No, it's alright," he said to her with a warm smile. He shivered under the cold wind. Even with his fiery scales, it was freezing on the Frost Island. He had turned off the burning surface of his scales to preserve the icy mountains anyway. "What did you see here again?"

She closed her eyes for a moment. "There's a whelp here. He needs help." She concentrated harder. "He's almost dead, but I can't see any way to save him. He's practically just a mangled corpse by now."

"Do we have any time at all?" he asked. *I can't let a whelp die here, not alone. I'd be there for any whelp in their last moments.*

Dying alone is awful.

Final opened her eyes and sped up, with Firebrazer following her. She hopped around the icy mountains with a grace that Firebrazer slightly envied with him scraping his talons on every ice mound and falling almost every time he walked on ice. By the time they got to their destination, Firebrazer had a lot of scrapes on his shoulders.

However, on the way, he managed to catch a glimpse of some kind of white creature in the snow. He paused to look over at it, and Firebrazer realised it was like a small Ice Furo, an arctic fox maybe. It was so small though, and there weren't any nearby. A closer look made him realize it was a white cat, and it indeed had a collar with an unfamiliar language written on it. Firebrazer looked up ahead and saw Final waiting for him, standing over a snow mound. He scooped up the cat and jumped into the freezing sky. Final was still looking at him, and he knew she wouldn't lose him. He flew up and looked around the frozen wasteland but spotted a flurry of lights in the midst of the storm. A young, white Furo was calling a name of some sort in a foreign language that they spoke.

"Moa!!!" the Furo called. It held a lantern, but even still it was hard to see her. "Moa!!!" Firebrazer landed in front of her and she leaped back at the sight of the large Ariash.

"Are you looking for this?" he asked, hoping she wouldn't be too scared of him. He held out the small, freezing cat in his talon, and the Furo snatched it quickly. A few other Ice Furo came out of the storm into view, staring in awe of him. The Furo right in front of Firebrazer was the smallest. She said something that sounded thankful to him. He nodded and he just stepped back and disappeared into the storm again.

Final was still waiting for him above the snow mound, and must've seen the whole thing.

"Sorry," she said.

"What?" he asked. "I didn't- What do you mean?"

"Oh- You... I know you want a cat." She tilted her head at him.

"Yeah, I know I can't have one though," he replied sadly. He quickly brightened up and pretended to stop thinking about the Ice Furo. "Let's find the whelp here." he knew Final could see his real thoughts, but it didn't matter.

Final nodded and continued on to where they were headed.

She brought him to a cave with a short way inside, and they could see the end.

"Oh my," Final said with wide eyes.

Firebrazer was horrified. A whelp about 2 or 3 years was lying lifelessly in the cave, blood pouring from his eyes, wings and legs. He could easily fit in the palm of Firebrazer's talon.

"My views are saying he's alive," Final said with a curious hint of surprise.

"I hope your views are right," Firebrazer replied, scooping the whelp into his arms. He could barely see his scales through the blood and snow. "But he isn't breathing still, that should be impossible."

"Cloud might know something." Final's scales flickering into CloudScraper for a moment.

It took about 3 hours to get back to Ashen. They didn't stop for anything, even food. Firebrazer carried the whelp the entire way, trying to feel some kind of life beneath the scales. There wasn't a pulse, he didn't move and didn't breathe. It gave him chills.

"There's something off about this one," Cloud said when they got there. She'd been inspecting him for a while, and Firebrazer was super anxious. They cleaned the blood off his scales to reveal a yellow-orange with black underscales and small black spikes on his back. His wings had a yellow and orange mix, and he wore a horribly-wrapped blindfold on his eyes.

"How so?" Firebrazer asked, fiddling with his claws. "Is he alive?"

"He's not dead, but he isn't alive either." Cloud sounded puzzled. "It's like he's-" she paused.

"What?" He asked again.

"It's like he's trapped between two realms," she said, amazed. "I think he might be a spirit that died when he got his constellation. If that's the case, then the moment he died, he got a constellation, but he was also dead at the time. That means he would have the age change that most spirits get when they return to this world. His will probably be random, which will make it really upsetting for a grown dragon to have the mind of a two year old whelp."

"So when he returns, he'll be alive?" Firebrazer's eyes lit up. Cloud nodded.

"He'll be that and so much more."

They both turned to Final. "What?" Cloud asked her. "How do you mean?"

"Because I would recognize this whelp anywhere," she replied, looking at him closely. "He's Meteor's brother."

Firebrazer's head snapped up. *Meteor... I remember her.* He remembered her being super upset and throwing him into the sea. He remember regaining consciousness later that day, trying to find her, only to be told she was taken by the prince. He felt dizzy thinking about that. Final gave Cloud a look and she put her talon on his back.

"I do believe she mentioned having a brother once," Final said, examining the whelp. "She said he died, but I guess she never saw him really die."

"Do we know his name?" Cloud asked. Firebrazer came back from his trance and looked up.

He knew his name. "His name is Prince Pyro."

Universal Energy Disguised as Green Flames

The Extivie clan would burn that night, but Parallel wasn't the real killer. No, no it wasn't his fault, of course. The flames flickered across the green grass and the black trees. He watched the Extivie kingdom burn, but didn't feel any remorse.

That's true, they deceived you, and now they will pay for it, the voice echoed in Parallel's head.

He smiled. *It was deserved, really.* He thought back to him. Parallel's black-green scales reflected the lime fire. He felt like a real spirit. He knew it was coming.

"You know, it's quite tragic, really." The voice replied. *"I'm actually no stranger to a clan's betrayal myself, yes. Dark clans are absolute menaces, it's quite a wonder, hm. Perhaps the Olvin will be more intelligent than its neighbouring brother clans."*

What do you want me to do? Parallel stalked the burning village and breathed in the black smoke. He let the lingering flames continue to climb around the forest, but didn't allow them to creep into the rest of the Dark Isle.

"Find my daughters," the voice said with an ominous glee. *"Twins. Yin and Yang, so to speak. Silver and Sacrifice. Also if you can; find my son. Siya. But I love naming all my whelps with a cruel pattern. Oldest to youngest, Siya, Sal, Skyex, Silver and Sacrifice. You can find and kill all of them except Skyex, she's the only one who isn't a disappointing worm. Then again, with my standards, I don't think even a gifted mage like you would be able to kill Skyex."*

I, too, have never been a fan of whelps, Parallel replied with a smirk. *My brother.*

Siblings are a scam, really.

I will find you below the Palace of Eternity, correct? He thought to the prince.

"*Correct,*" he replied. *"I've waited two years for this, child. Do not disappoint. I'd hate to have to wait another two years for another dragon to come along and want to get some justice."* The vision of a black-smoke dragon tilting his head in power filled his mind. He felt the prince's presence vanish from his body, the empowering feeling gone.

For a brief moment, the feeling of power returned. His talons glowed in bright green, he felt lightning in his chest. *About time,* he thought with a smile. A constellation opened in his claws, green squares floating before him. He turned his head north of where he was. He couldn't see most of it from behind and below the trees, but above the close horizon, he could see the top of it, spiralling black towers against a purple dome around the entire thing. Red and black rose vines covering the castle far away. He directed his attention and set towards it. To the Palace of Eternity.

Spring Waters in a Lake Filled with Flowers

The Shadowlings seemed to push the little whelp around, which was upsetting. *Am I a stalker?* Teal wondered. *No, stalkers like to stalk dragons for information. I'm just…* watching *a dragon for information.*

But I'm also going to save them, so I'm not the bad guy. A small plateau on the Northern Earth Island above the coast lined with trees, bushes and flowers made a nice view of the ocean. But the Shadowlings decided that a nice view and a tranquil river stream was a nice place to make their ridiculous campsite. *Also; right next to the Stone Furo? I mean, come on, they would tear these Shadowlings apart if they knew about them.* Teal saw the Shadowlings shove a young whelp, not too young as he looked about 14. *I'm not good with numbers, but I'm about three times his age. I'm 43, right? I think that's right. He looks Poseidonite. They age like, 4 times slower than other dragons, they all look naturally look young. I've been mistaken for a 21 year old, so I think it's believable that he'd be 14.* He fell onto the ground and they growled something behind him. He had a lot of bruises, something Teal wasn't happy with. She saw scales that looked kind of like hers, bright turquoise with a paler frill and wings. The Shadowlings just looked like they always had, with concerning smoke around their body and ominous pink lightning. Chains wrapped the other Poseidonite's limbs, but he could still move. The Shadowlings returned to their tents nearby, giving Teal a chance to talk to the whelp.

She got out of her hiding spot in the bushes and looked closely at him. He had two eye colours, bright hazel and a turquoise. Then he closed his eyes and he looked awfully upset, kind of like a tragic fox but blue. She lightly brushed his neck and he flinched, his eyes opening and he reeled back.

"Who are you?" He asked, panicked. "Where did you come from?"

She smiled in the warmest way she could. "My name is Teal, I was watching from the bushes. I-I do that a lot, surprisingly."

He stared at her with wide, curious and shocked eyes, but didn't make eye contact almost at all. He looked a bit scared. "I'm Pond," he said.

"Want to get out of here, or are these dragons your friends of some sorts?"

"Yes!" He gasped. "I mean... If you can do-." Before he could completely finish his sentence, she laid her talon on his chains and they shattered into a few pieces. Pond was awestruck by the magic as Teal did the same to his shackles.

"Incredible," he whispered.

Teal giggled. "My father was a mage and I learned a few things from him."

Teal brought Pond to the top of the plateau where her home was. She opened a leafy blanket covering a secret cave in the ground. A cave hidden by a moss blanket below ground with a skylight and moss carpets. Sunlight fell through the moss covering, but it was nearly impossible to see it from the top. Water pools sat around the cave and glowing stones hung from vines across the walls.

"So are you alright?" She asked him. From a wooden drawer she pulled out a few bandages.

"I'm fine, thanks," Pond replied. He sat down in a corner of the cave, the sunlight not reaching his face. "I'm surprised you're able to live peacefully here on the Northern Earth Island. I thought the Crystalians would've found you by now, or at last the Stone Furo."

"I had to hide my home so they didn't find me," Teal replied. She looked up at the skylight. "Can I just ask.. where are your parents?"

"I never knew them, I think." Pond looked to the ground. "My earliest memories are of the Shadowlings."

"I don't remember too much of my mother either, just my father's magic," Teal replied. *It's tragic, he didn't deserve those Shadowlings. What did they want from him anyway? I'm old enough to be this dragon's parent, maybe he could live with me?*

"You could always stay here," she offered. "I live mostly alone except for the sweet little birds outside." She gave Pond a cheerful smile.

He looked away, obviously trying to hide his interest. "If it isn't too much trouble…" he looked back at her with wet eyes. "I think I could stay here with you, Teal."

Sweet Crystal Purity Layered in Rose

The Crystalian resistance tunnels were still full, even after two years. The commanders took over, and the resistance was banished.

The cold, wet ground under Ruby's talons and the occasional scrape from the hard rocks already made her uncomfortable enough. But the ever-growing uneasiness of her throat and stomach combined with the current circumstances and King Cobalt ahead of her made her super scared. The cart she was pulling wasn't too heavy, but she was a very weak dragon.

King Cobalt called out another command, but she couldn't hear him from behind the other dragons. They travelled through the tunnels towards the Ox tribe, and nobody dared to turn back. Ruby glanced to the right. Beside her, Emeraldite carried her unconscious older sister, Kalista. He looked just as tired as she was. Kalista had been found outside the kingdom, clearly injured, but nobody was sure what hurt her.

"Are you alright?" Ruby asked him, offering to help him.

"I'm fine," he replied.

"We're almost there," she assured him. "I can take Kalista if you want."

Emeraldite shook his head. "It's fine."

Her younger sister hugged onto her side, holding Ruby's leg tightly. Ruby scooped her up and sighed.

Just around the tunnel was the main camp. A large area had been cleared out, just a big open space. The refugees started setting up their place there. Tents and fires were put up along with medical tables and supplies being opened. Ruby, Kalista and Emeraldite took the crates out of her cart in a corner, not wanting to be in the middle. Her little sister curled herself into the cart and drifted into sleep. Emeraldite placed Kalista in Ruby's tent before coming up to her side.

"I'm jealous that she can sleep so peacefully in this scenario," Ruby whispered.

Emeraldite brushed her wing. "You can rest if you want," he told her. "I can take your sisters." There was some commotion down the tunnels that lead to the Royalty tribe. Emeraldite drew his sword from the cart swiftly, prepared to fight. *I don't want you to have to fight for me,* Ruby thought with guilt. *But I don't want to fight... I don't want you to get hurt.*

Everyone was relieved to see who it was. "Crystalexite?" King Cobalt asked the scrambling messenger.

"The commanders said that a new queen is coming- or another living royal!" She exclaimed. Ruby and Emeraldite exchanged a look. Whispers flew around the cave immediately.

"A new queen?"

"There aren't any suitable royals, are there?"

"Is it Jewelem? Is he coming back?"

"Who stepped up for it?"

"Imagine if it's Amethyst again?"

Ruby became nervous hearing the late evil queen's name. At her death, she ran into the dungeons and found Emeraldite there. He looked much less rough than he did then, however. Once he got cared for.

"Emeraldite... Will we ever be able to return home?" She asked him.

"This is only temporary," he reassured her. "Home is wherever you want it to be- I personally have no problem eating rocks for dinner- But if you really want to return to the Royal City, then I can almost guarantee that we will be there soon."

Ruby snickered a little. Emeraldite was a good light in the darker tunnels of the resistance's journey. Everyone knew him, and he was amazing. The things he did for Kalista and Ruby made her happy. How he put everyone before himself and made every fight peaceful. The commander and the messenger proceeded into the main Ox City.

"I'm worried," Ruby said. She tried to keep her voice from breaking.

"Don't be worried, what is there to worry about?" Emeraldite put his wing over her back. "We can go into the Ox City tomorrow, we can look around. I asked around and found a candle shop like the place where Kalista volunteered for her classes. The commander said we were technically allowed to explore the city. I think most dragons would stay and recover. A lot of them seem pretty shaken after all that. If it would make you less worried, we could pick up a few things for the dragons around here." Ruby couldn't stop a smile from surfacing. She gave Emraldite a slightly bittersweet smile.

"All this chaos is going to end," he promised her. "Believe me."

"Then let's hope this new queen will sort it out," Ruby replied.

"

Bright Blazing Soul Past Enemy Lines

Prince Incinerator had been waiting for 18 years, *18 full years* for Red and Lassa's return. The back of his head was already throbbing from Volcanic beating him up, his back was hurting far too much for comfort, and he felt pain in all directions. But his mind was racing. They'd first met him when he was 2. It was a little bit after his father had died, and Lassa had met him someplace his mother had trapped him. She almost seemed to crawl through the window with her weapon raised. *Was it a crossbow? I think it was.*

Incinerator just stood on the top of the palace. Pyro had disappeared. He knew they were coming because of a signal that the dragon he was waiting for had given him. He'd set off a Glowing Phoenix Firework in the distance, and Incinerator had seen the golden springs in the air and just known. He knew that he was safe then.

He wasn't 100% sure that the Golden Phoenix was his friend's signal, but the sight of the freely glowing figure gave him a sense of hope. He hoped that the Golden Phoenix wasn't the only one, as fireworks were banned in the Ariash Kingdom by his mother, although he never knew why.

The palace was in flames, literally and figuratively. The queen was raging, Volcanic was raging with her and a few dead or injured guards were found. Incinerator had somehow made it out without too many scrapes, and he waited for Lassa and Red to find him. The volcano's rim poured smoke from inside the black cavern. He turned around on the thin circle of volcano stone to look into the deep flaming cavern. A black metal grate gave view into the Lava Chamber, but Incinerator called it 'The Infernium." 4 metal walls layered with flaming metal made a chamber of 4 bridges over a sea of lava. Ariash dragons could survive lava, but they never made it out of the room itself.

Incinerator shivered.

"There you are!"

He turned around to see a familiar dragon across the volcano rim. It was the same dragon he'd met 18 years ago, but taller and more amazing. A dark robe shielded most of the dragon's scales from Incinerator's eyes, and he could also see a hint of grey armour. He already knew who it was.

"Red?" He called to him.

"Incinerator!" Red squeaked, bounding over the circle to his side. "It's been 18 years, what's going on?"

"By the holy Ignis, it *has* been forever, yeah," he replied. Red looked so much older than he did when they met. *He was only 5 when we met… that means he's 23 now. I'm 20 now, but Volcanic is probably 23 as well now.*

"How has everything been?" Red asked him, taking Incinerator's claws and searching for injuries on him. "Are you alright? Is anything wrong?"

"I'm alright, Red, really," he reassured him with a small laugh. He tried to play it off casually, but he had lied. *I did something unforgivable.*

"Are you sure?" Red asked. "She's not here right now, but Lassa's group is at the base, just so you know. Also your head is bleeding, in case you didn't know. I'll take care of it later." On the other side of the rim where Red had come from was the back of the island, the edge of the kingdom. Incinerator stepped around to look over it and saw a camp of dragons below.

"The resistance?" He asked with wide eyes.

"Actually, we're the Revolution now," he said with obvious adorable pride.

"Well then, let's go meet them," Incinerator said with a smile. He soared down to the bottom of the volcano onto the thin bit of land between the back of the castle and the ocean. The camp seemed empty, but there was a cave under a large boulder that Incinerator couldn't see the end of. He looked back up at the volcano mouth, but he didn't see Red anywhere.

"Red?" He called up. He went silent to hear some kind of metal clashing, but he wasn't sure what it was. It felt like the noises were coming from far away, but something told him they weren't. A moment later, a flaming body fell from the edge. It landed near the coast of the island right next to Incinerator. He almost shrieked thinking it was Red, but he fluttered down from the top. But something was still off.

"What happened?" Incinerator asked. "Is everything ok?"

"Just some Ariash guards," Red told him. He sounded out of breath, as though he'd put up quite a fight. "Not much to worry about. Actually, there is this." Red moved the side of his robe, revealing dark bloodstains through his armour. "It hurts, but it's… probably fine." The sound of wingbeats made them both look over to see more guards coming towards them. A harpoon-like spear shot through the air and Red just dodged it by a centimetre. He spun out of the way and drew his red and gold-embedded wooden crossbow. In a flurry of black and dark red, he leaped over the rocky coast to defend against the opposing dragons. Incinerator couldn't see very well, but he saw that Red seemed to be an incredible fighter. All the guards were much bigger than him, but even they snapped commands to each other and shrieked in pain constantly. *I bet he could take on Magma, Volcanic and the entire Ariash palace himself,* he thought in awe. When Red held down the last guard, he turned and gave Incinerator a certain look. A look of a brief horror, but also a bit of sorrow and the beginning of terror. It was unsettling that Incinerator didn't notice the dragon behind him before he was on the ground.

There was a ringing sound, and his vision was super blurry, but he heard Red call his name. His vision cleared up a little to see two larger dragons holding Red back. His crossbow was laying on a rock near Incinerator, just out of reach from him. But there was also something under a rock nearby. It looked kind of like an explosive of some sort. *I guess it's my best bet for survival here,* he thought with fear. He craned his neck a little to see the dragon holding him down. None of the guards were anyone he recognized, but the one on him reminded him of Volcanic. The only way he'd ever broken free from Volcanic... it was a long time ago.

The guard was holding him down by his neck and back, meaning it would be harder for him to escape. He scrambled out from the dragon's massive claws and grabbed the nearest rock he could find. The guard growled deeply and Incinerator smashed it on their head before grabbing Red's crossbow. The guard collapsed while Incinerator set an arrow on fire and shot the explosive, ducking behind another boulder while the smoke set off. He covered his ears and kept his eyes shut as he heard the guards yell. He couldn't tell if it was anger, fear or both, but he didn't want to be on the receiving end of their fury. A warm talon grabbed Incinerator's arm and called something to him, but he didn't hear. It pulled him under something and around something else but his eyes were still closed. Eventually the noise was silent, the air was cooler, and it felt a lot wetter.

"You can open your eyes now, prince," Red told him. Incinerator opened his eyes into a dark tunnel with only a few torches. It was a more peaceful place than the original place they'd been it. Red inhaled and exhaled deeply at the sight of it and took off his hood. The firelight reflected his bright emerald eyes in a beautiful contrast.

"Are you alright?" Red asked him.

"Huh? Oh- yeah," he replied. "Are you ok?" He did wonder if Red had gotten hurt anywhere. "Didn't you get hurt someplace?"

Red pressed on a certain place in the wall and a compartment opened up from inside. There were bandages, wraps and other healing supplies. He sighed in a bit of pain as he wrapped something around his bleeding forearm. It looked like it had been clawed and torn apart by Volcanic. As for his side, he didn't do much except for drying the blood with his robe.

"Were you stabbed?" Incinerator asked nervously. "I-Is that a stab wound?"

"It felt like I might've been, yeah," he replied as though it wasn't a big deal. He winced in pain and Incinerator wanted to help, but didn't know what to do. Red took off his hood, revealing his dark red scales and orange wings.

"I'm kind of used to this by now," he said with a shrug. "Dragons get injured a lot in the revolution. I'm used to taking care of them."

"I understand that." Incinerator nodded and looked away a little. "In the war, dragons are always getting hurt. The difference is the other- I mean, *we* usually don't try to heal them." he thought about the scars on his body, the ones he never got treated for as a whelp. Red didn't seem to have many scars, only a few. Red took something and dried the blood from his head which was slowly creeping down his neck.

"You seem different from them," Red said thoughtfully. He took a torch off the wall and held it. He motioned for Incinerator to follow him through the tunnels.

"I've…done bad things, just like them," Incinerator said quietly. *Look what I did to her…*

"You don't seem like someone who would do that." Red looked at him with a skeptical curiosity.

He couldn't look Red in the eye, but he couldn't help but glance at him. He got a glimpse of the fear on his face. "I did some bad things. I hurt dragons who didn't deserve it. I don't even know if Lassa will accept me into the Revolution."

"She's a forgiving dragon," Red told him, his voice not much over a whisper. They kept continuing down the tunnel, even though Incinerator felt really bad about everything. He didn't want Red to have to deal with him.

305

Red stopped and faced him. Incinerator did the same. He sat down and took Incinerator's talons. "18 years ago, when you left, I kept asking my mother to find you and bring you back with us. I didn't care about the consequences at the time." He let out a soft laugh for a moment. "I mean… I was five, I didn't understand. Then for the next 18 years, I always thought about where you were. Lassa didn't let us into the palace without anyone to help in case we got hurt, and I was too scared to ask anyone. I'm the youngest soldier in the Revolution, I didn't think anyone would want to help me. I heard what happened to Pyro, it was an opportunity to find you again."

Incinerator realised what that meant. Red had spent the last almost 2 decades waiting for a chance to come back for him. *Oh, now I get it. He's afraid of me not going back with him… because he thinks I'll be too scared and I won't join him in the Revolution.*

"I'll go back with you," Incinerator promised him. "But there is something I need you to know." He didn't like how on edge Red looked, but he wasn't going to hide this secret until Red discovered it himself. *He'll be broken if I hide this and he finds out.*

"Red… I killed my sister."

Red's ears twitched and his eyes widened. "Princess Meteor," he whispered. "I heard of her when I was in the palace when I met you, trying to find my mother."

"No, I meant Princess Downfall," he said. "She hatched a few years after Meteor, but before Pyro and-" he stopped. "My mother told me to kill her. She was young, and a really unique peach colour. I thought she would love me if I did that, and I knew she would be proud of me… I didn't *want* to, but I wanted her to love me and-"

"Incinerator, it's ok," Red said to him firmly. He pulled Incinerator closer to him. "You're alright now, Magma doesn't have to love you. In the Revolution, nobody is going to hurt you. I'll make sure you're ok there. You won't have to hurt anyone, you can just be safe. I-we will love you anyway."

Incinerator closed his eyes. *I am safe here,* he thought. *Red will protect me.*

For now.